"*SWEET JESU*, LEANDRA, YOU'RE SO COLD. YOU'RE TURNING BLUE ALL OVER. . . ."

Wasting no more time, Garrett hooked his thumbs in the shoulder straps of her shift and peeled the wet garment from Leandra's body. His warm, strong hands brushed along her hips, her thighs, and the back of her knees.

She closed her eyes and let her head rest against him. "Being close is nice. Is this the love potion at work?"

"I don't care what it is," Garrett whispered, "I just need to know you're safe and well."

"I didn't think a love potion would work like this," Leandra said. "Don't you feel the attraction!"

"I feel it." Garrett's mouth hovered temptingly close to her face. Gently catching the back of her head, he planted a kiss on her lips.

"In a kiss, lovers share everything, Lioness, even their tongues," he murmured when she failed to respond.

"Really?" Leandra shivered, though no longer chilled.

Garrett leaned toward her again. "Like this . . ."

Books by Linda Madl

Sweet Ransom
Sunny
Speak of Love
A Tender Magic

Published by POCKET BOOKS

A TENDER MAGIC

LINDA MADL

POCKET BOOKS

New York   London   Toronto   Sydney   Tokyo   Singapore

An *Original* Publication of POCKET BOOKS

POCKET BOOKS, a division of Simon & Schuster Inc.
1230 Avenue of the Americas, New York, NY 10020

Copyright © 1993 by Linda Madl

ISBN: 0-671-73391-5

First Pocket Books printing March 1993

10 9 8 7 6 5 4 3 2 1

POCKET and colophon are registered trademarks of Simon & Schuster Inc.

Cover art by Lina Levy

Printed in the U.S.A.

To my parents, who taught me to cherish and respect the written word, to take pleasure in the beauty of the world, and to love.

Acknowledgments

Thanks to Earl Hoyt, expert traditional archer of Hoyt Archery Company, St. Louis, Missouri, for enthusiastically sharing his expertise. I have a new appreciation for the ancient skill of archery.

Nurse and fellow author Eileen Dreyer earns a special thank-you for her understanding medical advice. She helped pull Leandra through nicely.

Thanks too to all my friends, family, and colleagues who contribute in more ways than they know to my writing: Babette, Judy, Karyn, Ron, and Lori.

Author Betina Krahn deserves appreciation for her kind support of this project.

And heartfelt thanks to my editor, Caroline Tolley, for her faith and patience with *A TENDER MAGIC*.

Cupido,
Upon his shulders wyngs had he two,
And blynd he was, as it is often seene;
A bowe he bore and arrows brighte and kene.

—from THE KNIGHT'S TALE
by Geoffrey Chaucer

Prologue

Open in the name of Lyonesse," Leandra cried, pounding on the door of the witch's cottage. Silence greeted her. She glanced uneasily over her shoulder at her cousin.

Brenna lurked in the garden shadows, her face hidden by her cloak hood. "What did I tell you? She's gone. Let's go before someone sees us." No one in the forest clearing could fail to hear her hissing whisper.

Leandra turned back to the door, unwilling to give up so quickly. She feared failure more than discovery. She knew Brenna would never admit to making this clandestine visit, and Captain Ralph with his loyal mounted guards who waited at the garden gate were all sworn to secrecy. Still, she knew that someone might misunderstand this venture of hers.

But she had come too far and this mission was too important. Leandra renewed her knocking. "I say—"

Without warning, hinges creaked and the door swung open.

She paused, fist in midair, then blinked as her eyes adjusted to the dim cottage interior. A tall, brown-eyed, ageless beauty dressed in common russet faced her. Surely this was no witch.

"I seek Vivian of the Forest," Leandra announced, attempting to peer beyond the woman. Captain Ralph had assured her that this was the place.

"I am Vivian. I've been expecting you, Leandra of Lyonesse. And your cousin." With a gesture of welcome, the woman stood aside. "Please, enter. You've come for a love potion."

1

There was no need to say more. Leandra beckoned to Brenna and stepped through the doorway.

Close on her heels, Brenna chanted in her ear, "What did she say? What did she say?"

"She said she was expecting us," Leandra whispered back, tugging her skirts free of her cousin's feet. "She knows I want a love potion."

"Well, she might have guessed that." Brenna pressed close to Leandra. "All of Lyonesse knows of your betrothal to Reginald of Tremelyn."

Darkness closed around them as Vivian shut the door and turned to face her guests. Only a fire in the hearth lit the room. Leandra straightened her spine, summoning her courage. Brenna huddled closer.

"You are right to seek a love spell from me," Vivian said. "I understand that the earl was devoted to his late countess."

"Yes." Relief washed over Leandra. She did not need to recite all her carefully prepared reasons for obtaining the potion. "But he writes that he is ready for a new wife and family."

"We pray that he is over his grief," Vivian said, clasping her fine long hands in front of her in an oddly nunlike fashion. "But a potion should take care of any sorrow that lingers."

"Yes." The wise woman's understanding reassured Leandra. "Can you help me?"

"The brewing of a true love spell is an exacting business, fair lady," Vivian warned, wagging a slender finger at her. "It takes time and careful alchemy. First, the fiery heat. Then a delicate cooling. After that, the thaw must be prudently timed. Stewing follows. Through it all, one must stir tenderly."

"Of course." The explanation mystified Leandra, but she was too set on securing the potion to risk questions.

"I began preparations as soon as I saw your coming in the waters of my well." The wise woman waved toward two stools already sitting by the crackling fire—proof that they were expected.

Brenna began to protest. "Maybe we should leave and return when the potion is ready."

"Please sit, ladies," Vivian bade. "I will not keep you long. My apprentice will see to your needs and those of your escort."

"Sit, Brenna," Leandra ordered, unwilling at the moment to humor her petulant cousin.

Oddly silent, Brenna sank onto one of the stools, and Leandra joined her.

Singing soft incantations, Vivian retired to the corner table with her pestle and mortar—absorbed in her work— her visitors momentarily forgotten.

The apprentice, a courteous, chubby-cheeked young boy, served cups of the most delicious well water Leandra had ever tasted. After waiting on the men outside, he retreated to his corner near the hearth, where he crouched and stared, his worshipful gaze unnerving Leandra.

Brenna shifted uneasily. "If your father finds out about this, we'll be in a lot of trouble." She nodded for emphasis and began to rub her knees. "And Mother Mary Elizabeth, if she learns what we've been up to, she'll have us saying paternosters for weeks—months. I'll get calluses."

"Don't worry." Her teacher's reaction was the least of Leandra's worries. "I've taken care of everything. They'll never know."

"Why are we doing this anyway?" Brenna whined. "Tremelyn's first envoy practically drooled on your hand when he took it. No doubt the potbellied fool has given the earl a glowing report of your beauty. *I'm* the one who needs a potion to win a husband."

Leandra cast her pretty, dark-haired cousin a sharp-eyed look. Brenna had been first to ask all the questions of the envoy. What was my lord, the earl, like? Did he fancy dancing? Did he favor fine clothes? When the envoy presented Leandra with a small portrait of Lord Reginald, her cousin was the one who wrested the painting from her hand.

"What a fine-looking man, even with gray in his hair," Brenna had exclaimed, critically eyeing the picture. "But of course an earl, even an old earl, would be comely and charming. And a good lover, don't you think, Leandra?"

Tremelyn's envoy had blushed. Leandra snatched the portrait from her cousin's clutches, thankful that her father had missed Brenna's brazen words.

Now, Leandra sighed. How did a maid capture a man's heart? She had no mother to advise her. Only nuns and Captain Ralph served as her teachers. Brenna was no help. Her idea of winning favor was to flutter her eyelashes and show a little ankle. Instinctively Leandra knew there was more to love than that.

Tucking her feet beneath Vivian's stool, Leandra anxiously clasped her cold hands in her lap. She must please the earl. Anything less would be to fail Lyonesse and her father. They desperately needed the protection of the knight, the garrison, and the fighting men whom the earl was sending. With a love potion, she could be assured that Lord Reginald's grief over the loss of his first wife would fade and that this match would work.

Suddenly, from across the room, Vivian shrieked strange words. She seized her mortar and whisked into the back chamber. Curious, Leandra stared after the witch. Was she cooling or stewing now? The timid apprentice huddled deeper into his corner, until his mistress called his name. Reluctantly, he crawled to his feet and followed her.

Brenna and Leandra glanced questioningly at each other.

"What does she want him for?" Brenna whispered.

Leandra shrugged. In the next room crockery clattered. Metal rang against metal. Vivian's voice sang out in a language Leandra assumed must be magical. A cat yowled, and a lid slammed shut.

Unexpectedly, a black cat leapt into the room. Brenna and Leandra started. The green-eyed feline paused lightly on all fours, arched its back, and stared with unblinking interest at them. Firelight stroked its glossy fur.

"Sweet Mary, I hate cats," Brenna whimpered. She and the animal glared at one another in mutual dislike. The creature prowled toward them. Distaste twisted Brenna's winsome mouth, and she drew her skirts closer about her

4

feet. Tail lancing the air, the cat made for the hearth, slipping past them in a blur. Then bone by fluid bone the creature settled on the stone and regarded them once more with a wise, unwinking gaze.

For the first time, Leandra noted that the cat was missing whiskers on one side of its nose. What goes into a love potion? she wondered absurdly.

"Look at him, staring as if he knows everything," Brenna complained. "So sure of themselves, cats are. I don't like that." Brenna sniffed and studied the feline, her eyes narrowing. "I'll take that smug look off your face, sir cat."

Brenna launched herself at the animal.

"Oh, no, you don't." Leandra grabbed her cousin's arm just before the girl's booted foot came down on the creature's tail. "I'll not have you offend Vivian."

The cat fled.

"All I need is a potion brewed by an angry witch," Leandra snapped. "What if she decides to mix a spell to turn Lord Reginald into a frog? Sit down and behave yourself."

Brenna sank to her stool in a fit of giggles. "You and a frog on your wedding night."

"That's not funny." Leandra frowned. Her cousin always refused to take things seriously.

"You never do see the humor." Brenna giggled again.

Leandra settled on her stool and shook her head. That was her other shortcoming, she recalled, besides her ignorance. Her father and Mother Mary Elizabeth bluntly told her with a sorrowful shake of their heads that she lacked humor—a quality so essential in a charming woman. How could she make up for that? she wondered.

Unexpectedly, Vivian swept into the room, breathless with excitement. She held up a tiny silver phial stoppered with a silver-capped cork. "I have it."

"That's it?" Leandra asked, rising slowly, frogs and Brenna's foolishness forgotten. She stared at her future caught in a tiny bottle.

"Oh, yes." Vivian said. "It's colorless and tasteless. Only a few drops for you and a few for the earl will seal your fate."

"Only a few drops?" Leandra repeated. A powerful brew indeed.

With slow, deliberate steps Vivian approached the heiress to the realm of Lyonesse. "I have no qualms about giving you this potion, my lady, despite its power. Although you have seen only sixteen summers, I know that your heart is pure, your head is wise, and that you do not ask for this spell with a light mind."

Leandra nodded wordlessly, overwhelmed by the immensity of what she was doing, acquiring the means to take a man's will from him, to bind him to her whether he wished it or not. True, she wanted only to do the best for Lyonesse's welfare, but did she dare deny a man's right to choose his own destiny?

"This is no frivolous elixir," Vivian added, tapping the phial with her forefinger. "No simple magic ring nor enchanted cloak of invisibility. Nor is it a mere aphrodisiac to inflame passion or enhance fertility.

"My love potion will bind two hearts forever. You will love each other truly, above all things and all others. With passion. But most importantly, you will love with the courage to make any sacrifice to ensure the happiness of your beloved."

Leandra drew a deep breath and thought of the little portrait of Lord Reginald: his pleasant smile, his high, smooth, intelligent brow. But most clearly Leandra recalled his eyes. Surely a man with such dark, gentle eyes deserved to make his own choice.

"Can nothing break the charm?" she asked.

"Only a special antidote that's difficult to brew," Vivian explained. "It is used when one of the lovers dies, to free the survivor to wed again. Should you have need of it, my lady, I will brew it. But the antidote must be drunk fresh. So you see, release is not easy. Use this potion with great care."

Leandra accepted the phial from Vivian, holding the shining container up so that the firelight caught it and the silver glowed pure and innocent. Slowly she turned the bottle over and over in her hands, wondering at the wisdom of this plan.

"Well, now that's settled," Brenna said, rising from her stool with a clap of her hands, her fears and suspicions obviously overcome. "Mistress Vivian, do you have something to give me a dimple here? See? To match the one on the other side of my mouth. All my life I've had only this one dimple. . . . And seasickness. Do you have anything for that? I just know this voyage to Tremelyn is going to make me ill."

With a smile of forbearance, Vivian turned to her cluttered shelves. "I believe I can help you, too, Lady Brenna." The two filled the quiet cottage with their chatter as the wise woman mixed remedies for Brenna.

Leandra sank down by the fire once more, her heart heavy with the thought of this deception. She deplored dishonesty. Her hands began to tremble. She tucked the phial safely into the cuff of her brown surcoat. Her betrothal vows had already been said at the altar in Lyonesse chapel. She might not even need the potion, she thought. Lord Reginald had spoken his vows in the cathedral at Tremelyn.

They were promised to each other in the presence of God and their families, she reminded herself. Little could change that now. But what if they took a foolish dislike to each other? It was conceivable. What would happen to her people then? There was so much she didn't know—about Reginald, about his beloved countess, about marriage. So much rested on her shoulders.

Chapter 1

The West Country of England
The Year of Our Lord 1346

Why do you wish to become a knight, Garrett Bernay?"
Father John intoned as he stood on the altar in the rosy,
stained-glass sunlight. His clear, mellow voice carried easily
over Garrett's tawny head to a noisy congregation who
shuffled impatiently in their leather boots and wooden clogs.
"Is it with the hope of gaining personal treasure?"

In defiance of tradition, Garrett looked up from where he
knelt, his gaze drawn to the Bernay sword. High over his
head the cherished weapon—soon to be a knight's sword
once more—was held fast in the hands of his sponsor,
Reginald, Earl of Tremelyn.

"No, Father," Garrett responded, clearly and honestly.
He swallowed with difficulty, willing away the tightness in
his throat. But he could not keep his eyes from the newly
blessed blade that once was his father's and his father's
father's. Five generations of Bernays had sworn honor on
the weapon since it had been carried home from the Holy
Land. At last he had won back the right to do the same.

"Is it that men may show you homage?" Father John
quizzed.

"No, Father." Garrett looked to his longtime family
friend. A small twinge of guilt pricked at him. His reasons
were not quite so pure as that. He wanted to be a knight to
wipe away the darkness from his family name, the disgrace
of his uncle's treason against the king. He wanted his
brother, Wystan, and himself to be able to hold their heads
high again—as was their birthright—to walk proudly once
more among all the nobles of the land.

9

"I wish to be a knight so that I may serve the Church with a pure mind and heart," Garrett pledged and humbly bowed his head.

In truth this knighting ceremony was only a formality. He'd been knighted nearly a month ago on the battlefield.

The ambush was still etched vividly in his mind. They had been a small hunting party—just the earl, a few of the Tremelyn knights, some men-at-arms, and their captain, Garrett. The season's last snow flurried from a gray sky. Through the thickening snowfall they sighted a huge red buck. In the high spirit of the chase they let the quarry draw them into a narrow pass. They realized the danger only when outlaws rushed out of the whiteness from every side. The attack was so unexpected and so brutal that they lost several good men before making a stand.

The brigands fought ruthlessly toward Lord Reginald, greed and desperation in their eyes. It was as though more was at stake than mere robbery loot. What were they after? Ransom? Assassination? A frown darkened Garrett's brow as he recalled the fierce fighting. That question still plagued him.

Lord Reginald himself was seriously wounded by the time Garrett managed to fight to his lord's side and drive off the assailants. Weak and bleeding, Reginald struggled to his feet and, with his bloody sword in hand, bestowed knighthood on Garrett before the battle-weary knights.

Now, at the altar, Father John droned on. "In the name of the most Holy Lord, Almighty Father . . . who has permitted on earth the use of the sword to suppress the malice of the wicked and the treacherous, and to defend justice and the innocent . . ."

Garrett knew there were those present who doubted him still. Some said that like his uncle he lacked the loyalty to be a knight. Others pointed to his need for humility. But he knew they all were wrong. He'd lived humility for the sake of his mother, who died heartbroken, and for his father, who died hopeless and desolate without even trying to regain the honor lost. Garrett refused to surrender to despair. He grew strong and dauntless through years of training and service in France to one lord and another. Then Lord Reginald had taken him on as captain of the guard.

". . . and who for the protection of thy people hast deemed fit to institute the order of chivalry . . ." Father John was in good voice today, Garrett thought with pleasure.

Suddenly he felt old and young at once—his head light, his tawny hair shorn away like a green boy freshly tonsured. But the scarlet cloak he wore weighed heavily on his shoulders—even more heavily than his armor. The flowing red satin symbolized the blood he must be prepared to shed in defense of the Church and of his liege lord. He'd already spilled blood, and had little doubt that he would be called on to shed more—for the king, for the earl, and for the good of the Bernay name.

". . . do you, Garrett Bernay, swear to dispose your heart to goodness and never use *this* sword or any other to injure anyone unjustly?" Father John asked.

With confidence and a clear conscience, Garrett said, "I swear."

Reginald stepped forward to speak, still holding the sword high for all to see. "Do you swear to use this sword honorably and to always defend your liege lord, Reginald of Tremelyn?"

Gratitude rushed through Garrett as he lifted his gaze to meet Reginald's. No one man had been more help in his quest for knighthood. He knew he would forever be indebted—willingly and faithfully—to his lord.

"I so swear," Garrett vowed.

The final moment had arrived. He closed his eyes, took a deep breath, and braced himself. A hush settled over the congregation: fellow men-at-arms, knights, squires, barons, other vassals, and ladies. Garrett heard the flat of the sword blade cut the air, whisking past his ear to jolt against his shoulder with full force. He hardly felt the impact.

A sigh of relief escaped him. It was nearly finished. The mark against his family's name was almost wiped away.

From this day forward he would be Sir Garrett Bernay, knight and loyal defender of the Church and of his liege lord—no mark of treachery would mar the Bernays' Norman lineage again.

Reginald raised the finely tempered sword slowly and brought down the second blow just as forcefully on Garrett's other shoulder. Again, outwardly, Garrett remained unmoved, not even a smile touched his lips. But inside, elation soared. Lightness filled him. The burden of dishonor was lifted.

"Be thee dubbed knight, Sir Garrett Bernay." Reginald announced for all in the cathedral to hear. The earl raised the sword from Garrett's shoulder and with both hands offered it to him.

Without hesitation Garrett rose, towering over his lord to accept the gleaming symbol of his rightful place in the world.

Then Reginald stepped aside and Wystan came forward, blushing to the roots of his sandy hair. A youthful smile of pride spread across his face. He and Reginald together—a special honor—knelt to buckle on Garrett a shining pair of silver spurs, the symbol of a knight's honor and chivalry.

Next Reginald took a blue shield from Wystan, hung it about Garrett's neck and held him by the shoulders for a moment, his grip strong and warm. "Garrett, I could take no more pleasure in knighting my own son. I'm pleased and proud to have a Bernay among my knights. I have great plans for you."

They embraced, Garrett's heart too full for words.

A groom waited with Garrett's chestnut charger at the church steps. He stared at the fully armored mount in disbelief.

"You don't expect me to tilt with the quintain like some boy, do you?" he asked Lord Reginald. "I agreed to the required lock shearing. Why should I display arms against a straw-filled dummy as if I'm a stripling who needs to show off his fighting skills?"

"But, 'tis traditional," Reginald said with a laugh and a

hearty slap to Garrett's back. "'Tis our right to witness your valor."

So Sir Garrett Bernay rode forth into the cathedral square, mounted on his war horse, carrying his newly bestowed blue shield and feeling just a little foolish. Friends and well-wishers roared approval.

He grinned at them, then dropped his helmet visor into place. If they wanted a show, he'd give them one. He made six farcical charges at the dummy that everyone knew he could annihilate in one halfhearted sweep. On the final pass he scattered the poor spineless effigy. Straw fluttered on the breeze. Then iron horseshoes struck sparks on the cobbles and flashed against the sky as Garrett reined his horse around to salute his liege lord with the Bernay sword. Laughter, cheers, and applause filled the air.

Wine and ale flowed freely at the celebration feast that followed, and food-laden pages paraded forth endlessly from the castle kitchen. Garrett was touched that Reginald had spared no expense.

As the shadows grew long and the laughter raucous, the miller's daughter—a little dark-haired maid—lured Garrett beneath the winding stairs. On tiptoe she offered her congratulations, a lusty kiss. He accepted with pleasure, plying his lips to hers and savoring her eager response. He was tempted to take more, and it was offered. But in deference to his host, he tactfully declined, and was glad he did. When he reached the great hall, he found Reginald lingering at the doors.

"There you are," the earl greeted. Inside, the torches were being lit, and Garrett could hear the musicians tuning their instruments.

"Returned safe from the embrace of the shadows, I see."

Garrett merely smiled.

"When you are ready to wed, I think we can do better than the miller's daughter," Reginald said. "I was about to see to the feeding of the falcons. Join me."

Reginald led Garrett in the direction of the mews. "I have something I want to tell you before I proclaim the names of the knights who will join King Edward in France."

13

Garrett followed, the spring of confidence in his step. This was what he had been waiting for—the announcement that along with the other Tremelyn knights and squires, he and Wystan would defend Britain's holdings on the continent. The Bernays would once more have the chance to prove their loyalty to the king. This honor made all the rough camps, cold vigils, sore limbs, and bloody fighting worthwhile.

When they reached the mews, Reginald spoke casually over his shoulder. "I thought you should know that you are not going to France with the others."

Garrett halted in his tracks and let a long slow breath escape him. Had he heard correctly? "I'm sorry, my lord. What did you say?"

"I have another mission planned for you." Reginald stopped to peer into the hawk's cage, then moved on to the next coop. The earl ordered the falcon master to bring out the gyrfalcon.

Garrett clasped his fists behind him. Another mission? What could possibly be as important as the king's war? When he finally trusted his voice not to betray his anger, he said, "But I have experience fighting in France. What service can I perform for you that is more valuable than joining the king?"

"Restrain yourself, my new knight," Reginald cautioned, his tone low and patient. Without looking at Garrett, he pulled on a heavy leather glove and took his hooded gyrfalcon from the falconer. "I am to be wed, as you know. I dare not leave my holdings with all the unrest and the brigands at large. I have survived well enough so far, thanks to you, Sir Knight, but another trip abroad seems unwise just now.

"Fortunately, my betrothed, the Lady Leandra, understands and has asked only that I send my bravest and most honorable knight to Lyonesse. I also feel that she should have the best escort I can offer her."

"Yes, my lord." Garrett stood quiet and alert. He knew Reginald to be a just man. But like all good rulers, the earl never forgot what was owed to him—and Garrett owed him much.

"I want *you* to go to Lyonesse to bring my betrothed safely back to Tremelyn."

Garrett bowed his head humbly, but his thoughts rebelled. Sweet Jesu, he was being relegated to a lady's escort, a lady of whom he disapproved. "I'm honored that you would consider me qualified," Garrett stammered.

"I know you disapprove of this marriage." Reginald held up his free hand to silence the protest that came to Garrett's lips. "Don't argue. I've seen it in your face. But this alliance between Lyonesse and Tremelyn is important. They need our protection. We need their ships to transport our tin. I will not have the lady frightened off by a discourteous knight. Above that, I will not risk her safety."

Garrett waited impatiently as Reginald devoted his attention to feeding the gyrfalcon a tidbit of raw meat. In his opinion this match was unworthy of Reginald. It mattered little that Lyonesse's Highlord Aidan was said to have been a great warrior once. The man had turned to religion after the death of his wife and left his people leaderless. How he'd managed to hold his throne over the years was a mystery to Garrett. Now Aidan sought protection by marrying off his daughter. True enough, Leandra of Lyonesse was said to be young and fair, but what kind of female would such a man sire? What sort of wife could she be?

"I know you'd rather make your mark with the king in France," Reginald went on, offering the bird another tidbit. "But do this for me, Garrett, and I will petition the king for the return of Chycliff to the Bernays."

The offer jarred Garrett, and for a moment he forgot about the ignominy of being a lady's escort. Garrett shot the earl a quick glance. Securing the return of his ancestral home was what he wanted most, as Reginald well knew. Obviously the earl placed great value on the trip to Lyonesse.

"I am truly flattered by the generous offer, my lord, but I'm no diplomat," Garrett said, tempted, but at last moved to object. "I don't know the fair speeches that men of peace make. Surely there is someone better suited for this assignment."

"Don't act the rough soldier with me, Garrett," Reginald said in mild reproof. "From what the ladies say, you do well enough with words when you want to. Besides, the negotiations are done, only the signing of the betrothal contracts remains. Father John will accompany you to oversee the signing and to serve as proper companion for the ladies. You will remain long enough to establish a garrison and train men for it. An armed garrison is part of the agreement. Lyonesse is as troubled with brigands as we are.

"I don't want you to think of this assignment as merely a lady's escort, Garrett," Reginald continued. "I know that's what's on your mind. Think of it as rescuing a damsel in distress. Present her with my gifts. Make her long to see Tremelyn. I want my bride to come to me safe, happy, and smiling."

Garrett squinted at his liege lord. A damsel in distress, indeed. He was being ordered—if not bribed—to endure a nauseating sea voyage to a poor realm, play lady's escort, and all with no glory at the end. If he offered the right reasons, maybe he could escape that fate yet. "My lord, as much of an honor as this mission is, I'm not certain that—"

"There is one more thing you should know," Reginald interrupted. He cast Garrett a measuring, sidelong look. "There is the matter of Lady Leandra's other suitor. I believe you know the man. Leofric of Casseldorne."

The hair on the back of Garrett's neck prickled. He'd suffered more than one insult from the son of the earl of Casseldorne. As a soldier, Garrett was forbidden to challenge a knight. And Casseldorne took sneering pleasure in that. His interest awakened at last, Garrett moved restlessly to his lord's other side. "Casseldorne seeks the lady's hand?"

"He's been refused, but you know what a troublemaker he's always been," Reginald said, baiting the largest and most powerful of all trained falcons. Bells tinkled on the bird's jesses. The predator snatched the meat away and

16

greedily lifted its wings, mantling possessively over its reward. "'Tis you that must go, Garrett. No one else."

When Garrett made no reply, Reginald continued.

"Consider my choices. I don't dare send the lecherous Montgomery pup. He's not to be trusted within an arm's length of a skirt. I can't send Beaufort. Poor old Beau is half blind. He's probably forgotten what a pretty girl looks like. Not to mention that he couldn't win a battle with a quintain if his life depended on it.

"But you I can trust, Garrett. I know I can count on you to bring my bride to me."

Garrett clamped his mouth shut as mixed feelings roiled about in his gut. The prospect of meeting Leofric cast the undertaking in a new light. He reminded himself that a good soldier, a loyal knight, never bemoaned his orders.

Reginald returned the gyrfalcon to the falconer. Then he turned to appraise Garrett once more, satisfaction glowing in the earl's eyes. He gave Garrett a comradely slap on his back. "I'm glad you're going. So, now I must make the announcement of who goes to France." He strode toward the great hall, never looking back.

Garrett loitered in the mews, contemplating the cobblestones and softly pounding his fist on the gyrfalcon's cage, reluctant to rejoin the gaiety that no longer suited his mood.

Ruefully he chuckled to himself. One day he would be able to look back on this disappointment and laugh. This mission need be no more than a minor setback. That's all he would allow it to be. When he'd delivered the lady to the earl, he would sail after the others. He could still join the king, join the fighting. Yet his disappointment lingered.

The fact remained that when the knights of Tremelyn sailed for France toward war and glory, he and Wystan would sail west to the realm of Lyonesse—the last place on earth he wanted to go.

Chapter 2

Sharp alarm rang out from the peaceful bells of Lyonesse's chapel.

"Mother, have mercy!" Leandra started, then stared disheartened as an ink blotch spread from her quill onto the parchment.

"Pirates, again?" she muttered to herself, and resolutely stabbed the quill into the ink pot.

The discordant pealing echoed through the great hall where she worked, striking painfully against her ears.

In the castle keep she could hear the men shout "To arms! To arms!" as they raced to their combat posts, grabbing weapons as they went.

Hastily she rose from her worktable and reached for her bow. She'd prayed that they would be spared from another raid so soon after the last one. But she and Captain Ralph had not relied on prayers alone. The men were better prepared this time; they'd made certain of that.

The steward appeared to help her tie a quiver of arrows to her girdle. Determination set in her chin, she hitched up her skirts and climbed the steps to the castle tower.

At the top she went straight to the stone battlement and squinted out across the sea. How strong were the pirates this time? Beneath the gray sky she spotted only one pirate vessel bobbing at the mouth of the bay. She'd seen one boatload of these unholy brigands leave Lyonesse with crops aflame and fishing boats wrecked.

"But not for much longer," Leandra vowed aloud. "We will defeat you. I promise. If not today, then next time."

The panicked cries of the village women and children

drifted up to Leandra from the castle gate. Like geese with goslings, frantic mothers led their broods across the ramp into safety. Anger and guilt twisted her heart as she watched the sea breeze tug at their ragged garments. They ran on stick-thin legs, their faces pinched with fear and hunger. When had Lyonesse become a land where fearful children huddled inside the castle instead of playing in the sunshine? she wondered. She *would* bring this to an end.

"Is it the red-haired pirate as usual?" Brenna joined Leandra at the tower wall.

"They're not close enough to see yet. Did you find my father?"

"Yes, he was at his prayers, where else?" Brenna leaned against the battlements as if she were merely taking in a pleasing view. "He said he would pray for us and join you shortly." Then she added with a sniff, "Which means when the attack is over."

"Father does what he must." Leandra peered out over the whitecapped sea. She was alone in this once again. A cool emptiness stole through her, as it always did when her father abdicated his responsibility. But for as long as she could remember, he'd prayed to the heavens for protection and left her to sort out the realities of the world. She expected no more of him.

"Where's Captain Ralph?" she demanded.

"Right here, my lady." The stocky soldier's head appeared at the top of the stairs. His chain mail jingled as he marched to Leandra's side, concern on his dark-bearded face and deference in the slight bow he made. Leandra acknowledged him with a curt nod. "The bowmen are in position, my lady, and we are about to close the castle gate."

"Good. Have the pirates landed a party yet?"

"No, my lady."

"Is there any reason to think that there is more than one brilin?"

Captain Ralph hesitated, and Leandra knew without looking at his face that she wasn't going to like his news.

"My lady, the lookout on the point signals that three more

cogs, large ones, are moving in with great speed. They fly no colors."

"Cogs? Nothing so large has sailed against us before." Leandra glanced up at the captain in surprise. Icy fear touched her for the first time. Where did pirates find so many men and such vessels?

"Our men are determined, my lady. They have become skilled with the new longbows we've made. Nearly every ablebodied man and boy in the village is prepared. I think we can give them a good fight."

"We must do our best," Leandra said, refusing to reveal her despair. "The pirates must not land. Make certain that every man understands that. Let the ships sail into range, then launch a barrage of arrows. Hit them heavy and fast. We'll force them to turn away."

"Yes, my lady." Captain Ralph's boots clattered on the tower steps and he shouted orders as he went.

"Face it, Leandra, not even you can defeat three cogs full of men." Brenna leaned farther over the battlements and gazed curiously at the pirate ship. "I wonder, do pirates take wives?"

"You're never going to know," Leandra muttered through clenched teeth. "They'll not set foot on Lyonesse soil this time, even if I have to go down to the shore and put an arrow through the black heart of the red-haired captain myself."

"Prepare to attack!" Garrett roared, excitement surging through him. He gripped the cog's railing and looked across the sea at the small brilin sighted by the boy in the crow's nest. After two weeks of preparation at Tremelyn and two miserable days at sea, he was ready to do battle.

"Send up the earl's colors," Garrett shouted with a laugh of satisfaction that banished his dour mood. There might be some glory in this mission yet. "Let's show them who we are."

He turned eagerly to the men in midships and roared a challenge. "Let's send every last one of those scurvy knaves to the bottom of the bay!"

The fighting men on deck shook their fists and cheered.

"Aye, sir," said Cedric, Garrett's handpicked second in command, his voice as unruffled as that of a man just ordered to shoot target practice. The wiry little soldier resettled his sword belt on his hips and pushed his tunic sleeves back to the elbow like a man prepared to go to work. "To the bottom of the bay with them." He began to relay Garrett's orders.

Oarsmen took up battle stations. Bowmen donned helmets, secured shields, and nocked yard-long arrows in their longbows. Garrett waved Wystan away when the squire offered a helmet. "Not now. I must see everything."

The oarsmen heaved at the oars. The cog surged forward.

Garrett waited, marking the vanishing distance between the vessels. The ship plowed forward. Closer.

On the next command, designated bowmen prepared to set fire to their arrows. Garrett raised his hand.

Closer.

Garrett could make out the sloppy pitch job on the brilin's hull and the shaggy brown beard of the lookout who had not spotted them yet. The man watched the Lyonesse shore. Too late, the pirate lookout saw them and shouted a warning. His surprised comrades turned from the shore side and rushed across the deck toward the attacking ship. The brilin listed. The pirate captain screamed orders.

Garrett coolly calculated a moment longer. Timing often made the difference between victory or defeat.

The earl's bowmen became restless as the cog closed in. Cedric remained frozen, like a hound on point awaiting the next order.

Aboard the brilin, pirates fumbled with crossbows and grabbed for rigging ropes.

Garrett gave the command.

"Draw and shoot," Cedric relayed.

Battle cries went up. Flaming bolts flew. Steel-tipped shafts showered the brilin.

From the pirate ship shouts of alarm rang out. Smoke and flames leapt into the sky. Garrett's bowmen cheered.

"Again," Garrett ordered. A second volley of arrows flew.

"Their sail is afire, sir," Cedric reported.

Angry shouts carried over the water. The small brilin shipped oars and came about. A few pirate arrows halfheartedly flopped across the sea toward the cog, then dropped into the waves.

From the brilin a reckless, red-haired man jeered at them. He flung an obscene gesture and shouted words that the wind blew away. Garrett grinned and waved a derisive acknowledgment. Every defeated man deserved to have a last word, and Garrett would not slight him by ignoring it.

Pirate oars flailed in a splashing panic. Garrett almost laughed at the frantic maneuvers. Fanned by the sea breeze, the hungry flames ate at their sail and proclaimed their defeat. Smoke grayed the sky. Oar blades sliced into the sea. The pirates lunged against the sculls, rapidly putting distance between themselves and the earl's ship. They rowed for the open sea.

"Shall we pursue them, sir?" Cedric inquired, unmoved by the confusion.

But Garrett caught the glint of battle fever flashing in the old veteran's eye. Apparently he'd found the short engagement as unsatisfying as Garrett had. But a warning shout from the lookout finished any thoughts of pursuit. Garrett looked up to see the sky dark with a cloud of arrows.

"Sweet Jesu." With one hand Garrett shoved Wystan to the deck and with the other grabbed Cedric's tunic and jerked the man down behind the ship's railing.

The lethal barrage swooped down on them, clattering against the gunwales and raining on Garrett's unprepared men.

Bowmen and oarsmen alike threw up shields or flattened themselves to the deck, shouting curses.

"The Lyonesse bowmen must think we're pirates, too," Cedric gasped.

"Are they blind? We're flying the earl's colors." Garrett swore again, but he knew Cedric's explanation made sense. Apparently the earl's colors—blue and gray—had gone unobserved. If he didn't do something, they might suffer losses from another barrage.

"Get a white flag up there," Garrett shouted to the crow's nest. He'd never raised the flag of surrender in his life, and he hated to begin here. But it seemed the only thing to do.

The pale lad in his nest clutched his bleeding arm and valiantly ran up the flag of surrender. Garrett looked over the rail toward shore.

As soon as the white banner snapped in the breeze, he saw the Lyonesse bowmen throw down their longbows and toss their caps in the air.

Tersely Garrett issued orders for the wounded to be seen to and for the crew to make ready to land. He glared up at the walls of Castle Lyonesse. What simpleton would attack a ship without taking note of the flags—the most basic and vital of all battlefield civilities? He had a few words to say to that dolt.

The people of Lyonesse recognized the earl's ship as an ally at last and crowded the crumbling quay, waving their tattered hats and shouting welcome. Cheers rose from tailors, cobblers, bakers, coopers, fishermen, carpenters, and sailors. Women and children threw flowered boughs in the air as if the cog's crew were heroes.

"'Tis worse than I expected," Father John said, speaking the very words on Garrett's lips. The priest had joined Garrett, Wystan, and Cedric in the cog forecastle. "The poverty. But the people seem cheerful, ready to make us champions and victors."

"Nearly dead heroes, thanks to their foolish commander," Garrett said. All around he noted ragged clothing, pinched mouths, and eyes too large for hollow-cheeked faces. Skinny, long-legged pigs wandered in the street, and slab-sided cart horses drooped in their harnesses. He wondered how any lord could allow his people to be brought to this by mere pirates.

Garrett disembarked, eager to get his feet on solid ground again and to find Lyonesse's military commander. But his way was blocked by a stout fishwife who stank as badly as her trade would suggest. She offered him a big gap-tooth grin and shoved a great tankard of mead at him.

"Good fight, my lord," she lisped, the spray of saliva showering Garrett's shiny chain mail. The woman pounded his back with hearty praise. "We knew the earl's men would save us when they come. And here you be."

"Thank you, good mistress. But I must decline your hospitality," Garrett said. "I want to speak with your highlord."

Impatiently he signaled to Wystan and Father John to make their way to the castle overlooking the bay.

"You wish to see the highlord, do you?" the fishwife said. "Here, I'll be honored to take you. This way."

Without further delay she led them up the narrow cobbled street that curved steeply toward the weathered towers.

Cheering citizens of Lyonesse scampered along with them, their good spirits contagious. Garrett's anger abated some. Still, he would feel better when he'd taken one overeager commander to task.

Halfway up the hill they met a smiling, long-bearded holy man. A pair of pretty maids followed him. To Garrett's surprise, the fishwife halted. He knew immediately from the expectant silence that fell over the crowd that this white-robed man was of some importance. Despite the humble sandals that flapped on his feet, his stiff-kneed walk, and bowed shoulders, the people stood back in respect.

"Welcome to Lyonesse, my son," the man greeted, his lined face brightening when he saw Garrett. He enfolded Garrett in a hearty embrace and kissed him, first on one cheek, then the other. Garrett submitted. Were this man and the maids his official greeters?

"Thank you for defeating our enemies." With a wide smile and a blue, milky gaze the holy man stared up into Garrett's face. "You must be Sir Garrett, sent as envoy of the Earl of Tremelyn?"

"Yes, Father. I am the earl's envoy." Intent on his mission, Garrett looked beyond the wizened old man at the castle. "Forgive me my haste, but I must present myself at the castle to your Highlord Aidan. I would like to speak to the foo—captain who gave the orders to shoot at the earl's colors."

"You need go no farther. I'm that fool."

Garrett hesitated. Had he heard correctly? Had one of the maids just admitted to giving the order to attack? Impossible! But his eyes narrowed as he took closer note of the two girls, uncertain as to which one had spoken.

The dark-haired girl caught his eye first. She fluttered her lashes and cast him a coy smile that left Garrett unmoved. No flirtatious maid would have spoken with such sharpness. The bright yellow and blue of her attire along with the harp slung from her shoulder suggested that she might be the member of some musicians' troupe, no warrior. He sought another and purposely turned away.

The other girl glared back at him just as boldly. For the first time, he noted that she carried a bow and a quiver of arrows hung from her russet girdle. The plain dark leafy color of her gown deepened the verdant green of her almond-shaped eyes. She offered no smile, but regarded him brazenly with a stubborn set to her chin.

Up and down and up again she stared, her gaze piercing and her mouth solemn. She scrutinized him as if she searched for something unworthy and intended to find it.

"You spoke, my lady?" Garrett arrogantly returned the stare, half annoyed, half amused, and completely unconcerned whether she approved of him or not. But what an earthy, delicate creature to find in the company of a holy man! A common forester's daughter possibly, yet the golden wealth of her hair and the classic sculpting of her features made him think of a fair Diana.

A vision of a cool forest filled his senses. Life fluttered in the shadows, velvety green moss stretched along the floor, and the soft scent of fertile loam stirred his senses. Diana. The lithe and elusive huntress. Defender of Life. Virgin goddess of the Forest.

"I said *I* gave the order for our bowmen to attack," she snapped without offering an apology or an excuse. Green eyes flashed gold like a lioness's.

Garrett mentally shook himself and searched for the

25

anger that had nearly deserted him. It had been a long time since the sight of a woman had so muddled his thinking. He fought to clear his head. "What did you say?"

"I said I gave the order to attack," she repeated slowly, distinctly, as if she thought him addled.

"What! You?" Garrett sputtered. A woman captain? No wonder Lyonesse's defenses suffered.

"We would have defeated the pirates if some *fool* hadn't sailed into the way," she added, casting him a look of pure annoyance.

"Sailed into the way!" He stepped closer to her, set on making his point, almost ready to shake a finger in her face. "If we hadn't sailed into the bay when we did, your village would be afire right now. Did you not think to look at our colors?"

"Did you think to send up the earl's colors *before* sailing into the bay?" she demanded. Her chin jutted out a little farther.

The old man tugged at the girl's sleeve. "Daughter, dear?"

"How was I to know you'd attack anything that moved?" Garrett ignored the holy man's attempt to step between them.

"How could I be certain that you were not one of them?" she countered. "I would have endangered the men of Lyonesse to do anything other than I did."

Garrett clamped his mouth shut. The merit of her argument could not be denied, and that annoyed him even more.

Father John elbowed his way past Garrett and introduced himself to the holy man. "The battle is over and the outcome is happy. Let us give thanks and take pleasure in each other's company."

At the holy man's side, the golden-haired defender of Lyonesse pressed her lips together, obviously as reluctant as Garrett to give up on the disagreement.

"Welcome, Father John," the old man said with a kindly smile. "I am Highlord Aidan. Please let me present the ladies. This lovely maid with the harp is my niece, Lady Brenna."

A TENDER MAGIC

Still fuming, Garrett bowed to the flirtatious, dark-haired maid.

Then, touching the arm of the woman on his left, the old man added, "And this fair warrior is my daughter, Lady Leandra."

Chapter 3

Garrett's eyes widened at this revelation, and he nearly groaned aloud. Quickly he covered his surprise with a courteous bow. When he dared to look at Lady Leandra again, he stared in astonishment. *This* solemn-faced Diana was the heiress of Lyonesse? *This* was his future liege lady?

"My son, you are a hero here," Highlord Aidan said in obvious hope of easing the tension. "You have rescued us. Please come partake of our humble hospitality."

"'Twould be my pleasure, your lordship," Garrett said, unable to take his eyes from the old man's daughter. What had Reginald called her? A damsel in distress. Indeed. As much as he wanted to take her to task for forcing him to raise his first white flag, he didn't dare utter another word in anger. Not to Reginald's betrothed. Sweet Jesu, his first surrender was to a woman!

He glared at Lady Leandra and ground his teeth. Why hadn't he just refused Reginald's request and taken his chances on getting to France on his own?

She glared back.

Some thought occurred to her, softening her demeanor ever so slightly. "Were any of your men injured?" she asked.

"Yes, one," Garrett bit out, afraid to say more. Did this mere girl understand how miraculous it was they'd suffered only one wounded? "The boy in the crow's nest."

"Brenna? Please see to the injured man right away," Lady Leandra ordered. The dark-haired maid obeyed immediately.

"My niece is quite a good nurse." Lord Aidan flashed

Garrett a wary, disarming smile. "Your man will receive the best of care."

"Father, the food is being laid out for the men in the kitchen," Lady Leandra said with a suddenly uneasy look in Garrett's direction. Lady Brenna returned to whisper something in the lady's ear, something about "destroyed . . . and only enough bread for . . ."

"Your generosity is appreciated, my lady," Garrett began. It seemed Lyonesse was even poorer than he first thought. "However, we have our own stores aboard ship."

"But we have enough, Sir Garrett." Lady Leandra squared her shoulders and stiffened her back reed straight. "You cannot refuse Lyonesse hospitality after you have come to our defense."

Garrett bowed a grudging acceptance. Considering the poverty he saw around him, he had little inclination to indulge her pride. But to argue with Reginald's lady would be most ungracious and unwise. Already she frowned at him—the corners of her mouth turned down and a furrow formed between her softly arched brows—as though she were being insulted. As though she were the one who had been attacked.

What were the words and phrases Reginald had told him to use? Some of the expressions were so fawning that they refused to roll off Garrett's tongue. "Thank you for . . . your gracious welcome. It is a pleasure to step on solid ground again . . . on Lyonesse soil." That much he could say with all honesty.

"Then come, my son, and share with us," invited the highlord. He took Garrett companionably by the arm and led him up the street. "We of Lyonesse are most pleased with this union of our realm and Tremelyn. We have been preparing for days for your arrival, and all is nearly ready for a great banquet."

Garrett walked toward the castle gates, dreading the formality of the betrothal ceremony that would undoubtedly be part of the evening to come.

* * *

"Leandra, I've been looking for you." Brenna caught sight of Leandra walking into the great hall. Clog heels clicking against the floor, she charged after her cousin.

So many questions had tumbled about in her head as she saw to the Tremelyn boy's wounds that she had almost made a poor job of it and left the boy's arm bound too tight.

"So what do you think of Sir Garrett?" Brenna hissed at Leandra's back, intent on making her cousin speak to her. After the heated words between Leandra and the knight, Brenna just had to know what her cousin was thinking.

"Uncle Aidan likes him," Brenna said, trying to keep the anxiety out of her voice. She didn't want to appear too concerned, but if anything went wrong with the marriage arrangements, if she didn't go with Leandra to Tremelyn as a waiting woman, she'd probably never set foot in the world beyond Lyonesse's shores, never see the spires of London or learn the new songs and dances of real jongleurs. She wasn't about to let anything go wrong if she could help it.

Without replying, Leandra walked to the center of the hall, her eyes on the servants hanging green garland, her back to Brenna.

Abruptly Brenna stopped behind her cousin and planted her fists on her hips. Sometimes getting Leandra to talk could be a chore. "You're not going to take a dislike to Sir Garrett just because you didn't fancy the way he sailed into the bay, are you?"

Abruptly, Leandra turned to Brenna, concern written in the way she pressed her lips thin. "Did you see to the boy who was wounded? How serious is it?"

"'Twas little more than a scratch." Brenna snapped the hem of her blue gown at a hound that sniffed too close. "Shoo, dog. The boy will be fine if the wound doesn't fester. But you didn't answer me. You liked Sir Garrett, didn't you? I could tell by the way you scowled."

"He will do." Leandra frowned at Brenna. "A little arrogant, but I think Lord Reginald has done well enough for us. He sent us the knight that we need. A man ready to fight."

"Oh, he will do?" Brenna mimicked. "I thought he was perfect. Sir Perfect."

Thank heavens she wasn't going to have to convince Leandra of that. Her end was a little closer. She could already see herself in a beautiful cloak, her harp under her arm, standing in the bow of the cog and sailing toward the shores of Cornwall with the wind in her face and freedom spread before her.

"Uncle Aidan read the letter of introduction to me," Brenna said. "Sir Garrett has fought in France and has traveled to the Holy Land, and Lord Reginald recommends him most highly."

"Yes, I know," Leandra said.

"So what do you like best about Sir Garrett?" Brenna asked, casting a sly look at her cousin. Leandra seldom failed to take part in this childhood game of theirs. They never liked the same things. "I liked best his tawny hair and his long legs," Brenna offered as bait.

"Yes, more fresh garland over there." Leandra directed a servant to the place over a door and turned her back on Brenna again. "When you finish with that, be so good as to wash all the tabletops with rosewater. I'd like for the hall to smell like flowers."

"Roses, good," Brenna said, clapping her hands, but never forgetting her goal. "So appropriate for a betrothal celebration. No doubt Sir Garrett will have gifts and a betrothal speech for you. He'll be speaking for the earl, of course, but if one were to imagine Sir Garrett as—"

"Sir Garrett is the earl's man," Leandra interrupted, her voice curt and sharp. "Only a representative."

"Yes, of course." Her cousin's harshness startled Brenna. She sneaked a curious glance at Leandra's face. There was something odd about her cousin's behavior, odd even for Leandra. "So, did you like his blue eyes? Maybe we should be talking about whether he likes you? I'll wager if you'd been a man, he would have struck you down out there in the street."

"He was angry," Leandra agreed. "He had a right to be."

31

"So what do you like best about him?" Brenna prompted. "You've had thoughts. I can tell."

Leandra turned to her cousin at last. "If I tell you, will you stop chattering after me?"

Brenna nodded.

"I like best his age. He's old enough to have fighting experience the older men-at-arms can respect, yet youthful enough to claim the younger men's confidence. Captain Ralph has already shown respect toward Sir Garrett."

"Oh, rot me, Leandra," Brenna moaned and shook her head. "That's not what I was asking and you know it. Stop talking like a field marshal. What did you like about his person?"

When Leandra hesitated, Brenna looked down at her hands indifferently but leaned closer, eager to hear the answer.

"All right." Leandra thoughtfully tapped a finger against her lips. "I like the firmness in his jaw and the slight squareness of his chin. I think it reveals that he is decisive and not easily swayed from his decisions. Stubborn. But I think he is honorable. A true knight."

"A true, chivalrous knight?" Brenna asked. "Do you think so? You've never met one. My father was Lyonesse's last knight, and he died in battle so long ago that neither of us remembers him."

"But I'm sure he must have been very much like Sir Garrett," Leandra persisted with an unusual faraway look coming into her dark eyes.

"Maybe." Brenna wondered whether Leandra was withholding some thought. She liked the picture of her father that Leandra's words conjured. But she forgot the vision when she caught sight of a serving girl hurrying in the direction of the kitchen. Amice ought to be able to help them. "Come here, girl. Have you finished bathing the guests? Come tell Leandra and me what Sir Garrett and his squire are like."

"Magnificent, my lady, the knight especially," Amice said when she joined Leandra and Brenna in the center of the hall. A crooked-tooth grin gleamed in a face flushed from working over steamy water. She wiped her work-roughened hands on her apron. "I helped him undress, and he stepped into that tub bare as a babe at baptism."

"Don't be a rattle-pate, girl, give us details," Brenna demanded.

"Now, Lady Brenna, you know your uncle doesn't approve of such talk," Amice said, looking over her shoulder at the other servants in the hall. She lowered her voice, and she and Brenna put their heads together. Leandra remained apart, but Brenna noted that her cousin's ear was turned toward them.

Amice began, "Well, I can tell you Sir Garrett is broad of shoulder." She held out her arms in a wide measurement. "And his back is aripple with muscles. He's sensitive in the small of it. Near jumped from the tub when I scrubbed low, and cross like—in that deep voice—he bade me to move on."

Brenna sighed. "Yes?"

Leandra stepped closer, her ear nearly bent in their direction, but still she refused to join them.

"And his torso narrows to his hips like so." Amice's hands fluttered down into a vee. "I tell you, I never saw a firmer, rounder behind, my lady." She giggled and cupped her hands to hint at the shape. "His thighs! Long and hard."

"What else?" Brenna prompted. "Tell us."

"His chest bulges firm and 'tis covered with hair as tawny as the curls on his head, and it grows all the way down to a fine nest—well, that's enough for you to know."

"Oh," Brenna groaned in disappointment, then brightened. "The squire, what's he like?" She'd liked the younger man's looks, too. He hadn't rudely dismissed her as Sir Garrett had. "Are they brothers? Are they alike?"

"Oh, yes, my lady," Amice said. "Squire Wystan is built much like his brother, only slightly smaller, and his hair more sandy, of course."

"Do you want to ask something?" Brenna asked, tugging on Leandra's arm.

"No. Off with you, Amice. My only desire at the moment, cousin, is to complete the betrothal ceremony and sign the final contract," Leandra murmured, obviously distracted once more. "I just wish we had signed it today."

Brenna noted that her cousin's frown had grown deeper than ever. But she didn't take the expression too seriously. Leandra was always overly concerned with particulars. "Today. Tomorrow. What difference does it make? Lord Reginald is already fulfilling his part of the agreement. Uncle Aidan's signing is a mere detail."

"I'll just feel better when Father sets the seal to the contract," Leandra repeated.

An unsettling thought came to Brenna. "Are you thinking of Sir Leofric?" She shivered, always her reaction to the thought of this man who had courted her cousin. She found him handsome in a dark way, with his strange light-brown, almost yellow, eyes, and his smooth olive-skinned complexion. But his inclination to wear purple as if he were of a kingly rank offended her. The man presumed too much. "Do you think he will appear tonight and make a commotion about your betrothal?"

"I hope not." Leandra shook her head. "But you know how Leofric is given to displays."

Brenna twisted a dark lock around her finger. So that was what was on Leandra's mind. Sir Garrett might have passed Leandra's approval, but they were still a long way from Tremelyn.

The sounds of merriment seeped through the tall oaken doors of Lyonesse's great hall—doors lofty enough to admit the legendary giants of the land.

Garrett hesitated in the passage outside the portal. All he needed to do was present the ring and gifts, make a speech, and charm the lady over a meal. Lord Reginald had told him what was to be said. But the successful alliance of two houses rested in his hands.

Uneasy, he turned to look at the men following him. Out of long habit he walked from man to man—Wystan, Father John, and Master Cedric—inspecting their freshly bathed faces and clean dress clothes like a captain inspecting troops before a battle. The three stared back, their faces long with sober, doubtful expressions.

Satisfied with their appearance and preparation, Garrett turned back to the door. Before he could speak to the page, a warm, restraining hand gripped his arm. He glanced over his shoulder at Father John, flanked by Wystan and Cedric.

"Forgive me for saying so, my son," Father John began, "but you don't look like a man about to win a lady's favor for his liege lord."

Garrett looked at the others to see if they agreed. Wystan nodded. "'Tis true, brother. Your frown alone would lay waste to all of France for King Edward."

For the first time, Garrett became aware of the tension in his jaws and the tightness in his shoulders. His outrage smoldered anew with the realization that he was furious with the Lady Leandra, and even angrier with himself for being angry. "The lady did order an attack on us without taking note of our colors," Garrett growled as much to himself as to the good father. "For that a man suffers."

"'Twas an unfortunate way to make our landing at Lyonesse, 'tis true," Father John said, shaking his head in sorrow. "But little harm was done. I'm sure Lady Leandra regrets the incident."

"I think it's funny," Wystan offered with a derisive chuckle. "The reason you can't laugh, brother, is because you've never raised a white flag in your life, and you hate that when you did, it was against a woman."

"That's not so," Garrett snapped. He glared at his smirking little brother. But inside he knew it was true. His first deed as a knight had ended in a surrender—to a woman. How glorious!

Father John hid a smile with a cough.

Earnest Cedric stepped forward, apparently keen on lulling his commander's temper. "The men in the kitchen are well-satisfied with the hospitality. Though there is not overmuch to eat, the people are companionable enough and merry."

Resentfully, Garrett nodded.

"Do you have the ring?" Father John asked.

"Right here." Garrett pulled a blue silken veil from inside his surcoat. "Wystan has the other gifts, the fabrics and the jeweled bridle."

Father John said, "Do you know what you want to say?"

Garrett ignored Father John's question. "Why wasn't her father out there giving orders, I want to know." He shoved the veil deep inside his surcoat again. "What father puts his daughter in charge of the bowmen?"

"Garrett," Father John soothed. "I know you to be a more reasonable man than this. Where is your sense of humor? What lady could resist a knight who comes to her rescue flying a white flag? Just think of this betrothal as the recruiting of a worthy ally for your lord. Would Tremelyn not be in good hands if the Lady Leandra were left in charge of defenses?"

"Indeed, if first the Lady Lioness did not slaughter her own lord upon his return from battle," Garrett growled. He allowed a slow, rueful smile to ease his frown. He relished the vision of Reginald dodging arrows at his own castle gate. At the moment, the surprise that this marriage would bring the earl seemed no more than his lord deserved. "Stay near me tonight, Father. I may need your prompting to find the right words. Most of all to avoid the wrong ones."

"I'll be there, my son."

Garrett signaled to the page to open the tall, oaken doors, and the envoys of Reginald, Earl of Tremelyn, stepped into the great hall of Castle Lyonesse.

Music ceased and conversation lapsed.

Immediately Highlord Aidan and Lady Leandra rose respectfully from their tall chairs beneath the canopied dais at the far end of the hall. Benches scraped against the wooden floor as vassals turned from their talk and stood to greet the heroes of the day.

The minstrels in the gallery began a trumpet fanfare. Cheers and applause echoed against the hall rafters and brought a reluctant smile to Garrett's lips.

Careful to look stately and unhurried, he walked the

length of the hall with his head high, his shoulders square—
like a knight. He could feel all eyes on him. When he looked
ahead he saw that no forester's daughter stood next to the
highlord this evening. Instead, an heiress, dressed in a creamy
white gown trimmed in gold embroidery and overlaid with
a rich green surcoat, waited for him beneath the canopy. A
woven gold chaplet crowned her elegant brow, and her
golden locks were tamed into a thick braid.

The torchlight brought a pale rosy color to her flawless,
fair skin. She looked the true princess this night. Pure and
lovely. Yet there was about her still the tentative air of a wild
creature.

Garrett swallowed.

"Sir Garrett and gentlemen," Aidan greeted. "We are
pleased to have you join us. I trust Lyonesse's hospitality
meets your needs?"

"Your lordship has been most gracious and generous."
Garrett bowed slightly in Lady Leandra's direction. The
vassals' cheers and applause led him to think this was a good
start until he noticed that Lady Leandra neither cheered nor
applauded with the others. Her solemn expression remained
unchanged. His own smile faltered—for a moment only. He
forged on.

"Your lordship. My Lady Leandra. 'Tis my pleasure to be
of service to you, and it is my honor to represent Reginald,
Earl of Tremelyn, in presenting you with your betrothal
gifts."

Garrett stopped, allowing an expectant hush to fall over
the crowd.

To his surprise, Highlord Aidan sat down and the vassals
settled on their benches once more. Lady Leandra stood
alone with her hands at her sides and her somber gaze intent
on him.

"The honor and pleasure is ours, Sir Garrett," she said,
speaking in a rich, husky voice that all could hear. "We
thank you for your rescue this afternoon. We are most happy
to welcome you, Father John, and your men among us."

Garrett smiled at her. He thought those fair words

considering they had nearly done battle a few hours ago. Now if she would only give him some indication that she was a conventional maid susceptible to flattery and compliments.

"My lady." Garrett bowed slightly again and pulled the blue veil from his surcoat. "Upon leaving Tremelyn, my lord, Reginald, entrusted me with this silken veil and bade me give it to you and to you alone upon my arrival. For he wants you to know how pleased he is with the betrothal and how eager he is to welcome you to Tremelyn. He wishes for this ring and these gifts to seal your betrothal vows." He gestured to the goods Wystan carried.

Daintily Lady Leandra reached out to accept the silk without touching Garrett. Turning the fabric in her hands, she appeared to admire the blue color and the fineness of the weave. But she did not look as closely as Garrett knew she should. He clasped his hands behind him, wondering whether he was going to have to urge her to examine the veil again. Then she drew her hand over the silk slowly, hesitated, and peered intently at the knot.

Garrett relaxed a little. She found it.

The lady glanced up at him, her verdant eyes widening in surprise and a soft smile coming at last to her lips. A lovely, sweet smile that glowed with pleasure—and relief. Garrett realized she had been afraid there would be no betrothal ring—not from him anyway.

"It is engraved with your name and the earl's," Garrett explained as Lady Leandra eagerly untied the golden circle from the blue silk. "His lordship asked me to slip it on your finger on his behalf. If I may?"

After taking a moment to read the inscription, Leandra held the ring out to him.

Garrett took it and reached for her left hand. Her warm fingers, tiny and delicate, trembled slightly in his grasp. That betrayal of her anxiety gave him confidence. He cast her an encouraging smile, then holding her hand firmly, eased the golden circle into place.

The ring hung loose, swinging on her slender finger.

Sweet Jesu. Garrett stared at it dumbfounded. The cursed thing was too big. Enormous. It could slip from her finger without resistance. When the earl had first shown him the golden circle, it seemed impossibly small and dainty. Later, glorying in their cleverness like a pair of school boys, they'd contrived to present the ring tied in the scarf. He and Lord Reginald had never considered this complication.

Garrett opened his mouth to make some apology, but before he could get a word out, Leandra doubled her fingers into her tiny palm and yanked her hand from his grasp. She pressed the balled fist against her heart, covering it with her other hand as if she feared that he might try to reclaim the ring.

"Thank you, Sir Garrett," she said. The rare smile faded to a look of earnest gratitude that he knew he didn't deserve. "The ring is most beautiful, and I shall wear it as a constant reminder of the solemnness of my betrothal vows. Please be certain to send the earl my thanks in your next dispatch. I have a gift for him also. You will dispatch it to him?"

"Yes, indeed, of course," Garrett stammered, still uncertain what to do about the ring and only now recalling that tradition required that the lady also bestow a betrothal gift.

Lady Leandra signaled to a servant, who scurried forward with an ornately carved gift box. She opened it and lifted out a long lock of golden hair tied with silken threads through a wooden ring. Even from where he stood, Garrett could see that the ring was skillfully carved with an R entwined about an L and polished to a smooth, nearly golden sheen.

"This ring is of oak," she said, holding up the gift for all in the great hall to see. But she eyed Garrett as if she dared him to deride the humbleness of her gift. Everyone watched her in respectful silence. Garrett waited politely and prayed that no more went wrong.

"Oak is strong and durable," the lady went on. "Oak is cherished in Lyonesse. The sturdiest tree in the forest, yet humble enough to feed the squirrels and shelter the lowly ferns. Oak is the wealth of our realm. It is the material for our boats, and its leaf is the device, the symbol, we use on our arms. I hope the earl will tie this lock of my hair in his helmet as my favor to him and wear this ring as a symbol of my undying affection and faithfulness to him."

With that she replaced the shining lock and the ring into the box and handed it to Garrett.

He took it carefully, studying with great curiosity the long golden curl lying twisted on a cushion of green velvet. He glanced searchingly at Leandra again. She watched him with somber apprehension.

Something stirred inside Garrett's body, something deep, troubling, and forbidden. Something he didn't want to acknowledge. Yet to stare at the thick braid of golden hair resting on her shoulder enthralled him. To behold the loose lock of her hair in the box was daringly intimate. A sharing of something that she offered only to her betrothed—to her lover. With concentrated effort Garrett resisted the desire to caress the golden lock while all the people in the great hall watched.

Someone coughed and cleared his throat, someone who sounded like Father John.

Garrett dragged his gaze from the golden curl and remembered why he stood in front of all these people and this solemn, green-eyed young woman. He snapped the gift box closed and took a deep breath.

"My lord, Reginald, will be most pleased with such a distinctive and unique gift. I shall forward this to him immediately. I know that he will be eager to wear the ring of Lyonesse's great oak and to tie the lock of his betrothed's hair to his helmet."

Approval roared from the vassals.

A smile of relief flickered across the lady's face, soft yet brilliant, and so utterly disarming that Garrett's dislike of her nearly melted. He grinned, his confidence regained and his heart oddly lightened. Somehow he had said the right words. The lady knew how to smile, and she was truly lovely when she did. Success was still possible.

Chapter 4

The feast will begin!" Highlord Aidan called out. He struggled to his feet and motioned to the servants to set up the tables and spread the white cloths. The minstrels immediately began to pipe a lively tune. "Come, join your lord's betrothed for the meal, my son," Aidan called. "Sit, sit. There is room for your men, too."

Conversation filled the hall once more. Garrett relaxed a little when Leandra almost smiled at him as he sat down beside her. In silence and without touching, they washed their hands in the bowl of rosewater offered by a page.

The kitchen procession boasted platter after platter of delectable and artfully arranged courses. There was even a cockatrice—an amusing delicacy made of a spice-stuffed capon and a suckling pig sewn together and garnished with feathers and fruit.

Garrett watched a blush spread across Lady Leandra's face when the jester—complete in his bell-trimmed suit of colors—rode into the hall astride a donkey. In one hand he balanced a silver platter of a carefully wrought subtlety. The traditional marzipan had been sculptured into the form of cupid, complete with bow and arrow.

"The cupid," she said, glancing at him from beneath dark lashes. In her embarrassment she pinkened prettily. "'Tis in honor of the earl and me."

"Of course," Garrett said, distracted by the delicate color that flooded into her cheeks. Perhaps she was not a conventional maid, he thought, but near enough to deserve his best. Taking his supping knife from his belt, he began to carve

41

meat, his duty as a guest. She refused to eat much, but he attended her with pride because he knew—and he'd often been told—that taking care of a lady at the table was among his finer accomplishments.

Midway through the serving of the cockatrice, the abbey bells rang vespers and the hall grew quiet. The guests rose.

Bewildered, Garrett joined the assembly in rising respectfully. Leandra turned to her father and waited.

The feast marshal helped Highlord Aidan from the table.

"I go to my evening prayers now, children," the old man said, raising his hands in a gesture of blessing, much as a priest would. "Make merry and show our guests a good time." With a farewell nod in Garrett's direction, the highlord grasped his staff, stepped stiffly from the dais, and toiled down the length of the hall and out the door—a wise man sojourning to his mountaintop.

When the doors closed behind him, the assembly heartily resumed wolfing down food, guzzling drink, and doing their best to follow their lord's instructions. Garrett noted the lady seemed to find nothing amiss. Apparently she took so much on herself because her father was in his chapel.

As the trenchers were being cleared away, the highlord's niece ensconced herself in the vacant chair next to him.

"Remember me? I'm Leandra's cousin and her waiting lady." She planted her chin in the palm of her hand and leaned forward so that her breasts plumped against the scoop neckline of her gown.

She regarded Garrett with a look of admiration that made him sit back uncomfortably in his chair. "Mostly I'm waiting for a husband," she added. "I haven't had the great good fortune to have an earl ask for my hand."

Garrett smiled at her joke, but avoided letting his gaze linger on those ripe breasts. She was a pretty thing, with dark curls and clear gray gaze, complemented by her amber velvet gown. But the kind of coyness that glinted in her eyes and twitched at the corners of her mouth made him wary. "Yes, I remember you, Lady Brenna. I'm sure a lovely maid such as you will find a worthy husband soon."

"At Tremelyn perchance," she suggested. "Have you been telling Leandra all about Tremelyn?"

Leandra pushed her trencher aside. "Yes, Sir Garrett, we would like to hear about Lord Reginald's castle and about what you have brought us in the cogs."

"If it please you, my lady," Garrett began, with a glance at Leandra. She nodded encouragement. This was part of what he'd been sent to do. He cleared his throat and began with the things Reginald had told him to say. "Tremelyn is a fine castle with a vast great hall and a large orchard. It is appointed in every way to be a comfortable home. 'Tis well-built on high ground to withstand sieges. Just beyond the walls is a fine forest for hunting."

"What is the royal suite like?" Brenna asked.

"For the royal suite new silk has been spun and fine fabrics woven for the bed hangings. The earl's royal crest and Lyonesse's device is being sewn into a fine tapestry to be hung above—"

Lady Leandra broke in, tapping her finger on the table. "That all sounds very nice, Sir Garrett. But in truth, I'm more interested in what arms the earl has sent for Lyonesse's protection."

Garrett closed his mouth and stared at Leandra. Did she truly wish to speak of such matters here and now? The soft smile he glimpsed earlier was gone. She regarded him with sober expectation. As he struggled to make the mental leap from suitor-once-removed to knight, Brenna touched his shoulder.

"Leandra is our field marshal, so you see." She pulled a face that begged indulgence. "She doesn't wear armor like some ladies. But she is a tolerable archer. Do tell us about the wedding plans. Will there be a tourney with handsome knights like you there? For the feast, will the earl cut open a pie filled with live birds?"

Lady Leandra leaned toward Garrett, demanding his attention by putting a hand on his arm. "We'll talk of that in good time, cousin. Sir, how many men-at-arms? And weapons? What sort and how many?"

43

"The pirates are gone, Leandra," Brenna groaned, leaning across Garrett to talk to her cousin. "Who cares about weapons?"

With a growing sense of entrapment and disapproval, Garrett sat back and glared at one lady, then the other. The cousin talked like a bride and the bride talked like a captain of the guard.

"Arms and fighting men are matters best left to men," he said to Leandra. "Your father and I will talk of these things on the morrow, when the final betrothal papers are signed." Garrett reached for his goblet. He hoped that put an end to the matter.

Ignoring the silent Leandra, he favored Brenna with a reply. "Yes, I believe there will be the traditional pie with four and twenty blackbirds."

Lady Brenna clapped her hands in delight. "Oh, good. I love it when they escape and swoop about so everyone dodges and screams. Will there be a royal hunt? You know, the brigands have become so troublesome, we dare not even ride out to hunt without a heavy guard."

Before Garrett could reply, Leandra rapped him firmly on the arm. He turned to find her eyeing him with a fierce gaze, almost lionlike. The princess was gone and Diana the defender had returned. "You will discuss these betrothal details with me."

Garrett shifted uncomfortably in his chair. He'd never met a woman like Leandra of Lyonesse.

"Did not the previous envoy tell you this?" Leandra asked. "All agreements are made in my presence with my father's consent."

"That's true," Brenna agreed, pushing a crumb of bread about the white tablecloth with her forefinger. "Uncle Aidan always takes Leandra's counsel. But why can't arms talk wait until the morrow? Will the wedding take place in Tremelyn's cathedral?"

"No. Yes. I mean yes, in the cathedral. No, the envoy was ill. He did not give me details of the negotiations." Garrett sat back and refused to look at either maid. He knew exactly how Daniel felt in the lion's den.

A motion at the edge of Garrett's vision made him turn to catch a meaningful look from Father John, who sat just down the table from him. The good father's glare of admonition reminded Garrett that his duty was to win the lady and take her to Tremelyn. The rest was up to Reginald.

"How many men-at-arms?" Lady Leandra demanded softly in a husky voice nonetheless resolute.

Garrett swallowed his irritation and forced the information to his lips without looking at her. He did not like discussing these things with her. "His lord sent eighty-five men-at-arms. Thirty-five are bowmen."

"Experienced or new men?"

"All veterans. I selected them myself."

"Excellent," she said, as if she had every faith in him. His condemnation of her flagged a little. "What weapons do you bring?"

"Pikes, crossbows, axes, maces, and longbows—of good Spanish yew. Do you wish to see the manifest now?" He couldn't keep the derision from his tone.

"Spanish yew longbows. Excellent choices. No, I'll review the manifest tomorrow." She nodded in satisfaction, either ignoring or failing to catch the sarcasm.

Garrett continued. "Master Cedric is an excellent man to command the garrison. He is capable. Steady. Good with the men. He believes in thorough training and tolerates little rowdiness."

"Master Cedric?" Leandra asked.

"Yes. He will command the garrison."

"You mean you aren't going to be commander?" Lady Leandra exclaimed. She sat back and stared at him, surprise in the lift of her brows. "But you are the knight Lord Reginald sent. He promised me a knight."

"I am to set up the garrison and begin the training," Garrett explained patiently as he fingered the stem of his goblet. He sensed danger here. He was *not* going to stay in Lyonesse. "Then I'll escort you safely to Tremelyn. Those are my orders directly from the earl."

Lady Leandra regarded him in sharp silence. Inwardly Garrett cursed. What would she object to now? What was she going to demand? He had expected to sail into Lyonesse bay, to introduce himself to a simpering, grateful maid, and to start giving orders. What folly!

Once more he silently railed against Reginald for requiring this impossible undertaking of him—for pitching him against a deceptively delicate creature who long ago had given up mere female obstinacy for a lioness's determination.

"You have no faith in Master Cedric?" Garrett asked, hoping to regain whatever ground he'd lost. "I selected the man myself. The earl approved of him. Would you dispute the earl's orders?"

"Master Cedric may be a very skilled warrior, and he obviously has great concern for his men, but he was not the hero of the day. He does not have your presence," Leandra explained.

"My what?"

"So true, cousin," Brenna agreed.

Garrett shifted in his chair once more, uncomfortable under Leandra's appraising gaze. Brenna leaned over to whisper in his ear. "Please say you'll stay. If you don't, she won't go. Then what will we do?"

Lady Leandra went on, ignoring her cousin. "Sir Garrett, you are the hero today. The Lyonesse men will follow you. I think it better that you stay here. Captain Ralph can escort me to Tremelyn," the lady concluded as if the issue were settled and her pronouncement were as good as a royal earl's order.

"An escort of your own men is not what my lord intends." Garrett's forbearance frayed and he spoke through clamped teeth. "Great danger lurks on the road between here and Tremelyn. I will be your escort."

"Great danger lurks off the shore of Lyonesse," Lady Leandra countered without raising her voice. "Sir Garrett, are you not pledged as a knight to defend the weak? You have seen how weak we are."

"I am pledged to the earl, and he wishes—"

Tiny brass bells tinkled between their faces.

Garrett jumped and Leandra started. The noisome as-

46

sembly in the hall grew quiet, and the minstrels in the gallery above ceased playing.

Once more the jester shook his handful of bells between Garrett and Leandra. Brenna beamed, clapped her hands with victory, then thumped the table with an open hand. "It's time for my dance. You are going to watch me dance, my lady? My lord?"

Brenna tossed her head and fluttered her eyelashes at Garrett. He sat back in his chair, relieved to have this exchange with the iron-willed Leandra interrupted.

At a sign from Brenna, the minstrels started up the music, rich with the reedy strains of a pipe and the mellow strings of a harp. Brenna danced away, light on her feet, her dark hair swinging across her back.

To Garrett's surprise, Lady Lioness fell silent and watched her cousin's performance. He, too, was soon caught up in the music's lively beat and the airy melody. Brenna moved lithely, with grace and flow, the sort born of talent and the loving kinship of rhythm and song and body.

In dismay Garrett watched Wystan twist on his bench, craning his neck to stare spellbound after the swaying skirts of the young temptress.

When Lady Brenna caught Wystan's obvious looks of admiration, she laughed. Alluringly, she danced across the hall, took the squire's hands in hers, and drew the boy out onto the floor. Red-faced and mesmerized, Garrett's brother stumbled over his own feet, his gaze fastened on Brenna's reeling hips, his ardor beading his forehead and newly furred lip with perspiration.

Garrett groaned silently and rubbed a hand across his brow.

The rowdy vassals cheered their dancing guest, young Squire Wystan, stamped their feet and clapped their hands.

The hounds, full of banquet scraps, waddled across the floor, scampering a few steps to avoid being stepped on, and stretched themselves out on the hall's hearth, near the blazing fire.

Leandra settled back in her chair, her gaze on her lively cousin, but her troubled thoughts lingered on the handsome

47

man beside her. How could it be that this knight, the hero of the day, was not the warrior who would command the garrison guard? She had fought through all those long hours of negotiations to win just such a knight from the earl. Sir Perfect would not stay.

She clutched the heavy, oversized betrothal ring tighter in her hand, the smooth gold pressing painfully into her fingers. Sometimes miscalculations required adjustments, she reminded herself, as with the ring. She could make the ring fit. Ribbon wrapped around it would do. For Lyonesse's sake, she would make this work.

Before long others joined the dancing. The jester, Tyler Wotte, was out there, too. He capered about, making all laugh with his improbable, out-of-rhythm movements. Ludicrously he gamboled up to the head table, gave Leandra a stumbling bow, and invited her to join the dance. She could not refuse.

Courteously she turned to Garrett and invited him to join them. His frown was daunting. Relief swept over her when he accepted with a good-natured grin. He stood up, taking her hand full in his as a friend would—not by her little finger with his little finger as a lover would.

They joined the lively dancing, skipping around the hall in a great, thunderous circle. Sir Garrett laughed with the others and did his part to set the hall arumble with stomping feet.

Out of a gaggle of women in the corner stumbled Brenna with a veil tied across her eyes. "Beware! Beware!" she cried, her arms outstretched to grab the nearest body.

Leandra scolded herself for not remembering that a rowdy game of blindman's bluff was one of Brenna's favorite amusements when there was someone she wanted to kiss.

Brenna swept around in Sir Garrett's direction. He stepped neatly beyond her reach. Those nearby laughed knowingly. Leandra ducked beneath her cousin's grasp and turned in time to see Wystan approach. The crowd grew quiet. Small bubbles of laughter burst forth from moment to moment.

As was the custom of the game, the young squire tugged off his hood, worn loose about his neck, and with it swatted at the hem of Brenna's gown.

Brenna giggled. "What are you doing? Where did all of you go? I know you're there even though you whisper."

Wystan swept his hood out just enough to snap at Brenna's skirt again. She squealed and laughed, whirling in his direction. "Who was that? Leandra? Do you bait me?"

"Not I, cousin," Leandra called from behind Brenna.

She watched as Wystan stooped and whipped the hood about once more. Instantly Brenna staggered forward, nearly tripping over the squire. Garrett grabbed his brother's collar and dragged him from the lady's clutches.

The jester jumped up in Brenna's face.

Certain that she had whom she wanted in her grasp, the lady threw her arms around Tyler Wotte's neck without removing her blindfold and kissed him soundly on the mouth. The jester kissed back—a wet, smacking kiss.

Leandra smothered giggles behind her hand. The crowd shrieked delight, tears of laughter streaming down the faces of those who'd partaken heavily of the pear cider.

Suspicious at last, Brenna ripped off the blindfold to come face to face with the grinning jester.

"Augh!" she wailed. White greasepaint smudged her lamenting lips.

The vassals roared with laughter.

Tyler threw his arms over his head and shrank to the floor as though in fear of losing his life.

More laughter. Ever pleased to be the center of attention, Brenna's frown of indignation faded into a grin. She joined in the mirth, tossing her curls and wiping the smudge from her lips with the back of her hand. She turned on Tyler Wotte, shaking a finger at him.

"Shame upon you, Master Jester," Brenna cried with a smile. "Now you pay the penalty of being captured."

The jester hung his head and accepted the blindfold from Brenna with mock resignation. Soon ladies taunted him with their sleeves, and he stumbled about the room, unerringly knowing the ladies from the gentlemen—the pretty ones from the crones—kissing as many women as he could get his hands on.

Leandra noted that the older ladies demurred and protested his kisses—a little. The younger ladies were more elusive, but Tyler's efforts did not go unrewarded. Finally a frowning feast marshal stripped the blindfold from the young man's grinning face and returned it to Brenna.

"Leandra, you must be the blindman now," Brenna said, grabbing her cousin by the arm. "Our newly betrothed lady must take her turn."

"I really don't think—"

The crowd clamored approval, drowning Leandra's protest. Reluctant to spoil the people's good time, she allowed the blindfold to be fastened tightly over her eyes. Brenna spun her around until she thought she was going to stagger disgracefully to her knees. She swayed uncertainly for a moment, trying to regain a sense of rightness with the world. Sleeves and hoods whipped about the hem of her creamy white gown, first from one side, then the other.

To her right she could hear Brenna's stifled giggles and her rustling skirts. On her left she could hear the murmur of men talking in the background. Jester's bells jingled softly. Tyler darted in close, then withdrew. He was an old friend she'd known since childhood. She had no fear of him.

Purposely, Leandra turned away from the sound of the bells in hopes of luring Tyler to move in closer. She could hear Brenna's laughter again just beyond her reach. The tinkle of bells. A tug on the back of her skirt. With lightning speed Leandra swung around and threw her arms around her harasser. She embraced a solid body much larger than she'd anticipated. She leaned into him, still just a little dizzy from the spin Brenna had given her.

"Kiss, kiss," Brenna shouted, and giggled. "Go on."

"They are not going to be satisfied until we do this."

Leandra knew Sir Garrett's voice at once, and his scent—unfamiliar but welcome—was disturbing. Her reaction to his sudden nearness confused her and she tensed against the strong arms already slipping around her waist. She tried to pull away without appearing to pull away, but he held her fast.

"Think of me as your betrothed," he murmured, gently drawing the blindfold from her eyes while one hand remained on her waist. "A brief kiss so all the maidens can dream of their lovers tonight. 'Tis but a game. A little smile would be nice, too. You know, to make your face brighten has become something of a challenge."

Leandra stared up at the handsome planes of the knight's face. A softness settled on the line of his lips, and the warmth of good humor glimmered his blue eyes.

"Like this?" She forced a smile to her lips, an upward curve that seemed stiff and awkward. What harm could there be in the kiss? 'Twas only a game. She decided to submit quickly and without fuss.

"Nice," he said as he lowered his lips to hers, pressing warmth and moist firmness against her mouth in a gesture that was meant to be a simple kiss—an innocent, platonic display of goodwill for the throng.

She closed her eyes and concentrated on the kiss, tasted the knight, smelled the man, became aware of the strength in his mouth and the potency in the body she leaned against. His lips moved against hers as if about to take something from her. The sensation thrilled in her belly. A disabling tingle feathered down her spine and whispered into her limbs, leaving her more weak than dizzy. She sagged against him.

His hands tightened, warm and firm on her waist. She knew he'd sensed her weakness. She longed to rest against him an instant longer, drawing on his strength and taking comfort in the warm haven of his embrace. But the insistent chill of reality settled over her. She dare not risk the pleasure. Abruptly she shoved herself away from him.

With a look of confusion, he released her. Guiltily, Leandra gulped for air, not because the kiss had been so long, but because she simply could not catch her breath. She stepped back, staring up at him in fear—understanding at last what a danger this man could be to her. How easy it would be to succumb to him, to his handsome face, to his solid strength of will—to be quelled by the hard blue of his angry eyes or entranced by the sunny-blue humor that shone there when he grinned.

For the first time in her life Leandra understood desire— she desired this man, the perfect, loyal knight of her liege lord.

She saw the comprehension flash in Sir Garrett's eyes. The uncertain smile on his lips vanished, and a frown creased his brow. In horror Leandra realized that he'd recognized the longing in her eyes. She knew that he understood—that she wanted him.

Shame burned in her cheeks. What a wanton he must think her. She stepped back another pace and stared at the floor. Her braid swung down close to her face, hiding her flaming cheeks from Sir Garrett and from the people who crowded about them.

Vassals, men and women alike, hooted their approval of the kiss, and the minstrels played a wild, discordant fanfare. Tyler Wotte danced an antic circle around them, then threw himself between the pair, making a kissy face at Garrett. The knight grinned good-naturedly and shoved the comic aside.

Brenna hurled herself at Garrett, and with a hearty laugh he kissed her on the cheek and led her into the dancing crowd and away from Leandra.

Momentarily forgotten, Leandra retreated to the dais. As she sank into her chair, she muttered a prayer for some inspiration, any idea that would force the brave and loyal Sir Garrett to remain in Lyonesse. She did not want to travel long days and nights with him to Tremelyn.

Chapter 5

Lady Leandra never forgets them, the poor who come to the castle for help," Captain Ralph told Garrett. "She always has something for them."

The two men were crouched on the battlement above the gate where Garrett had come to inspect the postern gate house.

He'd risen before the ringing of prime—when the dawn's first light touched the treetops—to inspect defenses. Garrett had been pleased to find the outer curtain walls in better condition than he first thought, and Captain Ralph more capable than he had first credited him.

During the tour, they caught a glimpse of Leandra below them, doling out the remains of the betrothal banquet to a line of supplicants. From where he crouched, Garrett could not see her face, only the top of the simple white wimple she wore. He listened to the gentle tones of her husky voice carried to him on the morning breeze.

"She knows them all by name," Ralph continued. "Cook told me that she once saw Lady Leandra take her own bread and snatch a crust from her cousin's mouth for the women and children at the gate."

Garrett's emotions warred with one another as he leaned over the stone parapet to watch Leandra. He wanted to like her. But he clearly recalled the petal softness of her response when he'd held her in his arms, warm and yielding in a kiss that betrayed desire. The flash in her verdant-green eyes—that dazzling gold flame of passion, had angered him. Only his own cool discipline kept him from thrusting her away and embarrassing them both in the presence of the cheering vassals.

But what troubled him most about that kiss was his own reaction. Discovering desire in a woman's eyes had never troubled him before. Hardly. As often as not, he'd taken advantage of that yearning expression, depending on his mood and the appeal of the lady herself. Yet that look of longing in Lady Leandra's eyes had disquieted him, had stirred a sharp, regretful longing that he had never experienced.

"The lady is generous and honorable," Captain Ralph said, his voice full of pride. "Lord Reginald is getting a good wife."

Garrett made no reply. He studied Leandra at the gate, docile and guileless, giving away the food. She hadn't intended to betray herself with that kiss. He knew that, and he didn't believe she had intended to tempt him. She was not like Brenna. For a moment after the kiss she'd stared at him wide-eyed, like a startled doe suddenly trapped. With surprising strength she shoved herself away from him, then ducked her head, hiding behind her braid. The only chivalrous thing to do was laugh to throw the attention to Lady Brenna, who plainly adored the feel of all eyes on her.

"I'm certain Lord Reginald will be pleased with her," Garrett assured Captain Ralph. If he thought for a moment that Lady Leandra had willfully tempted him or any other man, he would not in all good conscience be able to complete this undertaking for his lord. His honor would not allow him to bring Reginald anything but a virtuous lady.

At midmorning Highlord Aidan summoned Garrett from his inspection of the castle to the great hall for the signing of the marriage contract, the final irrevocable step in the alliance.

When Garrett arrived, he found to his annoyance that Leandra was already reviewing the document.

"My daughter will be finished shortly," the highlord

explained to Garrett, then he turned to address Father John about a holy matter.

The morning sunlight streamed through the windows, bathing Leandra in a golden glow as she sat at the table, poring over the sheets of parchment. From where Garrett waited, back against the wall, he could see the understanding play across the lady's features as she read. She was dressed as demurely as she had been at the gate, covered like the lady of the castle, her bearing like that of a princess. Her white coif hid her hair and glowed pure against the innocent blush in her cheeks. Her fingers caressed the contract gently, lovingly.

After their banquet discussion, he should have known that she was well-acquainted with the terms and all the Latin phrases used to set them down. He prayed that she would advise her father to sign this document without more trouble over who would command the garrison.

Across the room below the cruciform, Lord Aidan debated amiably with Father John whether Christ had owned his clothes or not—an obscure theological issue that only churchmen could find worthy of dissection. Highlord Aidan appeared ready to argue either side, frontward or backward, with equal enthusiasm.

At the table, Leandra drew a slender finger down the ship's manifest. The number of weapons and the men-at-arms satisfied her. And the dowry terms—everything but the details about the garrison pleased her. She touched the precious document tenderly and once again noted Lord Reginald's signature and seal at the bottom. When Father John had unrolled the scroll across her worktable to reveal the earl's name, she had almost let out a noisy sigh of relief.

Her marriage and Lyonesse's future lay in the words of the contract before her. But it would never do now to rush, to agree to something she would regret later.

"Nothing is said about who will command the garrison," she said, glancing up at Sir Garrett near the hearth. She had avoided looking at him all morning, afraid that she would stare at his good looks and be lost in the weakness that had overcome her when they had kissed. What she saw when she raised her gaze to meet his was that the deep blue of his samite tunic matched his eyes. His short tawny hair shone like a polished gold helmet in the morning sun.

She gulped silently. For all she knew, he was an earth-bound angel sent to tempt her. Thanks to his kiss, she'd spent a sleepless night thinking of what she might do to entice him to stay in Lyonesse.

"I don't believe my lord expected command of the garrison would be an issue. Cedric is qualified." Garrett folded his arms across his chest and straightened, standing head and shoulders above the other men. "He was concerned that you have an escort proper for your station."

"I don't care who my escort is," Leandra began without realizing how her words would sound. She simply couldn't understand how this mistake had happened. "Appearances mean little to me. I want security for my people."

Garrett moved away from the hearth, coming to stand before Leandra's worktable.

Leandra reconsidered her words as she looked up into his frowning face. "I mean, I appreciate Lord Reginald's concern, but—" She decided a change in tactics would be best. "You are a bachelor knight, are you not? You have yet to win your lands?"

"Yes, my lady." Puzzlement crossed his brow. She might have hit on something here.

"I could offer you a manor along the southwest coast with a keep. 'Tis in need of some repair, but it's a fine, large fortification within an hour's ride from here. The holding offers hunting and fishing rights, as well as rich farmland and grazing. The men and women of Lyonesse are most grateful for your service yesterday, and I—"

Leandra broke off when she saw his face turn deadly cold, still as stone. His eyes, which she'd found so attractive only a moment ago, turned icy blue. She swallowed the sudden lump in her throat. Mother have mercy, what had she done now?

Inexplicably, her heart began to pound in her chest. She stared down at the marriage contract, unable to meet the knight's frosty glare. His anger sent a chill through the hall. Her father and the priest ceased their friendly debate.

Garrett leaned over the table. His shadow, like his anger, fell dark across the surface and Leandra. When he spoke, his voice was low and harsh. "My liege lord charged me with escorting his betrothed to Tremelyn safely. I will do that to the best of my ability. Offer me no gifts. I am no knight for hire. Do you understand me, lady? I am a loyal Bernay, and my fealty is pledged only to Lord Reginald."

He stepped back, his shoulders square, rigid with anger. His embittered glare swept the hall from Highlord Aidan and Father John to Captain Ralph and the Lyonesse guards. "I will challenge anyone to combat who questions that."

Leandra sat fixed in her chair as Sir Garrett's glare returned to her. Indignation narrowed his eyes and pulled down on the corners of his mouth, sending a frisson of fear through her. She'd never considered what an insult her offer might appear to be. She'd never dreamt he would take such violent offense to the proposal.

Highlord Aidan rose from the bench below the cruciform. "I'm certain no one questions your loyalty, Sir Garrett. Leandra meant no insult. She meant only to say that we appreciated your defense yesterday. We consider ample protection of Lyonesse of utmost importance."

"Of course, Lord Aidan, the earl and Sir Garrett know of your concern for Lyonesse," Father John chimed in, also rising from the bench, his gaze moving from Leandra to Garrett. As if he tread on eggshells, the priest crept to the knight's side and plucked at Garrett's sleeve. "Sit down, Sir Garrett. Allow Lady Leandra to finish her review of the contract."

Garrett shook off the priest, his angry gaze still searing Leandra.

She forced herself to meet his wintry glower. His blue eyes bore into her, drilling home the awareness that she was but a worthless sinner presented to a wrathful saint for judgment. She resisted the urge to cross herself. How was she to know that he would consider her offer an insult of the most grievous sort?

She took a deep breath for courage and chose her words carefully. "I see that you honor your word to your liege lord. I respect that. Please believe that no offense to your loyalty was intended."

As Garrett's anger subsided, he came slowly to his senses. The tense silence hovering in the hall rang in his ears. He looked at those about him. Everyone stared back, each frozen in place as if any movement would set off something dangerous. At his side Father John regarded him with a stricken expression. Alarm widened Leandra's eyes. Anxiety furrowed Highlord Aidan's brow.

Garrett rubbed a hand across his forehead. He had spoken too hastily, said angry words that were uncalled for. But before he could add anything, the tall oaken doors of the great hall were flung open.

The castle bailiff bolted into the hall, his face white, his cap askew.

Like the others, Garrett turned to stare at the shaken man.

"Sir Leofric has entered the city gate and is on his way here," the bailiff blurted out, gasping for breath. One hand clutched his heaving chest, and the other grabbed at his hood. Garrett feared the poor man was going to have a fit before he could tell all his news.

The bailiff scurried past Garrett, rudely stepping between him and Leandra's table. The man ducked a hasty but respectful bow. "Sir Leofric demands to see you immediately, my lady, and he demands that the Earl of Tremelyn withdraw his men and ships."

Garrett watched Leandra pale slightly and turn to the document.

"Leandra?" The highlord urgently crossed the hall to the worktable. His white beard trembled. "What do we say to Lord Leofric? You sent him our refusal, did you not?"

"Yes, I did, Father. He never responded to our invitation to the betrothal banquet."

To Garrett's surprise, the lady's solemn mouth, so soft and vulnerable beneath his the night before, hardened into a tight, stony line.

"Tell Lord Leofric when he arrives to wait outside," she

told the bailiff. "I will see him at my convenience. Serve him wine. Whatever he wishes."

"I will do my best, my lady." The doubtful bailiff scuttled from the hall, closing the tall doors behind him.

Garrett stepped to the table. He wanted a signature on the contract now. Leofric may have been refused, but the varlet was known for being unable to take no for an answer. Garrett wondered whether Leandra had heard the rumor that only last year the man ravished a lady who had lightly flirted with him. Then he killed her husband in a tourney.

But Lady Leandra was already reaching for the quill and ink pot, deliberately, without apparent haste.

"Father, sign this document, now."

"But, daughter, Leofric is a neighbor," Lord Aidan protested. "Is there a need to rush? Can we not offer him our hospitality?"

"No need to rush," the lady said patiently. With a steady hand she dipped the quill into the ink and held it out to her father. "No need to wait. Sign, Father. Is this the place, Father John? Sir Garrett, do you witness?"

"Yes, of course, and Father John also." Despite the lady's outward calm, Garrett detected determination in her careful actions and the cool quiet in her eyes.

Garrett took up the quill after Aidan and scrawled his own signature below the highlord's. He handed the quill to Father John, who hastily scratched his name on the parchment.

As the priest put the last flourish on his signature, loud voices filtered through the doors of the great hall. The clamor of boots on stone echoed in the passage beyond.

"It is done," Leandra sighed, a look of resignation on her somber face where Garrett expected to see at least a glimmer of bridal joy. But then the prospect of facing a man like Leofric brought pleasure to no one.

The commotion in the passage grew louder. Garrett and Father John stepped away from the table and followed Leandra's gaze toward the entrance to the great hall.

The towering doors split open with a force that banged them to the walls. Brass latches clanged against the stone and tumult flooded in. Armored men-at-arms tramped forth. Drummers beat a sharp march time. Trumpeters scurried in and raised their horns in a brassy fanfare.

Suddenly a great black horse thundered onto the wooden floor of the hall.

The dogs barked alarm and slunk away. The servants uttered cries of surprise and shrank against the walls. Wystan and Brenna followed in the rider's wake.

The purple-clad horseman sat straight and righteous in the saddle. An iridescent peacock feather in his cap bobbed with each prance of the war horse. The swarthy rider drew rein in the doorway. Behind him a herald carried a purple banner bearing the device of a gray boar.

Garrett's eyes narrowed as he recognized Casseldorne; here was the man who had insulted him and his family name when Garrett was but a man-at-arms and could demand no retraction. The memory remained clear-edged and raw.

Just last fall at one of the last tourneys that the Tremelyn earl and his knights had attended, Casseldorne had slighted the Bernays. Garrett and Wystan had been passing by a group of knights engrossed in conversation. When Leofric saw him, he immediately changed the subject.

"I am forever astonished that those Bernays show their face again and again among respectable knights," he had said, speaking from the side of his thin-lipped mouth. "You'd think they would stay in France, where traitors and mercenaries belong. They appear suited for that kind of common fighting."

Garrett had stopped in his tracks. But Wystan grabbed his sleeve and dragged him on.

Now the man insulted Lyonesse with this presumptuous entrance.

Cursing softly, Garrett reached for his sword, grasping only thin air at his hip. The marriage contract signing was a peaceful affair, and he was a guest. To parade about armed would have been discourteous. Annoyed, he forced himself to remain beside the table with Father John. He glanced apprehensively at Captain Ralph and the Lyonesse men-at-arms near the door. They appeared confused but stood their ground.

The Earl of Casseldorne's holdings bordered Lyonesse on the north, and though the earl's family made peaceful neighbors, menace wafted into the hall with the rider. Garrett recalled that Leofric and his father were given to displays of pomposity. He doubted the man would dare any violence in the presence of so many witnesses.

"My lady, I tried to tell Lord—" the bailiff said, trotting up beside Leofric's horse.

"Hush, man, I'm here now." The lord booted the bailiff aside and rode farther into the great hall to halt in front of Leandra's table. His long purple cloak billowed behind him, and the purple leather tack on his horse jingled and creaked.

Garrett frowned. Instinctively he stepped closer to Leandra, despite Father John's restraining tug on his sleeve.

"Ah, Lady Leandra, here you are," the dark-haired horseman greeted with an easy, artificial smile. He swept a grand bow from the saddle. He made no respectable move to dismount, Garrett noted.

"Imagine, my lady, your bailiff tried to delay presenting me to you, but I would have none of that," Leofric said with an indulgent grimace and a gesture of dismissal. "I knew you would want to greet me yourself immediately."

"Indeed?" Lady Leandra drawled, with a husky dryness in her voice that almost made Garrett smile. "I would have preferred that you leave your horse at the door."

She remained pale, but the contentious thrust of her chin betrayed her courage. Good, Garrett thought, the lioness was undaunted. He continued to quell his desire to challenge Casseldorne's bad manners.

"Did you not receive my message?" she asked.

"Yes. That's why I'm here. I came to express my disappointment in learning that your father has accepted the Earl of Tremelyn's offer of marriage in place of mine. Is it true?"

"Yes." Leandra extended a steady hand toward Garrett. "This is Sir Garrett Bernay and Father John, envoys of the Earl of Tremelyn."

Leofric studied them. His eyes narrowed and he sat back in his saddle, his gloved hand spread confidently across his thigh. Garrett knew the man recognized him, and he met Casseldorne's gaze steadily.

"So the earl is still so weak from his near mortal wound, delivered by outlaws riding his own land, that he had to send envoys to declare his betrothal vows?" Leofric gave Garrett a haughty glare of disapproval. "He sends the heir to the traitorous Bernay family no less?"

This time it was Leandra who stayed Garrett with a hand on his arm. She spoke before he could.

"My lord had pressing matters to tend to." Leandra held her head high. "If Lord Reginald trusts Sir Garrett, so do I."

Garrett shook off her hand. He didn't need her to come to his defense.

"The earl fares well enough," Garrett said, barely controlling his anger. "How well he feels, or how pressing his affairs are, is not for you to decide."

"Of course." Counterfeit contrition played across Leofric's darkly handsome face. Obviously the man knew he was treading close to danger. "I am glad to hear that the earl enjoys improved health."

With a sly look in Garrett's direction, Leofric asked, "Lady Leandra, may I speak with you and your father alone?"

"We have nothing to keep from the envoys of my betrothed. You may speak freely."

Leofric frowned at Garrett. "Lady Leandra, I have come with hope in my heart. To ask if there is any possibility that you would reconsider my offer of marriage over the earl's. Surely you understand that I can offer you everything he can—riches and, in time, the title of countess.

"Even as we speak, my esteemed father is with King Edward in France. The war goes well. No doubt he will return with more riches and lands. I am his legitimate heir. Then it would be only a matter of time until . . . Of course, it gives me no pleasure to speak of my father's demise. But I am a younger man than the Earl of Tremelyn. I can offer you a title eventually, more years of protection, and . . . other benefits." A lewd grin flitted across Leofric's face.

Anger flared in Garrett, hot and furious. He missed none of Casseldorne's tasteless innuendos about youth and potency. He knew from her round eyes and pale face that Lady Leandra also understood well enough. Garrett almost ordered the man out of the room, out of the castle, and out of Lyonesse.

But he seethed in silence. The lady deserved to remain in control of the audience. He wanted the pleasure of seeing Leofric bow before Lady Lioness's exquisite fortitude.

She tented her dainty hands upon the documents lying on the table. The sunlight glittered off her betrothal ring, and he wondered how she kept it from slipping from her finger.

"As for more riches or titles, I have little interest in those," the lady said. "I seek benefits for Lyonesse only."

The line of Leofric's mouth soured. Clearly he thought his charms should win the lady. "Then how does a union with Tremelyn benefit Lyonesse over a union with Casseldorne?"

"The Lyonesse ships carry Tremelyn and west country tin to markets that help the king in his war. Casseldorne has no need of our ships. You merely seek to add our lands to yours."

"But you are wrong, lady." A look of dismay softened Leofric's swarthy features. "Casseldorne also has goods to transport. You are but a maid. What do you understand of these issues? Leave this to me."

Garrett saw ire flash in the lady's eyes, and her chin jutted forth even more. With baleful pleasure he realized that Leofric would never recover his suit from that mistake.

"I can protect you from the pirates and the brigands," Leofric declared. "I have proof."

"We have appealed to you, our neighbor, to do that for the last two years, and we've seen little result," Leandra snapped, her husky voice edged with anger. "These days we are more at the outlaws' mercy than ever in the past. Sir Garrett here rescued us from attack yesterday."

"But he did not bring you a gift like this, did he?" Leofric asked. At the flourish of his gloved hand his men-at-arms marched forward, bearing between them an oak and ivory-inlaid casket almost as large as a small cooking pot.

At last Leofric jumped down from his black charger and approached Leandra. The men with the box stopped at his side.

Garrett started forward, once more reaching for the absent sword. He didn't like this turn in the talks. Father John's hand on his arm restrained him, and he allowed it only because Captain Ralph appeared at the ready.

Brenna, eyes bright with anticipation of a grand gift, crept closer for a better view. Reluctantly, Wystan followed her.

"Look upon this, my lady," Leofric said with a sneer, and threw open the box. With expansive gestures he peeled back a layer of red velvet and stepped aside. "For you."

A human head crowned in wild red locks stared up at Leandra. Eyes bulged. A purple tongue thrust from the mouth in obscene mockery. The fresh, bloody head glowed deathly white against the crimson velvet of the box.

All in the great hall gasped. Leandra turned white.

Garrett recognized the face of the jeering red-haired man on the brigand ship. How had Leofric's men tracked the outlaw down and dispatched him so quickly? he wondered. Did they know who he was and where to find him?

"Like the knights of old, I bring you the dragon's head, my lady," Leofric announced with malicious pride. "Like a knight returned from slaying a monster in a lady's honor. Do you not appreciate the tribute?"

The sound of retching caught Garrett's ear. He looked away from the gruesome spectacle, expecting to find Leandra sick or swooning. He found her composed. The retching was Brenna's. The dark-haired girl turned away from the scene and was violently ill down the front of Wystan's tunic.

"You overstep the boundaries of chivalry," Garrett muttered. Leofric only flicked him a glance, but Garrett knew he had been heard.

Leandra remained frozen beside the table, her face ashen, her lips bluish. As Garrett watched, she took a deep, steadying breath, tucked her hands into the sleeves of her surcoat. Garrett tensed. He was uncertain whether she was hiding her trembling hands or reaching for a weapon.

She leveled a cold gaze on Leofric.

"The decision has been made, Sir Leofric," she said, speaking quietly, without giving the slightest hint that a grisly pirate's head lay before her. Her fearlessness awed Garrett. "The contracts are signed. Only the intercession of the Church could change anything now."

"I'm afraid that's true, my son," Father John said, bravely moving to Leandra's side.

"I see," Leofric said, his features twisting into a gargoyle's grin. "So only an act of God can change this betrothal—or an act of the Grim Reaper."

That was enough for Garrett. He stepped forward, imposing himself between Leandra and Leofric. "Do you dare to threaten Lady Leandra? Before her father, her servants, the church? *Before me?*"

Chapter 6

Chain mail jingled menacingly as the Casseldorne guards drew their swords. Garrett was unarmed and afoot, but the force of his presence went undiminished. He was nearly Leofric's equal now, and the purple knight could no longer hide behind his knighthood.

The hush in the great hall grew deeper. No one drew a breath.

Leofric glowered disdainfully at the Tremelyn knight. His men-at-arms glanced at one another uncertainly, set the casket down at Leandra's feet, and stood ready to fight.

"Sir Leofric. Sir Garrett. Remember, this is the great hall of a Christian lord and his lady daughter, friends to you both." Father John hurried forward to stand between the knights. "Let us have no violence here. Not before the lady."

"I make no violence here," Garrett said, without taking his gaze from Leofric's cold, hard face. But he longed to beat the purple-clad Casseldorne to his knees and force him to beg forgiveness for bringing the vile head into Leandra's presence.

"Nor I," Leofric said, a look of righteousness composing his features. "I make no threat, no challenge. I simply bring proof that my word is good. I promised to help defend Lyonesse, and I did. What do I find when I bring the proof? That the ungrateful lady of my heart has accepted another."

"What did you say about the Grim Reaper?" Garrett demanded. He didn't believe a word Casseldorne was saying. The varlet was once more weaseling out of a challenge.

"I simply meant to say that life is but a game of chance," Leofric said. "You always make too much of things, Bernay. I took a chance on winning the lady's heart and I lost."

"Of course," Leandra's father agreed too quickly, too eager to ease the tension in the room. "The world is an uncertain place. None of us knows what may happen in the next month, week, day, or even the next hour. Alas, all our uncertain lives are in God's hands, just as this poor misguided man's was." Aidan gestured to the pirate head.

"True, and well put, your lordship," Leofric added, without warmth. "You are rich in wisdom. I take my leave of you, my lady, and wish you and Lord Reginald happiness in your marriage."

His envious gaze lingered overlong on Leandra, Garrett thought. Garrett stepped forward again, pushing Father John aside. Leofric cast him a look of cold hatred and swiftly swung up on his horse. Turning without a farewell, Casseldorne thundered out of the great hall, pages and guards surging in his wake.

Incensed, Garrett signaled for the guards to close the doors after the intruder.

The jester capered to the box where Leofric's gross gift lay. Gingerly he grasped the straggly red locks and lifted the bloodied head up for all to see. In astonishment Garrett watched the man take on Leofric's height and carriage. Casseldorne's curl of lip twisted Tyler's mouth, and his jaw firmed in an arrogant line.

"So only an act of God can change this betrothal—that or an act of the Grim Reaper," the jester mocked in a voice that echoed Leofric's with chilling accuracy.

"I believe that settles any question of me remaining here, my lady. I begin to train your men tomorrow, immediately after prime. We sail from Lyonesse in five days, maybe sooner. I will be your escort."

Leandra winced as the burly seaman dropped the last of her dower chests none too gently to the cog's deck.

"Stow it there," Sir Garrett ordered, and pointed to a

corner of the deck. "Lash all the baggage down well. Make haste man, or we'll lose the tide."

She was about to tell them to have a little more consideration for her life all packed up in those wooden boxes. The silver basin for hair washing. Her prayer book, a gift from Mother Mary Elizabeth. The small down pillow her mother had stuffed for her before she was born. But she pressed her lips together and decided to hold her tongue as she had done admirably well through the past five days.

Throughout the days of preparation and arms drills, Sir Garrett had growled and grumbled, prowling about the castle and grounds like a trapped bear in no mood to be baited with disagreement. Though they were about to set sail, Leandra noted that his temper had not lightened.

When he rounded to see her standing in the bow, he pointed an accusing finger at her. "I'll have a word with you, lady, as soon as these chests are loaded."

"As you please, Sir Garrett." What had she done now? Leandra wondered. Willfully she turned away to look for the last time at the village and the castle where she had been born and nurtured. The morning light washed across the face of each sturdy cottage, rinsing away the flaws—the cracks in the stone walls and the ragged thatching—to give Leandra a picture beautiful and familiar to treasure.

"Rot me, the man has been a bear these past few days." Brenna climbed onto the bow deck to stand next to Leandra. Her face was still puffy from sleep, and her eyelids drooped. "He growls here and bites a head off there." She paused to yawn. "So where is Uncle Aidan? At prayers I suppose."

"'Tis prime." Leandra studied each cottage with frowning concentration. She wanted to remember every detail in her head and in her heart. "Father prays for our safe journey."

Brenna sniffed and gave a virtuous toss of her curls. *"My* father wouldn't shuffle off to chapel and leave me to sail away alone. If he were alive, he'd ride down from the castle to see me off. He'd sit on a fine horse, a black one like Leofric's, and wave a heartfelt good-bye, after he gave me a costly gift, of course."

"Father and I have said our farewells," Leandra replied, patiently disregarding Brenna's insult. She had long ago accepted Brenna's need to create a mythical sire to replace the father who died before she was born. But a little encouragement from her own father would have been welcome. Defending one's home took one kind of courage. She was discovering that leaving home forever took another. "Our journey is long and dangerous, and we may need his prayers."

"I suppose prayers are useful," Brenna said, waving unenthusiastically to Tyler Wotte, the jester. "But the pirate is dead, thanks to Leofric. In the last few days Sir Perfect and Wystan made an army out of our fishermen and foresters. So, what's to fear? I found the training fascinating —all that sword swinging. Didn't you?"

"Yes, fascinating once we determined that Wystan was going to live," Leandra said, the vision of Brenna leaning over the stone battlements to wave at Wystan still clear in her mind. The unfortunate squire had looked up to return the greeting and been flattened by a mace-flinging farmer. Lord, Sir Garrett had snarled over that, and they'd been requested to cease observing the training sessions.

"So I can't imagine that we're in any danger with an escort of a brave knight and squire." Brenna looked around. "Where is Wystan anyway? Oh, there he is."

Without waiting for a word from Leandra, Brenna scrambled down the ladder to join the squire, whose head was still swaddled in bandages.

Leandra returned to memorizing Lyonesse's beauty. There probably was little danger ahead. But the image of Leofric and the gory pirate head in the gift box haunted her. She had always sensed something cruel in the heir to Casseldorne. Despite his pleasant overtures, there was always a gleam in his eye—something too bright and too intent—that spoke of dark currents and sinister appetites. Like the gleam that must have glinted in the serpent's eyes when it tempted Eve. How relieved she was that Lord Reginald had offered for her. She could only pray that he was as pleased that she had accepted.

"Lyonesse is in good hands," Sir Garrett said, his deep voice startling Leandra from her thoughts and bringing her back to the deck of the cog. "Cedric is capable. You have seen that for yourself. The best thing you can do for your people now is see to your own safety."

"How do you know that's what I reflect on?" she demanded. Actually, she had decided that Cedric was competent. But she still wished that it was Garrett who remained in command of the garrison. Was she so obvious? Even if she was, did Sir Perfect have to be so observant?

"Because that's what is always on your mind," he said. "I see it in your eyes sometimes. Where is your father? Does he not come to see you off?" Garrett peered over the railing as if in search of the highlord among the crowd.

"He is at prime prayers," Leandra explained for the second time. She bridled a little, annoyed that no one seemed to comprehend that her father and she understood each other completely. He did his duty. She did hers. She'd said all her farewells, and there remained nothing to do now but sail away to be married to Lord Reginald.

Behind them the ship's master shouted orders for the anchor to be weighed. Beneath Leandra's feet the ship took on life and edged away from the quay. She leaned forward, eagerly studying the villagers, trying to commit to memory dear faces, the bright sunlight on the tall oaks, and the ancient beauty of Castle Lyonesse rising against the pallid morning sky. The square sail snapped as the wind caught it, then billowed. Ashore, hands fluttered in farewell, and Leandra waved in return, her heart heavy but her eyes dry.

Her courage wavered and her throat grew achingly tight with tears she would not shed. At her side Sir Garrett leaned against the railing, and she heard him mutter something to himself. Her courage deserted her.

"Tell me about Lord Reginald," Leandra asked. She needed something to cling to, some reassurance to give her courage. "He is said to be a just man."

"Indeed, he is," Garrett agreed. She could hear the puzzlement in his voice.

"Tell me more," Leandra demanded. Little seeds of panic

threatened to bloom as Lyonesse grew smaller and smaller. Why hadn't she thought to ask for a potion against home-sickness? "Tell me what his first wife was like? The bards sing of his great devotion to her."

"I knew the lady only a short while before she died," Garrett said. His voice took on warmth Leandra had not heard since the night of the betrothal banquet. "She was a fair and kind lady. She was generous and devout. Graceful and smiling. Everyone honored her. Lord Reginald was loath to be without her company for long."

Leandra glanced up to find Sir Garrett watching her with a narrow-eyed look of assessment. He added, "She was said to be a lady of a powerful family, well-trained in the wifely skills, loving and gentle. Devoted to her husband. True and virtuous and pious."

"A paragon, indeed," Leandra muttered, her heart sink-ing. She could never live up to those standards, but she clung to her courage. "I have some of those skills." She couldn't think of a one at the moment.

"I'm certain you do." Garrett's face went blank. To Leandra's disgust he gazed at her, as baffled and unable to name one as she was. At least he had the good grace to appear embarrassed, and quickly added, "You are my lord's choice of wife, and I shall honor that."

Leandra regarded him for a long moment. "And the others. The barons, knights, and their ladies?"

"I'm certain they will show you every respect also."

"Even if they think me an unsuitable bride and Lyonesse unworthy of the alliance?" Leandra asked, watching him closely, waiting to see if he would deny the truth.

"They will honor you as I'm sure Lord Reginald will," he said. "But you are very young, and the responsibilities of Lord Reginald's wife will be great."

His doubts stung, but Leandra admired him for not disavowing his true thoughts. However, this was not the comfort she sought.

"I am a full sixteen years of age," Leandra said, squaring her shoulders and standing a little taller. "Our queen of England, Phillipa, gave birth to the Prince of Wales by the time she was my age. You yourself one day will take a bride perhaps as young or younger than myself."

She was surprised to see Sir Garrett blanch and turn away to stare out over the sea. "I have not thought of such yet. I'm more concerned about Wystan now. I have one favor to ask of you concerning your cousin and my brother."

"Yes, Sir Garrett?" Leandra frowned. "What about them?" Everyone had noticed that Wystan had eyes only for Brenna, and Brenna encouraged his shy attentions.

"I would prefer that they spend less time in each other's company. Clearly, they are unsuitable. Their natures are completely opposed."

"Your Wystan and my Brenna?" Leandra asked, astonished that anyone would consider another member of her family—even Brenna—unsuitable.

"I have plans for Wystan," Garrett said, his scowl deepening. He looked away as if he couldn't quite face her as he went on. "As soon as he wins his knight's spurs, he will go to the king's court. He is a gentle, inward soul, and I think he should marry a soft-spoken wife of fine lineage."

"What's wrong with the Lyonesse lineage?" Leandra demanded. Irritation grew, prickly and hot. She leaned back to look the knight square in the face. "Is your disapproval of me not enough? You disapprove of Brenna, too? She may be headstrong, but she will make some knight—even a Bernay knight—a fine wife."

Sir Garrett tensed and his features went hard as stone. They both turned abruptly to stare out over the bay in tortuous silence. She could almost hear him grappling with his anger, debating how to react. She scolded herself for being so petty, for bringing up the Bernay reputation in a way she knew would be hurtful. She'd only heard vague rumors about the Bernays and knew nothing of the truth.

Finally Garrett shook his head. "I do not mean to offend, my lady. Your Lyonesse lineage is fine and ancient. Surely Lady Brenna would seek higher than a humble second son. I wish only to do the best for my family, as I know you do for yours."

"I understand," she said, comprehending better than she

wanted to. Blunt, capricious Brenna would be a hindrance to an ambitious man at court. "You have no control over who weds your lord. But you can control what happens to your brother."

Sir Perfect made no denial.

Leandra looked away lest he see her mutinous expression. Momentarily she thought of encouraging Brenna and Wystan just to annoy him. She'd actually thought that Wystan's gentle ways might be good for her cousin. "Under these shipboard conditions I can hardly promise to keep Brenna from Wystan."

"No, of course not," he said, a look of relief softening his brow. "When the voyage is over. When we reach Penzance and start on the overland journey, I will need Wystan as a guard. Lady Brenna proves almost too much of a distraction for him. He was nearly addled forever that day during arms practice."

"Yes, 'twas unfortunate," Leandra hurried to agree. "Brenna did apologize. If you wish it, I shall speak to her when we land." Then she added, "You're wrong, you know."

"Wrong about what my lady?" He stepped closer, and she sensed him hovering over her shoulder—possessive, critical, and eager to part her company all at once. They had just cleared the mouth of the bay. Sir Garrett glanced ahead at the open sea and paled. "I must see to other duties. Tell me, quickly, how is it that I'm in error?"

Leandra ignored his strange expression and her chin came up a little higher. She fingered the tiny silver phial in her cuff to comfort herself. She held the power to make Lord Reginald love her, and in that love would lie her success and Lyonesse's safety.

"You'll see. I will make a fine countess and a good wife," she stated. The challenge sounded fine to her. Uttering the words and touching the phial made her feel stronger, ready to take on her quest. "I'm not too young. A year from now, Sir Garrett, I will have proved your misgivings unfair and unfounded."

* * *

A great sea swell heaved the bow of the cog up, and Garrett flung his head over the railing.

"Matins and all's well," called the helmsman from the stern.

Only midnight! thought Garrett, settling back on the deck and pulling the blanket over his head. Eternal hours stretched ahead until morning, until their landing at Penzance. The sickness had hit him, as he knew it would, as soon as they had cleared the quiet waters of Lyonesse Bay.

Thankfully, everything had been stowed and lashed by then and no trouble had appeared on the horizon, no pirates, no Leofric. Wystan seemed to have things in order, assuming Brenna hadn't robbed him of his senses again. Everyone was asleep, and if all went well, he would go unnoticed, huddled by the railing under the blanket.

Another swell and Garrett forgot everything—except the misery—and hung over the railing once more.

"Sir, what do you see on your watch?" a husky voice called softly from behind him.

Garrett drew a deep breath and struggled to remember who possessed that intriguing voice.

"Don't fall asleep, watchman," she said, the voice timbered with concern. "'Twould bring you to grief with the ship's master."

"I've already come to grief." Garrett groaned. "Go away. Sleep in your cabin, lady."

"Sleep eludes me this night," she said. "But 'tis such a beautiful evening, and I have too many thoughts in my head to sleep. I came out on deck to watch the moonbeams bounce off the waves."

"Augh." Garrett couldn't bear the thought of bouncing or waves.

On the deck behind them Father John snorted, snuffled, and turned on his side.

"Who are you?" Her voice had moved closer, and Garrett was vaguely aware of her standing over him at the rail. She hesitated. "Sir Garrett, is that you?"

Garrett pulled the blanket tighter over his head. "I'm not here. Go away."

She hesitated again. He prayed she was satisfied with that answer and would leave. But she didn't. "Sir? I wondered where you had gone. Are you ill? Do you need help?"

She stepped closer and leaned forward, her cool palm slipping beneath the blanket and covering his forehead. He shoved her hand away.

"Sir, you're ill. Even in this light I can see that you're as green as a moldy cheese."

"I'm not sick." Garrett shook his head miserably. "I'm, ah, merely occupied."

Another sizable swell rocked the cog and elicited a long, low groan of profound misery. "God, have mercy," Garrett pleaded. When the most serious wave of nausea had subsided, he managed to mumble, "Did I hear laughter? I warn you, lady . . . go away. I'll be all right as soon as we make landfall."

A wave of giggles burst from her lips, the laughter bubbling forth light and melodious. Garrett cast her a wounded look. "I'm fine on a horse. It's just the sea . . ."

She sobered. "Oh, I understand. Does Wystan know?"

"Yes, and where is he? He should never allow you to—"

"He's asleep outside the cabin door," Leandra said. She knelt down beside him, ignoring all his protests. "Does Lord Reginald know about this?"

"Oh . . . no," Garrett muttered. "Why should he? A knight fights on solid ground. A knight is a horseman, a conqueror of lands, not a rolling, gaited sailor. What cares a lord about my misery? Sweet Jesu, I can't even cross a river on a ferry."

Leandra gazed at him, her mouth carefully pursed like one trying to resist laughter. "I'm sure you're a fine warrior on land or sea." Despite her apparent best efforts, she chuckled.

Garrett frowned. "'Tis fine that the only thing that makes you smile is my misery. What kind of a lady are you? Have you no compassion?"

Leandra gulped back the laughter. "Yes, I have compassion. When it's needed. In fact, Sir Garrett, I have more than that. I have a cure for your illness."

Garrett shook his head over the railing again. "There is none. I have tried. Wise women's potions. Apothecary's powders. I even inquired of an alchemist once."

"This potion will work," Leandra vowed, patting him comfortingly on the back. "You'll see. Vivian's potions always work."

Chapter 7

All the way across the deck of the cog, Leandra choked back her laughter. She mustn't wake the others aboard. Besides, 'twas nigh sinful to laugh at the poor man's weakness. A seasick knight! Chivalrous, valiant, brave, and true, but at sea Sir Perfect was sicker than an overfed dog under a banquet table. He had a flaw!

With only the moonlight falling through the doorway, she located Brenna's surcoat thrown over a chest. Tucked in the cuff, just as Leandra had done with her love potion, she found the silver phial of seasickness remedy. Leandra saw no reason to wake her cousin to explain. Brenna had been so intent on entertaining Wystan and the other men with her harp that she had never succumbed to the ailment. She slept as soundly as a babe on her pallet. Leandra took the phial and tiptoed from the cabin.

"Can you keep water down?" she asked when she returned.

Garrett watched her pour some dark liquid into a wooden cup. "I'm not sure." What dreadful thing was she offering him? he wondered. At the moment he wasn't certain that it mattered. The way he felt, he would welcome poison if it ended this awful roiling in his gut.

"Here, try this."

In the moonlight Leandra's loose hair framed her smiling face like a gold-spun wimple. For a moment Garrett failed to notice the cup she held forth to him.

"Take it. I promise it will help."

With unsteady hands he took the cup and sipped at the water-laced potion.

He smacked his lips and peered into the cup. "It tastes brackish." *What* was she giving him? he wondered.

"'Tis just the remedy's flavor," Leandra assured him with the soothing patience of a mother. "Finish it if you can."

Another large swell interrupted Garrett's second sip, but with an encouraging gesture from Leandra, he put the cup to his lips for a third time and gulped down the contents. When he handed the cup back to her, he noted the pleased, upward curve of her lips. Sweet Jesu, she was enjoying this. The lady hardly ever smiled, but she grinned ear to ear while he suffered.

An uncomfortable warmth welled up in Garrett's gut, then suddenly subsided. He waited. Which would be more humiliating, sickness or blessed death? The nausea eased notably. Garrett relaxed a little, leaning his weary head against the ship's railing.

He gave a start when Leandra's cool, dry hand took his. He pulled away.

"No." She refused to release him. "Your hand is cold. When the warmth returns, we'll know the potion has worked."

Garrett nodded and left his hand in hers. He recalled now that was the way with women. The moment they thought someone was ill, they touched: a cheek, a hand, a brow. He sighed. But better a woman's touch than a foul leech put on your skin by some old barber. Garrett closed his eyes and found himself savoring her delicate touch.

They sat in silence. The ship creaked and the rigging rattled. The wind dried the dampness from Garrett's face, and he found himself taking deeper breaths of air. Was it possible the silly potion worked?

"Better?" she asked at last. "Your hand is warmer."

Garrett opened his eyes to regard her with a thoughtful gaze. She smiled up at him, a soft, tender smile that lightened her green eyes and quirked at the corners of a wide, luscious mouth.

"Yes, better, I think," Garrett admitted, unable to take his

78

eyes from her moonlit face. "Where did you get this remedy? I must have more."

"'Tis Vivian of the Forest's recipe," Leandra said. "The physician calls her a witch, but I think he is jealous of her skill. I've always heard that her potions are most reliable."

"She makes other remedies?"

"Yes, for illnesses and injuries." Leandra withdrew her hand and eyed him closely, leaning near, almost nose to nose, to peer into his eyes. Her lips hovered so near his, Garrett was reminded of a certain blindman's bluff kiss. "You do seem much improved," she conceded.

"What other potions of hers have you used?" Garrett asked, beginning to hope that those lips would move a little closer.

"Me?" Instantly, she retreated to the railing, looking a little alarmed. "Use potions?"

"Can Vivian change the gender of a babe, or some such thing that women always chatter about?" Garrett asked, wondering why he was so disappointed that she had moved away without touching him again.

"Oh, no, nothing like that," Leandra said, a peculiar expression of relief spreading across her face. "But she did give Brenna a dimple."

"Which your cousin used to beguile Wystan, no doubt."

"No doubt. But my cousin has other wiles."

"I am grateful to you, Lady Leandra, for sharing the remedy with me." Garrett decided they best stay away from the subject of Brenna.

"'Twas my pleasure to aid you, Sir P—Garrett," she said, rising from her place by the rail, an uncertain frown puckering her brow. "I bid you a good night and a pleasant voyage."

Leandra walked back to the cabin, lifting the hem of her gown to step over Father John, two soldiers, and a sailor who slept on deck. She could sleep now.

A small smile played across her lips as she went. Sir Garrett's flaw was forgotten. She cared little for that. She smiled for the success of his recovery. Now she was certain that Vivian's love potion would be as potent as she needed. She had little to fear from the dead countess.

"What do you mean you used all my seasick remedy?" Brenna wailed as they stood amid a maze of crowded market stalls. She ignored the heads that turned at the sound of her voice. Anger flashed hot in her heart. She whirled on Leandra and planted her hands on her hips. "That's just like you. Take what you want. You had a good reason, I suppose. You always do."

"Shh. Lower your voice," Leandra cautioned, glancing around awkwardly.

They'd sailed into Penzance Bay at midday under clear skies. When they docked, Sir Garrett had promptly sent them off to the market while the cog was being unloaded; to keep them out from under his feet, no doubt, but Brenna would never object.

On all sides of them Cornish and foreign merchants sang their wares. The pungent scents of tar and tidal water filled the air. Disappointingly like home, Brenna thought. Overhead, noisy sea gulls followed the fishing boats, but she heard a new sound here. Across the harbor tin-toting mules brayed and foreign tongues babbled throughout the market. Brenna had made it to Cornwall.

But Leandra's confession angered her.

"The remedy was sorely needed." Leandra turned from the fine woven goods she examined in a market booth. "I discovered one of Lord Reginald's men ill last night when I went on deck. You hadn't shown the least twinge of seasickness, so I gave him the potion."

"Who was it?" Brenna yanked an embroidered wimple from Leandra's hand and feigned interest in it. "Tell me. Tell me. Was it the black-haired sailor with gray eyes?" Brenna gasped at a new thought. "Was it Wystan?"

"No." Leandra pressed her lips together. "Someone else."

"I'll wager it was the blond soldier with the green eyes and big nose."

"I promised not to say."

Brenna sniffed, quickly realizing the futility of pursuing the topic. If Leandra had promised silence, she would be silent. But the thought of Wystan made her drop the wimple and stare off into the blue spring sky, dreaming of the squire's handsome face and blue eyes. "Of course it's not Wystan. He's too wonderful. Have you seen the way he smiles when I play the harp?"

Leandra turned away. "There is something I must tell you about Wystan."

Brenna held up the fine white embroidered cloth and ignored Leandra's earnest tone. She didn't want to think about serious things now. She wanted to buy things in the market and see the town. "Come try this over your hair."

"Brenna? About Wystan?" Leandra began, taking the wimple from her cousin without making an attempt to put it on her head. "Sir Garrett would prefer that you not distract his brother with your company."

"Me?" Brenna stared at Leandra, uncertain about the meaning of her cousin's words. "Distract Wystan? Is Sir Perfect still angry about the day Wystan was hit in the head? I told them both I was sorry. I tried to care for Wystan, but his brother sent me away."

Leandra cast Brenna an uneasy look. "Sir Garrett wishes his brother to marry into an influential family."

"What?" Brenna cried. "Influential family? He means that the house of Lyonesse—no, he means *I'm* not good enough for his brother? As if the Bernays are so good."

"I don't like the implications of Sir Garrett's request any more than you do," Leandra admitted with a frown. "I think it best that we comply for now. At Tremelyn there will be other squires and knights for you to meet."

"But what about how I feel?" Brenna complained. "What about Wystan? Does Sir Perfect consider how his brother feels?"

"Let's not offend Sir Garrett more," Leandra pleaded patiently. "Please consider that we still have a long journey ahead and the coming marriage to the earl."

"Of course, anything for your marriage to the earl."
Brenna pressed her lips together and turned away. "Humph!
Wystan's not the only man in the world."

"Indeed, not," Leandra said, her tone at last taking on the
indignation that Brenna liked to hear. "I'm certain the earl
will suggest some more appropriate candidate."

"Yes, I'm sure he will," Brenna agreed, and tossed her
head.

A cry of distress and the flash of pikes caught her
attention. She and Leandra turned to see a crone and an old
man shoved away from them by the two guards Sir Garrett
had sent along.

"My lady? We must speak with you. My lady?" the
woman begged, waving her walking stick at them. Brenna
instantly recognized the dusty black cloak the stooped
woman wore as that of a pilgrim.

"Cease that," Leandra ordered.

The guards froze, paralyzed by Leandra's best commander's voice.

Brenna grinned at them. Sometimes having a field marshal for a cousin was most amusing. "You dare to be unkind
to an old woman, and a holy pilgrim, too?" Brenna chided.
"Can you not see her badge? Let her come to us."

"Begging your pardon, my lady," one guard protested,
confusion and contrition playing across his face. "But no
one is to be near you. Sir Garrett ordered it so."

"What harm can there be in this pious woman?" Leandra
demanded. "Where is your respect for womanhood and the
Holy Church?"

The shamefaced guards exchanged frowns, then raised
their pikes reluctantly and stepped aside. The crone cast
them a triumphant look as she passed, nearly stabbing one's
foot with her walking staff. The bent old man hobbled along
after her, followed by a child—a boy of twelve or thirteen
years, possibly—with the hood of his pilgrim's cloak pulled
low over his face.

"Thank you, my lady." The old woman bobbed a curtsy
before Brenna and Leandra.

"Look at this, Leandra." Brenna studied the crone's

82

floppy-brimmed hat. "Mistress Pilgrim wears the cockle-shell badge of St. James's shrine." The lady pilgrim smiled a toothless, amiable grin that Brenna found contagious. Delicious excitement boiled up in her. "Tell me where have you been Mistress Pilgrim. What strange and new places have you seen?"

The crone waved her arms in the air as if to embrace the world. "We have traveled far and wide, my lady. Spain and France."

Brenna giggled with delight, feeling at last that the world was hers, ready to be explored and enjoyed.

"What can we do for you, Mistress Pilgrim?" Leandra asked, stepping to Brenna's side.

"The hostler says those be yer horses he is packing for a trip to the east," the old woman said.

"Yes," Leandra replied. "I suppose so. Why do you ask, good woman?"

"We've paid our homage to St. Michael's mount." The old woman gestured toward the isle in Penzance Bay. "Now we travel to Canterbury, me deaf husband and I and our grandson Alfred."

The old man ducked in a vague bow and grinned an ingratiating, yellow-toothed grin. Several days' worth of gray beard stubble gleamed on his chin. The hooded boy bowed, too.

"Me old man, he don't hear so good, so I do the talking," the woman explained. "We seek company to travel in, lady. It be not safe to tramp the roads alone. The thieves these days have no honor, no mercy. They rob merchant, noble, and pilgrim alike. Defy the will of God, they do. What has the world come to, I ask ye?"

"What indeed, mistress," Brenna agreed in sympathy. "We've had our trouble with pirates, right, Leandra? Tell me, you have been to Spain, to St. James?"

"We have seen great things in them foreign lands, my lady. Stories, I could tell such stories of our travels along the road to Compostela. We would be good company, my lady. I assure ye."

"Think what stories they could tell, what sights they've

seen," Brenna whispered into Leandra's ear. "It would make the trip go faster. Will Sir Garrett allow them along?"

"Of course, we cannot fail to give aid to holy pilgrims," Leandra whispered back. "Sir Garrett is pledged to protect the innocent and the Holy Church. Let me talk to him. He cannot refuse."

"No, absolutely not," Garrett said without blinking an eye and gazing straight into Lady Leandra's face. He could hardly believe that she had come to him with such a ridiculous request. She must understand that he would take no pilgrims under his wing and that there was no chance that he would change his mind.

He leaned against the stableyard fence, eager to finish selecting the hired mounts and annoyed with being interrupted. "No pilgrims, my lady," he repeated, even more irritated when he spied the crestfallen expression that she gave him—all innocent surprise. "Have you taken a good look at them? They're disreputable. They probably steal free travel like this all the time. Pilgrims, indeed."

"They *are* pilgrims, sir," the lady stammered, but she stole a look over her shoulder at the crone and her cousin, who loitered near the inn. "We have an obligation to them, Sir Garrett. You as a knight, I as a Christian lady."

"I know my obligations, Lady Leandra." He purposely stood a little taller and folded his arms across his chest as he held her gaze. He wished he didn't recall so clearly those verdant eyes gazing into his and those moist lips almost brushing his nose last night. Today it seemed more difficult than ever to say no to her. "No strangers travel with us. I've already refused a company of merchants who were willing to supply our food in exchange for our protection."

"'Tis but an old woman," Leandra persisted. "Her husband and their grandson. What harm could they be?"

"If nothing else, they'll hold us back." Garrett turned to look at the horses once more and hoped she would take the hint of dismissal.

"Oh, I think not," Leandra said, undaunted by his back. She leaned over the fence also, peering into his face. "They are seasoned travelers. They wear the cockleshell badge of St. James."

"I will take on no burden that might allow bandits or assassins to endanger us," Garrett said, refusing to look at her. "We're on my lord's land now, and I rule here. If you will excuse me, I wish to see to the final settlement for the packhorses."

Lady Leandra hesitated. Garrett suspected with growing irritation that she was gathering her wits, making ready to tackle him once more from another direction.

"But what if these pilgrims are angels in disguise, come for our help, and we turn them away?" Lady Leandra pointed out. "'Tis God's test, they say. Ask Father John."

Surprised and amused, Garrett chuckled. He looked back at the crone and her family. "Angels in the form of a pilgrim hag, a bent old man, and an ugly boy? I think not. The answer is still no, lady."

She drew a deep breath. Garrett almost winced. Sweet Jesu, did nothing discourage her?

"I am your liege lady, am I not, Sir Garrett? Would you deny me this?" she asked. "Besides, you owe me a debt for a secret kept."

In truth he had expected her to use this tactic earlier and was prepared. "I have sworn no fealty to you yet, Lady Leandra. Lord Reginald made my position clear. Your safety, first and foremost, is my charge. I will make the decisions I deem necessary to protect you. Secret be damned."

"I see." Lady Leandra stared at him, her face taking on a rosy hue. He waited for her to throw a tantrum, but she continued to speak calmly. "You were so amiable last night. I enjoyed your company. But today I find you as stubborn and overproud as ever. Is there nothing I can say to make you change your mind?" she asked.

"No, nothing." Garrett said. He preferred to forget about last night. He deliberately glanced away from Leandra. But Brenna's glare caught his eye and bore into him. "May I assume from the expression of disfavor your cousin casts in my direction that you have spoken to her about Wystan?"

"Oh, yes," Leandra said. "She was quite hurt. I hope she will get over it by the time we reach Tremelyn. She'll be terribly disappointed if you refuse these pilgrims."

"Not until Tremelyn?" Garrett asked, a little dismayed by prospect of a long, tense journey ahead.

"There you are, Sir Garrett," Father John shouted from the corner of the inn. A smile split his narrow, good-natured face, and he waved. "We've had great good fortune, my son." He beckoned to someone to join him. Two frocked churchmen appeared, one tall and thin like Father John and the other stunted and rotund. "This is Father Rhys and his clerk, Brother William. They journey with us on their pilgrimage to Canterbury."

Inwardly Garrett cringed. Father John could not be denied. A slow smile of victory spread across Lady Leandra's face. She had him and she knew it. With a nod of acknowledgment toward the priest and his friends, Leandra stepped closer to Garrett to stand—if she were taller—nearly shoulder to shoulder with him.

She whispered, her pretty pink lips barely moving, "Now, Sir Garrett, may I hear you refuse Father John and his holy pilgrims? Or will you welcome mine?"

Idly Brenna rolled the empty phial of seasickness remedy across the dining room table and back again with her forefinger. Then thoughtfully she plucked the love potion phial from the cuff of her blue surcoat and put the containers side by side.

"Reliable Leandra," Brenna muttered, as she sat alone waiting for the Tremelyn party to gather for supper. "Kept the thing tucked in her cuff where she put it the day we visited Vivian."

Just how did Leandra plan to use it? Brenna wondered, examining the phial closer. Would she pour it into the first cup of wine that she shared with Lord Reginald when they arrived, or would she wait until the bedding ceremony?

Brenna glanced up at the sound of footsteps in the passage. Hastily she slipped the phials out of sight. A dark-haired Tremelyn man-at-arms passed the door. When he saw Brenna, he paused to smile at her. She raised a hand in greeting, then turned away, purposely not inviting him to join her. She was waiting for Wystan, who appeared at that moment, elbowing the soldier aside.

"I received your message, and here I am," he greeted, grinning bashfully, like a man a little uncertain of his welcome.

"Join me while I await my cousin," Brenna invited, patting the bench beside her and making room for him. She liked his company and the reflection of herself in his blue-gray eyes. They showed her a maiden in bright colors, a laughing beauty, graceful and full of charm. Oh, how she loved herself in the mirror of Wystan Bernay. This squire, soon to be a knight, found her desirable. What did she care that Sir Garrett forbade them to enjoy each other's company?

Obviously heartened, Wystan sat down beside her, watching her as though reluctant to take his eyes from her face. "Will you entertain us after we sup tonight?"

"I don't feel like it today." Brenna pouted. "Your brother has taken away all the pleasure of the trip."

"What do you mean?" Wystan sat up indignantly. "What has Garrett done? Tell me and I'll talk to him about it."

"Your brother and my cousin have forbade me from being in your company on this journey," Brenna said, watching Wystan's face closely.

Surprise spread across his features. Satisfaction warmed Brenna's little heart. Just as she suspected. He knew nothing about his brother's decision. "Does your brother always dictate to you like that?" she asked innocently.

"Yes, well, I am his squire," Wystan said, turning away slowly, as if unable to face her. His indignation seemed to fade away as readily as a puff of smoke. "I must obey his wishes. But he said nothing to me about you."

"Well, he spoke to Leandra," Brenna said. "It seems he has some lofty ideas about your future, about whom you should marry."

When Wystan remained disappointingly silent, she added with disdain, "As if I scheme to wed you."

87

Wystan blushed and shrugged. "He did say something once—that he wanted me to marry a woman of some property. I am the second son, you know."

Brenna frowned and once more fingered the phials in her sleeve. She'd forgotten about that. But the title of knight sounded wonderful to her. That look of adoration in Wystan's eyes was what mattered. If he wasn't too poor, she could live on his adoration forever.

She squinted at him. But his short-lived anger disappointed her. Perhaps he didn't find her quite so beautiful as she thought. "Is what your brother thinks always so important to you?" she asked, hardly believing that she'd been wrong about her power over him.

"I'm his brother, his squire. I can't dismiss his feelings," Wystan said, seemingly absorbed in the weave of the white tablecloth before him. "Garrett has fought hard and planned carefully to regain knighthood for the Bernays. Don't let his good-humored smile deceive you. He knows exactly what he wants and how he is going to get it. He always achieves what he sets out to do."

"And you are going to let him tell you what to do?" Brenna demanded. She turned a frown on Wystan. One brother suddenly seemed nearly as bad as the other. "Is that what you are saying?"

Wystan wagged his head in confusion. "I don't know—"

An enormous shadow blocked out the overhead candlelight. "Where is Lady Leandra?" Garrett's voice boomed.

Brenna and Wystan started.

"Go tell her to gather here, Lady Brenna, and tell the pilgrims, too. The innkeeper is ready to serve us." The knight loomed over the table, the frown on his face chilling Brenna immediately. "Wystan, you come with me to call Father John."

The squire jumped to his feet and bounded out of the dining room to do his brother's bidding.

"Well?" Sir Garrett stared down at Brenna as if he were lord of the world. "Your sister has spoken to you about Wystan, has she not?"

"Yes, I'm going now," Brenna said, scooting off the bench.

She fumed all the way to the chamber she shared with Leandra. How she would like to plague his knightship, and Leandra, too, with troubles. She'd had enough of taking their orders. She and Wystan had a right to be friends if they wished it. A mischievous smile spread across her face. 'Twould serve them justly if she took the control out of their hands.

"'Tis spring," Father John declared, standing at the head of the table in the cramped private dining room. "When nature awakens from her winter sleep. When the sun warms the roads and gentles the wind. When *Englishmen* yearn to travel."

Agreement was murmured around the room.

Leandra watched the candlelight glint off the goblet the priest held in readiness for a toast.

"We celebrate tonight the beginning of a bridal journey for Lady Leandra," he continued.

"Thank you, Father." She reached for her goblet and acknowledged the toast with a polite smile.

Then he looked to the others. "And to the beginning of a holy pilgrimage for our friends, Father Rhys, Brother William, and the Pender family. To a safe and pleasant trip."

The guests chimed in agreement with a clinking of goblets and proclaimed similar wishes for good fortune. The supper proceeded without incident.

Wystan and Brenna served the plain food whenever the innkeeper or his wife needed more hands. The wine carafe went empty almost as soon as the innkeeper refilled it. Garrett sat near Father John, sober and silent, with Wystan at his side.

Leandra thought the meal was going well until Brenna, smiling mysteriously, poured herself a fourth goblet of wine. She leaned toward her cousin and suggested quietly, "We rise early on the morrow and ride far, Brenna. Should you drink so much wine?"

"I'll drink what I like," Brenna snapped, a frown spoiling

her pretty wine-reddened lips. "You're not my father, you know." She turned away from Leandra, obviously eager to attend to the storytelling.

The pilgrim family, the Penders, proved to be good company, telling engaging stories of their travels across Spain. Father Rhys also had stories to tell. His travels had taken him to Italy, a land that Sir Garrett spoke of with some knowledge and fondness, to Leandra's surprise.

The candles burned low and the greasy serving platters glistened bare when at last the Penders and the churchmen excused themselves.

As they rose to say their thank-yous and seek their beds, Leandra vaguely noted that it was Brenna who busied herself with pouring the remaining wine into the goblets of the four of them left in the room: Wystan, Garrett, Leandra, and herself.

"That 'twas a fine supper. Now I propose a toast," Brenna offered, swaying a little as she stood and held her goblet high. She looked to Garrett as if she expected him to object, but he didn't. Brenna went on. "To an amusing journey and a speedy arrival at Tremelyn."

"I'll drink to the speedy part." Garrett raised his goblet.

Wystan lifted his, murmuring agreement. Leandra sipped from hers, too, a little surprised by her cousin's unusually gracious gesture.

"Drink it all," Brenna warned. "Remember, 'tis bad luck to leave any in the bottom of the cup."

When they finished, she set her goblet down and peered first into Leandra's cup, then into Garrett's; apparently satisfied. An unusual grin spread across her face—a malicious smile that made Leandra shift nervously in her chair.

"This should prove to be a most entertaining trip," Brenna said. "Tell me, cousin, where is your love potion?"

Chapter 8

Leandra started as if Brenna had thrown a bucket of cold water into her face. What was her cousin up to? she wondered. "That is not something to jest about, Brenna. Not now."

"What love potion?" Garrett asked, cautiously setting his goblet on the table.

Leandra hesitated, but she had little choice. Garrett watched her expectantly.

"I have it right here." She reached for the phial in her cuff. She found nothing. It was gone!

"You see, I have it, or I did." Brenna held up the silver container for all to see. "Until I poured it into your wine. You two have just shared a love potion. How do you feel, Sir Garrett?"

In horror Leandra stared down the table at the knight. He glared uncomprehendingly at Brenna.

"Lady Leandra and I have *what?*" he asked, astonishment on his face, his voice ominously low. "Say that again."

Brenna slowly edged her way toward the door, a fiendish pleasure twisting her wine-stained lips. "You each have drunk of a love potion. You shall love each other hopelessly, eternally, above all things—just as Vivian said. Right, Leandra? No more bickering. No more scowls exchanged. No more vying to give the last order."

She beckoned to Wystan. The squire took one look at his older brother's threatening face and chose to remain in his place. Brenna wisely swept out of the room, leaving Garrett and Leandra to stare speechlessly at the closed door.

"What nonsense is this?" Garrett demanded. "Is what she said true? Was there a love potion in that phial?"

Leandra nodded, unable to speak and helpless to take her eyes from Garrett's grim face. How could Brenna have done this to them? To her?

"A love potion? One of Vivian's, I suppose?" Garrett stared at her, disbelief in his eyes. "Sweet Jesu, why do you have a love potion?"

Frantically Leandra searched for an explanation that would make sense to him.

"Because I wanted Lord Reginald to love me and I him," she stammered, staring up into Garrett's face, willing him to understand and knowing that he never would. "I want the best for your liege lord just as much as you do. I wanted ours to be a union true and strong."

Garrett's eyes had narrowed as he listened. Then he said, "You would deceive Lord Reginald with a village maid's aphrodisiac?" He stood up, the sound of his chair scraping the floor overpowering Leandra's protests. He turned his back to her and strode to the fireplace. "You would take away his choice, his free will?"

"I give up mine as well." Angered by his righteousness, Leandra also rose from her chair, hands spread on the table. Did no one care about the burden *she* bore? About the uncertainty she lived with, the insecurity? "I've had little enough choice in this marriage as it is. Lyonesse desperately needs Tremelyn's protection. And do you forget about the countess? I must overcome the earl's grief for his first wife. My skill with a bow won't help me there."

Garrett remained thoughtfully silent, the firelight glittering in his clear blue eyes. Shadows played against a jaw chiseled hard with anger and lips pressed thin with indignation. "Just what does the potion do?"

When Leandra didn't reply immediately because she wasn't certain what he asked, he gave an ironic laugh. "Well? Will I become mad to possess you? Will I chase you about the chamber until you surrender, moaning in my arms with passion?"

"No, no. Nothing like that," Leandra protested, staring at

him, unable to rid her mind of the very image he described —of a golden, impassioned Garrett pursuing her around a bed, his strong hands about to grasp her, to throw her down on the mattress, and his lips descending on hers. His body—

She shook her head, shaking away the picture from her mind. "I don't think so. Vivian said the potion is no aphrodisiac. It brings true love, forever."

Garrett gazed at her with an expression she could no longer read. Then he turned back to the fire. "True love? Forever? As serious as all that?"

"Yes, that's what she said. Maybe it will be ineffective on an unreceptive man," Leandra offered, desperate to give him and herself some peace of mind.

He said nothing for some moments, his gaze absorbed in the flames in the hearth. "But this is Vivian's potion, is it not? She who made the seasickness medicine?"

"Yes, Vivian," Leandra admitted, wishing for once that she had not sought out the best of all the wise women.

Garrett groaned and wiped his hand across his face. "What are we going to do? I can't love you. 'Twould be a betrayal of everything I believe in. I do not want to love you."

"Nor I to love you." Leandra sank into her chair and twisted her betrothal ring, strangely disappointed by his confession and all the while wishing she could say or do something to smooth the furrow from his brow.

"Is there some way to ward off the effects of this spell?" Wystan asked. "Or do we hope it's merely a maiden's silliness?"

"'Tis no maid's silliness," Leandra said, offended. She looked up at Garrett, at the handsomest face she'd ever seen, at the first man to stir passion in her with little more than a kiss bestowed in a child's game.

The temptation was great, but she would not compound Brenna's folly with a sin of omission. "Vivian told me that there is an antidote."

"An antidote?" Garrett's face brightened and he straightened, taking his elbow from the stone mantel. "See how simple it all is? There's an antidote. What do we do?"

"Yes, but Vivian must prepare it fresh for us," Leandra explained. "If we wish to take that, we must return to Lyonesse as soon as possible."

"Another sea voyage?" Garrett groaned. He ran his fingers through his hair once more. "I'm not setting foot on another ship. Not for a while. No. There must be another way."

"I don't know of any. Unless Father John—" Leandra began.

"Of course, the good father should be able to advise us," Garrett said. "Wystan, bid Father John to come to us."

Father John shuffled into the dining room, his fringe of white hair pressed flat on one side and crinkled into a cloud on the other. "You haven't had a change of heart about bringing the pilgrims along, have you, Sir Garrett?" the father asked, stifling a yawn. The priest's face shone rosy with sleep as he squinted at Garrett.

"No, Father. I—We asked you here for another reason."

Garrett explained about the potion. As the knight told the story, Father John's sleepy smile faded into a look of concern. Leandra could feel the heat of embarrassment rise in her cheeks as the priest looked from one of them to the other.

"Is this true, my daughter? You had a love potion with you?"

"That's not the problem, Father John," Garrett interrupted, diverting the priest's attention Leandra noted gratefully. "What are we going to do? Do you believe we will be affected? After all, the potion was not intended for me—us."

Father John said nothing for some moments. He paced the room in his sleep-wrinkled cassock. "Most potions are but the quaint recipes of old women who mean well. Mostly meant for young people who want to fall in love and would anyway.

"You both are honorable people, pure of heart, and true to the laws of the Church. Put it from your mind," the priest advised.

Garrett nodded and smiled at Leandra, relief coming to

his face. "There, see, 'tis all nonsense. We will suffer no ill effects."

Father John regarded Leandra for a moment more, then asked, "Lady Leandra, where did you obtain this spell?"

"From Vivian of the Forest, Father." Leandra knew Vivian was well-known, even beyond the shores of Lyonesse.

Father John's benign expression vanished. He put his fingers to his lips in sudden agitation. "Oh, my children, I don't know what to tell you except . . . Vivian? . . . Oh, ah . . . my goodness . . . when the spell takes hold, you must come to me. Confess all. Your lusts, your passions will be safe with me. Together we will pray to God for the strength to resist the desires until they pass."

"What are you saying, Father?" Garrett didn't like the priest's reversal. "That the potion might truly work a spell on us?"

He looked from Father John to Leandra, and she stared back at him, her face pale and her dark eyes wide. For a moment he thought he saw tears gathering. Before he could be certain, Father John walked between them and she lowered her head. Obviously she regretted this ridiculous situation more than Brenna ever would.

"'Tis possible," Father John said.

"I will go pray, Father," Leandra said, rising from her chair and clasping her hands like a penitent. With a wary look in Garrett's direction, she added, "I will make Brenna pray with me. Long and hard."

Quietly she walked across the room and turned into the passage.

Father John turned to Garrett. "Do I dare ask how all this happened?"

Garrett shook his head, unwilling to betray Leandra, even though the thought of her giving his lord a potion infuriated him.

"Then all I can say, my son, is come to me when—" He glanced out the door as if to make certain that Leandra was beyond their hearing. "You'll know when you need my help," Father John said. "I recommend that during this

95

journey you keep your distance from Lady Leandra and
bathe long and often in a cold stream."

Leandra slammed the chamber door behind her and
clenched her fists at her sides. Brenna stood half dressed in
the middle of their private chamber, her dark hair hanging
loose about her bare shoulders and wine still staining her
upper lip.

"What on *earth* do you think you're doing!" Leandra
demanded, angrier with Brenna than she'd ever been in her
life. She had survived Brenna's pranks before, but this one
would not be tolerated. "This is the most irresponsible thing
you have ever done. Have you gone mad?"

"No, merely incensed with being pushed here and shoved
there as if my feelings don't matter," Brenna asserted,
clearly not in the least disturbed by Leandra's rage.

"What is mischief supposed to accomplish? How does
this change any of that? You knew my plans for the potion.
Don't you care what happens to your homeland and your
uncle?"

"Oh, Leandra, don't be so dramatic," Brenna said, wiggling her gown down over her hips. "You're taking this love
potion thing too seriously."

"Too seriously? Who knows what is going to happen to Sir
Garrett and I under the potion's spell? Not only that, I have
nothing to ensure Lord Reginald's love. Suppose he dislikes
me on sight and sends you and I home?"

Brenna halted just as she was about to step out of her
gown. The thought of being sent home to Lyonesse appeared
to be a new one to her. "He wouldn't do that. The earl will
like you. Of course he will. In any event, I doubt the potion
would have been much use to you anyway."

"Just how is that?"

"You and Sir Garrett might fall in love. But I don't think
it will last long."

Leandra could hardly believe what Brenna was saying.
"What do you mean? You heard Vivian say it was eternal."

"Well, look here." Brenna pointed to her cheek. "See?"

"See what? What does your face have to do with this,"

Leandra demanded. She could see nothing on Brenna's flawless skin and her patience was gone. "And why should I care?"

"My new dimple," Brenna said, obviously irritated that Leandra had not noticed.

"Oh, the dimple that Vivian's remedy made for you? What about it?"

"It's gone. See? It only lasted two days and disappeared. I tried the lotion on it again and it came back sure enough, but only to disappear again." Brenna shrugged. "So if Vivian's love potion does take effect, I give you and Sir Perfect two days at the best."

Leandra dropped down on the bed. Was it possible, she wondered, that despite Vivian's claims, the potion was no more than an aphrodisiac after all? But the seasickness remedy had worked so well on Sir Garrett. Would the love potion be as effective as that remedy or as weak as Brenna's dimple brew?

Brenna added, "I can hardly wait to see something mellow that grumbling knight."

"I don't think giving him this potion is going to do that," Leandra observed. "He's as angry as I am, and he has every right to be."

What should she expect? Leandra wondered. If Brenna was right—two days? Surely she and Sir Garrett could resist each other for such a short length of time in the company of so many churchmen. And if she was wrong?

"What do you think Sir Perfect will be like as a lover?" Brenna asked, drawing a comb through her hair. "I don't think he's the type to recite poetry or sing love songs, do you? I fancy he's a fine kisser, though. And jealous. I wager he's a jealous lover."

The angry, jealous aspect of Garrett was easy for Leandra to see, too, but she didn't intend to speculate on the prospect of the knight as a lover. "Enough of this nonsense, Brenna. Regardless of how harmless you think this prank is, the fact remains that we've angered Sir Garrett once more. You have put us at great risk. I now have no potion to use on the earl when we reach Tremelyn."

"Well, the two of you have done enough to me that you can't ever make me feel guilty." Brenna heaved a long, exasperated sigh and blew out the only candle in the room. "'Tis no more than you both deserve."

What little sleep Garrett did get that night was filled with strange dreams of witches, all blond and resembling Leandra, bent over a steaming caldron of an evil-smelling brew. Nearby, innocent maidens, all dark-haired and resembling Brenna, prayed for forgiveness. Garrett awoke to the barking of a village dog. "No, that's not right," he muttered, rolling over. "Not right at all."

For a long time he lay awake, staring at the timbered ceiling above, listening to Father John snore, but his mind was filled with the vision of Leandra's anxious face when she replied, *Nor can I love you.* She had regarded him with those exotic eyes, wide and honest. Had he seen disappointment there, too? This time, when he finally drifted off, the witches in the dream were Brenna and the innocent maidens were all Leandra.

No hint of dawn had reached the eastern horizon when Garrett awoke again, frustrated, exhausted, and thoroughly irritated. But the strongest feeling that lay on him was the sense of having been betrayed by some unseen hand. He'd no idea what to call it or how to strike back at its unfairness. He knew only that he could sleep no more.

In the dark of the morning he whipped back the blankets, prodded Wystan on the shoulder, and started to bellow orders to soldiers and grooms.

"Why are you all lying about?" he roared. "We're wasting the good light of dawn. Up with you. The sooner we're on the road, the better."

The entourage that climbed the road westward out of Penzance was a tense lot. A fierce knight led the way, followed by two silent, belligerent women, one apprehensive priest, one baffled squire, five prayerful pilgrims, and a host of bewildered soldiers.

* * *

The cool water beckoned to Leandra, promising a soothing wade to tired feet and legs. As soon as she was certain she was alone, she'd dropped her bow and arrows, pulled off her green leather boots, and peeled off her hose.

Over her head a robin fussed and fretted, its shrill cries claiming her attention as she dropped her last garter and wiggled her bare toes in the grass.

"What's the trouble, mother robin?" Leandra asked. She had remained at the bubbling spring after the soldiers had watered the horses and mules and returned to camp. Sir Garrett had pressed them hard all day, keeping the horses moving at a steady pace despite the warm weather, and she looked forward to cooling her feet in the cold spring water.

Then the flapping of wings had distracted her.

"Is there a snake about?" she wondered aloud. "Here I stand barefoot."

She looked around for the source of the bird's alarm, half expecting to see a serpent slithering over the turf. Instead she spied a scrawny fledgling struggling on the ground. The ugly nestling raised a wobbly head and cheeped weakly in answer to its mother. Then its head drooped, its strength nearly spent.

"Oooh," Leandra crooned, instantly in sympathy with the separation of mother and young. "Where is your home?"

She gazed overhead again to find the nest, well-woven, snuggled tight in the fork of the tree branch. Returning the fledgling would be no great problem. As a girl she'd often climbed the orchard trees to pick fruit.

Once more she glanced around to their hillside camp to be certain no one was watching. Satisfied that everyone was busy with their own concerns, she looped her skirt up in her leather girdle, scooped up the soft bundle of feathers, and started up the gnarled tree.

When she reached the forking branch, she lay along the limb and tenderly placed the young robin in the nest with its sibling.

"There you go. Home safe." She lingered for a moment to watch the two birds call once more for their mother.

"You shouldn't be here alone," Sir Garrett warned, walking around one of the trees. He gave her such a start she nearly tumbled from the branch. When she looked down, she found him staring up at her as if he'd been watching every move she'd made from afar. Sweet Mother, had he seen her take off her hose? Leandra wondered.

His chain mail jingled and his sword clanked against his thigh as he leaned against the other tree by the spring. A frown of disapproval stretched across his face, and he added, "You know, countesses usually don't climb trees."

"I was restoring a bird to its nest," Leandra explained, annoyed with the censure in his remark. "When I'm countess, I can order you to do it. Besides, I'm not alone," she added. "I can see everyone and they can see me. I have my bow and arrows right here. Nothing is going to happen."

"I suppose not." Garrett sat down on one of the springside stones. "But I'll be here if anything does."

She wanted him to leave, but he leaned back against the tree, making himself comfortable for a long stay. What now? To climb down risked exposing more leg than was bare already. Her boots and hose lay on the ground right next to him. She couldn't dress without his observing every move. So she made a vain attempt to tuck her bare feet away and out of sight until he decided to take his leave.

"Look at Brenna," Garrett said, gazing across the moor at the camp. "She looks so innocent. Does she feel any remorse?"

"I think she believes it's a fine joke." Leandra was now becoming more disappointed than angry with Brenna's irresponsible act.

"Yes," he said. "Since I've had some time to think about it, this situation with the love potion is really rather humorous, isn't it? Nothing to get upset about." He spoke to her as if holding conversation with a maid lying on a tree branch were the most natural thing in the world.

Leandra shifted uncomfortably on the branch. "I'm afraid I don't see any humor in it. Last night you didn't, either."

"A long day's ride has given me a new perspective,"

Garrett explained. "You bring along a potion to share with your future husband, then the wrong people get it. 'Tis like the errors in a mummer's play."

Astonished, Leandra shook the tree limb, jostling the poor baby birds. "Are you becoming as addlepated as Brenna? This is no mummer's play! Do you realize what would happen if this potion works?" She hesitated a moment and lowered her voice. "What if . . . what if we . . ."

"What if we became lovers as the potion is supposed to make us do?" Garrett finished for her, gazing up without any apparent embarrassment.

"Yes, well, don't you see," she stammered on, unnerved by the thought of them together. The bedchamber vision popped into her head again. "You would betray your liege lord, and I would be unfaithful to my betrothed." She looked around to be certain that no one was close enough to hear. "We would both lose everything. Everything!"

"But only if the potion works," Garrett said, with a shrug of indifference. "Only if we become lovers."

His smile faded as he looked up at her, his eyes straying to her bare legs, which she had been unable to hide. "Tell me, do you believe this stuff will work? What are the first signs?"

"Well, I don't know," Leandra admitted with a frown. "I always assumed my heart would know. Vivian didn't say."

Garrett grinned at her mischievously, his eyes warm with good humor. "Are you falling in love with me, Lady Leandra?"

Leandra stared at him in horror. The sun glittered off his closely cropped hair and gleamed in his dark blue eyes— eyes as blue as a summer sea. His jawline would tempt an angel to kiss it, and the grin that twitched on his lips was beguiling.

Leandra shook her head. "Of course I'm not falling in love with you," she snapped. Her heart pounded as if she had just lied in the confessional. She talked on quickly, filling her head and her words with excuses. "You're far too arrogant and domineering to appeal to me, Sir Garrett."

Garrett sat up straight, surprised by her words. His captivating grin vanished.

"Arrogant?" he repeated. She thought him arrogant? He had worked so hard at being humble throughout this mission.

"Besides, I save my heart for Lord Reginald." Leandra placed her free hand over her heart and her betrothal ring glinted in the sunlight. "You're not falling in love with me, are you?"

"No, no. I favor a more docile woman," Garrett said, suddenly irritated with her and ready to give back as good as she offered. "One with dark hair."

But he caught himself gazing at her small feet, smooth and bare against the rough tree bark. He eyed the shapely line of her hips, tapering to a waist he'd fitted his hands around once already, and to round, firm breasts that he wanted to cup and to taste. The breeze fluttered her loose golden tresses, and he wondered about the texture of her hair. The golden goddess Diana—barefoot and innocent—stared down at him from above. Sweet Jesu, what was he thinking? Was this the work of the potion?

Chapter 9

Garrett straightened, and his eyes went to Leandra's face. Was she affected, too?

She stared back at him, her earthy green eyes wide and solemn, her expression strained and her lips tight with discomfort.

Understanding instantly, Garrett reached up for her. "Lady Leandra, let me help you down from there. It wouldn't do to save you from assassins and have you break your neck falling from a tree."

"I can get down myself." Leandra shrank from him, and a blush spread upward from her throat as she glanced down at her bare feet. "I was waiting for you to leave. Since I'm not properly clothed—as I'm sure a countess always is."

With a soft laugh he offered his hand again. "I'm an honorable knight, my lady. I promise not to look." He'd seen enough already.

After a moment of consideration, Leandra agreed. "I know you are an honorable knight."

She swung down, lowering herself carefully from the tree branch until Garrett could reach her waist. He spread his hands along her sides, wrapped his fingers around her rib cage, and lifted her down, allowing her to rest for a moment with her back against his chest.

Her hair smelled of roses and her body moved warm and vibrant in his arms, desirable enough to stir unchivalrous reactions.

Were she anyone else, he would have held her against him a little longer. But he set his lord's betrothed down promptly, his hands lingering only long enough to be certain she had her balance.

"Thank you, sir," she said without looking him in the eye. Immediately she reached for her boots.

Garrett stepped away. "I'll wait for you on the other side of the tree." With greater effort than he anticipated, he turned his back on her.

On the second day of the overland journey, Brenna began to complain that traveling wasn't as much fun as she thought it would be. She didn't like the fog that seemed to follow them, and she'd already tired of the pilgrims' stories.

"Have you noticed?" she added, leaning from the saddle to confide in Leandra's ear. "The old man always smells of garlic."

Leandra had noticed. It was impossible to miss. Even the guards had begun to avoid the old pilgrim.

"Mistress Pender seems more like a witch than Vivian did," Brenna observed and chattered on.

The foggy road that lay ahead suddenly stretched out beyond the ears of Leandra's horse—mile upon complaining mile.

Only the churchmen seemed to enjoy themselves, thrilled by the sight of every holy well and hallowed marker they encountered.

"Here it is, Sir Garrett, the way to St. Euny's well," Father Rhys said, pointing out the narrow track that disappeared down the hill into the fog. His fuzzy brown beard split into a toothy grin. "I recognize it now. We go by foot from here."

The excited priest jumped from his mule and trotted down the path, mist swirling in his wake.

"Are we stopping here?" Brenna asked. "Why were we in too much haste to stop at the fair in the last village, but have time to visit saint what's-his-name's well?"

"Yes," Leandra agreed. She had wanted to stop at the fair, too. "Why is that, Sir Garrett?"

"Because," bit out the knight who squinted at her from the other side of Wystan, "*your* pilgrims wish it."

"Oh." Leandra decided to say no more. Despite their

private talk, Sir Perfect's temper had improved little since Brenna had given them the potion. He scowled often, as though he wanted to commit murder every time he saw her cousin.

"I'd prefer the open moor to a close place like this, especially in this gloom," Sir Garrett was saying, his words meant for Wystan. "These hills remind me too much of that day Reginald was attacked and almost killed. Stay close and prepared."

His warning sent little chills down Leandra's back. She slipped off her horse without waiting for a groom, gathered her skirts, and strode down the path close behind the priests. Brenna followed her.

"Sir Garrett says this seems like a place for an attack," Brenna repeated, gazing fearfully at the shrouded hillsides.

"'Tis Sir Garrett's duty to be prepared to fight," Leandra said, without much interest. The gloom made her uneasy, but it wouldn't do to upset Brenna. They had no need to add hysteria to their problems.

"Lady Leandra?"

She and Brenna whirled around to find Mistress Pender and her family on their heels. The scent of garlic drifted to Leandra's nose.

"I didn't mean to frighten ye, ladies." The pilgrim lady, her husband, and grandson made no curtsy, no nod of respect. "But we wondered if ye will join us."

"I'll escort Lady Leandra." Sir Garrett strolled out of the fog to Leandra's side and gave the pilgrim woman a steady look.

Mistress Pender backed away, her husband and grandson huddling in the black wash of her pilgrim's cloak. Garrett's presence seemed to inspire deference.

"But I'm sure Lady Brenna would be glad to join you," he suggested, taking Leandra's arm.

"Of course, your lordship. Lady Brenna? We'd be pleased if ye joined us."

Leandra allowed Garrett to lead her on down the path, leaving Brenna behind to sputter some reply.

"Stay in the company of the group," Garrett warned. "No

wandering off to wade in the water or to rescue baby birds today."

"As you wish, your lordship." Leandra couldn't keep the rebellious sarcasm from her voice.

Garrett cast her a contemptuous frown.

"Surely you don't think anyone would desecrate a holy place with violence, do you?" Leandra asked, a little sorry that she had mocked his concern. He was only trying to complete his mission.

"It has happened before," he said. "Just don't wander off. If you wish to see something, take me—take a guard with you."

Leandra agreed.

At the bottom of the path, they found the natural stone grotto of the well. Leandra filled her lungs with the cool fresh air that hung over the spring and let the tension ease from her shoulders. Pristine water gurgled contentedly from the rocks. She pulled away from Garrett to peer into the clear brook that frolicked away through the ravine.

Over the grotto stood a chapel-like structure with an informal altar. Rich green moss dripped from the grotto ledges. Leandra watched in awe as the sky lightened and the sun came out long enough to make the dewy moss sparkle like emeralds.

Father John, Father Rhys, and the brother cleric busied themselves with prayers at the altar. Mistress Pender bathed her face in the water while her old husband sat on the bank across from Brenna dozing in the sun. Garrett paced like a sentry.

Farther downstream Leandra spotted Alfred wading in the water without taking off his wooden clogs, his hood pulled low over his face, as always. Leandra didn't like the way he constantly viewed the world from the depths of his pilgrim cloak. Furtively he looked up, and when he saw her watching him, he turned away. Leandra looked away. What's he up to? she wondered.

As soon as he thought he was unobserved, she saw him snatch coins from the water, coins tossed with prayers for a favor, a boon.

"Shame on you, Alfred." Brenna appeared at the stream bank and boldly gestured for him to throw back the coins. "Taking pilgrim's offerings! This is a holy place. Remember, thou shalt not steal. Return them."

At first the boy shook his head.

"Shall I say something to Father Rhys or Father John?" Brenna threatened.

After a moment of thought, Alfred grudgingly tossed the coins into the water. Abruptly he turned his back to Brenna and waded out of the water to join his grandfather, who slept against a tree on the other side.

Father John's invitation to prayer distracted Leandra, but later when they were back on the main road east, she touched Brenna's arm. "I saw you with Alfred at the well."

Brenna nodded. "Can you believe he took the coins? There's something strange about a pilgrim stealing from a holy place."

"I know," Leandra said. "I don't think he's a boy."

Brenna blinked at her. "Is he a maid? If so, he's a thieving maid."

"No, that's not what I mean," Leandra said. "I think he's older than he appears to be. Should we tell Sir Garrett?"

"After what we had to do to get him to bring them along?" Brenna asked, then shrugged. "The Penders probably fib about Alfred's age so they don't have to pay full fares for him. 'Tis dishonest, but harmless enough. Why tell Sir Garrett?"

"You're right," Leandra admitted, the stableyard scene still fresh in her mind. So what if the boy was older than he appeared? So his grandparents passed him off as a child to save on expenses? She and Brenna silently agreed to say nothing more. But Leandra decided that if she saw one more strange action from the Penders, she would have to say something to Garrett.

But Alfred's thieving was only the first of the odd events that troubled Leandra on the road across the moor.

That evening, just as they stopped to make camp, they were forced to the side of the road by a strange sound.

Chanting voices swelled in the gloom, eerily floating on the mist, rhythmic and sad. Garrett halted the company, though they could see nothing. In silence they waited, the chorus growing louder, then receding, only to grow again.

With apprehension Leandra watched the first blazing torches emerge from the fog, their smoke adding to the murk. Then came a rider followed by rank after rank of singing monks, their slow steps as harmonized as their mournful voices. On their shoulders rested an ornately carved casket. The sad hymn surged to new heights and surrounded the Tremelyn company.

Brenna cowered inside her cloak and whimpered, "I hate the sound of a death march."

Reassuringly, Leandra patted her cousin's arm.

At the head of the cortege rode a lady in fine black wool. Torchbearers marched at her side, and behind her filed the eight black-hooded monks bearing the funeral bier.

Leandra watched Sir Garrett inspect the group, a suspicious gleam in his eye. Had the man faith in no one, not even a widow?

The well-dressed lady stopped to exchange greetings with Garrett. Leandra overheard some of the conversation.

". . . died in the inn in London. I could not have him buried there. So impersonal a place, London. So I bring him home to lay in his family's crypt." Her voice was strong and hard, long accustomed to taking charge and to issuing orders.

Leandra urged her horse forward to greet the woman in black. "Will you pause and take some refreshment with us? Prayer with Father John and Father Rhys might be of some comfort."

Garrett shot Leandra a frown. She smiled back at him graciously.

"I would like that," the widow said. She introduced herself as Lady Adelle Chygwin.

The monks set down the bier. Proudly, Widow Chygwin insisted that Leandra and Brenna view her handsome dead husband. Brenna slunk away. But Leandra dutifully admired the deceased, a kindness she would do for any of her friends or villagers. She thought him a handsome, if sharp-nosed man. The fact that his widow could afford to hire the monks for this last journey home bespoke of considerable wealth.

"He was a good man, my husband, but so busy was he currying favor in court that he did not even spend his last Christmas at home," the widow complained over the cup of wine Leandra offered for her.

"Our petition for the return of disputed lands is still not settled. But I think my nephew will take up the cause," the widow explained. "With the king away in France, the process will take even longer."

The widow did not tarry over the bread and cheese she shared with them. Leandra saw her go on her way once more, the monks following with their sad burden.

A pall settled over the Tremelyn company—pilgrims and ladies alike—and the gloom about them seemed to deepen.

The beacon fire hung low in the eastern sky over Bodmin Moor—a misty, uncanny sight. Garrett stared at the orange flaming ball and debated the wisdom of making an early camp for the night. He'd been unable to shake off the melancholy that had settled over him after they'd met the funeral cortege. Maybe a good night's rest would do them all good.

"Is there water at the rock?" he asked Father Rhys, who proved to be a wealth of information about all the sacred corners of Cornwall.

"Oh, yes. There's a good campground. We must stop there. The hermit is an old friend of mine, and the place is most sacred. 'Twas once the hermitage of St. Roche, the first bishop of Cornwall."

"Wystan, as soon as we get there, you'll see to setting up the camp while we go atop the rock." Garrett ignored the pitiful look Brenna and Wystan exchanged. The place seemed almost too convenient a site for camp. Two days on the road and no trouble yet, he calculated. Another day and they'd reach the Tamar River. None too soon, as far as he was concerned.

Cold and gusty like a winter's gale, the wind caught at their cloaks as they began the climb up the rock. "The weather is worsening," Garrett called to the pilgrims, quickening his step to join them, to hurry them along. "Let's get to the top and down again before it turns foul."

Father Rhys led the way, with Brother William close behind him. Father John, the Penders, Leandra and Garrett, and Brenna followed, complaining all the way. Leandra was steady and nimble. They all trod cautiously on the granite steps, up a primitive ladder, and through a narrow stone passage.

"'Tis a bleak place to seek God," Leandra observed when they reached the top.

"Few distractions. Perfect for a hermit." Garrett noticed how the wind lifted her golden hair from her temple.

The priests joyfully greeted their solitary fellow and accepted an invitation into his cell. Brenna plopped herself down on a rock to rest.

They were alone. Garrett let himself admire the clean, delicate line of Leandra's profile. Desire stirred. Purposely he looked away to see Brenna join Mistress Pender at the altar. His need wasn't necessarily the work of the potion, he told himself. Other lovely women had tempted him before.

"Our journey is nearly over, is it not?" Leandra asked. "Nothing has happened."

"'Tis no time to let down our guard," Garrett said. "Outlaws may strike anytime or anyplace. They don't leave a trail like an army."

"I was referring to the potion," Leandra said. "Nothing has happened with the potion, has it? All our fears were for nothing."

Garrett forced himself to continue his study of the view. Was it possible that only he was affected and that she felt nothing of the stirrings?

"Nothing," he lied.

From the height the mist seemed lighter and the moors stretched out spring-green beyond them, dotted with distant black granite tors. The wind whipped about the cliff at their feet. Behind them the beacon fire, tended by a boy, danced and spewed embers.

"I do have a question for you," Garrett said. "I'd like to know why. I understand that you are concerned about Lord Reginald's devotion to the first countess. But why not give nature . . . ah, Cupid, an opportunity."

Leandra blinked at him. "Why the potion?"

"Yes. Do maids commonly use love potions?"

"Oh." Leandra stared ahead, the heat of a blush flooding into her cheeks. She hoped he'd forgotten about the potion. She had, for a while. It seemed to be having no effect. "I don't know what other maids do. I don't even know what wives do. You see, that's why I obtained the potion. Mother died when I was born. I've had no one but nuns for teachers."

"No mother?" Garrett repeated thoughtfully. "What did nuns teach you about wifely duties?"

"Well, what do you think?" Leandra asked, heat rising into her cheeks once more. "Needlework, which I hate. Household management, and, of course, the appropriate prayers. You know, prayers to say over the butter, over rising bread, over the cheese-making or a sick child. For childbed."

"Women pray for that?"

"For children, of course, and a safe delivery. What greater blessing?"

"I think I begin to see." He chuckled more softly this time, a gentle derisive yet understanding sound that made her face burn even hotter. She was certain she must be absolutely glowing. "You had so little faith in prayers, in nature, or in Lord Reginald, that you decided to use a love potion?"

"It's not a matter of faith," Leandra protested, annoyed with his amusement at her expense. He was a worldly man and couldn't possibly understand how wide and mysterious the future looked to her.

"It's a matter of ignorance," she said. "Brenna and I asked the midwife questions once, but she refused to tell us anything without Father's permission, and he said we were too young." Leandra found her old frustrations rising to the surface again, and despite the delicate nature of the topic, she spoke on in earnest, wanting him to understand. "Maybe men know these things already, about bedding and loving. Are you born with the knowledge? The process is not quite so obvious to a maid."

Garrett's expression sobered. With a glimmer of hope, Leandra realized that he was considering her words. "No, we are not born with the knowledge," he admitted. "Men also need to learn. A woman of experience is usually the best teacher."

Leandra stared at him, then looked away with a little pang of envy stinging her heart. Who had his teacher been? Where was she now? Did he still love her? Before Leandra thought about how the words might sound, the question slipped out. "Did she have dark hair?"

"Did who have dark hair?"

Leandra huffed. "Your teacher. Who else?"

Garrett grinned. "Why, yes? How did you know?"

Leandra gave an elaborate shrug to her shoulders and turned away, feigning indifference. But her cheeks burned. "'Tis unfair. Women are not allowed men teachers."

"Are you jealous?" Garrett asked. He leaned toward her, and Leandra recognized the teasing tone in his voice. "Has the potion taken effect yet? Are you seized with overwhelming desire? Is it passion that pinkens your cheeks?"

"Of course not," Leandra snapped. "Nor do you appear to be enthralled by my presence."

Garrett chuckled. "Have you discovered how we will know when the potion takes possession of us?"

His laughter was so goodhearted that Leandra smiled and decided to join in the fun. "I'll be seized by an irresistible obsession to embroider your tunics, and you'll spend endless hours below my window, reciting poetry."

"Yes, only a strong spell could do that," Garrett agreed.

The image was so ridiculous and delightful that they both began to laugh.

He sobered and again looked out over the moors. "Now

you have no potion to give Reginald. What do you plan to do?"

The humor of the moment disappeared for Leandra, and an unaccountable gray cloud settled over her spirits. She wanted so desperately for Reginald to be pleased with her. She longed to be as loyal and steadfast a wife as the Widow Chygwin had been. "I will simply have to do my best," she confessed. The thought of loyalty pricked Leandra's conscience. "Sir Garrett, there is something about the Penders that I should tell you about. Yesterday, at the well . . ."

"Yes, what about yesterday?"

"We saw—" A tug on her cloak startled Leandra and she whirled around to find Mistress Pender at her elbow.

"Sorry, me lady, I didn't mean to startle ye," the old woman pilgrim said. "Please, pray with us?"

"Oh, Mistress Pender," Leandra said. "I'll be right there." She glanced hesitantly at Garrett, curious about his pensive expression. Maybe this was not the time to tell him of the strange incident at the well. "We can talk of this later. Excuse me, sir."

Garrett nodded and turned back to the moorland view before him, oddly aware of a sense of loss when Leandra left his side. The use of a potion made sense as she explained it. She secured the spell as an aid in her duties and responsibilities as a wife. She meant no harm to Lord Reginald, and she was so young. Too young to have carried the weight of Lyonesse on her shoulders.

"Sir Garrett? Sir Garrett?" Alfred, the Penders' boy, loped up from behind. "Father John wishes to see ye in the hermit's cell. He says it's important."

Annoyed with the interruption of his thoughts, Garrett frowned at the odd boy who constantly ducked his head. The lad never met anyone's eye when he spoke.

"He wants ye right away," the boy added, and fidgeted impatiently with the corner of his cloak hood.

"All right," Garrett said. He walked toward the stone doorway where he'd seen Father John, Father Rhys, Brother William, and the hermit disappear earlier. When he reached the door, he knocked. No one answered.

"Go on in. He expects ye," the boy said, pushing the door open for Garrett. One glimpse of the three churchmen bound and gagged on the floor gave away the trap.

Garrett swore—at the boy, and at his idiotic lapse. He whirled around, bringing his elbow up to catch the boy's chin. But he was too late. With the strength of a man, Alfred slammed a shoulder into Garrett's stomach, nearly knocking him off his feet. Garrett grunted with the pain and staggered back into the hermit's cell, fighting to recover his breath. He reached for a wall to steady himself, but found none. He crashed to the floor.

Pender appeared from behind the door and kicked him viciously in the ribs. Chain mail was no protection against the pilgrim's wooden clogs. The ceiling flashed white and black, but Garrett refused to lose consciousness. Another kick rolled him over. A clog stomped painfully into the small of his back. Cold steel pressed against Garrett's jaw.

"Make a sound, and I'll put this sword through yer face, Sir Knight." From the corner of his eye Garrett could see old man Pender standing over him, tall and straight with sword in hand. "Take his sword, Alfred."

The boy's hood fell away from his face, revealing clearly now a small, wiry man—with coarse features like a dwarf. He thrust a knee into Garrett's back, cut away his sword belt, and began to bind his hands and feet. Garrett resisted. Pender's steel pressed tighter against his jaw, and blood trickled down his chin. Garrett allowed himself to be gagged. He knew Leandra well enough to realize that a warning call would only bring her to the cell, not send her flying in escape as he wanted.

"Now, Sir Knight, let's finish this business quickly," Pender said.

When he grabbed Garrett by the hair and yanked his head back, Garrett knew exactly what was coming next. He wasn't about to die like a butchered sheep with his throat cut. Why hadn't he seen these pilgrims' swords? Had they hidden them so well? His anger at his own stupidity and the pilgrims' duplicity added to his strength.

He ducked his head, brought up his knees, then struck out

with his feet. He put all his strength into the strike. He caught Alfred solidly on the shin. The little man yowled and hopped backward, out of Garrett's reach.

Pender cursed, his hand full of nothing but strands of hair. Savagely he swung his blade up. "Give it up, Bernay. There's no escape. Yer going to die."

Chapter 10

Garrett lay silent on the cold stone floor, staring up at Pender's sword blade. Every rasping breath came with pain and effort. Regardless of the danger to himself, he had no intention of making anything easy for these devil's spawn—his murder or Leandra's kidnapping. Garrett caught Pender's gaze and held it.

He willed the moment of hesitation. The ploy worked. Pender faltered. The sword blade paused in midair. In one swift kick Garrett's feet caught Pender in the stomach. Air whooshed from the man's body. The cloaked pilgrim doubled over, clutching his belly, dropping the sword. Garrett rolled away. Pender stumbled backward and plunked onto the floor.

Garrett kicked at Alfred. The little man flattened himself against the cell wall just beyond Garrett's booted feet. His eyes bulged in panic at the sight of the infuriated knight's face. Pender moaned. Alfred grabbed the sword, seized his gasping partner under the arms and dragged him from the cell. He slammed the door behind them. Garrett could hear the two muttering to each other as they frantically lashed it closed.

Through the window he heard Leandra call out, her voice full of concern. "Where is everyone? Garrett? Brenna?"

Brenna screamed.

Garrett struggled to his feet and made his way to the window. Father John, Father Rhys, the hermit, and Brother William mumbled and muttered at him through their gags. Garrett ignored them. In the growing darkness he could see

116

Leandra still standing near the fire, her face tense, a pale oval against the gray mist. Her alert gaze was fastened on the altar where Mistress Pender and Brenna had been. Those women were beyond Garrett's view. He saw no panic in Leandra's face, but he knew—whether Brenna deserved it or not—that Leandra would never hold out against a threat to her cousin.

"Sir Garrett and the priests are bound and gagged in the cell. No one is going to come to your rescue, lady. Your knight is lying on his back as helpless as a turtle."

Under his breath Garrett cursed the near truth of Pender's statement.

"So do as we tell ye and we won't hurt anyone," Pender said.

"Who are you?" Leandra demanded.

Garrett knew she was stalling, hoping as he was that Wystan would realize something was wrong and raise the alarm. He cursed himself for leaving his brother below at the camp.

"No questions," Mistress Pender ordered. The woman stood straight and more youthful than she had appeared before. "Come over here to me, or I'm going to make little slices of your cousin."

Leandra made no move to obey, and glanced in the direction of the cell again.

"Leandra?" Brenna whimpered.

The Penders exchanged uncertain looks. Garrett knew Leandra's cool hesitation surprised them; they'd expected him to be the problem, not the lady.

Leandra began to sidestep toward the rock's edge. "Release my cousin and I will consider going with you. Otherwise, I jump. Take that knife away from her throat, I say."

He heard Brenna whimper again. Then the girl scrambled into his view. She stumbled, casting fearful glances over her shoulder at Mistress Pender, and threw herself at her cousin's feet. Leandra never flinched. She stood with her head high, her chin jutted forward, her gaze steady.

Garrett would have smiled if he could. Leandra and Brenna were only a few yards from the steps.

"Your courage is magnificent, lioness," he muttered into his gag. "Are your wits up to the challenge? You don't have to keep your word."

He closed his eyes and prayed that Leandra would forget her offer to go with the Penders, and instead grab her cousin and run. But when he opened his eyes, he was disappointed to see that she hadn't moved. Still she refused to put herself within Pender's reach. The fraudulent pilgrim motioned toward the hoist, and she walked obediently toward it. Garrett groaned.

Pender reached for Brenna. The girl screamed. "Louder! Louder!" Garrett shouted into his gag. Wystan, where are you? Behind him the churchmen's gagged protests grew clamorous.

Leandra pulled away from Mistress Pender, who stood by the hoist. "Let Brenna go."

Immediately Pender released Brenna. The dark-haired girl scuttled beyond his reach.

Garrett was beginning to understand what the Penders were going to do. He remembered all too clearly the wood cart that waited at the foot of the rock. Perfect for hiding someone. The commonplace vehicle would drive away, and no one, not a single guard in the entourage below, would think to ask questions. Garrett cursed and began to struggle against the rope bound about his wrists.

When he looked out the window again, he saw Leandra offer her unstrung bow to Mistress Pender. When the crone reached for the bow, Leandra brought it up under the woman's chin. Her head snapped back. She clutched her throat and fell backward over a stone stool. Pender dived in then, but Leandra saw him coming and caught the man against the side of his head. Yew cracked. Pender yelped and staggered away. Then Alfred was on her.

Garrett roared frustration through his gag and threw himself against the tiny stone window until the pain in his shoulders stopped him. Silently Garrett praised her courage and prayed now for her safety.

The boy threw her to the ground and held her down while Pender began to pull a huge bag over her head.

Leandra turned toward the cell, and Garrett realized that she caught a glimpse of him. Her look tore at his heart. He knew he would forever see that expression on her face—reassurance masking carefully restrained terror. *Never fear. I will be all right until you can come for me. I know you will come for me,* she said with her eyes in that briefest of glances. The bag covered her face. Garrett's heart stopped beating.

He pulled away from the window, unable to bear the sight of Leandra bagged and tied. He cursed the Penders again, himself, the Fates. The only comfort Garrett found in the situation was that these people obviously wanted Leandra alive. If they didn't, she would be dead by now, just as he was supposed to be. Mistress Pender was with them—a rough woman, but a woman. Surely that ensured Leandra's safety against abuse. But he couldn't be certain.

The pulley on the hoist squeaked. Garrett peered out the window in time to see the Leandra-size bag disappear into the mist. Pender lowered the rope slowly and Mistress Pender watched over the edge.

A muffled shout finally penetrated Garrett's musings. For the first time he truly heard the strangled protests of the churchmen seated against the wall of the cell. Father John in particular seemed to be saying something vital into his gag.

Garrett knelt with his back to the priest. Father John leaned forward, bringing his face as close to Garrett's hands as he could. The action was slow and awkward. Garrett couldn't see what Father John was doing and could only wait to grasp the gag with his fingers when he could. During the agonizing moments, he could hear the squeak of the pulley. He knew that with each creak of the wood and rope, Leandra was being taken farther from him.

In two tries he had the gag out of Father John's mouth. "They took Lady Leandra?"

Garrett nodded.

"I'll untie your hands," Father John said, turning around so that his back was to Garrett's. He began to fumble with the leather on Garrett's wrists.

"They were fakes all along," Father John said as he worked.

Garrett nodded again, his gag still in place.

"Did you know? I thought their behavior at the well curious, but I never suspected anything like this."

Garrett shook his head. Impostors or not, that mattered little now. The gag prevented him from telling the good father to shut up and get the ropes loose.

"Surely, they won't harm her," Father John babbled on. "Lord Reginald's bride. The heiress to Lyonesse. Ransom is what they want, I think. This isn't Leofric's doing, is it?"

The leather loosened at last, and Garrett pulled and twisted his wrists free of the bindings, the pain unheeded. He yanked the gag from his mouth.

"Who else's would it be?" Garrett demanded. "Who else threatened her life? Who else made it plain he opposed her betrothal? He could kill her, or he could force her into marriage to him. Either way, I've failed—Lord Reginald and Leandra."

Garrett stopped, his own cold words ringing in his ears. Leandra's trusting expression loomed vividly in his mind. She knew he would come after her. She counted on it. Suddenly his sense of failure seemed of little importance. Getting to Leandra was what mattered.

Garrett launched himself at the door. By the time the wood splintered apart from his onslaught, the Penders and Leandra were gone. Brenna huddled in a weeping heap not far from the fire. He found the hoist tied, with the loose end of the rope lowered down the side of the rock where Pender had left it after lowering himself over the edge. The cart was gone and no sign of the Penders or Leandra remained. Even the fire boy was gone. Taken as a guide? Garrett wondered. Garrett flung himself down the narrow steps, shouting all the way for Wystan, for horses, arms, and guards.

They found the empty fuel cart abandoned in the valley beyond Roche's Rock. The horse had obviously been ridden off by one of the party.

"This was well-planned," Wystan said. They stared down

at the tracks in the wet moorland. "Someone with horses must have been waiting here for them."

Garrett agreed. The mist grew thicker with the gathering of darkness, and a light rain began to fall. Behind them the beacon fire burned orange in the fog. The tracks marked the route the mounted group had taken across the moors, a dangerous move unless they had a guide who knew the lay of the land as the fire boy probably did.

"Bring the hermit to me," Garrett demanded. "He will be our guide."

"You mean to follow them in the dark?" Wystan asked.

"They travel through the night." Garrett's gaze fixed on the direction he knew they had taken Leandra. "We will, too."

Wystan gave the orders and the guards rode back to the camp to do as they were ordered.

The going was slow. The animals picked their way slowly along the stony high ground. The bottomless bogs in the low areas could mire down man and horse and had to be avoided. The wind came up and flung rain in their faces. They nearly lost a man and horse in one bog. Garrett was forced to leave a man with the near-drowned rider and the injured animal.

Mounted atop a mule, the old hermit blustered that he knew little of the moor because he so seldom left his cell. And darkness obscured the kidnappers' trail. At times, with only torchlight, Garrett's men could find no tracks to follow and could only assume that the pilgrims carried their hostage south and west, away from Tremelyn.

At first light, when they'd reached a river valley near the coast, they found a green tassel from Leandra's cloak caught on a low tree limb beside the narrow track of a road. Until then Garrett almost doubted they were on the right trail. At the sight of the frazzled silken tassel he'd seen on Leandra's cloak only the day before, Garrett's blood ran cold.

Abruptly he ordered Wystan and a guard to escort the hermit back to his cell. Then he turned to the last two men who rode with him. They were the best fighters of the lot he'd brought along from Tremelyn.

He held up the tassel for them to see. "I think we're in for an ugly battle."

"We're ready, sir," the one named Tom said. "'Tis been a quiet trip until now. We could use some action." To Garrett's satisfaction, the other agreed.

"Loosen her bindings, but if she touches her blindfold, tie her again," Pender ordered, the sound of his voice grating against Leandra's ears. Then she heard his horse trot on down the road.

Mistress Pender's chapped hands tugged at the ropes on Leandra's hands. "Mind what he says, now. We don't have to keep ye tied so tight. By the mass, yer hands are nearly purple. There. Leave the blindfold in place. Hear me?"

"Yes, I hear." Leandra's eyes had been covered since Pender pulled the bag over her head at Roche's Rock. The ride in the back of the wood cart hadn't lasted long. To her relief, she was now allowed to sit astride her mount with her hands free enough to cling to the saddle bow. Blindfolded, she could only guess who rode near her and where they were headed.

Without warning, her horse started forward again, throwing her off balance. Leandra struggled to stay in the saddle. Her body was numb with cold and her mind was befuddled with exhaustion. Her cloak and gown hung on her wet and heavy with the rain that had fallen all night. Hard as she tried to understand all that had happened to her in the last dark hours, nothing made sense. Who was this fraudulent pilgrim? Where did he get the money for the horses? The money to hire the men who rode with them? She could tell from the sounds around her that at least two others besides the Penders were making this ride.

She had no idea how long it would take Sir Garrett to catch up with them, but she knew he would come. He would never let Lord Reginald down. She sighed and thanked heaven once more that Brenna was safe in Garrett's and Wystan's protection. Distractedly she toyed with the braid trim of her surcoat. Until Garrett came, she would have to do the best she could on her own.

"Ride on," growled the guard behind her, slapping her horse's rump with something. "We haven't far to go now."

Again Leandra's horse leaped forward, jostling her. She grabbed the saddle bow to steady herself, but made no protest. She'd save her energy.

"Stop that, you," Mistress Pender complained to the guard. She held the reins to Leandra's horse and seemed to consider herself on equal footing with the men of the band.

Since dawn both the Penders and Alfred behaved notably relieved, Leandra thought. The two men rode ahead laughing and apparently at ease. Were they indeed near their destination? Wherever that was.

At the top of a hill the group drew rein again.

"There it is," Pender called back to them. Leandra could tell by the directness of his voice that he'd twisted around in the saddle to speak to the riders behind him. "They'll take care of ye there, my lady."

A chill shook Leandra and her grasp on the saddle bow slipped. The damp cold seeped painfully into her bones. Water dripped from her curls. In the grip of cold exhaustion her faith lagged. Where was Garrett? Had he given up the pursuit? Had he decided that Lord Reginald would be better off without her?

She shook her head. No, Garrett would do his duty. He wouldn't allow his personal feelings to interfere. There must have been other complications. Someone had been hurt. Brenna? Her cousin had been in a heap on the rock when she last saw her.

Leandra heard the men slap one another on the back, congratulating themselves on the reward that would soon jingle in their purses. Who was paying this reward? she wondered. In the distance she heard the baying of hounds and the thunder of horses' hooves on the road.

"Is his lordship coming to meet us?" Mistress Pender asked.

"'Twould seem so," Pender said, but Leandra could hear suspicion in his voice.

She cocked her head, longing to hear more. Lordship, who? Say more, she begged in silence.

"He don't look friendly," Alfred offered.

"No, he don't," Pender agreed.

The thunder of hooves was close now, and Leandra knew Pender spoke of the riders approaching them.

From a distance someone shouted, "Bandits! Outlaws! Kill them, but spare the lady."

"What's this?" Pender cried. Swords raked against scabbards, and crossbows creaked as they were being cocked.

This was her moment to escape. Experimentally, Leandra pulled on her mount's reins. Her mare refused to respond.

"I got ye, me lady," Mistress Pender warned. "Don't be anxious to ride away."

"I wants me money," Pender shouted. "I'll fight fer it if I have to."

The galloping horses were close now. Leandra heard the release of a crossbow, then the thud of an arrow piercing a body. Someone cried out and her horse nickered and shied, leaping away from something, nearly throwing her to the ground. She heard a strangled cry. Then something fell to the road, something large and soft, like a dead man. A rapid, terrifying, incomprehensible chorus followed. But Leandra could feel that her horse was free now.

She yanked off her blindfold and bent over the mare's neck to grab the reins. There was no time to take in what was going on around her. The panicked animal bolted away from the melee, taking a stone roadside fence. Without the blindfold, Leandra easily regained her seat. She worked frantically with loosely bound hands to take up the slack in the reins. The mare galloped headlong into the woods. But a runaway horse she could handle.

Gradually, with a steady hand, she drew rein, easing the horse into a wide circle. She drew tighter and tighter until the horse calmed, slowed her gait, and came to a halt, sides heaving. Leandra sat breathless and confused, listening for more sounds from the battle she had just escaped.

Behind her she heard the tattoo of hooves and started. Friend or foe? What should she do now? Then a purple-clothed rider on a black horse broke through the greenery. "My God, can it be? Lady Leandra!"

Chapter 11

"Sir Leofric!" At the sight of the heir of Casseldorne, tentative relief flooded through Leandra. "I am so glad to see a friend. Some men kidnapped me. Then we were attacked and I broke free."

She didn't understand what he was doing in this part of Cornwall, but he was her neighbor and a welcome sight. "Will you help me?"

"But of course, my lady." Leofric peered at her closely as he rode up. "'Twas my men who attacked. I was out hunting with friends, and we could see the men with you were outlaws." A look of genuine concern crossed his face. "Are you hurt? I saw your horse bolt. You look soaked through."

"I am only chilled," Leandra said, unable to resist a shiver that shook her. She held out her hands to him. "And bound. Will you release me?"

"Gladly." Leofric immediately slipped a knife from his belt to cut the rope around Leandra's wrist. When he tossed away the bindings, he took off his cloak. "Here, take this. You are turning positively blue."

Gratefully Leandra pulled the fur-lined garment over her shoulders. The two sat side by side in silence, listening to the distant shouts of attack, the clang of the swords, the alarmed nicker of horses and strangled cries.

"These parts have been sorely troubled by outlaws of late," Leofric said. "My men are only too glad to rid the woods of them."

"These woods are yours?" Leandra asked. She thought all the Casseldorne holdings lay to the north of Tremelyn and Lyonesse.

"Oh, 'tis but a small manor that belongs to my mother's sister," Leofric said, reaching for the reins of Leandra's horse. "'Tis fortunate that my men and I came upon you and the outlaws. Come, let's leave the fighting to my men and get you to some warmth and food."

Cold, hungry, and bewildered, she allowed him to lead the way out of the woods and down the road to an ancient round Cornish keep. Apprehension shivered through her when the odd castle and its moat first came into view.

Guardianlike, it sat atop a conical mound, windswept, the gate gaping open to make the structure look almost like a giant's head, windows for eyes, the gatekeeper's portal for a nose, and a watery moat for a smile.

In the courtyard Leofric sprang from his mount. His black boots thudded resolutely on the cobbles and a pleased grin spread across his dark face as he reached for Leandra. Only the absence of his purple cap and the disarray of his black hair gave away that he had just ordered men into battle.

"At last, you arrive at a safe place, my lady." He seized her around the waist and tried to pull her from her horse before she could free her feet of the stirrups. "'Tis difficult to believe that Bernay could let this happen to you."

"It was my fault," Leandra blurted out, struggling against Leofric to set her feet on the ground. "I insisted on bringing along the pilgrims. But they were outlaws in disguise."

"God's wounds, outlaws disguised as pilgrims," Leofric echoed, and shook his head at the disgrace.

"We must send someone back to tell Sir Garrett that I'm well and that I'm here," Leandra insisted. She shivered again and pushed away Leofric's hands, which remained pressed against her sides. "I don't think he's far behind me. Put me down, please, sir."

Leofric's yellow-brown eyes narrowed and he abruptly released Leandra. When she dropped to the ground, the impact sent sharp slivers of pain through her numbed feet.

"Bernay is in pursuit? Are you certain?" Leofric demanded. He grasped her by the shoulders and gave her a firm shake. "How would he know where to find you?"

His explosive reaction to the news that Sir Garrett was close disturbed Leandra. She swallowed the answer. No need for Leofric to know everything. "He will find me because he's a good soldier." She shifted from one painful foot to the other and edged herself away from the purple knight. "'Twould be kind to send someone to save his searching."

"Save him searching, indeed," Leofric said, red-faced and nearly sputtering in anger. "If he can't keep you safe, I'm not going to help him. You're in my care now."

Garrett paced the roadside restlessly. "Come on, Tom," he muttered to himself. "Come on. What have you found? Is there a trail for us to follow?"

His stomach growled with hunger, but he paid no heed. His rain-soaked surcoat clung to his chain mail, and the quilted jerkin beneath was wet and cold, but he didn't care. The only discomfort he would acknowledge was the tightness in his chest, or was it his heart? The kind of pain that came with caring too much.

He'd halted their search only because their horses required rest and his men needed food. Beside the road one man bolted down the bread and cheese that Garrett had purchased in the last village with the only gold he carried on him.

The other man, Tom, he'd sent on foot ahead to look for a trail. Garrett stopped pacing when Tom loped down the road toward him, a grin splitting his weathered face. With glee he held up a piece of green fabric.

"From the hem of Lady Leandra's gown, I think," he called.

Garrett suppressed a groan and resisted the urge to slap the joy from the idiot's face. The man was pleased with the discovery! "Where did you find it?"

"On a tree limb on the right fork of the road. They're working their way west and south."

Garrett grabbed the precious cloth. He clutched it tightly in his palm, scrutinizing it as if the fibers might tell him what had happened to Leandra, what fear she knew, what pain she suffered. Pender must be pushing them hard for tree limbs to be ripping at her clothes.

"We can't be far behind them now," the soldier babbled on, apparently thrilled with the find. "With Lady Leandra's help, we haven't taken a wrong turn yet."

"What do you mean with the lady's help?" Garrett demanded. He almost grabbed the man by his woolen hood, but gripped his shoulders instead and shook him. "Only good fortune kept us from turning east at the last village. If the innkeeper's wife hadn't noticed the heavily hooded lady riding with the pilgrims and brought us the silken cord from the lady's cloak, we would have ridden in the wrong direction."

The man's grin vanished and he peered at Garrett uncertainly. "Do you think a lady in disguise riding along the highway is so strange these days? You think these things were left by chance? Oh, no. With respect, Sir Garrett, have faith in the lady. She shows us the way. We have but to follow."

Slowly, thoughtfully, Garrett released the soldier.

"Let's ride, sir."

Garrett stared after Tom, astonished. Why was he so muddled? How could he have missed the obvious? Aside from the tassel, they had been given a piece of trim from her cloak, found by a shepherd at the crossroads near the south fork. Then a hostler at the last village gave them a shred of her surcoat, confirming that she and the Penders had ridden through. Now with a tatter from her gown . . . Garrett shook his head. Of course Leandra showed them the way.

With a laugh at his own witlessness and at Pender's carelessness—a laugh that came with an immense measure of relief—Garrett threw himself onto his mount and led the way down the road. If Leandra had enough wits about her to leave them a trail, then she must be all right. Knowing that eased the aching tightness in his chest, in his heart.

At the fork in the road they rode west through the woods.

They hadn't ridden far before they came upon a gathering of peasants and a friar tending bodies scattered along the roadside—the outlaws.

"Did anyone see what happened here?" Garrett asked of the friar and the peasants who gathered about the scene. They shook their heads.

Garrett walked among them in the growing darkness: Mistress Pender, Alfred, and two others. He was inured to the carnage; his only fear was that of finding Leandra among them.

A friar bent over the last body, Pender. The outlaw lived, barely, with sword wound in his gut and a purple knot on his head from Leandra's bow. He mumbled his confession to the little friar but croaked when he saw Garrett loom over him. The outlaw grasped the arm of the friar and tried to sit up.

"Traitor!" Pender brayed.

Garrett tensed, his hand on the hilt of his sword, ready to end the misery of one who would call him names.

"Casseldorne is a traitor," Pender cried, obviously eager for Garrett to know more.

The friar moved away. Garrett knelt beside the man. "What about Casseldorne?" he asked, slipping a hand beneath the outlaw's head to support him as he spoke.

Pender's pale gray eyes were glazed with pain, but he knew what he was saying. "He wanted the lady. He promised a reward. A big reward." Pender closed his eyes, and with his last breath he mumbled, "This is what we got."

"Where's Lady Leandra?" Garrett demanded. But he was too late. The outlaw was dead. Garrett called the friar to the man to finish his business.

Pender's accusation against Leofric didn't surprise Garrett. But the circumstances didn't fit together. Was Casseldorne here in Cornwall? Was Leofric truly responsible for these deaths? Did he take Leandra with him? Where to?

"Where does this road lead?" Garrett demanded of the friar.

"Forestell," the friar said. "'Tis Sir Chygwin's keep. The

good old knight died recently, but his nephew did not know that when he arrived."

"Who is this nephew?" Garrett asked. "Do you know his name?"

"A man of wide travels and great wealth," the friar said. "Why, Leofric of Casseldorne."

Leandra was unable to stop shivering, and the desire to sleep was beginning to overwhelm her. The torchlit hall draped in black frightened her. Abruptly she turned away from the funeral bier and the ornately carved casket that sat to one side of the room. How long would it take Garrett to find the trail? she wondered. She really had no desire to stay here.

"We must get you into some dry clothes, my dear," the black-clad woman with a familiar face said. Her nose seemed about to touch Leandra's. Leandra squinted back at her, wondering who she was.

"Do you hear me? You do remember me, don't you, dear? I'm Widow Adelle Chygwin. We met on the road."

"Oh, yes." Slowly Leandra recalled the plain, practical widow who'd ridden at the head of the funeral cortege. "Of course, I remember. May I stand by the fire? I'm so chilled."

"Dry clothes first," the widow said, gently shoving Leandra in the direction of the stairs. "Then something warm to drink. My dear, your hand is absolute icy. We must warm you. This way."

Leandra put out her free hand and braced herself against the wall. The shivering seemed to have taken all the strength from her brain, but she knew she should wait near the door for Garrett. He would be along any moment, and he would expect to ride away without delay. Besides that, an annoying voice in her head was telling her that she didn't want to stay under the same roof with Leofric for any reason. "No. Please, uh, Widow Chygwin, just let me sit by the fire."

"As you wish, my dear," the widow agreed. "But I really think you should put on some dry clothes. Sit here. I'll have the fire tended to and bring wine, hot and spiced. Sit here, my dear."

Battered down by the Widow Chygwin's torrent of words, Leandra nearly collapsed into the chair.

"So, you're a neighbor of Leofric's," the widow continued. "You can imagine my surprise when I arrived home with my husband and found my nephew here waiting for us. Leofric hadn't heard about the death, you see. But it has been such a comfort to have him here. So reassuring."

When the wine arrived, Leandra clasped the cup between her hands, allowing the warmth to seep painfully into her frozen fingers. The spicy aroma tingled in her nose, and she began to awaken to her senses again, but the shivering refused to stop. If Garrett would kindly make his entrance soon, everything would be as it should be.

"There you are." Leofric's eyes lit up when he spied Leandra and Lady Adelle. Dressed in fresh purple hose and jacket, his hair neatly combed, he grinned covetously and seized Leandra's hand as soon as he reached the fireside. He bowed over her cold fingers, murmuring foolish compliments to her fair beauty, which Leandra knew couldn't possibly apply to her. As soon as was polite, she withdrew her hand from his grasp.

The leather of the chair next to her creaked as Leofric seated himself. Something about his nearness always made Leandra wary of his touch and uncomfortable with his attentions. With a stiff, polite smile, she sank deeper into the chair, grateful at least for the heat of the fire and the warmth of the wine.

She closed her eyes, soaking up the heat and yielding to the desire to sleep. Another fit of shivering shook her.

"You have been through such a trial," he said, leaning toward her. "Here I was pining away, thinking that you were safe and happy with Bernay, on your way to Lord Reginald, but you were in the hands of those outlaws. Being abused by them. I'm only sorry that I was unable to come to your rescue sooner."

"I was not abused. Only taken away against my will," Leandra snapped. His possessive tone and his attitude that she'd somehow been compromised by the outlaws annoyed her. She sat up a little straighter in her chair. "Those outlaws were taking me somewhere for some purpose. Did your men learn anything from them? Have your men found Sir Garrett?"

"Ah, no." Leofric glanced uneasily at the door of the great hall, as if someone might burst in at any moment. "As soon as we know what has happened to Sir Garrett, we will send a messenger to Tremelyn and let the earl know of all that has happened to you and of your safe rescue. I know he will be most grateful. But let us trouble ourselves over this no more."

Leofric snapped his fingers at the steward. "Bring more wine for the lady. Where is that minstrel? Come sing us a song. Something soft and soothing for the lady." He leaned closer to Leandra. She could feel his warm breath on her cheek, and it took all her self-control to resist leaning away from him.

"We will take care of you, my lady," Leofric assured her. "You are safe here."

She began to wish that she'd ridden back down the road toward Garrett when she'd gained control of her runaway horse.

The minstrel sang on. Outside the castle the wind rose and rain beat down, clinking against the glass windows. Leandra sipped the warm, spiced wine and listened to the songs with half an ear. Exhaustion stole over her. She leaned her head on her hand and fought back the sleep that threatened to overcome her. Such an insult to her host. The influence of the wine, she thought. She shivered again and pulled herself up in the chair.

"You wear Lord Reginald's betrothal ring," Leofric said. He stroked Leandra's hand, a finger lingering on the gold circle she wore. "'Tis large for your finger. See how easily it slips off."

Leandra's awareness sharpened. Her hands were so cold that the ribbon wound inside the ring did little to prevent Leofric from taking it from her. She struggled to sit straight in her chair. "My ring. Give it back, please."

"Don't set your chin like that," he murmured. "You forget how long I've known you, sweet Leandra, since you were but a child. I know what that set of your chin means. Such stubbornness. I only ask you once more to reconsider this betrothal."

"No," Leandra said. "Please, my ring."

"Obstinacy is an ugly attribute in a woman," Leofric admonished. He took the wine cup from Leandra. "Consider my request. What has Lord Reginald done for you? Sent a knight known to come from a traitorous family? Garrett couldn't even protect you from renegade pilgrims."

She tipped her head back to squint at Leofric. "The pilgrims were my fault." The room swayed a bit. Leandra was uncertain whether she was ill or had merely imbibed too much wine. She took a deep breath to clear her head, but weakness nearly overwhelmed her. Her head became unbelievably heavy. Sleep beckoned, seduced her. She tried to rise from the chair, thinking she would gladly lie down on the floor to sleep. Maybe then the shivering would stop. But her feet were lead. She sank back heavily, terrified that she was going to lose all her senses to the encroaching darkness.

"Well, the earl's knight certainly has failed in protecting you," Lady Adelle said. "You should be grateful for Leofric's brave rescue."

"Oh, indeed I am," Leandra muttered.

"There is no time to lose," Leofric said. She could hear him talking over her head to his aunt. "I will have an answer from her tonight, before Bernay comes."

Then he peered at Leandra, leaning closer until his dark features filled the whole of her view like a face in a rounded mirror. She closed her eyes against the dark, unpleasant sight and turned away.

"Aunt Adelle, bring your chaplain here to witness her change of heart," Leofric demanded.

"Witness? Chaplain?" Leandra repeated, trying to make sense of what was being said around her. "No, I don't need a chaplain."

"Oh, yes, dear," Lady Adelle piped cheerfully. "A chaplain would do no harm."

"What is the matter with you?" Leofric demanded when Lady Adelle disappeared from the room. He bent over

Leandra and grabbed her under the arms, trying to drag her from the chair. "Don't go to sleep on me. God's wounds, your wet clothes will ruin my new suit."

Leandra struggled against him. But his strength seemed too much for her. So she let herself become dead weight. Surprised, Leofric almost dropped her. He cursed her defiance.

"I won't do it. Whatever you want, I won't do it. Never, never, never," she chanted. She liked the sound of the word and repeated it again. It seemed to relieve the heaviness of her head. "Never, never, never," she sang. If she kept saying that, she thought, surely she'd be safe.

"The words are 'I will,' my lady." Leofric swung her up into his arms and spoke into her ear. "Say, 'I deny my betrothal to Lord Reginald. I will become betrothed to Sir Leofric,' then I'll let you sleep."

"No," Leandra said. "Never, never, never. I can't say 'I will' to anyone. Not you. Not Reginald. I can love only Sir Garrett."

"What's this?" Leofric asked peering into her face. "Stop shivering and explain."

"I love only Sir Garrett. And he loves me. Faithfully. Above all things. Whatever your plan, Leofric, it will never work. Never, never, never. It's because of the love potion, you know."

Leofric started across the room, Leandra still in his arms. She was remotely aware of a chaplain, and of Leofric and Lady Adelle staring at each other.

"Why didn't I think of that?" Leofric hissed at Adelle. "A love potion. She would have fallen in love with me, and Reginald would never have had a chance."

"You want to wed the girl?" Adelle asked. "Lord Reginald's bethrothed? But she's such a dear thing. Called your uncle a handsome man when she viewed him."

The door banged open. A gust of wind swept about the room and dragged at Leandra's skirts. Torches flickered and flared. Rain showered into the hall. Unholy shouting rang painfully in her ears. She covered them with her hands and twisted around to find the source of all the noise.

Too late, the guard at the door tried to take a defensive position, but he was forced to retreat with one swipe of the intruder's huge blade. The minstrel and the steward cowered in a corner. Frozen in place, Lady Adelle, the chaplain, and Leofric stared at Garrett Bernay.

He towered just inside the door, his sword in one hand and the nape of Leofric's captain of the guard clutched in the other. Tom lingered in Garrett's shadow, no squire. Leandra swallowed hard to ward off the tears of relief that threatened. The knight's dark golden locks were plastered shiny wet to his head. The tunic that clung to his chain mail was mud-spattered, and water dripped from his chin. At the moment Sir Perfect was hardly the vision of knighthood in full bloom. The wrath of a warrior god burned in his dark eyes.

No one dared move except Leandra.

She couldn't take her gaze from Garrett's face. He was the one person in the room who seemed real to her. She squirmed her way out of Leofric's arms. "Mercy, I'm glad to see you."

Chapter 12

When Leandra's feet hit the floor, she found the stones untrustworthy. She staggered slightly, stretching out both arms to find her balance. Finally the faces and the furniture steadied.

"I've been waiting for you, Sir Knight." She planted her hands on her hips and listed a little to the right, shivering the entire time. "I told him 'never.' But he wouldn't listen. So I told him about the potion that binds us. I'm afraid I couldn't do any more."

Garrett stared at Leandra, annoyance and relief washing over him, hot and cold all at once. The sight of her wrenched his gut. Sweet Jesu, her eyes were too round and lustrous, her lips almost blue, and her face whiter than pale.

"What have you done to her?" Garrett demanded. He wanted to snatch her up and whisk her away, out of Leofric's reach, beyond the prying eyes of all the people in the hall. He wanted to hide her somewhere, to wrap her up in safety and warmth, to make her well.

"She drank too much wine, that's all," Leofric said, shrugging his shoulders, meanwhile regaining his composure enough to step forward. "What is this, Bernay? Release my man. You have no need to charge into my aunt's keep, armed and hostile."

"Your man? This man tried to ambush me," Garrett said. He shoved the trembling captain of the guard sprawling to the floor.

"I'm sure 'twas a mistake," Leofric said. "Put away your sword, Bernay, and I'll send the guard out. We're all honorable knights of King Edward here."

"Indeed," Lady Adelle agreed. "This is a house of peace."

"Then dismiss them," Garrett said. He pointed to the guard and the captain and waited.

Leofric gave the men a curt nod of dismissal.

Each of the two soldiers scurried out into the rain. Garrett didn't regard the chaplain and the lady as threats, but he noted that Casseldorne remained armed.

Leandra tottered across the hall toward Garrett.

Leofric's eyes narrowed. Anger drew hard lines in his handsome face. He reached out to retrieve her, but the lady lurched, staggering a few steps just beyond his reach. Garrett stepped forward to draw Leandra to his side.

Leofric folded his arms across his chest. "Just where have you been, Bernay? The lady was in need of your help. Outlaws carried her off. Who knows what would have happened if she hadn't had the good fortune to ride into us in the forest."

"Good fortune, hah," Garrett scoffed. "You planned this from the beginning, didn't you, Leofric? Rescue her from her captors and wed the grateful lady."

"'Twas mere chance," Leofric protested with a patronizing smile.

"Pender wasn't quite dead when we found him," Garrett said. "He told me about the reward you offered to any who would bring the lady to you unharmed."

"Is that true?" Leandra asked, swaying unsteadily against Garrett. Her eyes grew rounder and darker in horror. "Pender was your man? You killed your own man?"

Leofric shrugged and looked around at the company, Lady Adelle and the chaplain, as though he didn't relish them hearing these details. "I killed the red-haired pirate, too. Sometimes a man has to deal with people he would never ordinarily speak to. What did Pender tell you?"

Satisfied that there was no immediate danger, Garrett sheathed his sword. "He told me about you and your father's disappointment in the king's refusal to help you further your fortune, and about your plot to take over Tremelyn," Garrett said, guessing at some truths and weaving in the certain facts. All the while he talked he worried about Leandra's blue lips and trembling limbs.

"You know more than I thought." Leofric smiled ruefully. "You should be thanking me. If it weren't for my paid assassins, you wouldn't have gone to Reginald's rescue. If you hadn't rescued him, you wouldn't be a knight today. You'd still be toiling away as a humble captain of the guard."

"I would have defended Lord Reginald whether the threat was yours or another's," Garrett said. "That was my pledge. Your assassins made no difference."

Innocent men had died because of Casseldorne's greed, and some not so innocent, but men had been betrayed. Anger boiled up inside of Garrett, though he knew that emotion had no place in dealing with a man as ruthless as the purple knight.

At his side, Leandra turned to him as if she sensed some change. He ignored her look of inquiry.

"But Lord Reginald lives," Garrett said. "And you have yet to win Lady Leandra—"

"Who is bound to you, I understand." Leofric grinned maliciously and wagged a finger at Garrett. "She told us about the love potion. Were you that desperate, old man?"

"The potion was none of our doing," Garrett said as calmly as he could. He frowned at Leandra, but she appeared too confused and cold to understand their words.

"But I can see you're besotted with her, and for me to have her, I'll have to fight you, won't I?" Leofric clasped his hands thoughtfully behind him and turned to the fire. "Sit down, Bernay. We're both men of the world. Surely we can do business."

"I'll listen," Garrett said, ever mindful of the guards just outside the door, ready at Casseldorne's beckoning. He drew Leandra with him to a pair of chairs by the fire. Tom remained near the door.

With a great show of being a thoughtful host, Leofric ordered dry towels for Garrett and hot wine. Garrett accepted the towels and refused the wine.

When Garrett was finished drying himself, Leofric turned

in his chair and began. "I know what you want. You and I are alike in a way. We have ambition. You've won back the Bernay knighthood. Next you want the family holding that was forfeited. Am I right? What was the place called—"

"Chycliff," Garrett supplied. He glanced around to see that Leandra was sinking into a sound sleep in the chair at his side, yet she continued to shiver even in her sleep.

"Yes, Chycliff." Leofric leaned forward in his chair, speaking directly to Garrett. Firelight lit one side of his face and cast the other in shadow. His words fell from his lips rapidly, soft and hissing like the serpent in the Garden of Eden. "I can petition the king for the return of Chycliff as easily as Reginald can. I can even see to it that you have the lady, if you want her. I'd planned to take her for myself. But it really doesn't matter who weds her, just as long as she bears no heirs to Tremelyn. Pledge your fealty to me, Bernay, and the lady and Chycliff are yours."

Slowly Garrett turned to gaze upon the dozing Leandra. Her head nodded to one side and her sable lashes fluttered against her pale cheeks.

"Yes, look at her," Leofric whispered. "Fair and lovely Lady Leandra. When her lips aren't blue. Think of her at your side."

Unbidden pictures flashed in Garrett's head. Leandra seated beside him in the great hall of Chycliff, where his father and mother once reigned. The sunlit orchard a-riot with blond, green-eyed children, their laughter tripping along on the breeze. The glimpse brought such astonishing sweetness to his mind that he could almost taste it.

"Think of her in your bed, Bernay. She must be a virgin. Ripe for the taking," Leofric tempted softly. "So ready to learn whatever a man wants to teach her. I imagine you'd enjoy the instruction. Or have you taken care of that already?"

"Some knights are more honorable than others," Garrett said, although he didn't feel honorable at the moment. He'd already imagined Leandra in his bed. The thought came upon him soon after their first meeting. Such an idea was not to be contemplated. She was Reginald's betrothed.

He glared at Leofric indignantly, but the image of his hands on her naked skin persisted, slipping into his dreams at night and invading his mind during mundane exchanges with the lady. He saw her—long-limbed, smooth, and soft. In this fantasy she was pink and white with golden curls wreathing her face and fair downy ringlets adorning her femininity. In his mind's eye she sighed and moved incitingly beneath his hands. *His hands.* No one else's. Not Leofric's. God forgive him, not Reginald's.

Leofric edged forward in his chair. With a start Garrett realized he'd betrayed his thoughts.

"You want her. Fall in with me, Bernay." Leofric eyed Garrett intently, obviously thinking he had him hooked. "I can give you all that you want."

Garrett shook his head.

"Why do you hesitate, man?" Leofric waved away imaginary objections. "Of course the treachery will cause a stir now. But the king is in France, unable to take any action. You of all men know how these infamies go. In a few years no one will remember or care what happened here this night."

The insult was all Garrett needed. He lunged forward and grabbed Leofric by the throat, dragging the man to his feet. "They remember traitors, Casseldorne. I know. Everyone remembers. I'm no traitor. Nor is the lady. Each of us has made pledges, spoken vows before the holy altar, and we will not betray those. Not for you. Not for anyone."

"You hypocrite!" Leofric shouted, fury curling his lip and lighting his eyes. With a mighty thrust he brought his arms up between Garrett's and broke the hold.

"Gentlemen. Gentlemen." Lady Adelle stepped between the men. "We don't need to grapple like peasants."

Both men ignored the lady.

"Hypocrite!" Leofric pointed an accusing finger at Garrett. "You owe me, you pretentious Jack fool. Your family name isn't fit for Casseldornes to wipe their feet on. Never was. Bernays are nothing more than Norman upstarts. Your grand ancestor looted his way to knighthood along with the rest of William the Conqueror's army.

140

"You owe me, Bernay. *You* have benefited from my efforts. All you have to do is take the maid. You want her. It's written all over your face."

A muscle in Garrett's jaw flexed. He held his silence, clenched his teeth, and worked furiously to regain control. He thanked the heavens that Leandra was asleep and had not heard the insults. He wanted to flatten Leofric's aristocratic nose into his face.

Taking a deep breath, Garrett clamped his fists against his sides, determined to see this through his way. Mentally he shook off the bittersweet images of Leandra and Chycliff.

When he spoke, he used a quiet voice. "I owe you nothing, Casseldorne. As I see it, the scales are balanced at last. I have built my life honoring my vows. I will never exchange that for land or riches. Here and now, I challenge you to combat for the insult, sir. The insult to my family, to the lady, to Lord Reginald."

Leofric stared at him uncomprehendingly.

"You must fight me now, *brave knight.*" Garrett twisted the last two words with sarcasm. "You can no longer throw an insult at me and hide behind your knighthood as you did once. I am your equal, Sir Leofric of Casseldorne. Remember, you have made me so. We will fight knight against knight."

Leofric's mouth went slack.

"What wonderful irony," Lady Adelle observed. She turned to Leofric. "Your uncle would say 'tis a fair challenge, nephew."

"Whose side are you on, Aunt Adelle?" Leofric snapped. "What do you know of challenges?"

"Well, I never understood whatever it was that you planned for the Lady Leandra." Lady Adelle cast Leofric a solemn look of disapproval. "But a knight's challenge to a knight is a matter between chivalrous men. A matter of honor. Do you refuse it?"

Leofric paused, obviously considering that possibility.

"You would shame the family name, my husband's honor, by refusing a challenge in his presence?" Lady Adelle asked, gesturing to her husband's casket.

Leofric sighed warily. "So be it. I choose swords."

"Swords," Garrett confirmed, unsurprised by Leofric's choice. Casseldorne was well-known for cheating while jousting, but was known just as well for his showy, expert swordplay. Garrett had never considered his own skills better than they needed to be.

"Lady Adelle will act as referee," Garrett suggested, for want of a better candidate. She was as trustworthy as her nephew.

"Me?" the good widow sputtered. A pleased smile played on her lips. "Of course. I will be honored."

The two knights retreated to opposite sides of the hall. The minstrel and the steward hastily cleared the chairs. Garrett motioned to Tom to wake Leandra. The soldier obeyed.

Leofric stripped off his fashionable jacket and walked to the center of the hall. Garrett peeled off his wet surcoat and chain mail, down to his leather jerkin.

He disregarded his aching muscles and his exhaustion from long hours in the saddle. Finally he faced the man who'd ridiculed the Bernay name more than once. With each insult, petty pleasure had glowed in Leofric's yellow eyes as if Garrett's shame added to the Casseldorne prestige.

Leofric struck first. The initial parries took them from one end of the hall to the other, then around the funeral bier. Garrett suspected that Leofric was taking his measure. He followed Leofric's eyes. He knew the man searched for a weakness, an unguarded side, a delayed reaction. Garrett used the exchange to do likewise.

"What are they doing?" Leandra cried to Tom, grasping his wet sleeve, blinking sleep from her eyes. "Garrett does little more than defend himself."

"He knows what he's doing, my lady." The soldier patted her shoulder. "Don't watch them if it troubles you."

Leandra couldn't take her eyes from them.

The purple knight backed off and they circled again, still on guard. By the gleam in Leofric's light eyes, Garrett surmised the man was eager for victory. Too eager, Garrett hoped.

Once again Leofric swung in on the attack. Garrett began to suspect that the man had spotted his exhaustion. In a flurry of strikes, Leofric drove Garrett toward the stairs.

The steward scrambled out of their way. Garrett ducked. Leofric struck a riser. Garrett swung in from the side. Swords clanged as Leofric parried the strike.

The clamor sliced into Leandra's head. She winced. As her head cleared, she began to follow Garrett's every movement. The clearer her head became, the greater her anxiety grew.

Yet she found herself grimly fascinated by the duel, the first she'd seen. Reluctant admiration held her as she watched the two men parry, attack, repel, and lunge. Both men were fair to the eye, well-made—broad shoulders, narrow hips, and slender limbs. Their movements took on a grace, a style, and a rhythm. The pace grew and fell much like a dance, a deadly dance.

The pair fought their way across the room, Garrett always giving ground. Leofric, apparently eager for a quick end, was beginning to get careless. Near the fireplace his wild swing struck one of the rusty firedogs. The steel sword sang. Leandra covered her ears.

Garrett smiled. Renewed rage snarled on Leofric's lips. Cursing his own poor performance, the purple knight backed away. Garrett held his ground.

Leofric circled again and lunged in, bringing his sword down across Garrett's shoulder, but Garrett spun away just in time, his jerkin slashed, but no blood drawn. Leofric waved the shred of leather in the air victoriously.

Leandra pressed her cold, trembling fingers to her mouth to catch her gasp. She wanted to turn away, but didn't dare. If anything happened to Garrett, she must know. She prayed that God would grant him the strength to overcome his exhaustion.

Undaunted by the close strike, Garrett turned to advance, sending Leofric into a rapid retreat toward the funeral bier. He parried Garrett's attack and returned his own. The thrust missed Garrett and struck the casket.

Lady Adelle cried out and marched between the swordsmen. "Watch your blades, Sir Knights. I rented that casket from a London casket maker and must return it to him when my husband's own is ready. Have care."

Garrett acknowledged the request with a quick bow.

Leofric attacked from behind the casket with a flurry of thrusts. With a burst of strength Garrett knocked the last one aside and brought his sword up to Leofric's throat. Only the men's rasping could be heard. Leandra held her breath, her eyes on the life throbbing in Leofric's neck. Deliberately, Garrett nicked the vulnerable flesh. Blood trickled from the cut.

Lady Adelle gasped.

"First blood. Do you yield?" Garrett demanded.

"No! Never," Leofric growled. "Kill me."

"That was a bit unfair of you, Sir Garrett," Lady Adelle said. "You set upon Leofric when he was taking care for the casket. No yield? We go another round. Back off now."

"No! Garrett won," Leandra cried indignantly. She strode into the center of the room. "You saw it, Widow Chygwin. First blood. The fight is over. Sir Garrett is the victor."

"Stay out of this, Leandra," Garrett warned, without taking his eyes from Leofric's face. "Tom, restrain her if you have to. We fight until Sir Leofric of Casseldorne is satisfied."

Leandra opened her mouth to protest, but Garrett fastened his dark blue eyes on her. Weariness lined the corners of his mouth, but the strength of pride filled his gaze, striking her breathless. She thought she almost heard his voice in the power of that look. *This is my fight, Leandra. Leave it to me.* When Tom took her arm, Leandra reluctantly allowed him to lead her from the floor.

The two swordsmen circled again. Leofric's shirt was soaked with sweat and streaked with blood. The mood of the action changed, slowed, became more watchful, more deadly. The men's stances became more guarded, alert. Leofric's glance grew wary, sly, and he appeared less eager to engage Garrett now.

When Leofric attacked, the clang of the swords made Leandra start. They parried and feinted, lunging across the floor and back. Breaking free, they circled once more. The action was coming faster. Exhaustion was telling in Garrett's stance. For a moment he lowered his sword and Leofric struck out, slashing the back of Garrett's sword hand.

Leandra clamped her hands to her mouth to silence her scream. When she started toward Garrett, Tom yanked her back.

"'Tis but a scratch." Garrett held up his sword hand to show his opponent.

To Leandra's relief, it appeared to be no more than that, but she worried about Garrett's grip on his sword.

"Let's finish this, Casseldorne."

"To the finish," Leofric challenged. With that, he began an attack that took them around the hall once more, even around the casket. The blades flashed in the torchlight. Boots thudded against the stone floor and steel rang against steel.

The minstrel had to duck out the door into the chapel. Lady Adelle scuttled aside as the knights lunged across the room. Leandra and Tom flattened themselves against the door when the swordsmen neared them.

The pace was beginning to tell on each man. Blood trickled from Garrett's hand. Perspiration dripped from Leofric's chin.

Leofric sprang up the stairway and turned to fight, using the height against Garrett, bringing his blade down from above. Suddenly he dropped to one knee and thrust his sword at Garrett's midsection. The blade slashed across Garrett's tunic. Garrett leapt clear and brought his sword down on Leofric's. The blade clattered to the floor. Garrett stepped on it and placed his blade tip to Leofric's throat.

"To the death, Sir Leofric? Is that what you truly want?"

With a sob of relief Leandra turned away, rested her forehead against the door and let the tears roll down her cheeks. Garrett was safe. He was the victor.

Her knees shook so that she feared she was going to slide into a heap on the floor. She'd rather fight the fight herself than have to watch anything like this again.

"Death isn't necessary." Lady Adelle rushed to them. "'Twas a fair fight. I witnessed it. But not to the death. Not under my roof. Come away, Sir Garrett. Put aside your sword."

Garrett lowered his weapon and stepped away.

"I will not yield to a man who doesn't deserve to be a knight," Leofric gasped, clutching his middle as if his belly ached. "I will not."

To Leandra's disbelief, Garrett threw back his head and began to laugh. "And they said that *I* lacked humility."

Lightning quick, Leofric reached down and yanked with all his might on the rush matting on which Garrett stood. Leandra tried to cry a warning. Garrett instantly brought up his sword, slicing open Leofric's arm nearly to the shoulder.

The purple knight yelped and spun away, grasping the arm against his chest.

"That's the finish," Lady Adelle said with a final authority that brooked no dispute. She put herself between the men.

"We get safe escort to the next village." Garrett held his sword ready, uncertain of the lady's intentions. "Tonight."

"You shall have it," Lady Adelle said, "provided nothing of this is said to others. To Lord Reginald. Or to the sheriff. I will not have my sister's son disgraced. You have a secret of your own to keep. Remember, we know of the potion."

Chapter 13

"I'll have a fire for you right away, my lady." The shy serving girl knelt at the hearth in the bedchamber and with a trembling hand fed tinder to the hot coals.

Leandra leaned against the fireplace for support and sleepily wondered where Garrett had gone. He'd brought her upstairs then disappeared again.

"Are you a princess?" the girl asked in her broad Cornish accent. She fixed her gaze on Leandra's gold chaplet and touched her own forehead.

"No, only a lady," Leandra said through shivering lips. The question made her smile. "What is your name?"

"Isabelle," the girl murmured, still staring.

The tinder flamed to life. Leandra eagerly stretched her shaking hands out to the heat. A low groan escaped her lips as aching warmth spread through her fingers and up her arms. She clamped her mouth closed to still the chattering of her teeth. Hastily, Isabelle laid more wood on the fire.

With numb fingers Leandra reached into her purse to find her last pence, the only one she hadn't spent at the Penzance market. She handed the coin to the girl. "Here, Isabelle, for you. Save it for the May Day fair."

"Thank you, my lady. I will."

The desire to close her eyes and savor the heat was nearly overpowering, but sword blades flashed in Leandra's mind every time she tried. She could hear the fabric rip, see the slash across Garrett's hand. She opened her eyes and took a deep breath. Garrett could have been killed in that fight. Those disapproving, but ever-so-blue eyes had almost been lost to her.

At her feet the nervous serving girl tended the fire. Then she bobbed a curtsy and stared up at Leandra, awe and admiration shining on her pale face.

Garrett ducked through the low doorway, his force spilling into the room, stirring up eddies of urgency and impatience.

"Off with those wet clothes," he ordered. Then he swung back to the doorway to call down the stairs. "Mistress Innkeep, bring up bricks to warm the bed. Plenty of them and more clean blankets." Then he turned back into the room. "You, girl, help the lady to undress."

In open-mouthed terror the girl backed away from the towering knight. She nodded but made no move to help Leandra.

"Off with this," Garrett repeated. With an insistence Leandra didn't understand, he took her roughly by the shoulders so that she faced him, then he began to untie her cloak.

"I've seen men die of such a chill," he muttered as he worked at the silken cords of her cloak.

Unable to resist, Leandra touched his jaw. How close he had come to death for her. "This cut? I saw Leofric strike your hand, but this—"

"'Tis nothing. Pender's work. That outlaw won't trouble us again."

"And Leofric? Is it over?" she asked, her mind still filled with the image of the purple knight and his sword. "Or do you think he will send someone after us?"

"He doesn't dare," Garrett said with a crisp certainty Leandra found reassuring; but she didn't totally believe him.

"What makes you so sure?" she asked.

"The House of Casseldorne would prefer not to have Leofric's nasty little plot revealed, I'm sure," Garrett said. "'Twould be especially embarrassing should the king hear of it."

Rain had poured down on them from the moment they rode away from Forestell. Tom led the way. Garrett and

Leandra followed, both on his horse. She was glad because she was afraid the shivering had rendered her too weak to sit her own horse. The other soldier rode behind them. More than once she caught Garrett looking over his shoulder at the road behind them. He seemed not so certain after all that Leofric would not send pursuit.

As they rode, Leandra's clothes became soaked through once more. Now she had been cold for so long that the chill was part of her. She was almost unaware of her constant shivering.

"So, we're safe?" she asked through chattering teeth. She wanted to believe him. The tightness in her chest eased a little, but not enough to stop her shaking.

"No, you're not if we don't warm you up soon." Garrett let the wet cloak drop to the floor, turned her around and began to work on the laces of her gown. "Your teeth are chattering so loudly I have to raise my voice to make myself heard by you."

Leandra's chill-muddled mind snapped awake the moment Garrett's warm fingers grazed the base of her neck. Immediately his hands dropped to his side, and she knew he'd heard her gasp. He moved away. "Girl? Help the lady. 'Tis your job."

With a wary eye on Garrett, the whey-faced girl crept around the far side of Leandra. She took up the task of unlacing the gown only when she saw Garrett seat himself on the bed. He unbuckled his sword belt and leaned it against the tall bedpost.

"You intend to stay here, sir?" Leandra asked, suddenly aware that she was stripping down to nothing with a man in the same room.

"Yes, I intend to stay," he said matter-of-factly. "This is the only private chamber in the inn. No offense intended, my lady, but so far, for you, I have raised the white flag of surrender, spent more time on the sea than I ever intended, and dueled around a funeral bier. I do not intend to add to this adventure the discomfort of sleeping in the public room with a lot of mumbling peddlers, snoring friars, and drunken sailors."

"I would not think of asking you to suffer discomfort, Sir Knight." Leandra pressed her wet gown to her breasts. What he said made sense. She did owe him her rescue.

Quietly she turned to the girl and asked her to bring a blanket from the bed and to hold it up as a screen so that she could continue to undress. Garrett seemed satisfied with that solution. As she peeled the wet gown from her arms, she could hear him pulling off his boots and unlacing his wet leather jerkin. He was as soaked as she and surely as exhausted. Each time she spied the bed, her longing to forget everything else and climb in grew stronger. She could barely hold her head up.

"Put the blanket over my shoulders," she told Isabelle once her wet gown was off. With her back turned to Garrett, Leandra used the light of the fire to work as quickly as she could to untie the laces on her shift, but the soaked fabric defied her numb and trembling fingers. She tugged at it with her soft, wet fingernails, succeeding only in pulling the tiny knot impossibly tight. The girl tried to help, but the tangle defied her, too.

Longing now more than ever for the comfort the bed promised, Leandra muttered in frustration.

"What is it?" Garrett asked. She heard his weight shift impatiently on the bed. "You've got to get out of those clothes."

"Ah, well, we can't loosen this," she admitted, talking over her shoulder to him.

His feet hit the floor and he strode across the room to them, his frown dark and determined. In his hand, the blade of his meat knife flashed. The horrified serving girl threw herself between Leandra and Garrett, her arms stretched out wide to hold the blanket and keep him away from the lady.

"What the d—" Bewildered, Garrett stared at the child for a moment before Leandra was able to catch his eye.

She sent him a small smile that begged patience. "'Tis all

right, Isabelle, he only means to cut the lace." She held out her shaky hand to take the knife from Garrett.

While she cut at the lace, she could feel his eyes on her, much as they had been that day by the spring when her ankles were bare. He stared with such intensity and fascination that day as she lay in the tree, Leandra could have sworn he didn't know that women had feet.

This time he wasn't looking at her ankles. His gaze caressed her hips, traveled up to her waist, then lingered a little on her breasts. She realized with embarrassment that her puckered nipples were plainly visible through the wet linen.

When the lace was cut, she returned the knife to him and peeked up into his face. The anxiety etched in the lines around his mouth startled her.

"Sweet Jesu, Leandra, you are turning blue all over," he gasped. He touched her bare arms. "You're so cold. Girl, go ask your mistress where those bricks are. Bring them this instant."

The frightened girl circled Garrett and dashed from the room.

Wasting no more time, Garrett hooked his thumbs in the shoulder straps of the shift and peeled the wet garment from Leandra's body. His warm, strong hands brushed along her hips, her thighs, and the back of her knees. When he dropped to his knees so that she could step out of the garment, his breath tickled her belly. A great shiver shook her. With a trembling hand on his shoulder to steady herself, she stepped free of the shift. In a swift movement Garrett grabbed the blanket that had fallen to the floor and wrapped it about her.

Then he pulled her into his arms and began to vigorously rub her back, much as she'd seen him rub down a horse. The scratch of the wool against Leandra's skin brought warmth back into her body. She clutched the blanket around her and leaned into him, her arms pressed against his chest. She closed her eyes and let her head rest on his shoulder. She was warm and secure at last.

He stopped rubbing.

"Being close is nice," Leandra said. She peered up into his face, glad to see that his anxiety was fading into a gentler expression of concern. "Do you think this is the love potion at work?"

"I don't care what this is," Garrett whispered, his arms squeezing her even closer. "I just need to know that you're safe and well."

Without warning he swept her up into his arms and carried her to the high-backed fireside settle, where he sat down and dropped her into his lap. Gratefully she sank against his hard body and let him tuck the blanket around her toes.

"I didn't think a love potion would work like this," Leandra said, too sleepy to understand the import of what she was saying. "Don't you feel it? This attraction to touch and be touched. 'Tis the potion."

"I feel it," Garrett said, his voice hoarse, his lips temptingly close to her face. He removed her chaplet and laid it aside. Then he pulled at her braid, untwisting her wet hair, combing his fingers through the damp strands, spreading the tresses across her back so the heat from the fire could dry them. Leandra closed her eyes, taking pleasure in his sure, steady touch, absorbing his warmth. She sighed.

Gently catching the back of her head, he planted a kiss on her lips.

The kiss surprised her, but she didn't resist. She obeyed her instincts to melt against him, lifting her chin to make her mouth more accessible. She let his lips press against hers as long as he wanted. This was too pleasant to stop. The firm, sensuous movement of his lips moving over hers pitched a funny little drop in her belly and curled her cold toes.

Then, unexpectedly, his tongue darted over her lips. The intimacy shocked her out of her shivering lethargy and frightened her a little. He wanted more of her, and she was uncertain how to respond.

"Lovers share everything, lioness," Garrett whispered, his nose brushing against hers. "In a kiss, even their tongues."

"Truly?" Leandra shivered again. Vaguely she recalled

Brenna and Amice discussing the intimacy of kissing once, but she hadn't listened. It sounded too revolting—sharing one's tongue. As she gazed at Garrett, the idea took on a different appeal.

He must have recognized her interest because he leaned toward her again. "Like this," he said.

She closed her eyes and waited. Her breath came in short little gasps, and all her senses tingled through her lips as if that was the only part of her that existed. Lightly, with slow deliberation, Garrett drew his strong, wet tongue along the length of her lower lip, leaving a path of pleasure in its wake. He kissed her cheek when he reached the corner of her mouth. "See? That's how it's done. At first."

She blinked at him and her gaze fell immediately on his finely formed lips, still glistening from the kiss. She was suddenly hungrier for the taste of those lips than she was for any other kind of nourishment.

"You mean like this?" Freeing one hand from the blanket, she slipped it around his neck and lifted her lips to his again. He tensed. Why? she wondered, but she didn't let his reaction keep her from drawing her tongue along his lower lip with tantalizing slowness, just as he had done to her. He remained tense and frozen.

When she was halfway along his lip, Garrett groaned. His grip on her grew almost painful. His body became restless beneath hers. Just as she reached the corner of his mouth, he pulled away—only to return to her, slanting his mouth over hers.

He demanded admittance this time. Startled and thrilled, Leandra parted her lips and opened to him. The intimate sensations of this contact were strange and new, but oh so wholly right and complete. She needed no further instruction in the art of kissing. She accepted his teasing exploration and returned to his lips with her own. Passion, new and untried, rekindled Leandra's body heat, warming her right down through frozen toes—curled in pleasure against the back of the settle.

Garrett let Leandra pull away from the kiss first. To his relief, color was returning to her lips, and she no longer shivered constantly in his arms. Her eyes fluttered closed. She settled deeper in his embrace and laid her head against his shoulder.

He drew in a deep breath and released it slowly. Her expertise in kissing had certainly improved since their first exchange during blindman's bluff in Lyonesse. Enough to painfully remind him of how much he wanted her. Though he'd scoffed at the idea of the love potion, he knew no amount of denial and protest would change his body's and his heart's desire. He wanted the impossible. Leofric had made him face that fact. He wanted Leandra for himself. But he had resisted—except for the kiss.

Someone tapped on the door. "Here are the blankets and the warmed bricks you wanted, Sir Garr—" Tom stood at the door.

Over Leandra's head Garrett put his finger to his lips.

"Oh, she's asleep already?" Tom said, stepping farther into the room. He closed the door behind him. He shifted awkwardly from one foot to the other. "Mistress Innkeep assumes that you are a knight with his lady."

When Garrett didn't answer immediately, Tom thumped a fist to his chest. "Sir Garrett, you're still my captain. I promised to follow you when you first came to Tremelyn to lead the guard. I'll follow you now. You can count on me and Ned, too. Your concerns are safe with us."

The pledge brought a small smile to Garrett's lips.

He hesitated, warring with himself. He looked down into Leandra's face. Although her breathing was even and her shivering had subsided, her coloring still troubled him. He'd seen this kind of chill weaken soldiers, even kill them. He doubted that she'd be ready to travel again for several days—for the first time in his life, he seriously contemplated the benefits of dishonesty.

If he admitted to being a knight of Tremelyn, their credit would be good and the whole sleepy fishing village would stir to do their bidding. On the other hand, the earl's name and the unusual circumstances would send rumors flying, even from so isolated a hamlet. Something neither Reginald nor Leandra needed.

154

"Let Mistress Innkeep think what she likes," he said to Tom, without taking his gaze from Leandra's pale face. "Get some rest. Tomorrow I'll have a message for you to take to Wystan. He should be camped along the Tamar River with Lady Brenna, waiting to hear from us."

"As you wish," Tom said. He slipped the bricks into the bed and departed hastily, closing the door behind him.

Garrett carried Leandra to the bed and tucked her in, careful not to disturb her sleep as he placed the heated, linen-covered bricks around her. That done, he stripped off his own wet clothes, wrapped himself in another blanket, and lay down beside her atop the covers.

He chuckled to himself, the image of a defeated Leofric still fresh in his mind. He grinned into the darkness, more pleased with himself than he'd been since his knighting.

Leofric had flaunted temptation in his face—offered him money, Chycliff, and the woman he wanted—and he'd defeated the man. He'd defeated temptation.

Next to Garrett, Leandra stirred in her sleep and sighed, her warm, sweet breath caressing his cheek.

Chapter 14

Leandra drowsed in the sunny warmth pouring through the opened window.

"Lady? Lady? Are you awake?" a little voice whispered, tickling Leandra's ear. "You must awake. Tomorrow 'tis May Day."

Leandra lifted one wary eyelid to spy Isabelle leaning over her. The girl brightened. "I have fresh bread for you."

When Leandra stirred, her muscles ached and her joints protested. Vaguely she was aware that Garrett no longer lay beside her.

"How long have I slept?" Leandra asked, her voice little more than a hoarse whisper.

"Two days and two nights." Isabelle set a tray of bread, milk, and honey on the edge of the bed. "Your knight sent me with food so you can break your fast. He's been very concerned. Here, eat. You need to build your strength."

Leandra obeyed, at first because Isabelle had shoved a bread crust into her hand. But after a sip of milk and another bite of the bread, she discovered she was starved. She ate like a beggar. Isabelle busied herself tidying the chamber.

The chill, the harrowing sword fight, leering Leofric, and the kidnapping—all of it wavered, blurred, and shrank, the ghostly part of a long-ago past, a bad dream. Dim memories of strangers' faces peering at her drifted through her mind. A man. A physician perchance? An old woman. Mistress Innkeep. But Garrett had always been there, too. Leandra recalled his assurances that Brenna was safe with Wystan near the Tamar River.

Leandra munched on her meal with half an ear tuned to Isabelle, who danced about her duties chirping in delight, like a Cornish piskie. Outside, Leandra could hear the songs of children trebling along the breeze. The bass rumble of cartwheels thundered across cobbles. The villagers were preparing for May Day.

"We'll have a maypole and all kinds of contests and green food," Isabelle chattered. "You'll stay for the festivities, won't you, lady?"

"Perhaps," Leandra said. She certainly didn't feel like traveling, and she had to admit, May Day was one of her favorite celebrations.

Leandra wondered whether Garrett would agree to stay a day longer for the spring festival.

"Who's there?" Isabelle ceased jabbering when the chamber door opened a small way. She went to greet the visitor and returned quickly to Leandra. "My lady, my mum and a gentleman are here to see you."

"I'm not prepared to speak with strangers," Leandra said, suddenly aware that she was nude beneath the bed covers.

"Please, Lady Anne," the girl begged.

Leandra started at being addressed as Anne. Now she recalled Garrett had warned her before he left that they were known only as Sir John and Lady Anne to the villagers.

Isabelle trotted to the chair by the fireplace to retrieve Leandra's surcoat, and helped her into it while she remained in bed. "My mum is pleased to learn you are recovered. She and the mayor have something important to speak to you about."

Leandra debated for a moment, arranging the surcoat so that she looked as presentable as possible. Finally she said, "A brief word only, and you will remain with me, please."

"Of course." The girl opened the door and ushered in the lady innkeeper and a gentleman wearing a fine blue wool tunic that strained across his belly and a rabbit-lined, threadbare brown surcoat. When the gentleman bowed too low, his blue wool hat flopped over his brow and threatened to cover his eyes. Embarrassed, he hastily pushed it back into place to cover his thinning gray hair.

The lady innkeeper dropped a curtsy.

"My lady," they both began, then flashed each other a resentful glare. Apparently they had made no agreement on who would speak first. Condescendingly, the lady innkeeper waved a hand toward the gentleman.

"My lady," the man began. Self-importantly, he stuck his thumbs in his belt, leaned back and spoke. "We wish to express our pleasure in your recovery. I'm Mr. Amdale, merchant and mayor."

"I'm pleased to meet you, sir." Leandra repressed a smile with some effort. What an amusingly officious man, she thought.

"Yes, we are most pleased that you are recovered from your illness," the Mistress Innkeep said, clasping her hands beneath her apron in a proprietary manner.

"We know Sir John has been most anxious for your health, as we all have been," Mr. Amdale continued.

The lady innkeeper smiled and blushed at the mention of Garrett, and agreed with a furious nodding of her head. Leandra frowned. Garrett often seemed to have such an effect on ladies, young and old.

"I thank you for your well wishes," she said, still wondering what this call was about. She looked to Isabelle for a hint, but the child merely gave her a wait-and-see shake of her head. Leandra turned back to the pair.

"Have you seen what is going on in the market square?" the lady asked. "We are preparing for May Day."

"Oh, yes, how wonderful. I have not looked out the window this morn, but I can hear the preparations," Leandra said. She really must try to get on her feet soon, she decided.

"Indeed, my lady," the mayor said. "We have come to ask you to do our village the honor of being May Queen this year."

"Me?" Leandra exclaimed. It was the last request she'd expected to hear from these people who hardly knew her. To be the May Queen was a great honor in any village, on any manor. The queen of the annual spring ritual led the flower cutters into the woods at dawn to gather greenery. She bestowed the prize bells on the game winners and led the Maying-Round-the-Merry-Maypole.

All of these doings were part of the effort to force spring back into the earth. The revelry was the peasants' merrymaking, with the gentry joining in only as guests and observers. Not even Brenna had ever been asked to be May Queen in Lyonesse. "But why me?"

"We ask you for your fair beauty," Mistress Innkeep said.

"For your green eyes," Mr. Amdale murmured, averting his gaze from her face to his feet like a bashful boy.

"To share in your good fortune in overcoming your illness," the lady innkeeper added, earnestly tucking her hands into the sleeves of her russet surcoat as if she suddenly feared that Leandra would say no.

"We often ask a guest of honor," the mayor explained with another shy duck of his head.

For a moment Leandra thought of refusing. Surely there was a maiden in the village who would take the flowered May Queen crown with delight. Yet the thought of May Day brought to mind carefree romps in the May woods, dancing, and hobbyhorse games. 'Twould be such fun.

Still she hesitated. What did Garrett plan for them?

From behind the two visitors, Isabelle frowned at Leandra. She emphatically shook her head with an expression that said Leandra would miss the fun of a lifetime if she didn't accept.

The thought of being in a quiet fishing village where they were simply thought of as another knight and his lady made Leandra feel strangely free of responsibilities. Who would know what they did here? What harm could come from taking a day in their travels to celebrate the coming of spring with these good, simple people?

She smiled maliciously to herself. Just how would Garrett, Sir Perfect, feel about gathering flowers in the woods and dancing around the maypole? He would glower and growl like a bear until the fun of the day won him over.

Her grin grew broader. How could she possibly be in love with a man that she so enjoyed aggravating?

Her breath caught in her throat and her heart gave a little leap. Love? Why did she think of loving Garrett? Why had she dissolved in terror and tears as he fought with Leofric? Because she feared for his life, his happiness. She loved him. Because of a potion?

"My lady," Mistress Innkeep said. "Would you like for us to return later for your answer?"

"What? No. I would be delighted to be your May Queen," she said at last. Her heart began to patter lightly, rapidly, as it did when she knew she took a great risk, and the reward, if successful, would be a thrilling one. "'Twould please me much if Sir John can be the Lord of May."

Joy lit the two callers' faces. "Of course, my lady," they chorused. "We would ask no other."

Leandra began chuckling. Just how would Sir Perfect, dignified knight in leather and chain mail, look in the May Lord's traditional bright green tunic and hose?

The next morning the pearly dawn barely glimmered pink in the east when Leandra presented a newly awakened Garrett with the May Lord's clothes.

He raked his hair from his brow and scowled sleepily at the green wool tunic Leandra held out for him. "I've decided that the May Lord is an improper part for a knight to play."

What had ever possessed him to give in to this May Day idea of hers? If only Leandra hadn't greeted him with such a dazzling, heart-stopping smile when he'd returned yesterday. She looked so well, so fully recovered! She could have asked for his own head on a platter and he probably would have agreed to cut it off for her himself. "Don't you think the May Lord should be younger?"

"But you agreed to do it, Sir Knight," Leandra reminded him in a voice full of confidence.

He had the feeling she was fully prepared for any argument he might try.

She added, "You can't refuse now. You'll disappoint the entire village."

"The truth is, the less notice the village takes of us, the better," Garrett said. In the candlelight he squinted at the tunic she held.

"I think the Lord of May should be a man who turns all the ladies' heads," Leandra said, shaking the tunic at him. "That's you." Then she whispered. "Mistress Innkeep absolutely blushed when she spoke your name."

Garrett grinned in spite of himself and took the tunic from her. "Flattery is definitely your best weapon, lioness."

She cast him that little smile of pleasure that seemed to render him powerless. Defeated, Garrett stripped off his leather tunic and threw it across the bed.

Without thinking, he raised his arms over his head, ready to pull on the costume. Leandra's stare stopped him. She gazed at his bare chest—no, feasted—her eyes ardent, almost caressing him. Garrett suddenly felt naked, though he still wore his leather chausses. As he watched, a pensive longing softened Leandra's full lips, and a curious tenderness darkened her loden eyes when they flicked up to meet his.

His mouth went dry. Her look of desire awakened parts of his body he thought were better left asleep.

Her eyes, bright and liquid with confusion, betrayed her innocence. He was certain for the first time that she understood less of what she was feeling than he did. Hastily, Garrett pulled the tunic over his head and yanked it down over his hips without meeting her gaze again.

"So today we lead the way for the gathering of the May flowers, your highness, the Queen of May," he said in an effort to break the spell. He turned away to take up his sword and strapped it on. In his experience, danger seldom took a holiday. He had allowed his vigilance to slip once before. He had no intention of letting that happen again.

She offered him her hand. "Yes, I can hear the villagers awaiting us in the square below, my Lord of May."

They led the singing merrymakers, old and young, into

the woods along the stream that emptied into the harbor. The dew dampened the ladies' skirts and brushed against their faces as they skipped through spring's first greenery.

Garrett remained constantly at Leandra's side, his gaze ever sharp. Wildlife vanished ahead of the revelers' noisy singing and the blare of their May horns and whistles. Their laughter filled the air as they stamped the ground to awaken the sleeping spirits of the earth.

Before long Garrett's dour mood dissolved amidst the villagers' gaiety. But he remained vigilant. He followed Leandra deeper into the forest, noting that groups and couples stopped along the way to gather the flowers that Leandra pointed out as she ran along. The undergrowth grew thicker, and the morning light softened into green shadows.

When a woodsman stopped Garrett to ask him about the merits of a tree that the men had selected for the maypole, Garrett lingered to offer his thoughts. But his eyes followed Leandra as they talked. Behind them he saw a maid duck into the bushes with her swain in hot pursuit, the boy's hand grabbing at the hem of the girl's skirt. When he looked around for Leandra, he glimpsed another couple, the giggling maid's bodice loosened and slipping from her shoulders. Her partner dragged her down behind a fallen log.

The freedom around him made him suddenly uneasy. He'd received a few inviting glances himself from the village maids. No doubt some lads were eyeing Leandra. Suddenly aware that her graceful form had just disappeared into the forest beyond, Garrett bolted after her, cursing himself for losing sight of her. He strode down the hill, leapt along the stepping-stones in the stream, and worked his way through the undergrowth.

He found her exploring only a little distance ahead of him. When he caught up, he glanced back, uneasy about their distance from the others.

"Let's go back." He tugged on the sleeve of her green gown.

"No. Oh!" Leandra started and turned suddenly on Garrett, her face pinkening. She bit her lip.

"What is it?" Alerted, Garrett dragged her behind him and reached for his sword. He'd take care of Leofric this time, if the man dared appear. He peered through leafy greenery, almost wishing for a glimpse of Leofric's purple plume. Instead, through the spring leaves he spied a heap of legs and arms flailing in the ferns. The girl's russet skirt was rucked up about her waist, and the boy's bare bottom shone from beneath his tunic. His hose wrinkled about his knees.

"Is that lovemaking?" Leandra asked, her whispered words tickling Garrett's ear. The impassioned couple loved on, blissfully unaware of the presence of the May Queen and Lord. "Is that what the love potion is supposed to do to us?"

Garrett eyed the energetic work of the boy and berated himself for not thinking of this very reason for not allowing Leandra to run free in the woods. Many a maid lost her virtue on May Day. Garrett turned and with a firm hand on her shoulder guided her toward the merrymakers behind them. She resisted.

"But how is it done?" she asked softly, guileless confusion plain in her rosy face. "'Tis a mystery to me. A man and woman are made to fit. I know that. But how is a thing so small and soft tucked into where it belongs?" Her hands fluttered in a flopping gesture that almost undid Garrett.

He fought back his laughter, then turned away to hide his embarrassment and amusement. Did she really know so little about the man's part of mating? Gently he took her hand and led her away from the scene. This time she followed him. "Didn't the serving girls' talk make these things known to you?" he asked.

"Father and the nuns were very strict about our talk," Leandra said. "I know Brenna won't admit it, but she doesn't understand any better than I."

"You think I should teach you?" Garrett asked.

"You admitted that there is a benefit in having a teacher," Leandra said, hopefulness lilting her voice and shining in her eyes.

Garrett clasped her hand tighter and quickened his pace through the woods toward the others.

"Need you walk so quickly?" Leandra asked. After a

pause, she added, "Surely you must understand that this is how we got into this difficulty in the first place."

"What difficulty?" Garrett asked, slowing his pace a little so that she didn't have to trot to keep up with him. He should never have allowed her to explore on her own.

"With the love potion," Leandra said. "I know so little. Most girls have their mother or an aunt for their questions. When I asked Amice, she made some kind of pantomime of the thing growing."

Garrett stopped and looked back at her incredulously. "You didn't believe her?"

Leandra bumped into him as she, too, lurched to a halt, her body pressed dangerously close to his. "Should I? I never know what to believe with Amice. She's like Tyler Wotte, always full of jokes and tales."

As she spoke, Garrett's arm burned where her breast had grazed it. He gulped as he noted how the green linen stretched and slackened across her breasts, rising and falling from the exertion of their brisk walk. She looked up at him, wide-eyed, an innocent blush still staining her cheeks, a truly virginal May Queen.

"Is that what happens? Does it grow? That sounds so strange and terrible."

Garrett cleared his throat with difficulty, trying to dismiss his desire. Her curiosity and apprehension touched him. He'd never considered how foreign the act might seem to a true maiden.

"'Tis not my place to talk of these things with you," he said gruffly, ignoring the look of disappointment that crossed her face.

Ahead he saw that the people of the village had gathered, their arms full of flowers and boughs, awaiting the return of their May Queen and Lord. When he turned back to Leandra, he caught her studying him, her features settling into an expression of earnest inquiry.

"Then who will? How does a woman find a teacher?" she asked with a soft but determined glint in her eye. "'Tis unfair, don't you think? A man can go to a woman to learn, but a woman, if she learns too much, is thought less of."

Garrett turned away, unable to look into her face. With a sudden tug in his gut, he realized how much he wanted to give her the answers to her questions. He ached to take her into his arms and show her all of those strange and terrible things that she professed ignorance about. He longed to watch her green eyes widen in surprise, to feel the excitement build in her lovely body, to taste the sweet sigh of pleasure he could put on those innocent lips.

Garrett mentally shook himself and stared at the stream in their path. Was that water cold enough? he wondered, remembering Father John's advice about bathing. Sweet Jesu, he needed a cold swim now.

He passed his hand across his brow, stunned by his own lack of discipline.

"No teacher is necessary for a woman other than her husband," Garrett growled, knowing that he lied. A man took a virgin for a wife to be certain of his heir. Otherwise, an experienced woman was most gratifying. God's wounds, why must she stare at him with such disbelief and disappointment?

A delicious "why?" formed on her pink, tender lips.

He dragged his eyes from her face, away from those lush, inquiring eyes.

"Because no more is necessary," Garrett explained.

"You won't even answer my questions?"

"No." He waved to the other revelers. A group danced around the tree chosen to be felled for the maypole. The sooner they left the forest, the safer they'd both be, Garrett decided. He almost wished they'd found Leofric in the woods instead of the lovers.

He gave Leandra a low mocking bow and offered her his arm. "Our subjects await us, my queen."

She studied him a moment more, her embarrassment gone and her expression quiet. He waited, wondering whether she would press him more, but she didn't.

Without another word she took his arm and they returned to the safety of the merrymakers.

The lord of May marched along in scowling silence, his tawny brow so low over his eyes that Leandra wondered how he could see where he was going. She walked at his side, almost afraid to look him in the eye again and puzzled by his sulky annoyance with her.

For the benefit of the other merrymakers, who were dragging the maypole back to the village, she forced a smile to her lips.

"Smile," she muttered to him. "For the villagers, at least."

Still Garrett refused to look at her. He'd been such a fine companion until they'd stumbled onto the lovers.

"How was I to know those lovers were there?" Leandra hissed, keeping her voice low so that the others didn't know they were arguing. How was she to know her questions would upset Sir Perfect? "I only thought as a man of experience, as my knight and elder, you would answer a simple question," Leandra added. "No need to take offense. After all—"

"Elder?" Garrett grumbled.

"Well, you did show me a lover's kiss, did you not?"

Garrett halted, then took up the pace again. "That was no lover's kiss."

"But you said—"

"I was relieved to have you out of Leofric's grasp." Garrett quickened the pace, and Leandra skipped a few steps to keep at his side. He added, "'Twas no more than a kiss of victory."

Chapter 15

Kiss of victory?" Leandra repeated in disbelief. Victory merited lips to cheek only. Brief and congratulatory. Nothing mouth to mouth, lip to lip . . . Nothing lingering. Nothing that curled a girl's toes.

"Yes, victory," Garrett confirmed staunchly. "The subjects of kissing and lovemaking are now closed. 'Tis not appropriate between us."

Leandra decided to let it pass, for the time anyway.

Back in the village square she joined the other women as a grimly enthusiastic Garrett and the other men threw themselves into hefting the maypole into place. The women sang as they trimmed it with more fresh garlands, bright ribbons, floral bouquets, and tingling bells. Beneath the maypole they gathered to crown a radiant Leandra with a chaplet of flowers.

She lost herself in the revelry, graciously responding to the pleasure she saw reflected in the people's eyes. She was unable to see herself as they did—the delicate pink hawthorn crown enhancing the blush in her cheeks, and the rich green leaves highlighting the color of her eyes. Little did she know that every man at the May Day festivities longed for at least one kiss from the queen.

Once she was crowned, Garrett approached her in the spirit of the day and presented himself. "As Lord of May allow me to be the first to pay my respects and pledge my liege."

"My lord." Leandra proffered her hand with a haughty movement that bespoke of queenly disdain. Then she laughed. Garrett's frown faded and he grinned at her before he bent to kiss her hand.

Pleased to see him enjoying the festival again, Leandra smiled down on the top of his golden head. He seemed to hesitate a long moment, his lips softly brushing her hand. What did he find so fascinating, she wondered, that he must linger, massaging her fingers between his palm and thumb?

Suddenly Leandra's left hand seemed bare, naked. She tried to pull her hand free of his. Garrett's head came up and he looked her in the eye, his face full of questions. He refused to release her hand. But he could not prevent her from looking down to see that her betrothal ring was gone.

The smile fell from her face. She forgot the presence of the singing villagers. "My ring! I forgot that Leofric took it. I was so weak, so confused, that I couldn't stop him. Then you arrived. Everything happened so fast."

She pressed her fingers to her lips to stifle the cry of dismay that threatened. With the ring gone, her tie to Reginald was lost. Gone was the betrothal gift that brought protection to Lyonesse. She closed her eyes against the uncertainty that shook her. She couldn't allow herself to believe that all was lost because Leofric possessed the ring.

"You didn't take it off, then?" Garrett questioned, his whisper harsh and low, as if he suspected her of some betrayal.

"No, never." Leandra nearly sobbed. How dare he think she would take off her betrothal ring. Pain and anger set her spine straight and rigid. "You know what that ring meant to me. I know you know. I saw it in your face."

"I believe you," he said. Leandra let him draw her closer to his side. "Don't trouble yourself over it now," he murmured, squeezing her hand until she was forced to look him in the eye.

Garrett met her gaze steadily, reading the wild panic there. He remembered well how she'd clutched the ring to her heart, how she'd worn it despite its size, keeping the circle on her tiny finger by some miracle, with determination.

"You've been dragged through so much," he said sooth-ingly. He took her into his arms, rubbing her back, willing the anxiety from her body, from her face. The villagers cheered, unaware of their crisis. He grinned at them before he went on. "Forget it for now. Be my May Queen."

He gave her a sound kiss. The villagers roared and called out for more from their May Lord and May Queen. Garrett ignored them. He watched Leandra press her lips together, refusing to display her despair. No tears from the lioness. She gave him a determined nod.

"We'll find it. I promise," he whispered into her ear, without the slightest idea of how he would fulfill that vow. But he would. He must, for her sake and his.

Brave and smiling, Leandra reigned over the festivities. She announced each game with regal poise that awed the villagers and bestowed the May bells on each champion with a victory kiss that made Garrett oddly uncomfortable. Nothing was meant by the little rewards. He knew that. But each time her lips touched a champion's, Garrett recalled their fireside kiss.

The lads that won the foot race, the longest leap, the farthest throw of a ball—each blushed when the lady planted a May Queen peck on their fresh country faces. The little girl who won the contest for the longest-held note kissed Leandra back, and the old man who won at the most accurate ring toss angled for a wet kiss on the lips, which Leandra handily avoided. The winners cavorted round the maypole, jingling their newly won bells, then placing them on the hooks for such trophy gifts.

The final game was a contest of archery—a skill King Edward III required yeomen to practice. Until then Garrett politely refrained from joining the games. But the urge to earn the approval of the crowd and a victory kiss from the May Queen was more than he could resist. So when Leandra announced this contest, Garrett grinned and was among the first to step forward.

"What is this, my Lord of May?" Leandra chided. She spoke loud enough so that all could hear. "You would compete with these sharp-eyed bowmen, fresh from target shooting last Sunday?"

The villagers cheered for their archers.

Leandra grinned at their goodwill. "What does a knight know of archery?"

"I've not always been a knight, your highness," Garrett said. He took a longbow offered by one of the village men. "A captain of the guard learns many skills."

"Well, then I think I shall have to join in this contest," she said.

Garrett glanced at her, surprised but willing to meet the challenge.

The villagers clapped and cheered again, and a bow was found for Leandra, a boy's bow somewhat shorter than the average six-foot weapon. Straw-filled dummies were tied in place along a stone wall. The contest began.

Cornish villagers were better fishermen, shepherds, and miners than archers. Before long, with no regret on the part of the crowd, the contest narrowed to the pretty May Queen and the handsome May Lord. The ladies took the queen's side; the men rooted for the lord.

The marksmanship of each was consistently good. Between each volley the opponents eyed each other warily and with some amusement.

"How are we going to settle this to their satisfaction and ours?" Garrett asked under his breath as they waited for a boy to pull the arrows from the dummy that was their target.

"You could let me win," Leandra suggested. She selected an arrow from the quiver tied to her green girdle and cast an eye along the shaft, measuring its straightness.

Garrett also selected an arrow and gave it the straightness test. Then he examined the fletching. Leandra's expertise pleased him. She seemed quite good with the bow— confident and at home with the patience and concentration needed to be a good target shooter. Silently he congratulated Captain Ralph on his training of the lady. Without looking up from the arrow, he said, "If you win, everyone will know that I allowed it."

An unladylike huff escaped her and her bow and arrow flopped to her side as she turned on Garrett. "Is that so?"

"Of course," he said, still intent on his arrow and determined to return some aggravation at last. He was also pleased to see that she'd forgotten about the missing ring.

"Well, we'll see about that," Leandra snapped. She whirled around to face the target. Without delay she smoothly drew her bow.

Garrett admired her graceful form. At full draw with her elbows at shoulder level, her breasts lifted in a pert way that charmed Garrett and stirred him. He wished they weren't being watched so closely. She released the arrow perfectly, the spun flaxen string rolling off her fingertips.

"Bull's-eye!" one of the former contestants shouted. The villagers murmured approval, breaking Garrett away from his admiration of the lady's form.

He turned to the target to see that she'd indeed made it difficult for him to win this one. He glanced at her, and she returned the sweetest of mocking smiles.

He eyed the target. Sweet Jesu, how had he gotten into this mess? Escort to an innocent lady warrior. Victim of a love potion. Surely God had a design in all of this, but what it could be was beyond Garrett.

He took note of the wind, eyed his arrow again, then licked the dark feather. Slowly he nocked the shaft and took aim. He hoped to do something he had never succeeded in doing in the past. He released the flaxen bowstring carefully, without plucking, sending the bolt straight for the end of Leandra's.

The villager's heads snapped around toward the target, and they groaned in satisfaction as Garrett's shaft struck the same hole as the May Queen's. It plowed into the target atop her arrow. Garrett grinned and bowed to the crowd's applause.

"Very nice, my lord," Leandra conceded, her lips pressed together, the flesh about her mouth tight and white. Garrett smiled inwardly. She was a spirited competitor. "I challenge you to another trial."

"But of course," Garrett said, shrugging his shoulders toward the villagers as if he could do nothing but comply with the lady's ridiculous request.

"Bring the rings from the ring toss," the May Queen ordered.

Garrett maintained his smile but groaned inside. Surely she wasn't serious. He'd seen a trickster at a London fair perform with the rings from the toss before. But no archer he knew practiced this kind of shooting. "Is this a trick you learned from Captain Ralph?"

"Yes," she said. "It requires a fine eye."

"Nothing wrong with my eye," Garrett said with supreme confidence. Lord, how was he going to win this one? he wondered. He watched her nock an arrow in her bow. "Talented soldier, that Captain Ralph."

"Indeed." Leandra nodded to the man who tossed the ring upward between her and the dummy target. She drew her bow. An instant after the toss, she released the arrow and cleanly pinned the ring to the dummy's heart. The crowd murmured in approval, and applause broke out. Leandra stepped back, a smile of pure satisfaction on her lips.

Garrett admired the marksmanship and swore silently. Nothing else had gone right on this undertaking. If only she'd missed that shot. Slowly he took an arrow from his quiver, licked the feather and nocked the arrow in his bow. If he was to have any glory, any luck on this journey with Lady Leandra, now would be a good time. He nodded to the man who tossed the ring. Garrett spotted it and released. The arrow thudded into the dummy, pinning the ring to the straw just inside Leandra's ring.

The village men shouted cheers and danced in the street. Garrett grinned.

Leandra frowned. "Good shooting, May Lord."

"Thank you, my lady," Garrett said, giving her a little bow. "One more contest? Which of us can shoot the most arrows into the air?"

Leandra frowned. "That's not a fair competition. You are bigger and stronger and can use the bigger bow."

But the crowd liked the idea, and the archers gathered around them with arrows and advice on how to shoot rapidly enough to have at least six in the air at once.

The boys and women took Leandra's part. The men surged around Garrett, several offering him their finest shafts, well-fletched and known to be lucky.

"Are you ready? You first," Garrett said.

Leandra's frown vanished. A smile played on her lips and the gleam of challenge sparkled in her eye. Garrett grinned back, knowing that she was going to give her best effort. Women grabbed their children and cleared the square to stand beneath the overhang of the inn or the eaves of the cottage shops. Silence fell over the crowd.

Leandra rapidly shot five arrows high into the air before the first fell to the thatched roof of the inn. The crowd cheered once more. Garrett suspected that among the village archers, few could do better.

Leandra stepped aside to allow Garrett his turn. He took up his stance and swiftly put seven arrows into the blue sky before the first bolt fell to the roof of a nearby cottage.

The archers cheered.

Garrett turned to Leandra. "Can we do better together?"

"What? How?"

"I'll shoot," Garrett said. "You hand me the arrows, ready to nock. Hold them here like this. An archer team is deadly. I've seen it done in France with the crossbows. Yes, like that."

Leandra scowled at him at first, as though she thought he was playing some trick on her.

"How many did I get into the air?" Garrett asked her.

"Seven," she snapped. "But only because you are stronger."

"We'll get eight into the air," Garrett assured her.

"Eight is impossible."

"Hand the arrows to me as I showed you."

Rebellion smoldered in Leandra's green eyes. But she stood at his shoulder as he had told her, annoyance radiating from her like heat from a blacksmith's fire. The game master gave the signal to begin. She offered each arrow to

Garrett as he'd instructed, concentrating so intently on the task that she didn't even look up to see the arrows fly into the sky, but she counted aloud with the villagers.

Once more the crowd stood back and counted.

"One. Two. Three. Four." Her hand trembled when she handed him the next one. "Five."

"Keep them coming," Garrett muttered without a break in his movements—nock, draw, release.

"Six," Leandra counted, a soft breathlessness in her voice.

Another. And another.

"Eight!"

The first arrow clattered to the cobbles at their feet.

"We did it!" Leandra said. She stared up at him in disbelief. Then she threw her arms around his neck and smacked a kiss on his lips.

Astonished, Garrett set her away from him. "Of course we did it. I told you we would together. You must trust me."

The smile faded from Leandra's face and she spoke in a low, husky voice that only he could hear. "But I do trust you. Completely. I have trusted you from the very first."

Garrett stared down at her, totally disarmed by her words and excruciatingly aware that she no longer wore Reginald's betrothal ring.

After the hobbyhorse games played throughout the narrow streets of the village, the May feasting began. The shadows grew long and the cool of evening settled over the village with the dusk.

Leandra and Garrett sat side by side, sampling strange green foods and exchanging stories and conversation with the villagers.

Leandra found herself comfortable again in Garrett's company. Something about his victory kiss set things right between them. The feeling was strange and indistinct, but it surrounded them like an invisible halo, and he sensed it, too. She could tell by the way he turned to her, speaking at times in a voice soft and velvety, meant only for her ears. Sometimes his hand lingered on the small of her back. She smiled up at him, delighted with the way he joined in with the people, not reserving himself in a haughty manner as other knights might have done, but laughing with them, delighting in the simple things that pleased them. He could easily bellow at bawdy jokes and bait the men for fishing stories. He would have been the perfect knight for Lyonesse.

She took pride in him, of how he'd impressed the villagers with his prowess and charm, of how he'd turned her loss into a victory. Sir Perfect was so much more than a knight, and she knew that she loved him. She didn't care whether it was the potion's doing. She loved him nonetheless. The knowledge made her sad, because they could never love each other like the boy and girl rolling in the ferns. In lusty innocence and abandon. She could never ask that of him.

Compline bells rang. Bonfires glowed on the cliffs along the sea, and couples slunk away into the darkness. Leandra yawned into her hand, aware that she'd yet to recover her full strength.

"What is expected of the May Queen and her lord now?" she asked Garrett.

"I think they usually slip away into the night," he said. "Just as we are going to do." He took her arm and led the way to the inn.

He closed the chamber door behind them and barred it. With no more explanation, he knelt in front of the hearth and began to heap wood onto the fire.

Leandra stood beside him to bask in the growing heat. She yawned again. To her surprise, Garrett reached up for her arm, pulled her down beside him and held her close. She studied his face. The firelight gleamed in his tawny hair, and his jovial smile, worn for the day's gaiety, faded into a curious, tender solemnity. Leandra took advantage of his tranquil mood to rub her nose against his.

He accepted her touch and followed it with a light kiss to her lips. She closed her eyes and sighed, soaking in the comfort of the fire, of his embrace. She thought of the words she wanted to say, but remained silent.

"No use denying it any longer," he whispered, his lips grazing her brow.

"Denying what?" Leandra asked, sinking into his arms.

"That Vivian's love potion has worked," Garrett murmured, his lips against her temple. "I have known it for days, but I refused to believe. I even told myself it was just the spirit of May Day. But I can no longer deny it. I love you, Leandra. Though I can hardly believe it's so, I think you love me. I've seen it in your smile. Heard it in your voice, too. A solemn maid like you would never smile with such warmth at a man she didn't care about."

Leandra sighed, relieved to hear her own confession on Garrett's lips. She touched his face with the back of her hand. A calmness settled over her. This moment was so fated that it seemed almost familiar. "'Tis true, I'm afraid. I love you."

He took her hand and kissed it.

Leandra closed her eyes, allowing the ardor of his kiss to tingle through her hand and up her arm to her heart. Her sleepiness vanished, and the vivid memory of the couple wrestling among the ferns popped into her head.

"I didn't think this was how the potion would work," Garrett said. "So slow and quiet and compelling. An irresistible force."

"Yes." Leandra refused to open her eyes. The tingling in her arm had yet to stop, and she wasn't ready for it to. She wanted this magic moment to go on and on. She let him draw her closer, until she sensed his lips against her hair and the fresh stubble of his beard scratching her cheek.

He nuzzled her ear. "I want to be your lover."

Leandra's eyes opened and she almost pulled away. She could tell by the sudden iron in his grip that he'd anticipated her reaction. "Garrett, I know we've been given a potion and 'tis May Day, but—"

"I know," Garrett whispered, his lips closer to hers now, his breath moist and warm against her cheekbone. "I promise that we will not break our vows. There are many ways to love, Leandra. You said today that you trust me. Will you trust me in this? I will reveal the mystery to you. I'll give you what you need to know. I will take nothing. I promise. I swear."

Briefly she thought of the morning to come, when they would see the world in a new light. But in truth she cared nothing for tomorrow. All she could think of was this moment and him—a night of passion and love—more powerful than any thoughts of the future. She wanted to lie close, skin against skin, mouth brushing mouth, legs and arms entwined. She'd tuck whatever needed to be tucked into wherever it needed to go because she longed to hold Garrett, and she could see in the tense lines of his face that he wanted to be held.

"Tell me what you want," Garrett said.

"I want to touch you." Images of the morning, of Garrett pulling the tunic over his head, of rippling muscles and gleaming hair, still danced vividly in her head.

Garrett stiffened in her arms, drawing away from her slightly. "I know you're curious, lioness. But don't you think that's, ah, too familiar to begin with?"

A blush heated Leandra's cheeks. "Touching your chest is too familiar? After we've shared a lover's kiss?"

"My chest?" The tension eased from Garrett's face. He chuckled, shaking his head in a self-deprecating manner. "Forgive me, sweet lady. I thought you referred to something else. I forget that you are virgin."

Garrett pulled the green tunic over his head and cast it aside. He took her hands in his and placed them over his heart. "Is that what you desire? You have already touched me more ways than you will ever know."

Beneath Leandra's hands his heart beat strong and steady, and between her fingers his golden chest hair curled crisp and wiry. She caught the tantalizing scent of him, warm and male. He leaned closer. A delightful weakness tickled her nose and spiraled down through her belly.

"Remember the lover's kiss?" Garrett asked.

She nodded, offering her lips to him, and he took them, stroking and parting and teasing until she kissed him back. She pressed closer, returning Garrett's passionate attentions, exploring territory, new and strange, yet so natural, so nearly a part of her. Without uncoupling, she sighed, melted against him and offered more of herself. To her surprise, he grabbed the back of her head and took her surrender, delving greedily into her mouth, forcefully yet delicately seeking her. Leandra's world shrank to nothing but the feel of him. And she wanted more.

Garrett pulled away first, only to descend on her throat, his lips doing things that thrilled down through her breasts and swirled into her middle. His fingers fumbled with the laces at the back of her gown.

Leandra took his hands away and put them on her thighs. "You need only to pull up my skirt," she whispered. "Like the boy and girl we saw in the woods."

"Oh, no." He drew her closer and resumed his work with her laces. "This is no lusty mating stolen in the woods. I'm not a lover to be content with bare thighs. This is a true loving. There."

Leandra felt the laces loosen.

"The defenses are breached," he said, soft amusement in his voice. Gently he slipped her gown and shift from her shoulders, following the fabric down her arm with light, teasing kisses. But he stopped just as he bared her breasts. Leandra held her breath, achingly aware of a heaviness in her that longed for his touch.

He lifted his face to hers, his eyes half closed, his lips fuller and more sensitive than Leandra remembered. His grip bit into her arms. "Do you still want the mystery revealed, Leandra? Nothing will ever be the same after this night if we yield to the potion."

"What choice do we have?"

"I believe we always have a choice." Garrett lifted his head, his eyes widening and his stormy blue gaze searching her face. "At least, I believed that until I met you."

"Then let's choose tonight," Leandra whispered, uncertain what he meant about choice. She needed him, and he wanted her. What other choice was there? She put her fingers to his lips in a gesture of appeal. "Will you choose it with me?"

"Yes," Garrett said without hesitation. But he closed his eyes against something painful, something Leandra understood but refused to think about. Vows and promises, duties

178

and obligations. She would not admit them. Not this night. He offered her light in dark hours of May Day, and she would take the light for herself, for him. These hours would be theirs alone.

He kissed her fingertips. Then he slipped her gown down, freeing her arms and exposing her breasts. Cool air stirred across her throat and teased the aching heaviness. She glanced at him, wondering whether a man wanted to touch a woman's breasts as much as she wanted him to.

She never asked. He took a ripened nipple into his mouth. Leandra gasped in surprise, then pleasure. But the satisfaction brought was only momentary. She threaded her fingers through his hair and arched her back to help the pleasure spread through her body. The touch of his lips and the flick of his tongue stirred hidden needs in secret places. She shifted in his arms. For the first time she understood the weakness that made a woman willingly open herself to a man. Offering him all. A strange, tender magic.

She didn't ever want the sensations to stop. She tugged greedily on his hair when he pulled away.

"Patience, lioness." He kissed her lightly on the lips. "Let's take our loving in comfort." He reached for the counterpane on the bed and spread it before the fireplace. Then he pulled her back into his lap, nestling her between his thighs and deftly slipping Leandra's clothes over her hips. She kicked her legs free of the gown and leaned back against him.

With one arm wrapped around her waist, he stroked her thigh and kissed her shoulder. Each stroke moved tantalizingly closer to her inner thigh, coaxing to life sensations Leandra had never experienced. A moist heat flooded through her lower body. She tensed, clamped her legs together, afraid that he might discover this peculiar reaction.

"Relax."

"What if something is wrong?"

"What could be wrong? Does something feel wrong? Have I hurt you?"

Leandra shook her head.

"Then let me decide if something is wrong," he said. "These things are new to you."

When she relaxed, her thighs parting slightly, Garrett encouraged her to open more, drawing her own leg up alongside his, her bottom pressed tight against his hard groin. One strong hand held her against him, fingers spreading across her ribs and brushing the underside of her breast. His other hand teased her secret curls, stroking, brushing closer each time to the source of the moist, aching warmth.

"You are lovely," he whispered into her ear. "You are right not to hide anything from me." She realized that he stared down at her body over her shoulder. The firelight kept nothing from his eyes, not even her most private places. Gone was the modesty that she'd always been so certain she would never surrender to a man.

His fingers slid into the dewy warmth between Leandra's legs. She tensed. He crooned softly into her ear, his fingers moving over tender folds of flesh.

Leandra sank back into his embrace unaware of her sighs or of the gentle movement that her hips made against him.

"Yes, dance as you please," he whispered. "'Tis my pleasure, too." Wonderful feelings dissolved her body, leaving her mindless beyond the reality of his hands, his lips, and his body. At some point Garrett groaned. Leandra stopped, fearful that she'd done something wrong. She tried to pull away. "What—"

Garrett clasped her against him, even tighter than before. "No," he groaned again. "Give me your hand. What Amice told you is true."

He pulled her hand back against his groin. She found something long, hot, and remarkably hard.

"It does grow, and it needs no tucking when the time comes," Garrett whispered hoarsely. "It finds its way to love with only a little help of passion and care."

"How does it feel?" Leandra asked, leaning her head back to look into his face. "I mean, does it hurt?"

"It only aches to find a home in you," Garrett said with a smile.

"And if we don't—"

"One of the things I learned from my teacher is that there are many ways for a man to find satisfaction." Garrett kissed her ear and caressed one breast with a feathery touch. "Move against me, sweeting, as you were doing."

Leandra yielded once more to the seduction of Garrett's hands, the strength and warmth that tenderly built pleasures in her that she'd only suspected existed. She was unprepared for the brink when it came. A glimmer of pleasure blossomed inside, spreading throughout her body. Bright and promising, she arched her back reaching for it, knowing instinctively that this was the joy she sought with Garrett. The pleasure radiated through her, welling up from deep inside, and pulled her over the sweet edge of elation. She plunged, showered through brightness. A cry escaped her, muffled with a sigh of pleasure. She sank back into Garrett's arms, exhausted and glowing.

She snuggled closer, only to turn her face against his bare shoulder and wrap her arms around his neck. The musky male scent of him filled her senses, and she fervently kissed his throat, tasting the dearest man in the world. She pressed her bottom between his leather-clad thighs. His grip on her tightened. He tensed and his great body shuddered.

Leandra froze, uncertain of her role, but little by little realizing from the pattern of his breathing that he'd experienced something similar to her own pleasure. "Garrett?"

"It's all right," he sighed into her ear and held her close. He stroked her back, a faraway look in his eye. "Now you know how loving works between a man and a woman."

She nodded. "'Tis truly beautiful for something that looks so strange."

"We broke no vows, Leandra," Garrett whispered. "You are more knowing, but still unknown by a man. You are still a virgin."

"But I love you," Leandra murmured, too weak to move. Before she slept, she sighed, "My heart is yours."

Chapter 16

Garrett awoke abruptly to the harsh gray dawn with Leandra snuggled against him. No fire burned in the hearth. But Leandra's naked body lay toasty warm next to his half-clothed one in the bed where he'd carried her during the night. Despite the cold of the pale morn, her skin glowed with the blush of a contented woman. Her breathing was deep and even, sweet and untroubled.

Beyond their chamber the inn and the village slept peacefully.

"Sweet Jesu," Garrett prayed, and closed his eyes against the morning light, against reality. He would not deal with that just yet. Instead he let himself drift on the remnant of last night's pleasure—in the blissful ease that weighed down each limb. He had no desire to move. He wasn't even certain who he was. For the moment he was satisfied to be a man lying with his woman at his side. All he wanted was to dream once more of the sweet submission, the slow possession, and the final wondrous fulfillment.

"My heart is yours." He could still hear her words. Leandra had given him her heart!

A smile touched his lips and he drifted on. Wrapped still in the fading fragment of their pleasure, he slowly became aware of something else. Inside of him something different ticked along steady and true. The sensation was new and strange, but pleasant and welcome: a serenity, a harmony, a wholeness of being that left his mind and heart as blissfully happy as his limbs.

Leandra made him whole. The realization both astonished and frightened him. Could he ever give her up?

Down the lane from the inn a dog barked. Along with the sunlight, cold truth crept through the cracks in the window shutters.

Garrett frowned at the unpleasant thoughts that crowded into his head. Reginald may have asked him to help win the lady, but not like this. Oh, yes, there were excuses. Fate worked against them. Certainly the wanton spirit of May Day was an influence. So were the coupled lovers they'd stumbled upon. And Leandra's frank questions.

Beside him Leandra sighed in her sleep.

The sweet scent of the crushed May flowers still woven in her hair filled their private world. With a new smile he reached for her, tenderly touched her hair and brushed a finger along the pulse in her throat. He'd found a life as dear as his own; dearer. Last night he'd discovered paradise in living. With dawn's first light, reality snatched it away.

He closed his eyes and flopped back down on the pillow. He could blame the potion. Without it he would never have dreamt of falling in love with Leandra. "Damn Brenna. Damn her spiteful hide." The words were out before he realized he'd spoken. Leandra stirred again.

"Damn who?" Warm lips touched his cheek and a firm breast pressed against his bare shoulder. Newly awakened desires tingled through Garrett.

"You're awake. I can tell by your breathing," Leandra whispered into his ear. Passion stirred. Garrett didn't dare touch her.

"Damn Brenna," he repeated, clenching his fists at his sides. In repeating the curse, he realized how much he meant it. How he longed to throttle Leandra's cousin. "I know that she's your kinswoman, Leandra, but damn her for doing this to us."

Leandra raised herself up on one elbow and considered him for a moment. Garrett refused to meet her gaze. Apparently she didn't like what she saw. She drew up the sheet to cover herself—to Garrett's disappointment. His body was already reacting to her touch and to the tempting glimpse of her tight pink nipples just as she pulled the sheet between their bodies.

"I'm not certain Brenna deserves your curse," she said, a wary edge in her husky voice. "I'm the one who brought the potion." She rolled to her back to look up at the canopy above them. He could see the stubborn thrust to her chin.

"Then damn the Fates, if that makes you feel better." He almost reached out to put an arm around her and offer comfort, but decided that would only lead to other things. In the light of day those things were best avoided. "Aren't you angry about what the potion has done to us? Thank God we've broken no vows yet. But soon we face a life of dishonesty, denying our love day after day in the presence of *my* liege lord and *your* husband."

She relaxed and gave a little sigh that puzzled him. "Well, neither Brenna nor the Fates are here to damn, so what should we do?"

"We must leave here before anyone realizes who we are," Garrett insisted. Fortunately, she didn't seem about to go hysterical on him. "Do you think you are strong enough to ride today? You understand why we can't stay, don't you?"

"Yes," Leandra said. Garrett thought he heard a desire in her voice to say something more—to argue, no doubt. Or did she want to talk about last night? He hoped she wouldn't. He didn't want to recall any more than he and his body already did.

"Your chill aside, and love potion or not, our sharing this room could be difficult to explain," Garrett said. "Even to a reasonable man like Reginald."

"Yes, I suppose so," Leandra agreed.

They both lay silently staring up at the faded fabric stretched above them, obviously reluctant to leave the curtained world they'd shared so passionately during the night.

Although they no longer touched, Leandra could feel the tension in Garrett's body, a tautness that spurned her touch. The rejection hurt. He admitted that they loved each other. They'd shared the secret things that only a husband and wife would share. They were joined in pleasure, sweet and beautiful. At least she thought it was. But he wanted to go on as if nothing between them was changed.

Offended now, she sat up, putting more distance between them and wrapping the sheet around her, covering her confusion and pain. She turned on him and made no effort to hide her anger. "What if I'm got with child? Is it not true that when a woman takes pleasure with a man, she conceives. What then?"

For an instant Garrett stared back at her, astonishment on his face, as if he didn't believe his ears. Then laughter began to shake him, slowly at first, then with more violence, sending tremors through the entire bed.

Leandra's face burned with shame. There was something here she did not understand. "How can you laugh about such a thing?"

"Sweeting, I've heard that churchmen believe that a woman takes pleasure when she conceives, but that assumes that the man took his pleasure *in* her," Garrett said, continuing to chuckle. "We did nothing to get you with child, Leandra. Nothing that makes you less virtuous than you were or will be for your wedding—" Garrett's voice broke. The light of laughter vanished from his eyes. He whipped back the covers and swung out of bed.

"So where do we go, then?" Leandra asked, wondering at the anger etched on his face as he prowled around the chamber, his chest gloriously bare, gleaming with golden curls in the pale morning light.

"To rejoin Wystan and Brenna?" she suggested. Her cheeks still burned; not in response to Garrett's laughter, but because she realized to her surprise that she wanted his child. She longed for a laughing, blue-eyed baby with tawny locks to brush around her fingers.

"Yes, then after Wystan and Brenna are reassured, we find an antidote to the potion and swallow it," Garrett said. He found his shirt, pulled it on, and reached for his boots.

"But only Vivian can make the antidote," Leandra reminded him. His confidence perplexed her. She suspected that a simple antidote—even Vivian's—was not the solution to their problem.

"That's what she said." Garrett still worked at lacing his boots. "But there is more than one love potion, so there must be more than one antidote that could help us."

"Oh." Obvious male logic, Leandra thought. Reasonable, irrefutable, and lacking any consideration of the heart. But she was soon lost in watching his long fingers work with the leather laces. Vivid memories of his touch overwhelmed her. Suddenly she saw again her fingers tangled in his gleaming chest hair, knew the pressure of his thighs alongside hers, and felt the tenderness of his fingers stroking places on her body she never thought to touch or expected a man to seek.

"If the spell is lifted, then we are free of this passion for each another," Garrett was saying as he gave a final determined yank to his laces.

Leandra shook the intimate visions from her mind. "That's what you want?"

Garrett stared at her, his face grave. Then he rose from the chest where he sat and stalked across the room, swooping down on her like a gyrfalcon seizing its prey. Leandra froze, naked and tangled in sheets, unable to escape. He grasped her chin in one hand and bent to bestow a fierce, yet overwhelmingly tender kiss on her mouth. Every thread of her being yielded to him, reached for him, and gave to him in return. His power over her was as masterful as the night before. She forgot her confusion and fear, forgot everything but his lips, firm and warm, moving needfully over hers.

"That's what I want." His voice was a harsh whisper when he released her. "Because I love you, and I know that I can't give you up to Reginald as long as I feel like this. The antidote will free us."

Leandra gathered the sheet tighter to her chest, not out of modesty, but in a struggle to catch her breath and to keep her thoughts from fluttering off with the light-headedness his declaration brought. He loved her! The night was not forgotten. She gazed up at him, memorizing his expression: open, earnest, tender, hard, and forbidding all at once. She wasn't so certain she wanted to be free.

"What if—" Leandra swallowed in an effort to find her voice. Still she could only summon a whisper. "What if I told you that I can't become Reginald's wife, that I can't take vows of faithfulness to him because I love you? What if I told you that I would go anywhere with you?"

Garrett bowed his head and sank to his knees before her, taking her hands, which still clutched the sheet, his fingers warm against her heart. Sunlight gilded his hair— glimmering strands of gold, bronze, and ivory. When he looked up, his eyes were clear and dark. He wore the gentlest, most loving expression she'd ever seen on a man's face. A lump ached in her throat, and tears sprang to her eyes.

"If you told me that, lioness, I would remind you that this feeling is only from a potion, not from our hearts. Your future and Lyonesse's are under Reginald's protection. Mine is as his loyal knight and as a warrior in France. A love between us has no future. When you break a vow, when you are disloyal, everyone knows."

Leandra looked away, ashamed of her weeping, unable to face the love and painful honesty she saw in Garrett's face. She wanted to deny everything he said, to think of some exception, some happy ending, but none came to mind. Garrett wiped away her tears with his thumb, then gripped her hands even tighter.

"Listen to me. I know about the price of betrayal. No one forgets betrayal or forgives it. They make you pay over and over again. Men like Leofric spit on your pride and walk on your honor.

"Because of my uncle's treason against the king, my mother died of shame. Chycliff was forfeited to the crown and my father died drunk. I have struggled and fought for years to regain what we lost."

"Why did your father not fight like you have done?" Leandra asked, a glimmer of understanding coming to her. "Why did he let himself and you suffer for his brother's crime?"

"My father was unjustly implicated." Garrett hesitated,

as if he were gathering strength to say the words. "My uncle was a small man, one who took satisfaction in taking others down with him. He claimed my father had a part in the plotting. There was enough association to make Father look guilty though he was innocent, of course. But the accusation coming from one he loved crushed him. To the day he died he tried to make excuses for his brother." Garrett shook his head without releasing her gaze, his blue eyes captivating hers. "My father deserved a better fate. But he would not fight for it. I won't do that. I won't accept whatever comes my way, not if it isn't what I want."

"Your father was like my father," Leandra said, the whole picture suddenly becoming so clear to her.

"No, not like your father," Garrett contradicted, with an emphatic shake of his head. "Your father hides in his chapel."

"Oh, indeed, like my father," Leandra repeated. "He was crushed by the death of my mother. He turned to the Church. Your father simply took refuge in drink when he lost his brother to betrayal."

She watched Garrett contemplate her words for a moment, denial softening into consideration. "I see some truth in what you say."

"So we have taken up our fathers' battles, you and I," Leandra finished.

Garrett nodded and went on. "I covet the honor of the Bernays. You fight to protect Lyonesse. Are you willing to endanger your homeland and your father?"

"Never!" Slowly Leandra shook her head. Her tears freshened as her loss struck her anew. "No. Nor do you wish to give up the honor of the Bernays."

"I'm not being selfish, Leandra. Do you know what happens to illicit lovers—to runaways? They are never received in any respectable household again. Never. Sometimes the Church excommunicates them. They lose their home, their family, their friends. They are condemned to wander. They belong nowhere. Do you understand what I am saying, Leandra? The price is *too high*. I have paid once. I could again. But I would never ask that of you."

Leandra bit her lip, refusing to shed more tears. Like it or not, she understood what he was saying. Her heartache became a burning pain.

Garrett squeezed her hands again. "Are you brave enough to face this? Will you come with me, or shall I go for the antidote alone? Once we have it, the rest will be easy. There'll be no hurt. No dishonesty. We will be a loyal knight and a lord's faithful lady. Maybe we won't even remember last night."

Leandra met his persuasive gaze. She had no desire to forget about their night together. She would never willingly give up the memory of their blending of hearts and bodies.

She knew with the instinct that women are born with that there was no turning back. Nothing would ever be the same between them, as much as Garrett wished it. Regardless of how many reasons he could give. She loved him and he loved her. Their relationship was forever changed.

"We'll go together," she said at last. "You have a plan? You know where we can get an antidote?"

"I know an old alchemist not far from Tremelyn," Garrett said. "He has traveled far, is learned, and has many ancient books of spells and alchemy. I think he might be able to help us."

Confidently, Garrett kissed her hands and stood up. "Now dress while I see to our accounts and hiring a horse for you."

The ride exhausted Leandra, but she never complained. Garrett was an attentive escort. He stopped frequently to allow her to rest, and he hovered over her at every crossroad inn, checking the tack on her horse and ordering hot food and refreshment. Leandra appreciated his concern. When their eyes met, she knew without a word from him that he still loved her as much as he had the night before. That knowledge comforted her, but she sensed an eagerness in him to rejoin the safe company of Wystan, Father John, and Brenna in the camp on the Tamar.

With her quiet compliance, she told him that she understood his need to fulfill his duties and to uphold his honor. She respected that.

But as they rode, she began to envy what she saw as Garrett's content. In his mind things were very clear. He'd laid a battle plan, resolving for himself the conflict that still weighed heavy in her heart. She had no more desire than he to betray Reginald, but she believed that freeing themselves was going to be harder than Garrett foretold.

They arrived at the camp on the Tamar River late and unannounced. Fires were burning even though daylight lingered on the horizon. As soon as word of their arrival was called out, Brenna came running from her silken pavilion with her arms wide open and tears streaming down her face.

"Cousin, cousin," she cried, flying at Leandra's horse so that the mare shied. "Are you all right?"

Astonished, Leandra slipped from the frightened horse to console Brenna. Sweet Mother of God, what had happened? she wondered. "What is it? What's the trouble, Brenna?"

"Nothing, nothing," Brenna wept. "I'm so glad you are well and so happy to see you. We've never really been apart until now."

Leandra allowed her cousin to wrap her in a heartfelt embrace and realized that Brenna was right. As children they'd never been separated. The anger Leandra suffered over the potion trickled away in the face of Brenna's obvious distress over her absence and pleasure in her return.

Leandra looked around to see that Garrett was similarly occupied with Wystan, who also rushed to him as soon as their arrival was known. Father John appeared, an expression of pleasure mixed with apprehension on his face. She and Garrett exchanged understanding looks. They each had duties to fulfill, people's needs to see to. Arm in arm with her cousin, Leandra strolled into the ladies' pavilion, where she set about finding out what was afoot.

"Wystan's been awful," Brenna complained as she brought Leandra a pillow to sit on in an uncharacteristic gesture of servitude. "How's this? I have some wine here and bread and cheese. You must be starved. You look so thin and pale. And you're so quiet. Have you recovered? Didn't Sir Perfect see that you were attended by a good physician?"

"I'm fine." Leandra nibbled on the bread and sipped the wine. Garrett was probably listening to similar words of complaint from Wystan. Then she wondered where this sudden instinctive knowledge of Garrett came from.

"But you look so distracted, Leandra. Why that puzzled smile? There's something different about you."

Leandra shook her head to free herself of sweet, distracting thoughts. "I'm fine, really. Tell me, why is Wystan such a problem?"

"Oh, you know. He's like his brother."

"Really?"

"Well, not exactly. He hated being left behind when Sir Garrett rode off after you. He thinks ill of me because I told you and Garrett that I gave you the love potion." Brenna's voice rose a pitch and she began to wring her hands. "He won't forgive me, even though I told him you and Sir Garrett weren't upset about it. I told him you said you experienced no effects. But he wouldn't believe me. It's not fair."

Then Brenna heaved an enormous sob, filled with unspeakable misery. "He blames your illness and Sir Garrett's absence on me and the potion. He's acted so strangely, almost suspicious, as if you two were going to become forbidden lovers."

Leandra choked on the dry bread and took a sip of wine to wash away the cough.

Brenna babbled on about daily messengers to and from Tremelyn. Lord Reginald sent notes of concern and offers of medicines and more men-at-arms. But Wystan refused them and assured the earl that Garrett had matters in control. Brenna paused to gulp for a breath before chattering on about passersby on their way to Tremelyn to attend the wedding. "It seems like all of the countryside is traveling to join the Earl of Tremelyn in celebrating his marriage." Brenna's face brightened at the prospect of festivities. She wiped her tears away on her sleeve. "You know who came riding by only this morning? Sir Leofric and some relatives. He had one arm wrapped in a bandage. He told some story about being injured when he slayed a wild boar. Do you believe that? I didn't think he'd come to the wedding after the dreadful stir he made at Lyonesse. But he said he's on his way to Tremelyn to join the wedding guests there."

Chapter 17

Leandra closed her eyes, willing herself to be calm.

"Leofric has no pride," Brenna babbled. "What rejected suitor would want to appear at the wedding? You really don't look well, cousin."

"Unless he intends to bait the bride," Leandra said. "I'll be fine." Light-headedness overwhelmed her, and she had to set her goblet down and lie back on the pillows. The two men-at-arms who witnessed the combat between Garrett and Leofric had been sworn to secrecy. She and Garrett agreed to say nothing about the fight with Leofric, but they assumed they would hear no more from him. Surely after the kidnapping attempt he would not have the courage to present himself at Tremelyn. "Leofric knows about the potion," she said.

Brenna touched Leandra's hand. "I'm sorry, cousin. Truly, I'm sorry for all the trouble I caused. I never really thought you and Sir Perfect would . . . I mean, have you . . . ? 'Twas all in jest."

"Everything will be well soon," Leandra whispered, trying to reassure her cousin of an outcome she herself was uncertain of. Maybe Garrett was right. The only thing to do was to search out an antidote. Then no matter what Leofric said or did, they would be free. They could stand before Leofric, Reginald, and even Father John, and honorably vow that they did not love each other.

"Where is the silver phial that contained the potion?"

"Why?" Brenna hesitated, then took a phial from the cuff of her surcoat and held it up to the lamplight. "I have it here. Why do you want it?"

"I want to take the phial." Leandra told Brenna of Garrett's plan to visit the alchemist. "Maybe the residue in the container will help him discover the antidote."

"But if you have noticed no effects, why do you want an antidote?" Brenna asked. She turned away, oddly absorbed in picking at her skirt.

"Because Sir Garrett and I have at last come under the spell," Leandra said, renewed anger with her cousin suddenly filling her. "Look at me, Brenna. Isn't this what you thought would be so funny when you fixed our wine in Penzance?"

"No!" Brenna cried, her voice full of a remorse that Leandra knew did not come easily to her. Fresh tears large as raindrops poured down Brenna's cheeks. "Never. I never expected anything this ghastly." She shook her head, flinging huge tears onto the silken pillows, refusing to meet Leandra's eyes. "Even Wystan hates me."

Leandra softened and slipped a comforting arm around her cousin. It was impossible to remain angry with someone who truly regretted her actions. "The trip to the alchemist will set everything right. Maybe then Wystan will have a change of heart."

"Thomas Charnock is a skilled alchemist very learned and dedicated to the study of his art," Garrett said as he and Leandra rode side by side toward Exeter two days later.

He wore leather chausses and a light wool tunic, like an ordinary soldier—a handsome ordinary soldier, Leandra mused with a half smile on her lips. Likewise, she was dressed like a common soldier's wife, in a plain green gown.

She was delighted to have Garrett to herself again. "How did you meet this distinguished alchemist?"

"I sought him out about my seasickness when I was about to undertake my first voyage to France." He chuckled. "You see, I knew even then that I'd never be able to make the channel crossing without some help."

They laughed companionably and rode on. Tom, in the

guise of a groom, followed them as protection against outlaws.

The day before, the entire Tremelyn party had traveled. By mutual consent, Leandra and Garrett kept their distance from each other. Except once when they consulted briefly with Wystan and Brenna. Wystan accused Brenna of being a traitor and refused to be more than coolly civil to her.

"That's not fair," a tearful Brenna had wailed. "You'll see."

Garrett simply shook his head and, without meeting Leandra's gaze, said in an enigmatic tone, "Let them be. If they are going to love, they will."

After that, amid the company of a moping Brenna, a stoic Wystan, the churchmen, and the half-dozen men-at-arms, Garrett and Leandra managed easily to keep apart. But the temptation to seek each other out with their eyes proved to be more difficult to overcome.

She would urge her horse, resisting the desire to look toward him. But she failed every time. She would always catch his eye, and there in the blue depths she would find his acknowledgment of their secret devotion.

It warmed her, glimmered about her head and shoulders, she feared, like the radiance painted around the saints in the church. Loving and being loved were new delights, a joy she would never have been able to imagine even through a lifetime of listening to love songs and poems.

Knowing someone cared brightened the colors of the world and sweetened the scents on the wind. It lengthened her patience and lightened her heart. Garrett's love made her smile.

She simply couldn't help it: the corners of her mouth tipped upward. Often, when he didn't think anyone was watching, Garrett smiled back. If the others noticed her new glow or their loving exchanges, no one said so.

When the Tremelyn group settled in another camp, Leandra and Garrett rode toward Exeter on the excuse that she'd promised to see to the delivery of a letter from her father to a Benedictine friend at the priory. She had indeed made such a promise, never dreaming that she would actually go to Exeter herself in search of a love potion antidote.

"But I thought an alchemist made gold from base metals, not remedies," Leandra said as they rode along under a clear sky. "My teacher, Mother Mary Elizabeth, says alchemists are in league with the devil."

"No more than your Vivian," Garrett said with a sidelong glance that challenged Mother Mary Elizabeth's words. "But a successful alchemist can make gold. Master Thomas explained it all to me then. First he creates the perfect white pebble, which eventually turns into the reddish philosopher's stone. With that he can cure human disease as well as turn ordinary metal into gold. Some say a good philosopher's stone can even restore a man's youth. Surely it works on love potions, too."

"Did it help your seasickness?" She wondered what it was that gave Garrett so much confidence in Thomas Charnock's skills.

"No, he'd not made the stone then, but he was certain that he was close." Garrett turned to her and smiled, a bittersweet curve of his lips, and his eyes took on a sorrowful smoky blue. "Don't fret. I'm sure he will help us."

As they neared the prosperous riverside town of Exeter, traffic on the road grew more frequent and diverse. Here the westernmost Roman road led east to London. Leandra stared about her, lost in watching the people, trusting her horse to follow Garrett's lead. Peddlers passed, stooped under their load of wares. Richly garbed merchants rode at the head of caravans of pack mules. Shepherds herded flocks of newly shorn sheep.

Other travelers like themselves hurried along the road. Leandra stared at the ladies' dresses and at the men. None were nearly so handsome as Garrett. She observed that the other ladies in the crowd noticed Garrett's good looks, too.

Dust rose from beneath the many hooves. Leandra sneezed and urged her mare on. Even Fair Day at Lyonesse was never like this: so noisy and colorful, full of new and mysterious costumes and smells.

Farther along, they entered the city gate, where a gaily

decorated wagon provided a stage for a minstrel and players. A boisterous crowd was gathered about the wagon. Their masked enactment of *Reynard the Fox* caught Leandra's eye. She forgot about her horse and Garrett and became so engrossed in the players' exaggerated gestures and falsetto voices that she didn't realize she was left behind until Garrett called her name. Tom took her mare's bridle and led them on.

"Leandra?" Garrett's exasperation drew her attention immediately. He smiled, a strained but patient smile. "If we're to be back at camp tonight, we cannot tarry. There will be players at your wedding. You can watch then until your heart is content."

She frowned at his back, almost ready to tell him that her heart was content right this moment, amid this crowd and dust, with him at her side and the better part of the day stretching ahead of them. But that answer served no purpose. She settled for trying to remember details of the play to describe to Brenna.

Inside the gate to the north of them rose the red stone castle of the city, Rougemont, and ahead of them soared the twin square Norman towers of the nearly completed Exeter Cathedral. The way narrowed between the two-story stone and timber houses, and streets led off one side of the way, then off to the other. Leandra had never seen so many lanes. "Do you know the way?" she asked. "Exeter must be as big as London."

Garrett glanced at her in surprise, then laughed. "Oh, London streets go on and on and on. Exeter is a small city. Sir Thomas's dwelling isn't far from the cathedral, as I recall."

Leandra gave up trying to make sense of the maze. Even Penzance was not this large and confusing.

They left the horses with Tom at the White Hart Inn. Down a shaded narrow way, no wider than the length of a longbow and even narrower above their heads, where the houses leaned toward each other, they found the alchemist's laboratory.

A noxious odor issued from the open doorway.

"I think this is it," Garrett said, stopping before an ordinary two-story dwelling that looked much like the others crowded next to it. Leandra noted that the front window was heavily draped and the windows above were shuttered even on so sunny a day. The children playing in the water that trickled down the street sniffed the air, mumbled among themselves, and scampered away.

Leandra tried to give Garrett a pleased smile, but the odor was so strong that she was forced to put her perfumed sleeve to her nose to fend off the sting. Her eyes teared.

"I know," Garrett said with an expression of apology. "It smelled bad to me the first time, too."

He knocked on the wooden door frame. "Master Charnock?"

A thin, angry voice bellowed something inarticulate from the bowels of the darkness.

A boy with large front teeth appeared at the door. He brushed his hood back from his forehead and looked Garrett up and down before asking pointedly, "Who's calling?"

Garrett gave his name and offered the boy a coin. "Tell Master Charnock I knew him when he was nearing the creation of the white pebble."

The boy eyed him with renewed curiosity, then disappeared into the gloom of the house. Leandra and Garrett waited in apprehensive silence. Voices rumbled within. Above, they heard the shutters thrown open. Soon the boy reappeared and beckoned them into the murky depths.

Garrett took Leandra's hand, and she followed him into the keeping room, still blinking away tears. But fresh air was quickly carrying away the smell.

"Garrett Bernay?" The greeting came from a tall, angular man, wearing spectacles, stooped over a table of books. His undisciplined iron-gray beard bobbed as he spoke. His long brown surcoat, much too heavy for the weather, was streaked with stains. "*Sir* Garrett Bernay? You have grown, my boy, and made your mark on the world. Knighthood?" The old man smiled, offered his hand, and removed his spectacles.

Garrett strode forward to accept the hearty handshake.

They fell to exchanging greetings and news, leaving Leandra to look about her as her eyes adjusted to the darkness. Drawers, cupboards, and assorted cubbyholes lined the wall—each filled with scrolls, books, jars, and other secrets. The sooty dust of tallow candles layered everything.

From their conversation, she learned that Master Thomas had yet to perfect the philospher's stone which was Garrett's hope of an antidote.

"But I've learned much since you visited me, Garrett," Master Thomas was saying. "In my experiments I found that the mixture in my retort changed almost daily. Sometimes it was dark and smelly, and I despaired of ever reaching my goal. Then, other days, the substance would be white and at times almost clear. I would think I was near . . . that I had merely made some miscalculation . . . and I would study even harder. But, alas, over time I have learned that the substance merely reflects my moods."

Leandra stepped closer to the shelves to read the spines of the books and the labels of the jars. Some were marked with strange symbols, characters like the Greek alphabet she'd studied. But others were even stranger, more exotic, more ancient—triangles with horns, circles with T tops, flatbottomed W's, and L-footed H's. The strange shapes made her shiver. Her father and Mother Mary Elizabeth would disapprove of her looking at such things. Leandra clasped her hands behind her back. Her palms itched to take the strange tomes from the shelves and browse through their mysteries and riddles.

A noise from the room beyond drew her away from the books. Through the doorway that led even deeper into the house, she glimpsed an oven. Firelight flickered against glass shapes unlike any she'd ever seen, round-bellied with bent necks. On an odd-step stove sat tiers of copper pots draining down into other copper pots.

"For distillations, my lady," Master Charnock said, suddenly looming at Leandra's shoulder. "So, Garrett, you have acquired a lady, too. 'Tis my pleasure to meet you, Lady Bernay. Here, let me move this. Sit, please. My boy is bringing us ale."

Leandra, who'd agreed reluctantly to let Garrett do the

talking, glanced uneasily at him as she took the chair Master Thomas cleared for her. He dropped the manuscripts on his table, and dust swirled into a golden cloud, glittering in the shaft of sunlight that slanted through the doorway.

"That's the reason we are here, Master Thomas," Garrett said, resting a hip on the arm of Leandra's chair. He put an arm along its back in a gesture both familiar and protective. Leandra closed her eyes, pretending that she was his lady and that his arm belonged there.

"It's a long story, Master Thomas," Garrett said. "To put it simply, the lady and I have been given a love potion. She is promised to another. We have come to you in search of an antidote."

"You want a what? An antidote to a love potion?" Master Thomas shook his head. "I don't ordinarily deal in love potions, Garrett."

"We must break the spell, Thomas," Garrett said. "'Tis no ordinary potion."

"Vivian of the Forest brewed it," Leandra added.

"I thought with all your books and your knowledge, maybe you could help us," Garrett said.

"If it will help, I have the phial that held the potion right here," Leandra said. She took the silver container from the leather purse tied to her girdle. "I brought it because I thought the phial might contain some clue to help you determine what it is."

"Ah! Clever. Clever." Master Thomas cast Garrett an appreciative glance as if to compliment him on his lady before taking the phial from Leandra. He unstoppered the container and sniffed it, staring off into the murky air, his thoughts clearly sorting through possibilities.

He shook his head, then wiped the opening with his forefinger and sampled the residue, his mouth moving in search of other likelihoods. "Hmm. Not unlike a remedy for stomach ailments. Yes, I suppose there might be a relationship between stomach ailments and love." Thomas chuckled to himself.

A chill suddenly settled over Leandra. She didn't like his comparison.

Garrett smiled tolerantly at the old alchemist and touched her shoulder sympathetically. "Our experience indicates the potion definitely affects the heart."

"A potion did this to you?" he said. "Put that soft look in your eyes when you gaze at each other? I thought you were newlyweds. Are you certain you wish to do away with this bond you have found? Even if it came from a bottle, love is a rarer blessing than most people think."

"We must, Thomas. We have other obligations, unyielding ones," Garrett said. "We need an antidote to set us free to fulfill them."

Thomas nodded gravely. "You say Vivian of the Forest brewed this? Indeed. Her remedies are known to be most powerful. I've never heard of her love potions. I don't know. But I have one book . . . here."

The boy brought the ale. Master Thomas spent the next hour going through a large, red leather-bound book he took from his bookshelves. Garrett joined him at the table, and Leandra pulled her chair closer.

"No, this wouldn't do. Nor that. This one is for warts. That is for cattle breeding. Here? No." Thomas turned a page and read on. When he exhausted that book, he sought another—a green one this time.

On the floor the small shaft of sunlight from the open door vanished. Leandra looked to Garrett, whose face was wearing long. She clasped her hands in her lap, tucked her feet under the chair and waited, knowing that from moment to passing moment their chances of an antidote were fading.

Master Thomas shook his head and closed the book. "I would like to help you and your lady, Garrett, but I have nothing here. You say Vivian can't help you unless you return to Lyonesse?"

Leandra found herself shaking her head along with her knight. "There is no time before the wedding."

"And you, Garrett, I suppose, don't wish to cross the sea again," Master Thomas supplied with an ironic smile. "I don't know what to tell you."

"Do love potions wear off?" Garrett asked with an uneasy glance in Leandra's direction.

"The ordinary ones wear off by the next morning," Master Thomas said. "Sometimes even in a few hours, to the regret of many a man and maid. But I can see that this is no ordinary spell."

Garrett rose from his chair. "The sun rides low in the sky. We must go." He took Leandra's hand. She could feel his disappointment spreading into her own body, smothering the happiness that had been hers that morning.

"I will continue to search, Garrett," Master Thomas said. "But I can promise nothing."

They said their farewells to the old alchemist and his boy and rode out of the city gate in sober silence. The players were acting a different play. A family of jugglers was entertaining a crowd near the city wall, but Leandra didn't have the heart to take interest in them now. They rode west toward camp.

The sun soon dropped out of sight, but spring twilight still lingered and would light the way for hours yet. Garrett suggested that they stop to rest the horses. But he sent Tom on to announce their return.

Near a pleasant brook Garrett helped her off her horse and, speaking in quiet tones, gave her his plain cloak. He suggested where to place it beneath some trees so they might sit while the horses rested.

No other travelers were in sight. They had not spoken since leaving Exeter. Leandra was not surprised. What was there to say? They were still bound by the potion, and release seemed unlikely.

Leandra spread out the cloak and sat down to unpack the wine, cold meat, and bread that Brenna had packed for them. She wasn't hungry, and when Garrett joined her, he also refused the food. He sat, legs drawn up and elbows resting on knees, and stared into space.

The day was still warm. Leandra pulled off her wimple and loosened her braid to cool herself. She turned away from Garrett, unable to witness his disappointment and her own. She wanted desperately to know what he was thinking, yet she was afraid to ask.

Uncertainly, she took the container from her purse where

she'd put it when Master Thomas returned it to her. She glanced into his face to measure his mood. His mouth was tight and his eyes glistened a hard and bitter blue.

The glint of the silver phial caught his eye. His roar shook her. He grabbed the tiny vessel, leapt up from the cloak, strode to the stream, muttering curses that would have scorched a groom's ears. Leandra didn't understand the words, but she heard the outrage. Defiant. Dark. Despairing. Frightened for his peace of mind, she ran to his side.

She barely reached him when he brought back his powerful arm, nearly striking her. She staggered backward. With all his might Garrett hurled the phial into the stream. Water spumed. The offending container vanished, swallowed in eddies and bubbles. He stared after it as she did.

An absurd satisfaction spread over Leandra. It was only a harmless container, empty, but she was glad the thing was gone, ignobly drowned in cold waters, to be washed into the sea where it would lie among fishes, never to trouble anyone again. The love potion phial was no more.

She found herself seeking Garrett's face again, thinking of his despair, wanting to bear his pain, and knowing all the time that was impossible. The only thing that kept her from touching him was her certainty that he must blame her. The potion was hers.

Her heart ached. She knew he'd insisted on believing that their dilemma would be solved, that he could triumph over this adversity as he had so many others in his life. But this time was different. Confronting the impossibility of their plight brought numbing sorrow. After the numbness came heavy sadness and then raw anger. He faced all that now, and she was helpless to ease his pain.

"Master Thomas did his best for us," Leandra said, anxious to hear his voice, to know what he was feeling.

"I know," Garrett muttered, looking up at the twilight sky, refusing to face her.

"What do we do now?" she asked, half expecting him to turn on her like the avenging angel she'd called up when she'd offered him a bribe to stay in Lyonesse. The anger was there, if not on his face, in his stance—tense, hard, and rippling with heat.

"We do our best to forget about the potion, about May Day, and the antidote, and we do our best to serve Reginald," Garrett said, his voice low and guttural.

"Yes," Leandra agreed reluctantly. "I didn't know it was possible to want two things so impossibly opposed."

"Nor I." Finally Garrett gathered enough control of himself to look down at the stream where the phial had disappeared.

He tried to remember that Leandra was hurting, at least as much as he was. Theirs was an invisible pain that offered no wounds, no blood, nor missing limb as evidence. Yet to him it was a ripping apart as surely as if he was being stretched on a torture rack. He didn't know what to do about it—how to ease his pain or hers.

Garrett glanced at her. She shed no tears, but that did not surprise him. His lioness would face her fate as bravely as any warrior. When she looked up at him again, they reached for each other.

She slipped her arms around his neck and, with a look of tenderness and compassion, pressed her lips against his.

The first wonder of her willingness almost blinded Garrett to the doom that hung over them. He pulled her down onto the grassy bank, loosening the laces of her gown as they sank to their knees.

The neckline opened. Gown and shift slipped away, baring her throat and her shoulders and releasing her eager breasts. He told her of his love and his pain not in words, but with his lips along each collarbone, across the fullness of each breast, against her heart. The powerful pleasure of her quickening shuddered through him.

Tenderly, he cushioned her head from the hard ground with one hand, and with the other, protected her bare back from the scratchy grass. He brushed his lips across the smooth swell of her breasts and kissed the damp valley between. He continued, drawing her gown down around her waist. He tasted her, losing himself in the pleasure of the tight, warm bud of her breast against his tongue—the pressure of her fingertips working his scalp. Her love filled him, left no room for his anger, crowded out his anger and frustration. Garrett wanted to exist nowhere else in the world but here in her arms.

Her heart thrummed strong and swift against his cheek. Her breath ran rapid and hungry against his ear. She drew him closer. The heat of her lips against his brow offered her own passion, told of her pain. He wanted to take it from her. He longed to promise her a future, give happiness, but there was none.

The sweet familiar scent of her filled him with need. He nuzzled her stomach and kissed her navel, long and well. Then he rested his head against her belly, gasping for breath, searching for the strength to do the honorable thing.

Finally Garrett rolled to his back, spreading his hand across her bottom to pull her atop his body, crushing her to him, aching to make her part of him, lacing his fingers through her hair, longing to taste her forever, accepting her kisses and treasuring the words of love she murmured against his throat. All the time, his conscience would not allow him to forget that they were doomed.

Leandra was a passionate woman, and so new to love-making that Garrett knew he must take responsibility. With a steely will he put her away from him. He took a deep breath of cool night air, trying to clear his head.

If he breached the protection of her skirts, if he touched her center again and she opened to him, he knew there would be no stopping. His body and heart cried out in sore need, louder than ever, but he could never lead them close to union again and stop.

He pushed her away and began to rearrange her gown, drawing the bodice over her breasts, covering temptation. She protested. He silenced her with a finger to her lips. "For the first time in my life, I'm sorry I was born a Bernay," Garrett said. "I wish I had been born a humble freeman."

"Why?" Leandra asked. Surprise erased the sadness from her face. Her eyes, wide and clear like liquid emeralds, blinked in disbelief.

"Because if we were simple people, say I were a freeman

and you a miller's daughter, then no one would care whom we married. We'd have no family honor at stake. Lyonesse's safety would not rest in your hands. Lord Reginald would have little care about us."

Leandra offered him a sad smile. "'Tis a nice wish. When I was a little girl, I liked to make wishes. But when I grew older, I learned that wishing for the impossible brings only frustration. 'Tis better to spend the effort wishing on things that are real and can be changed."

Garrett took her hand and kissed it. "What a funny, solemn child you must have been, Leandra. As you say, no more wishing."

Leandra turned away and began to dress herself. "No course is left to us but dishonesty?"

"But only for a short while," Garrett said. "First, I will get your betrothal ring back. Yes, I know. Wystan told me about Leofric. I'm certain he will have that ring with him. He's an opportunist. He may be thinking he can do something with it. As soon as the wedding and the festivities are over, Wystan and I will leave for France to join King Edward's forces. Reginald will think nothing of my departure. I planned the journey before he sent me to escort you."

"I would have you safe near me at Tremelyn."

"'Twould be impossible," Garrett said. His heart eased a little, knowing that she didn't want him to leave. "I could not live day in and day out watching you and . . . Leandra, this is the last time we will be alone together. I say that not only because it is so, but because it *must* be so. We cannot chance being alone together again."

Leandra turned to him, a question in her eyes, astonishment on her face. "But tonight, we could—"

Garrett shook his head. "Turn. I will help you dress." She did as he bid and lifted her hair so that he could see what he was doing. Impulsively, Garrett kissed the back of her neck, quick and light on the pale skin always hidden by her tresses. She gasped and shuddered.

He would not deceive himself nor her. "As much as we may wish otherwise, 'tis impossible to steal an eternity of loving in one twilight, sweeting."

Quickly then, before any other forbidden thoughts overpowered him, Garrett began to knot the laces.

Despite the lateness of the hour, fires blazed and torches flared against the darkness when Leandra and Garrett rode into camp. Leandra was surprised to see Wystan standing with the guard, awaiting them. He was breathless. Agitation and relief played across his young features when they drew near.

"Lord Reginald rode into camp today," Wystan announced without preamble. He took the bridle of his brother's horse while Garrett dismounted. "He was most kind, but he wanted to see his bride. His disappointment was obvious when he found she wasn't here. Lady Brenna and I told him about your delivering the letter. I think he accepted the excuse, but he was not pleased."

Leandra listened as Garrett helped her from her horse. She'd never expected Reginald to come looking for her. Garrett's expression remained unreadable, and he let his hand linger possessively on her waist. As soon as her feet were on the ground, he touched her cheek so that she turned to him, and he studied her face in the glow of the torchlight.

"Reginald is ready to claim his bride," Garrett whispered before anyone stepped close enough to hear or observe them closely. "This must be our farewell."

"I'll never be ready to lose you," she murmured. She wanted to kiss him but knew she didn't dare in front of his brother and Father John.

"From now on we are no longer lovers," Garrett said, releasing her abruptly. Leandra sagged against the horse to steady herself. The day was ending too soon for her. Reality was closing in. Garrett went on. "Tomorrow I will be the Earl of Tremelyn's knight, and you will be his betrothed. No more."

Faced with the quiet pain in Garrett's face, Leandra wanted to say something comforting, something to ease the dull ache. But there were no such words. Without saying any more, Garrett led their horses away.

"Oh, Leandra, thank heavens you've returned," Brenna

called, peeking out of her pavilion. Wrapped in a cloak, she brushed past Wystan, clearly ignoring him, and reached for Leandra's arm. "Lord Reginald was here today. Did Wystan tell you? Are you tired? Are you hungry? Did you get it? The antidote, I mean. Come into the tent and tell me."

Leandra allowed Brenna to drag her off to the pavilion.

"You are right about Lord Reginald's eyes," Brenna said, excitement in her voice and interest bright on her features. "Big brown eyes so nice. But, oh, can he frown. He has a mouth that can be hard as iron when he is displeased. He was displeased that you and Garrett weren't here, Leandra. He's not in a mood to be put off any longer. I'm afraid he's beginning to think something is wrong."

Leandra said nothing. She took off Garrett's cloak and folded it neatly, lovingly. She'd send Brenna to return it in the morning. Slowly she sat down on the cushions and tried to listen to what Brenna said, to make sense of her cousin's words and her distress. Leandra knew she should be concerned about Reginald, but her thoughts remained with Garrett, with his decision that they should not be alone together again, that he would leave her. The resolution made perfect sense, but she wanted to object to it, to think of some reason why they should be able to have a few moments, no matter how short and how painful, to be together.

"Did you find it?" Brenna asked, shaking Leandra's arm to break into her thoughts. "Did you find the antidote?"

"What? The antidote?" Leandra looked at her cousin, who leaned forward, regarding her with surprising eagerness, as if the future of the world depended on her answer. Brenna's concern touched Leandra, and she took Brenna's hand. Her cousin seemed truly sorry for the trouble she'd caused. Leandra bit back a bitter reply. "No, we found no antidote. Master Thomas couldn't help us."

"Oh, no." Brenna sat back and chewed on her lip in uncharacteristic anxiety. "I wish he had. I mean, that would have been the perfect answer."

"Garrett was so angry that he threw the phial into a stream along the way," Leandra said. " 'Twould be best for us stay away from him."

"You mean *I* should stay away from him," Brenna translated, that resentful, rebellious gleam returning to her dark eyes. Her remorse seemed forgotten.

"He has a right to be angry, you know," Leandra said. "What you did was very unfair. If Garrett were not such a strong, honorable man, it could have spelled disaster for both of us. And you, too."

"I know." Brenna's bottom lip began to tremble as it always did before the tears rolled down her cheek. She hung her head and clasped her hands in a penitent gesture that made Leandra feel guilty for her angry reply. Yet Leandra found herself eyeing her cousin suspiciously, uncertain whether Brenna truly felt as dejected as she looked.

"We'll arrive at Tremelyn tomorrow, and amid the guests and the festivities, it won't be difficult to stay away from Sir Garrett," Leandra said, hoping that Brenna was really taking all this to heart. "Stay out of Sir Leofric's company as well. He's planning something. I just wish I knew what it was."

Chapter 18

Blessed Mother," Brenna gasped, her gray eyes wide and her mouth gaping as they rode into view of Tremelyn for the first time. "'Tis bigger by two times than Lyonesse with the village."

Blue and white swallow-tailed pennons fluttered in welcome from all towers of the earl's castle. Leandra reined in her horse alongside Brenna's to stare at the white, carved stone battlements gleaming in the spring sun.

A prosperous village spread itself at the foot of the castle mount. From where they halted their horses, Leandra could look down on cobbled streets winding between half-timber houses. A stone Norman church loomed on one side of the market square, and the water-powered mill stood beside a bubbling stream just beyond the town wall.

'Twas grander than anything Leandra had expected to rule over.

"Just think, cousin." Brenna turned a new look of appreciation on Leandra. "You will be lady of it all."

"Countess," Leandra corrected, as much for her own benefit as her cousin's. Once the prospect of bearing that title thrilled her. Today, after a sleepless night with Garrett's farewell echoing through her dreams, she could only look at that imposing castle and think of herself as a prisoner.

"Countess," Brenna echoed thoughtfully. "Leandra, Countess of Tremelyn. That sounds lofty."

To Leandra, it sounded cold and haughty, not at all how she wanted to be known for the rest of her life. It sounded like the name of another woman, a stranger, a lady of years with sharp lines at the corner of her eyes and lips pressed thin. A dry woman, cold and unspeakably alone.

Leandra shivered.

"Well, if Lord Reginald is really as eager to see you as he would have us believe yesterday, he will ride out to meet you," Brenna said, her gaze locked on the castle gate. "Not wait until we have paraded through the streets."

Ahead of them riders jostled about and horses stamped hooves, but the line didn't move forward.

Brenna leaned out from her saddle to spy the trouble. "Here he comes, Sir Perfect. Inspection time."

Leandra watched Garrett, with Wystan at his side, ride back down the line, his mouth set in a forbidding line, his gaze flicking over each man and horse, instantly spotting out-of-place tack, sloppy tunics, unpolished armor. He snapped orders to each offender. The deep furrow in his brow made it clear that he would tolerate no excuse.

When he reached Leandra and Brenna, he reined in his charger. Leandra met his sober, demanding gaze with silence. In the day since their trip to Exeter, a change had come over him. He'd become a faultless escort: cool, courteous, and distant. But Leandra found no humor in his eyes, no hint of a smile on his lips. Though she understood what he was doing, she heartily disliked it.

He greeted her and Brenna with a grudging nod. "Ladies. Do you wish to pause to refresh yourselves before your ride through the village and into the castle? The people will line the way to see their new lady."

His frown was so daunting. Did she look that bad? Leandra almost raised her hand to smooth her braid before she realized what she was doing. She glared back at him and inwardly cursed the heat of embarrassment that burned in her cheeks. She was not to be ordered about like one of his men.

"Has a wart grown on my nose since I looked in my mirror this morning?" she snapped.

Only Brenna laughed. Wystan paled.

Garrett's frown deepened and his voice sharpened. "No,

my lady. I wished only to offer you the opportunity to prepare yourself to meet your betrothed."

"So kind of you, sir, but there is no need." Leandra purposely turned away from his grim countenance to look at the castle. She could be as stiff and cool as he. "I'm quite ready to meet Lord Reginald. I see no reason to delay."

Then, as if on some signal in Leandra's words, a trumpet fanfare blared from the castle's battlements. The town gates parted and a flock of riders spilled forth in a bright flurry of blue banners and gay finery. Jewels flashed in the sun, and the bells of caparisoned horses jingled.

"'Tis him," Brenna cried, bouncing in her saddle like an excited child. "And all his nobles. See? Lord Reginald rides at the head on the white horse. Look how tall he is. Square-shouldered for such an old man, I think. Lord, have mercy, I hope he likes you, Leandra."

Garrett glared at Brenna, the venom in his expression so potent that Leandra almost threw herself between the two. Even in her excitement, Brenna saw the dangerous gaze and took the hint, shrinking back into her saddle, her mouth clamping shut.

Without another word, Garrett rode away to hail his liege lord.

As Leandra watched the two men, she fingered the ring she and Brenna had found among their few jewels to wear in place of her betrothal ring. Meeting Lord Reginald could not be put off much longer. Silently she prayed that he would find her pleasing. She now possessed no potion to ensure the outcome of her marriage. Undoubtedly the vassals were already comparing her to the earl's first countess.

Tall on his horse, the Earl of Tremelyn rode easily, wearing a merry countenance. As the portrait promised, his beard was a distinguished gray and his smiling eyes were a warm brown. Befitting the occasion, his tunic was of rich blue samite, and his white horse was decked in blue and gold. With a tinge of jealous disappointment, Leandra understood Garrett's unswerving loyalty to the man. The Earl of Tremelyn was a lord to be proud of—a worthy seigneur and no doubt a reliable benefactor, to whom any knight would be glad to swear undying fealty. A lord husband to whom any woman would be pleased to pledge her faithfulness.

"Lady Leandra, at last you have arrived," Lord Reginald called to her after giving Garrett only the briefest of greetings. He rode toward her, his voice warm and hearty, full of pleasure. He showed no concern about a formal introduction. "We've been concerned for you. Ah, here is your delightful cousin, Lady Brenna."

He doffed his cap and bowed in an endearingly humble manner, revealing a receding hairline that gave his noble face a broad, intelligent brow. "I trust, Lady Brenna, that you are as well as you were when we last met. Lady Leandra, your cousin entertained me most charmingly yesterday."

Brenna smiled coyly, an unusual maidenly blush staining her cheeks. "'Tis fine to see you again, my lord, and I assure you 'twas my pleasure to play and sing for you."

"I'm so glad you were well-amused, my lord." Leandra cast a quick, uncertain glance at Brenna. Just how had her cousin entertained him? Dancing? Singing? Brenna hadn't bothered to tell her that. "Indeed, I'm sorry I missed meeting you then. But there was an errand—"

"So I understand, for your father," Lord Reginald supplied. "Your daughterly devotion is admirable. But you are here. The festivities can begin in earnest. First, we will ride through the town. The people are eager to see you."

He urged his horse closer and leaned toward Leandra, examining her face at length. Embarrassed by his scrutiny, Leandra looked down at her hands and held her breath. Had a wart indeed popped up on her nose?

He held out his left hand to her, fingers extended. "I wanted you to see that I wear your betrothal ring that Sir Garrett sent ahead. A circle of finely carved oak, 'tis a fitting jewel to come from Lyonesse."

Leandra stared at the ring he wore, suddenly terrified that he would see that the ring she wore was but a poor substitute. "It has meant more to me than you know to wear yours," she mumbled.

"Are you all right, my dear?" He took little interest in the ring she wore. "You look pale and so sober. Are you recovered from your illness?"

"Thank you for your concern, my lord. I'm quite recovered." Leandra remembered that she must smile at him, as clumsy as the expression seemed. She forced a wan curve to her lips. "My color is slow to return. Please lead the way. I'm as eager to greet the people of Tremelyn as they are to see me."

Lord Reginald slapped his thigh and grinned. "That's good to hear." He waved to the party riding behind him: a swarm of feather-capped lords, wimpled ladies, and spur-sporting knights. Their well-fed faces looked so alike to Leandra that she despaired of ever learning all of their names and titles.

One of the party, a rider in purple, lifted a hand in greeting. Sunlight glinted off a gold ring on the little finger of his bare hand and caught Leandra's eye. Startled, she looked closer.

"Hello, lady neighbor," Leofric called, a smirk on his lips.

Leandra nearly choked. He dared to taunt her with the ring? Carefully forcing fear and guilt from her mind, she glanced at Reginald, who turned his horse around to ride at her side.

He smiled at her once more, pride and pleasure obvious in his expression. She forced a smile to her lips in return.

"Shall we show ourselves to the people, my lady?" Lord Reginald asked. "No, Lady Brenna, please don't drop behind. Ride alongside us. The people of Tremelyn will be glad to welcome my bride's kinswoman."

"As you please, my lord." Brenna colored to the roots of her dark hair and grinned broadly at Reginald. Leandra realized the earl had already learned that Brenna hungered to be admired.

"So kind of you, my lord." Leandra urged her horse forward with Reginald's. He held her hand high so that the crowd could see that she was his intended. She felt all eyes upon her, measuring her worthiness. Did they compare her to the other countess?

"Leandra!" hissed Brenna, pinching her arm. "Smile."

Leandra clenched her teeth together and stretched her lips upward in what she hoped looked like a smile. With determination, she avoided looking in Leofric's direction.

Church bells chimed. Through the gate and into the town they rode. People crowded in around their horses, cheering, waving, and tossing flowers. Some walked along, keeping pace with the horses and shouting salutations.

Leandra briefly glanced over her shoulder, looking for Garrett, wondering whether he saw her betrothal ring on Leofric's finger. But like the men-at-arms, he'd fallen back, disappearing in the crush of guests and well-wishers. The guard had done their job.

Leandra faced forward, her expression suddenly stiff with the counterfeit smile. In her heart she died a little. Garrett was already gone from her life, though his departure for France was weeks away. Oh, she would see him again among the wedding guests. He might take her hand and say a few polite words. But there would be no secret exchange between them, he would never dishonor Reginald that way. Was there nothing left to them but this painful fading from each other's lives?

Reginald's grip on her fingers tightened, and Leandra could feel his eyes upon her. She turned to him. He offered her a reassuring pat on the arm meant to give her courage. What a dear man he was. He deserved so much more than she was going to be able to give him. To please him, she tried earnestly for a genuine smile. But she knew no amount of courage or smiling would change the truth in her heart.

Flags, flowers, and boughs of greenery decked the entire town and the castle for the arrival of Leandra of Lyonesse. Brenna craned her neck to see it all. No countess-to-be could expect more, she thought. She frowned at Leandra, wishing her cousin would at least make an attempt to be grateful and to appear happy.

"You are going to have to do better than this," Brenna fussed as soon as the door of their bedchamber closed behind them. But Leandra merely swept past her, sank down onto the bed and buried her face in a pillow.

"You've always been humorless, Leandra, but this is strange, even for you. Are you still ill? If you don't snap out of this, Lord Reginald is going to send us home and seek a more agreeable bride."

Then where would she be? Brenna thought, eyeing her gloomy cousin. Returning to Lyonesse held no appeal and, more importantly, no future.

"Leofric wore my ring. Did you see it?" Leandra muttered without raising her head from the satin-covered cushion. "I just need to rest. I'll think of a way to get it back. Then all will be well."

Brenna put a hand on her cousin's brow. "You're not feverish. In fact, you seem chilled. What are we going to do? Reginald expects us downstairs shortly to receive the guests. Did you see all those people come to the wedding? What an important man he is. Nobles flock to Tremelyn, so 'tis like a little king's court."

"Please get something warm for me from the kitchen," Leandra asked. "I think a warm drink would help. I've just taken a chill again."

"Yes, that's it." Brenna agreed. She wouldn't mind something hot herself. "I'll find the kitchen and get us some refreshment."

"While you're gone, I'll look through your face powders and find something to help my color," Leandra said.

"Here are my pots," Brenna volunteered. "Put some powder on your nose, a little rouge on your cheeks. I'll be right back."

Brenna closed the door softly behind her and paused, torn between concern for her cousin and curiosity about the castle. Leandra was never ill. Something was terribly wrong. But Brenna couldn't bear to be closed up in one room when an entire castle waited to be explored.

At the bottom of the stairs a blue-garbed page—one of the earl's own—politely directed her out the side door of the great hall and on to the half-timber kitchen. Enthralled with her surroundings, Brenna strolled across the exercise yard and past the well, where a group of giggling laundry maids were drawing water. Around the corner, near the front entrance of the great hall, stood a group of nobles, richly attired and fine-looking men. Brenna admired the snugness of their hose and the shortness of their fashionable jackets. Their comeliness brought a smile to her lips. One of the men dressed in yellow caught her eye and grinned encouragingly. Brenna grinned in return. An earl's castle was truly a marvelous place.

Taking heart, the young man swept off his feathered cap and bowed in her direction. Handsome heads turned. "My lady," he said, his invitation plain.

Oh, how Brenna wanted to join them, to toss her head, to quip some clever phrase that would make him and his fellows laugh, but she knew it wasn't proper. Not for the cousin of the bride, who had yet to be introduced to them. When she saw Leofric in the group, she forgot her smile and hurried on. She must think of appearances and Lord Reginald.

The rich, ripe smell of brewing grain reminded her of her real goal. Brenna walked toward the kitchen next to the brewhouse. If she didn't find something to restore Leandra, this adventure could end for both them with a quick, disappointing return to Lyonesse.

Smoke poured from all six kitchen chimneys. At the door she dodged cooks, pages, brewers, soldiers, and grooms— many of whom were seeking the favor of an extra bite of food or a measure of ale.

Heat and the sharp scent of spices engulfed her the moment she stepped into the kitchen. A fire burned in each of the gaping hearths. Lyonesse's kitchen boasted only two hearths, and the second one was built not long ago, upon Leandra's orders, Brenna recalled.

At one hearth a perspiring kitchen scullion cranked a spit heavy with a haunch of venison. In another fireplace kettles steamed over glowing coals. Aromas of baking bread drifted from the brick oven at the far end of the kitchen. Brenna turned slowly, staring in wonder at the number of cooks and the quantity of food being prepared. In the center of the room, at a bed-sized table, women with well-muscled arms floured to the elbow worked over pastry dough.

Suddenly something or someone loomed over her shoulder, a huge presence, casting a dark, ominous shadow. Her hair prickled on the back of her neck.

"Is Leandra unwell? Does she need something? A physician?"

Brenna instantly recognized Sir Garrett's voice, deep and velvet with the quality it took on whenever he spoke of her cousin. She ducked her head, refusing to look at him. Involuntarily her hand fluttered to protect her throat. Ever since she'd told him and Leandra that she'd given them the potion, she'd sensed his great restraint when he was near her. He watched her with keen, narrowed eyes, as though he could barely hold back his hands from encircling her neck and squeezing.

Brenna gulped, but shrugged so as to appear unconcerned. She would give no man the satisfaction of seeing her fear. "She's weary and wants refreshment, that's all."

"Are you certain? Don't mislead me."

"I'm not misleading you," Brenna protested. She peeked at him out of the corner of her eye and spoke out with more courage than she felt. "Do you believe me a liar? Your dislike of me, sir, is unfair. I don't deserve it. Leandra has forgiven me. Why can't you?"

"Leandra is ill because of you, that's why." Sir Garrett glowered at her with fiendishly bright blue eyes. "She suffers because of your spitefulness. I should have sent you back to Lyonesse when you told us what you'd done."

Brenna almost winced, but the threat angered her. "Her ring. She suffers that loss, too. You were her guard. You let Leofric take it from her."

Garrett drew a sharp breath. This time Brenna cowered. His chest broadened and his height seemed to increase by two feet.

"She needs rest and food," she rushed to plead. "As soon as she joins in the festivities, she'll be all right. She loves to hunt. And dance. She'll dance with Reginald, and everything will be all right. You'll see."

"Then see to it," Garrett ordered. With that he turned on

his heel and left the kitchen. Brenna took a deep breath of relief. The aroma of food cooking assailed her again, and she remembered what she was there for. She talked to one of the cooks and was soon bearing a tray heaped with warm bread, honey, an oatmeal pudding, half a meat pie, and fresh milk.

The crowd gathered at the front door of the great hall was drifting across the exercise yard to the side door that Brenna used earlier. Curious and anxious now to get back to Leandra, Brenna skirted the gathering. But soon she realized that the throng blocked her way, so she began to elbow her way through the bodies, edging sideways.

"Pardon me. Pardon, please." She protected the laden tray with her elbows and shoulders. When she'd nearly reached the front, she found herself staring again at Sir Garrett, and this time he loomed over Leofric, who was backed against the stone wall. The heir to Casseldorne smirked, his yellow-brown eyes bright with amusement, the curve of his full lips smug and satisfied.

"You know what I want, Casseldorne," Garrett growled.

"God's teeth," Leofric swore. He shrugged his shoulders and appealed his innocence to the onlookers. "I don't know what you want of me, Bernay. Tell me what it is. Speak out. Why would I withhold anything from you that is rightfully yours? Do you call me a thief?"

Brenna stopped. The tray began to tremble in her hands. Garrett glared at Leofric, his fine features warped with a wrath that even Brenna had never seen before.

She knew that Garrett dared not demand return of the betrothal ring before the crowd, and Leofric knew that, too. No doubt if he were accused of taking the ring, he would reveal that Garrett and Leandra had been given a love potion. Leofric was truly evil, Brenna decided. He needed a niceness potion.

The side door swung open and Lord Reginald strode forth. "Sir Garrett and Sir Leofric. What goes on here? Some new game for amusement, I hope?"

Brenna tightened her grip on the tray and stepped forward. "Begging your pardon, sirs." She forged ahead between the knights and even edged Lord Reginald aside. "I have a tray of food for Lady Leandra, and she bade me to be quick with it." She flashed Reginald a smile as he stepped aside. "She'll be refreshed soon and ready to receive her guests, my lord. Never fear."

"Indeed," Reginald said, offering a chivalrous bow. "We look forward to her company."

Brenna nodded and nearly flew up the stairs, bursting into their bedchamber. She kicked the door closed behind her and paused a moment to catch her breath.

"I was almost trapped between them," Brenna cried, the horror of the possibility suddenly more real than ever. Pottery began to clink on the tray in her trembling hands.

Leandra looked up from where she sat. She'd been sorting through Brenna's chest of cosmetics pots—some from the wise women of Lyonesse and some from peddlers who had called at Castle Lyonesse.

Brenna well remembered selecting each pot, with dreams in her head about the place each one came from. She chose a rouge to give her cheeks and lips color—'twas from Paris, so the peddler claimed—and a fine white powder to take away the shine on her nose. From Italy.

But the silver phial in Leandra's hand made her bite her tongue. Oh, rot me, she cursed inwardly. Leandra would have questions to ask now. She wouldn't like any of the answers.

Slowly, as if she thought it might burn her, Leandra pointed to the phial. She turned it over in her hand gingerly, and it shone deceptively innocent in her palm.

Leandra held the phial near her ear and shook it. "What is in this phial, Brenna? It sounds as if it's full."

Brenna remembered the tray in her hands and set it down on the chest at the foot of the bed.

Leandra pulled out the stopper and touched the colorless residue on the lip of the neck. Thrill prickled in Brenna's belly.

"This is tasteless." Leandra tipped the container slightly

over her palm, and a clear liquid dripped from it. "The container was full. What is this, Brenna?" The impatience in Leandra's husky voice, so seldom sharp, made Brenna uneasy. "Tell me now."

"Well, what does it look like?" Brenna said, holding her head high. "'Tis the love potion."

Chapter 19

Leandra said nothing, just stared at the phial in shock. "I told you all along that I didn't deserve your anger. I never gave you and Sir Garrett the potion."

Brenna waited, certain that when Leandra understood her meaning, she wouldn't be so angry. "'Tis all still there in the phial. You can give it to Lord Reginald just as you planned."

Leandra moved at last, turning to stare at Brenna. "Let me be certain that I understand what you are telling me, cousin." Disbelief faded from her pale face and a frightening, harsh calmness replaced it. Involuntarily, Brenna took a step backward.

Leandra lifted a skeptical brow. "You never truly poured the potion into my wine cup and Garrett's? You only told us so and held up the phial? Is that correct?"

Brenna nodded and held up her hands in innocence. "You see, no real harm done. How was I to know you'd go all cow-eyed over Sir Perfect?"

"But why?" Leandra's voice was but a breathless whisper, as if someone had knocked the wind out of her.

"Well, rot me, why do you think? First, you took my seasick potion—and gave it to Sir Perfect! Then you sided with Sir Garrett about Wystan. You didn't care about me! I thought you both deserved to know what life is like when you're at the mercy of everyone around you. Ordered here, ordered there." Brenna let her bottom lip tremble and sobbed. "Not even allowed to bestow my heart where I wished. I thought you ought to have a taste of the problem. Who thought you two would do more than be shocked at the idea for a day or two?"

Leandra shook her head. "Bestow your heart? Don't try to tell me you love Wystan. I know you better than that."

"Well, I like him." The trembling lip didn't fool her cousin, Brenna realized, and she began to chew on the corner of her mouth. "I truly do like Wystan. Or I thought I did."

"I don't believe this," Leandra muttered, staring at the phial in her hand once more. "What am I going to tell Garrett?"

"Do you have to tell him?" Brenna's hands fluttered to her throat and she choked. She could almost feel Sir Garrett's hands on her neck. "Can't we make up some story? Let's say that the spell fades if the lady weds another. When the wedding is over, he'll fall out of love."

Leandra cast her a withering look. "He deserves to know the truth. 'Tis only just."

"Is there a way to explain the truth without telling the truth?" Brenna pleaded. "You know what I mean. If you tell him the truth, he'll murder me. I know he will."

"Why didn't you think about that before?" Leandra demanded.

Brenna shrugged, regretting for the first time her short-sightedness.

Sudden color flooded back into Leandra's face. Anger hardened her eyes. She actually shook a fist at Brenna.

"You have endangered Lyonesse, Garrett, and even Wystan. I don't consider what you've done to me of any great import, but that you would endanger our people and Father . . . Brenna, I've no concern about Sir Garrett's strangling you, because I intend to have that pleasure myself."

Brenna planted her hands on her hips. "I think you're taking this far too seriously, as usual."

"This *is* serious." Leandra turned away, afraid that if she didn't, she might leap across the room and do her cousin bodily harm. But she couldn't keep herself from saying the thing that she knew would upset Brenna the most. "You have meddled with people's lives. With hearts. I should send you home."

"Oh, no, don't do that," Brenna wailed. She clasped her hands before her in a pleading gesture. "Please don't."

A tinge of satisfaction seeped into Leandra's heart. She needn't admit to Brenna that she wouldn't send her away. Let her stew over the prospect for a while.

Leandra stared down once more at the phial in her hand. She and Garrett fell in love thinking all the time that they were victims of a spell. But there was none. Nothing. The potion remained in the phial, ready to be given just as she planned from the beginning.

The whole idea of the potion turned her stomach now. She longed to be rid of it, to pitch the troublesome brew into the fire, just as Garrett had hurled the other container into watery depths. Destruction by fire seemed appropriate, cleansing, final. But the hearth was cold.

Then another troubling thought occurred to Leandra. She knew she loved Garrett. She was not victim of a spell. Did he *truly* love her? Or had he succumbed to the idea of the potion? Had he believed he had no choice but to love her? Would his love evaporate into thin air if he knew that they had received no potion?

Leandra put her hand to her heart. Her breath was coming in quick and short gulps, almost in sobs, when a third troubling thought dawned. What would Garrett say if he knew of the trick played against them?

With a glance in Brenna's direction, Leandra decided her cousin might have reason to fear for her safety. If Garrett knew what had actually happened, he would turn into that fiery avenging angel and swoop down on them both, strangling Brenna for her duplicity and . . . well, she was guilty in her own way, Leandra thought, for acquiring the potion in the first place.

"You're not going to tell him, are you?" Brenna begged in a whisper. She wrung her hands.

"I don't know." Leandra put a hand to her temple, where a headache blossomed behind her eyes. What about the potion that she possessed? Did she still want to give the elixir to Lord Reginald? The more she thought about what Brenna just told her, the more complicated everything became. "No, I won't tell him. Not yet anyway."

Relief whistled between Brenna's lips. "Good. Didn't you say he's going away when the wedding is over? The problem will take care of itself. No need to worry. Here, come have something to eat. Though I must say your color seems to be returning nicely."

A regretful smile twisted Leandra's lips. How like Brenna to put the issue behind her so quickly, while she herself would suffer and worry over the consequences. Brenna would go her merry way. It had always been so between them. Leandra peered sharp-eyed at her cousin, suddenly jealous of Brenna's carefree ways. Brenna dismissed everything easily, with a wave of her hand and a smile on her lips, while she would carry the responsibility for them both, frowning and fretting until the outcome fell into place. Leandra had never longed for things to be different, until now.

"Do you mind if I have the meat pie? I thought the oatmeal pudding looked good, too, but you can have that." Brenna bustled over to the tray, handing Leandra the milk and peering into each bowl and cup.

"The pudding is good," Leandra said, trying to put things out of her mind. But the food lay like a lumpy sweet substance in her mouth.

"Yes, see. The bread is so soft and fresh." Brenna was about to pour a generous glop of honey on a crust when a knock on the door interrupted her.

Brenna crammed the bread and honey into her mouth and licked each finger as she walked to the door. Leandra pushed the pudding away, more interested in their caller than in food.

A groom greeted them, a man in simple gray wool with the sign of the purple boar worked onto the shoulder of his tunic—Leofric's man.

"I seek Lady Leandra," he said, eyeing Brenna skeptically.

"Yes, I'm here." Leandra exchanged a look of curiosity with Brenna as she approached the door.

"My lady, Sir Leofric sends word only for your ears." The groom gave Brenna a meaningful glance. Leandra waved her cousin away. Brenna ducked behind the door, out of sight, her eyes wide and her ear almost against the door.

"Speak," Leandra ordered, knowing her cousin listened. She wasn't about to take a message from Leofric without a witness.

He bowed and recited, obviously from memory. "Sir Leofric requests that tomorrow during the hunt, you ride to his side so that he may return to you that which is yours without the notice of others."

Wariness stiffened Leandra's neck. What was Leofric up to now? "Does your master wish an answer?"

"No, my lady." The groom shuffled his feet. "He said only to add that you have no need to tell anyone else. He will keep your secret, certain that you will keep his."

"I see." Leandra's wariness retreated in the face of cool anger and frustration. Leofric had the ring, and she must force him to return it. "Tell your master that I will no doubt see him during the hunt tomorrow."

She closed the door soundly. "So Leofric seeks to threaten me over our secrets. What does he gain, I wonder?"

"Don't trust him." Brenna backed up her warning by telling Leandra what she had seen happen in the exercise yard between Garrett and Leofric.

"I mistrust him, but I must heed his invitation. How else can I get the ring back?" Leandra said thoughtfully. She had been ill when she witnessed Garrett and Leofric's sword fight, but she remembered clearly how the enmity between the men had filled the hall. A hot and seething force.

"I must seek the ring's return," she said. "If those two fight again, I fear it will be to the death."

The next morning the Earl of Tremelyn's noisy hunting party thundered over the hill and galloped along the length of the country lake. Laughter and friendly name-calling danced on the spring air. Cap feathers fluttered in the breeze. The reflection of bright beribboned cloaks streaked across the blue lake, sparkling rich and radiant on the water's surface like shining jewels. But the sight held no charm for Garrett.

At the head of the party rode Reginald, all in blue on his white horse, and by his side rode Leandra, garbed in green on the gray mare Garrett had personally selected for her.

In the past the hunting party's gay colors and easy camaraderie would have captivated Garrett's good humor, but not this morn. He and the other bachelor knights had been out before sunrise searching for any trace of outlaws. He'd seen a few suspicious tracks, but the area seemed clear and safe. With the spring weather, the criminals seemed to have retreated to a more profitable highway and forest.

When the party reached the forest's edge, where a picnic breakfast had been set up, the nobles abandoned their horses to the grooms. Without delay they blighted the long, cloth-covered tables like a buzzing cloud of biblical locusts heedlessly devouring the array of foods offered. Reginald, generous as ever, begrudged his guests nothing and spared little to entertain them and to impress his bride-to-be.

Garrett wandered through the crowd, greeting friends and acquaintances and longing to catch Leandra's eye. He needed to speak to her, but Reginald and a bevy of ladies and gentlemen surrounded her constantly. He would have to bide his time.

"Did you see whom Sir Leofric is with?" Wystan asked, appearing at Garrett's side.

"Yes, I saw," Garrett said, scrutinizing Leofric, who sat at the side of a dark-haired noblewoman. "The lady is well known for her generosity with her charms."

As Garrett watched, the heir to Casseldorne turned toward the lady, obviously too enamored with her every word to look in his direction. But Garrett suspected that Leofric knew he was there. He wanted the purple boar to be aware of them. He wanted Leofric to know that he dare not so much as twitch an eyebrow in Leandra's direction—or in Reginald's.

"Do you think he intends to cause more trouble?" Wystan asked, his gaze following the purple knight.

"I'm certain of it." Silently Garrett thanked Brenna for having the sense and the courage to seek him out. She'd surprised him, reached out from the shadows beyond the great hall while dinner was being served last night. She wasted no time, but spoke up in a quavering voice, telling him about the message Leofric had sent to Leandra.

Casseldorne may have hinted that he would return the ring, but Garrett suspected that the man still hoped to prevent Leandra's marriage to Reginald.

"He will cause trouble," Garrett said quietly to Wystan. "Follow him during the hunt if you can."

Wystan nodded and returned to the horses.

Garrett ate little breakfast himself. He didn't relish riding across country with the hunt on a full belly. Besides that, he was too interested in keeping an eye on Reginald and Leandra. They sat at the center of the table, where Leandra, with a new bow still slung over her shoulder, picked at her food and offered her guests and her lord a weak, distracted smile. Garrett disliked the darkness beneath her eyes and the new hollows in her cheeks. She looked as if she'd slept little and needed a good meal.

Around them the nobles of the hunting party ate, drank, and paraded about with hooded hawks on their arms. Their boisterous laughter filled the air and grated against Garrett's nerves. So did the picture of Leandra and Reginald that he saw. She was worthy of the title she soon would possess, but she apparently took no pleasure in it.

He found himself torn by jealousies and satisfactions, watching her sit at Reginald's side as his betrothed, a vague smile on her lips. That pained smile pleased Garrett in a dark way. She had what she wanted. Yet when he glimpsed the unhappiness it truly mirrored, he regretted his mean feelings. Most of all, he wanted her happiness—just as the potion had promised.

Garrett wandered along the table, his eyes on the food, his ear tuned to the sound of the beaters and the hounds in the forest beyond them.

"My lord and my lady." Garrett addressed Reginald and Leandra with a bow. Despite the awkwardness, he must pay his respects. To fail to do so would be more curious than a tongue-tied greeting.

"Bernay, here you are." Reginald smiled, a warm and genuine reception. "Please, 'tis good to see you. Leandra, Sir Garrett selected your mount for today."

"Yes, indeed," Garrett said. "I decided on the gray mare because she is reliable and responsive, yet spirited enough for your accomplished abilities, my lady. I hope you are pleased with her."

"Yes, I am," Leandra said, meeting his gaze at last. The darkness beneath her eyes and the weariness about her mouth tugged at Garrett's heart. He longed to lean across the table and say so many things to her. He wanted to tell her to smile, to be happy, to show Reginald what a courageous heart she possessed. Most of all he wanted to tell her to ignore Leofric's message.

A huntsman suddenly plunged from the forest. Panting for breath, he stumbled to a stop in front of Lord Reginald.

"'Tis a great hart, my lord," the young man gasped. Remembering his manners, he pulled his hood from his head. "Sleek he is, my lord, and with a great rack on his head." The lad held his hands out at arm's length on either side of his head to demonstrate the size of the antlers.

"Shall we hunt hart?" Reginald called, addressing his guests.

"To the horses!" they shouted.

Nobles threw themselves at the grooms and horses.

Garrett followed Leandra, took the gray's reins from the groom, and offered to help her mount. She hesitated a moment, long enough to see that Reginald was already on his horse and ready to be off.

Garrett offered his hand once more. Leandra stepped into it and swung up on her mare. When she leaned forward for the reins, Garrett spoke. "Don't go near Leofric. Ignore his message."

"How did you know about that?"

Garrett shrugged. "Just stay away from Leofric."

"But I must get the ring back," Leandra protested. "It was Brenna, wasn't it? She told you? She had no right."

"I'll get your ring for you," Garrett said. "Leave it to me."

"No, Leofric took the ring from me," she snapped. Her chin took on a willful thrust and the spirit of a warrior flashed in her eyes. "He will return it to me, Garrett. You are no longer part of this."

"I am pledged to your safety," Garrett said. "That makes me a part."

Reginald took up the oliphant and blew it. The hunt horn's mellow tones soared up and through the forest. Then he led the way into the woods; Leandra and the wedding guests followed.

When the last of the nobles had ridden off, the knights fell in at the rear. Garrett bided his time, waiting for the party of riders to spread out. Once the hunters spied the hart, all ceremony would be forgotten and everyone would ride for the kill.

Ahead, the baying of the dogs—the huntsman's siren—became clear. Someone shouted that the hart was sighted. Reginald sounded his horn again, leading the hunting party over the crest of a ridge. They burst into the blinding sunlight of a clearing, Leandra still following her lord, but riding a little behind him. Then they all vanished again into the dim forest. Already the riders straggled out across the hillside.

In the depths of the forest, the cool shadows made recognition of individual riders difficult, unless their horse or colors were plain. The heir to Casseldorne rode a huge black stallion, nearly the size of a war horse.

Leandra's gray was decked out in green, blue, and white. Her fair hair, braided down her back and crowned with her chaplet, almost glowed even in the darkest shadows of the forest. If she intended to meet Leofric, she would have to leave Reginald's side and strike out on her own. Garrett knew she was capable of that, brave enough, and now, maybe even reckless enough. She would have her ring. He had no intention of allowing her to face Leofric alone.

Garrett could hear horses crashing through thickets.

Hooves thundered over hard ground. Frustrated riders shouted curses at their mounts. Garrett heeded none of that, focusing only on the flying white tail of Leandra's gray.

At the bottom of the ridge they splashed through a stream and started up the slope. Garrett spied Leandra still riding beside her lord.

Brenna rode with them. She shouted, the thrill of the chase shrill in her voice. "You won't lose me. I'll be at the kill." With a laugh she spurred her horse on.

Garrett had sworn her to secrecy about coming to him, and he warned her to stay away from this meeting with Leofric. She willingly agreed to obey.

In the dense forest, Garrett lost sight of the three of them as the hunters lunged up the next slope. He turned his chestnut in the direction where he'd last seen Leofric, but he didn't catch sight of the purple knight again.

At the crest, Garrett saw Leandra head her mare east, away from the sound of horns. She disappeared into a thicket of pines.

"Sweet Jesu, I knew it," Garrett swore under his breath. "She's going to join Leofric."

Chapter 20

Garrett lost sight of Leandra for a few agonizing moments.

Then he caught a flash of the gray's white tail along a game trail and he charged after her. Abruptly she turned back south, down the slope, farther away from the hunting party again. He lost her again, only to glimpse her golden head beyond a grove of oaks at the foot. Garrett plunged down the slope into a clearing. There he found Leandra facing Leofric.

They stared at him—Casseldorne appearing speechless for once, Leandra scowling in annoyance. Garrett didn't rein in his horse until he was almost between them.

"Give her the ring and be off," Garrett ordered, drawing his sword.

Leofric curled a lip and turned to Leandra. "How did he learn of our meeting?"

"I think Brenna told him. She overheard the message your man delivered." Leandra cast Garrett a cutting look that should have mortally wounded him. Apparently she truly intended to deal with Leofric on her own. "What difference does it make? You promised to return what is mine. Give me the ring and we'll be gone."

"No need to rush about this," Leofric said, swinging down from his horse. "The others will be chasing that stag for some time. I would enjoy the lady's company."

"No games, Casseldorne," Garrett warned. Instantly alert, he sat a little taller in the saddle, peering into the shadows of the woods. He'd never doubted that this was a trap set for Leandra. The quicker Leofric played out his game, the better. "Hand over the ring and be done with this.

The wedding takes place tomorrow, and there is nothing you can do about it."

"Will you share a cup of wine with me, my lady?" Leofric asked, disregarding Garrett. He untied a wineskin from the saddle and from another bag he took a cup. "I wish to admit my defeat and to drink to your health."

"So generous of you, Sir Leofric!" With unstudied grace, Leandra dropped to the ground in a rustle of gold skirts and green surcoat. Her fair braid swung free down her back, and her gold chaplet gleamed in the sunlight. Only the furrow between her brows betrayed her anxiety.

"No," Garrett protested, determined that she would not step within Leofric's reach. But Leandra had already started toward the purple knight.

"Stay out of this, Bernay," Leofric cautioned, his eyes on Leandra and nearly aglow with anticipation. "You and I will meet in the tourney lists during the wedding jousts. We'll settle our differences then. This is between the lady and me."

A stealthy smile spread across Leofric's face, and his tongue flicked across his lips, reminding Garrett of a greedy snake about to gulp down a tender baby bird.

His confidence alarmed Garrett. Sword ready, Garrett leapt from his horse and imposed himself between them.

"Get away, Leandra," Garrett demanded, his back to her. "Where is the ring, Casseldorne?"

"I have it here," Leofric said, without deigning to take his eyes from Leandra. He held up his hand once more, wiggling his little finger in the soft shaft of sunlight that penetrated the narrow clearing.

At the sight of the golden circle a stricken look crossed Leandra's face and her hands fluttered as if she wanted to reach out for it. Garrett despised Casseldorne for baiting her—with her honor, with the symbol of Lyonesse's safety. He loathed Leofric for tormenting Leandra a thousand times more than for any insult he'd ever uttered against the Bernays.

"Drink with me, lady," Leofric invited again, his voice

soft and hissing like a serpent's, tempting Leandra with the one thing she wanted. He flashed Garrett a lewd look. Did he play for time, or was there something in the wine? Garrett wondered.

"Drink with me, lady, and I will give you the ring." Slowly Leofric lifted the cup to his lips and drew a sip. Then he blatantly licked the rim of the cup, his wine-reddened tongue caressing the lip slowly, sensuously. Then he held the cup out to Leandra, almost reaching around Garrett.

After a moment's hesitation, she reached for the goblet.

Garrett struck. A lightning thrust flipped the cup from Leofric's hand, splashing red wine down the front of the man's purple tunic. Garrett shoved Leandra aside.

"The ring," Garrett demanded, his free arm forcing Leandra to remain behind him. "Return the ring to her. Now."

Wine dripped from Leofric's chin, and anger twisted his thin mouth and narrowed his pale eyes. He seized his sword, the blade glinting in the light as he leveled it at Garrett's throat.

"No, no!" Leandra threw herself in front of Garrett despite his efforts to prevent it. "There is no reason for this. Not another sword fight. I couldn't bear that. Garrett, put away your sword. Leofric, give me the ring. Settle your quarrel at the tourney, if you must. 'Tis the proper place."

Leandra's tone was low, firm, and determined, oddly reminiscent of a good commander's. Warily, Garrett lowered his sword as Leofric did the same.

Leandra beseechingly held her hand out to the purple knight.

Beyond the trees Garrett heard movement in the forest. He didn't think the hunting party was near. The baying of the hounds rang far to the north and the west now. Without taking his eyes from Leofric, Garrett turned his ear toward the trees, listening for the slightest stir of a leaf, the faint snap of a twig. Silence. Even the birds had ceased to sing.

"The ring." Leandra stepped toward Leofric. But he defied her demand. His gaze also flicked toward the woods.

Garrett could feel the presence now. The thickets had eyes. Someone was about to ride down upon them, and there was no more time to waste. He shoved Leandra aside again and lunged against Leofric, seizing his hand. With a quick twist Garrett swung Leofric around, wrenching his arm behind his back, and began to wrest the ring from Leofric's finger.

"Get on your horse, Leandra," Garrett ground out as he strained against a struggling, cursing Leofric. The ring was almost free.

"What are you—" Leandra hesitated, startled and confused.

Bowmen crashed into the clearing. Men swarmed from the woods, and everywhere Garrett looked a grim-faced outlaw drew down on him with a bow, a crossbow, or an ax. The ring slipped free of Leofric's finger. Garrett threw the man aside, jammed the ring into his belt and flourished his sword again.

He grasped Leandra's wrist and dragged her behind him, putting the gray mare to their backs.

Leandra deftly unslung her new hunting bow, strung it, nocked an arrow, and took up guard at Garrett's flank.

Leofric staggered to his feet, uttering curses. He lifted a wobbly sword in defense and backed toward Garrett and Leandra as if he expected help from them. No one else moved.

Slowly, deliberately, one of the outlaws rode from the forest on an old but still proud war horse—stolen, Garrett suspected. A shock of dark hair split the outlaw's brow, and something about his stubbled chin was familiar to Garrett.

The man bowed toward Leandra. "My lady. Sir Knights. I seek Leofric of Casseldorne." The outlaw leaned forward over his saddle bow and stared pointedly at Leofric. "He who sent me word that he offered a reward for the capture of the lady."

"'Tis me, you fool," Leofric said. He dropped his guard, lowering his sword. "I promised you the reward. I thought you'd never arrive. There's the lady. Take her."

The outlaw glanced thoughtfully at Leandra and Garrett,

who remained armed and ready. He settled his gaze on Casseldorne once more. Instinct warned Garrett to make no move yet. The air was too thick with betrayal. He sensed Leandra at his back, alert, fearful, but collected.

"And the reward?" the outlaw said. "You think I'm knave enough to ride away with the earl's betrothed without seeing the color of your coin?"

"Of course." Leofric went to his horse, moving slowly so that the bowmen would not mistake his actions. He took a bag of coins from his saddle and tossed it up to the outlaw. Garrett watched the man pull open the purse strings with one hand and his teeth. He fingered the contents, weighing them in his hand. Apparently satisfied, he drew the purse shut and stashed the reward inside his surcoat.

"Seize him," the bandit ordered. Bowmen descended on Leofric, overwhelming him like rooks flocking to a corpse.

"No! No!" Leofric shouted at the top of his lungs, his yellow-brown eyes wild with fear. So many swarmed so quickly that his lowered sword was useless. He struggled, but each leg and arm was restrained.

"You, Sir Knight, and the lady are free to go," the outlaw announced to Garrett and Leandra, loud enough for all to hear.

"No! No! This is a mistake," Leofric protested, his swarthy face nearly as purple as his tunic. "You take the lady. The gold is for taking the lady. I don't care what you do with this—this traitor's son who thinks he's a knight."

The insult bounded off Garrett like an arrow off a stone battlement. When had Leofric lost the power to wound him? Garrett wondered. When had he learned that he was no traitor and no one's accusations would make him one?

"I make no mistake, Sir Leofric," the outlaw said. "Sir Knight, you and the lady may go."

Still screaming, Leofric was lifted off the ground and borne into the forest by the men.

The outlaw watched impassively. A boy appeared out of the melee, grabbed the reins of Casseldorne's black, and led the horse away.

The black-haired bandit turned to Garrett and waved

toward the baying of the hounds in the distance. "Tell your earl that you escaped capture narrowly. Tell him there was nothing you could do. You were outnumbered and would have risked the lady if you had saved the heir of Casseldorne. There is no lie in what I'm saying. You can send out armed men if you want, but we'll be gone to ground and more difficult to flush than the innocent of the forest."

Garrett stared at the man, recognition dawning. "Who are you?"

"My name is Trevail," the outlaw said. "My kinsman was named Pender. Perchance you knew the man?"

"I knew your kinsman," Garrett admitted. He would never forget the dying man who told him of Leofric. "I know the name."

"Then let this be," Trevail warned. By ones and twos the bowmen silently slipped from the clearing. "Casseldorne is rightfully mine." The man whirled his horse around and trotted from the clearing, forest-green shadows closing behind him.

"What will they do with Leofric?" Leandra asked. She peered over Garrett's shoulder at the empty, peaceful meadow.

"I don't think they're going to put him in the pillory," Garrett said with a harsh, cynical laugh.

Convinced that all was clear, he allowed Leandra to step out from behind him at last, and they both stared around in disbelief. Only a moment ago they were surrounded by outlaws. When they looked to where Leofric had stood, they saw only his purple cap, the blue-green peacock feather waving softly in the breeze.

Beyond the clearing the baying of the hounds grew louder, the barking frenzied and insistent. Garrett knew that the quarry was cornered; the hunt was nearly over.

He drew Leandra back to her horse. "We'll have to send out a search party, but I doubt we'll see Leofric or Trevail again."

"The ring," Leandra said, touching his shoulder. "Did you get the ring?"

Chapter 21

Yes, right here." Garrett reached inside his sword belt, where he'd hastily shoved it when the outlaws had descended on them. Victoriously, he held it up for Leandra to see. Polished gold glimmered in the sun, and the frayed ribbon wound through it to make it fit glowed soft and white. "We won back the ring."

She reached for the symbol of her betrothal, but Garrett took her hand.

"No, I'll put it on," he said. "'Twas my charge in the first place."

"Let me take this one off." Hastily Leandra removed the replacement ring and offered her hand to Garrett.

He poised the ring to slip onto her finger. But he couldn't do it. The ring was as large as ever and would easily glide onto her slender finger, but he couldn't do it. He couldn't make himself push the ring beyond her fingertip. His hand began to shake.

"What's the trouble?" Leandra asked, her hand remaining steady, her eyes questioning. "Why do you wait? Put the ring on. I hear someone coming."

Garrett heard the sound of a rider coming through the woods, too—from the direction of the hunt. He took a deep breath. This was foolish. Nothing kept the ring from slipping easily into place. He tried once more. But he could not make himself replace the betrothal ring on Leandra's finger.

"I can't," he said. He swore under his breath. "I know I put it on your finger once, before I loved you. I was glad to perform the honor then. But I can't now. Leandra, I can't—too much has happened. The potion. May Day. I was glad when you told me Leofric took the ring. You were set free to be mine."

He glanced up, wondering whether his confession would shock her. She stared back, her eyes round, shining, and dark with understanding. "I know. I remember."

A hunting horn sounded close, almost upon them.

"I don't want this wedding to happen," Garrett admitted. "I ache every time I see you at Lord Reginald's side. I want to stand up and say he doesn't deserve the Lady Leandra. He hasn't defended her from her enemies. He hasn't held her when she was ill." Garrett peered into Leandra's eyes and lowered his voice. "He hasn't touched her secret places and coaxed the first passionate sigh from her lips."

"Garrett, don't," Leandra said, her voice unsteady. She turned away, anxiously watching the woods beyond them. "You torture yourself—and me. Remember 'tis but the work of a potion. You know you would not betray your lord for that."

Quickly, she snatched the ring from his trembling hand and slipped it onto her finger.

At that moment Wystan bolted out into the clearing. His cap sat askew, and his horse's sides heaved.

"There you are," the squire gasped as soon as he reined in his mount. "I lost Leofric on the ridge, and I missed you at the kill. So I thought I'd better come in search.

"They got the stag. Brenna was there. The hart put up a great fight, but Reginald slew him. An arrow straight to the heart."

Brenna smacked her lips together, swished her tongue about her mouth, squinted, and gazed off into space, concentrating on the tart flavor on her palate. Smoke filled the kitchen where she stood. One of the hearths had belched the sooty cloud before it warmed enough to draw a new fire. Brenna took no notice. The sourness in her mouth faded, the acid taste lingering to pucker along her taste buds and onto her lips.

"Oooh, that's ghastly. Really dreadful. Almost appallingly

loathsome," she muttered to herself. With a wrinkle of her nose she stared appreciatively at the bottle of cloudy vinegar the cook had set before her. "Yes, the vinegar will do nicely for a start. What else?"

She looked up at the shelves above the table. What to sprinkle into this concoction to make it truly convincing? She thoughtfully tapped the empty, blue glass bottle and looked up at the drawers of spices in front of her: ginger, pepper, saffron, cloves, cinnamon, and mustard. The steward had unlocked the drawers for her, fully believing her excuse that she was concocting a headache remedy for Lady Leandra. This was probably going to be her only opportunity to make a potion. She must do it well. Leandra would have no reason to complain.

Brenna gave a determined nod. No reason at all. While she mixed and stirred, she pretended she was a wise woman like Vivian—beautiful, knowledgeable, and experienced in the ways of magic, witches, and the devil. Wait. Did wise women meet with the devil? Brenna gave her head a haughty shake. Of course, and he'd better beware when he dealt with Brenna of . . . whatever.

"Did you find what you wanted, my lady?" The gray-haired cook appeared at Brenna's elbow, wiping her wet, pudgy hands on her apron.

Brenna started like a child caught licking out of the honey jar. "Oh, yes." She leaned against the table in an attitude of nonchalance. After all, one didn't dare let on that one was creating a potion, especially to the castle underlings. "Found everything I need. What's here will do nicely. Thank you, cook."

"Good. Good." The ham-armed woman turned away, her eyes lighting on other duties that begged attention. "I'll leave you to it then, my lady. We have our hands full with this hart to prepare and the coming banquet."

As Brenna watched the cook bustle off, she saw Wystan enter the kitchen. She turned her back to him, hoping that he wouldn't see her, but he spotted her immediately and started her way.

"Oh, rot me," Brenna cursed. She covered the bottle and

vinegar with a linen towel, muttering all the time. "When I wanted to spend time with him, he was too good for me. Now he's everywhere I go."

"Is Lady Leandra all right?" Wystan asked as soon as he reached her. "Garrett wants to know."

"Of course she is." Brenna sniffed. "Leandra has faced brigands often. What makes Sir Garrett think she'd become faint of heart now?"

Wystan shrugged. "Why has she kept to her rooms all afternoon?"

"We've been having a talk." Brenna decided to add to the lie. "Naturally she's disappointed that the wedding has been put off for another day while the search is made for Leofric."

The news of Leofric's unfortunate capture troubled the wedding guests—some. He was not a man well-liked. But Lord Reginald was outraged that such a thing would happen on his own lands, to his guest, and he immediately sent men out to track the outlaws.

Wystan moved to Brenna's other side. "Garrett wants to see Lady Leandra today. Alone. Is there a time when she might take air in the orchard or stroll in the garden?"

"Yes, the orchard." Brenna immediately smiled to herself. This was going to work better than she and her cousin had planned. "Leandra wishes to see Sir Garrett also. She has something for him."

"Truly?" Wystan looked at her in surprise.

"Yes, but it is not to be shared in the presence of others," Brenna said, and turned away to make it clear that she could not be tempted into telling more.

"When in the orchard?"

"Tomorrow morn, after we break fast, when Lord Reginald is busy with his bailiff and steward." Brenna and Leandra had already discussed this. "Tell Sir Garrett to be there then."

Wystan nodded, but he didn't leave as Brenna hoped. She fingered the towel. What was he waiting for? "Is there something more?"

"I was just wondering if you will be staying in Tremelyn

241

with your cousin after the wedding?" Wystan asked, leaning against the table and toying with the edge of the linen towel, his hand near hers, near her secret potion. "I mean, you did a brave thing going to Garrett about Leofric. I thought maybe we—"

"Ah, well," Brenna said, nervously eyeing Wystan's hand. "You and your brother are sailing for France, aren't you? That's what Leandra said."

"Yes, well, but a war doesn't last forever." Wystan stepped closer, and Brenna got that tingly feeling that came when a man stood close. "We will return, and I was just wondering whether you might still be here then?"

"I don't know," Brenna said with a twinge of guilt, unable to look Wystan in the eye. She'd already begun to look higher than a mere squire. During the hunt she'd even ridden briefly beside the young man in yellow who'd bowed to her on her first day at Tremelyn. She'd liked him. Her interest blossomed when she learned that he was the first son of a baron. The young man would inherit a fief along the road to London with a toll bridge that brought in a nice revenue.

"You'll find a lady in France," Brenna said. "Rescue her from some danger and wed her to keep her safe."

"Maybe," Wystan said, obviously unconvinced. "At least promise you will dance with me at the wedding banquet."

Brenna couldn't keep the smile from her face. "My pleasure, sir."

With that, he left.

Humming the tune of a romance ballad to herself, Brenna added another pinch of mustard to the potion in the blue bottle, corked it, and left the kitchen. This stuff would make Leandra happy.

The next morning Leandra broke her fast as usual, then sat in the sun in the castle orchard, aware that she appeared to the others as shaken as she felt. But she was certain she was doing the right thing.

When she first returned from the ordeal, a few of the ladies had kindly offered their services. They brought her wine, patted her hand, admired her courage, and whispered that she was fortunate to have had Sir Garrett there to protect her. But her continued silence puzzled them, and they wandered away to take part in a game of ball.

Leandra owed the outlaws much, she decided, as she twisted her betrothal ring on her finger. They'd whisked away Leofric, averting a danger to her and Garrett. They'd given her an excuse to look pale and distressed.

But Leofric had nothing to do with her demeanor. Garrett's heartfelt confession over the ring had nearly destroyed what little composure remained to her. His every word had pierced her heart and weighed like a stone on her conscience. Loving her had endangered everything he took pride in, his loyalty, his reputation, his ambitions—for himself and Wystan as well. She'd ridden from the clearing with her betrothal ring on her finger and the knowledge in her heart that she must free Garrett from the belief that he loved her. Nothing else was fair or just. He did not deserve the unhappiness that she and Brenna had brought to him.

The orchard gate squeaked and Leandra looked up to see Brenna marching across the orchard, her dark curls bouncing with each hasty step.

"Well, here's the antidote," she said, plopping down on the bench.

Leandra took the blue glass bottle from her cousin, shook the container to assure herself of the contents, peered through the glass, and finally uncorked it to sniff the concoction.

"Whew!" Leandra waved the stench away from her nose. "What did you put in this?"

"Spices and things from the kitchen," Brenna said. "What do *you* think an antidote to a love potion would taste like?"

"Dreadful," Leandra agreed without hesitation. "Sour. Sharp. Sir Garrett won't believe this is a real antidote if it tastes nice and sweet. You've done well."

Leandra studied the blue bottle as if the solution within solved all her problems. In a way it did. The inspiration had come to her on the ride back to the castle after the hunt, when the pain and astonishment on Garrett's face as he tried to put the ring back on her finger was still fresh in her mind.

The suffering in his eyes had twisted Leandra's heart. If she and Garrett had received no potion—only the idea of a potion—then they needed no antidote, only the idea of one. Wouldn't it be better if at least one of them was free? And she knew who could help her carry out her plan.

Brenna leaned toward her and whispered, "Do you really think a fake antidote is going to work? Even if Sir Garrett takes the stuff and falls out of love with you, won't you still love him?"

"Yes, forever." Leandra spoke from her heart. Her love for Garrett was real and true. She prayed only that his love for her was less profound. "But how I feel is not what's important here. I have to set Garrett free to find another. 'Tis the only fair thing to do."

She stopped to take a deep breath, hurt by the thought of Garrett in another woman's arms. The painful image haunted her dreams all through the night, leaving her exhausted when dawn broke. But she was certain that she was doing the right thing.

"Oh, I see Wystan," Brenna said. "Sir Garrett must be on his way. I'll wave from the gate if anyone is coming." She rose and hurried away.

Leandra looked eagerly to Garrett as he walked through the orchard to the bench where she sat. His dress was casual and light, his blue tunic open at the neck, the hue the perfect match for his eyes, as always. The wind ruffled his tawny helmet of hair and flapped the tunic edge about his well-turned knees.

Leandra thought his expression bland: pleasant, ready to charm, without betraying his true mood or emotion. How proper for an earl's knight, she thought.

"My lady," Garrett said when he reached her. "I trust you have recovered from the shock of our encounter yesterday with the outlaws."

"Oh, yes, indeed," Leandra said. Their words sounded

bent and brittle to her. "Please sit with me a moment, Sir Garrett."

The walls of the castle towered over them, gleaming gray-white in the morning sun. Leandra knew, as she was certain Garrett did, too, that they were visible to anyone who cared to look out of windows or from the battlements above. She had no fear of being seen in his company. He was her knight, after all. But in the orchard, where the spring-green leaves of the pear trees already rustled in the breeze, there was little opportunity for them to be overheard.

"You wished to see me?" Garrett asked, inclining his head impersonally toward her, refusing to meet her gaze.

"Yes." Leandra took a deep breath and dived into the story she'd made up. "Garrett, yesterday while we were out hunting, a messenger arrived from Master Thomas, the alchemist. He sent us the antidote."

His head came up, and interest gleamed in his eyes as he turned to her. "Is that so?"

Leandra nodded and drew the blue bottle from her sleeve. Slowly she held it up so that the morning light flashed against it. With great effort she kept her breathing normal and her hand steady. She prayed for the strength to still the fluttering of her heart, to quell the sense of panic that was creeping over her. She didn't want to hear her own words— her own lies so carefully created to send Garrett away from her forever. She was snuffing out the one light in her life.

"Master Thomas swears in his message that this will break the hold of Vivian's potion in a matter of hours." Leandra took another deep breath and stared at the phial she held up between them. Garrett stared, too, but she could not look at him. She did not want to see the hope grow in his eyes. "This is the answer. We share a few drops of this, and all of our problems will be gone."

Guardedly, Garrett took the phial from her, turned it over in his hand, and studied it.

"Is this what you want?" he asked, his voice low, his eyes on the bottle. "To end it all with the antidote?"

"Of course, 'tis the release we've been searching for these

past days." His question surprised Leandra. Her throat had tightened, so she was afraid her voice would crack and betray her emotions. "'Tis the freedom you talked of the morning we left the inn. Remember? We can take the antidote here and now. Then the deed will be done. In only hours we will be ourselves again. Without betrayal or dishonesty. Free. No smear against you or your family. No uncertain future for Lyonesse."

"In only a few hours?" Garrett asked. "So quickly. So easily?"

"Yes, that's what Master Thomas said in his message." If she were going to tell an untruth, Leandra decided, it might as well be a big, practical one.

"I can hardly believe after all the searching we did that he found the antidote. That here in this tiny bottle is the end to our torment and to our joy." His unreadable expression turned to one of grave wonder. "It hardly seems possible."

"I know," Leandra lied. She stole a glance at him. How grim he looked. How stony his jaw. How cold and questioning his eyes when they met hers. She looked away. Her heart began to race. Did he detect the lie?

"In the days since we visited Master Thomas, I've had a lot of time to think, Leandra," Garrett said, turning the bottle over in his hands again. "Loving you has changed my life, brought me something I never knew I was missing."

He paused, and Leandra was uncertain as to why, so she said nothing, stared at her hands, and waited for him to speak the words that he seemed to be holding back.

"Not being able to take you . . . as wife is painful. Still, I have truly loved you. I have learned to value another's life and happiness more highly than my own, for more reasons than mere honor and riches. I know I must travel to escape the pain of seeing you beside Reginald, for I cannot bear to remain here and watch your wedded bliss."

Leandra shook her head, fighting back the tears. "I would never ask that of you."

"But you see, I have a choice other than taking this antidote. If I leave Tremelyn without taking this, I will part knowing that I was once loved." He touched her heart lightly, then his own.

"I will know that you loved me. That you, brave Leandra, knew me, knew my thoughts and my heart, knew my faults and my virtues, and loved me nonetheless. You cared not for my name or my rank, you cared for me. 'Tis a treasure I would not give up for all the gold, for all the fiefs, for all the titles in the world. You have given me the greatest blessing of all. For what are honor and riches if one has not loved and been loved in return?"

Tears rolled down Leandra's cheeks. "Oh, Garrett, don't say such things."

Garrett went on without looking at her, and Leandra wondered whether his heart ached as much as hers. "I wanted you to know how I feel. I wanted you to know that I love you. The antidote is of no importance."

The sob in Leandra's throat vanished. Sweet Mary, was he refusing the antidote?

Garrett smiled at her, a thin-lipped, ironic smile. "So here it is. Antidote fresh from Master Thomas."

Without wasting another moment, Leandra signaled her cousin to bring refreshment. He couldn't refuse it. She wouldn't let him. "Master Thomas went to such trouble for us. You will take it, won't you, Garrett? 'Tis really the best way."

Garrett said nothing, argued no more. Leandra decided to take the silence as agreement.

When Brenna arrived, as arranged, with a tray bearing a flagon of wine and a goblet, Leandra motioned for her to set it down on the other side of the bench and to pour. Brenna finished filling the goblet and stood aside, her face uncharacteristically sober. Leandra took the goblet and turned to Garrett.

He held the blue bottle still, staring at it curiously, fingering it thoughtfully. Then, to Leandra's dismay, he uncorked it and sniffed. "Whew, what's in this stuff?" He thrust the bottle away at arm's length.

Leandra and Brenna shrugged in unison. "Only Master

Thomas knows," Leandra said, without daring to look at Brenna.

"How could the potion be so tasteless and the antidote so terrible?" Garrett asked, holding the bottle up to the sunlight.

"Who knows?" Unable to stand the suspense any longer, Leandra closed her eyes. Please, Mother Mary, have mercy and let this be over soon, she prayed. "Pour it, Brenna."

"Yes, Brenna," Garrett said at last. "'Tis fitting that you should be the one to do so."

"Oh, don't be cruel," Brenna cried. To Leandra's surprise, great tears began to roll down her cousin's cheeks. "I didn't mean to cause so much pain. I never did. Truly. You must believe me."

"Pour," Garrett ordered, his voice harsh now, his patience apparently worn thin.

With trembling hands Brenna took the antidote and poured it into the goblet, the sharp fumes of the elixir drifting up about them.

Leandra seized the goblet and offered it to Garrett. "Hold your breath and drink quickly," she cautioned. She would allow him no other opportunity to back down.

Without any more protest, Garrett took the goblet, but hesitated before he put it to his mouth. "Remember that I loved you, Leandra. I loved you well and above all things."

"I will remember," Leandra promised in a whisper. Her heart twisted into a painful lump that lodged itself in her throat.

Garrett drank. When he finished, Leandra took the goblet and sipped the last of the wine and potion; the liquid rolled sour in her mouth, bitter on her tongue, and stung all the way down her throat. She almost choked.

"'Tis done," she whispered when she finished and could speak again.

Garrett regarded her for a long moment, no pleasure in his face, no satisfaction in his eyes. "If Master Thomas is right, by sundown we will no longer love one another."

* * *

Wystan picked up a battered greave and held it so that the late afternoon sunlight glinted off its dints. "If the smith can hammer these out," he said, "this piece will be as good as new."

"Umph" was Garrett's only reply. He stared unseeing at the armory walls, his old chain mail in his hands. He cared nothing about the metal shin guard his brother was examining. He sat heedless of the armor that lay scattered around them, waiting and listening for his heart to stop aching. But the dull pain hammered on, potent as ever.

"If I didn't know better, brother, I'd think your heart isn't in this voyage to France," Wystan said, letting the greave drop to the table. "You haven't listened to a thing I've said since we started to sort through our equipment for the journey."

"The antidote isn't working," Garrett said. The sun had traveled nearly its full arc, and he felt no different than he did in the orchard that morning when he confessed the depth of his love to Leandra, when her tears nearly moved him to refuse the antidote.

"Give it a little more time," Wystan said, his tone impatient. "Maybe Brenna knows why. Ask her about it when she arrives. You know, before you met Lady Leandra, you were ready enough to sail to France. You didn't care how long the voyage was. You were so determined, I was afraid you'd defy even Lord Reginald when he ordered us to Lyonesse. But now you don't care a bit about France."

"I know," Garrett said. So Wystan had noticed it, too. Garrett shook his head, as mystified by his behavior as his brother. He knew other knights with ladies and wives who never lost their interest in war, journeys, and jousting. In truth, it was often the married men who seemed the most eager to fight, to seek new lands, or at least to enjoy different company. He wanted the antidote to set him free. Soon.

"Tell me again what you saw Lady Brenna doing in the kitchen last night."

"I've told you twice," Wystan complained. "Why again?"

"Because I think there's something important about it," Garrett snapped. "Tell me."

"She really wasn't doing anything while I talked with her," Wystan said. "She was standing near the spice cabinet, and a jug of vinegar sat on the table, and a towel was thrown over a bottle and things. I couldn't see exactly what."

"A blue bottle?" Garrett asked again.

"It might have been a blue bottle." Wystan threw up his hands in a gesture of frustration. "I'm not sure. She said she was fixing some remedy for Lady Leandra, and I thought no more of it. I was there to deliver your message. Ask her yourself when she gets here. She'll be here soon. She's too curious to pass up my offer to look at the armory."

"Good. How did the stuff she was mixing smell?" Garrett persisted.

"Stunk worse than the slop from a brewhouse," Wystan said, wagging his head like a man who has repeated a story too often.

Garrett nodded. "So did the antidote." He wasn't sure what he suspected, but there was something about this antidote that didn't make sense. "You're certain the guard at the gate wasn't mistaken?"

"By the rood, Garrett." Wystan shoved the greave away from him so it rolled across the table and clattered to the floor. "Do you think I make up something new every time you ask me to tell it? I thought you wanted the truth?"

"I do," Garrett said. "The truth is precisely what I'm after. What did the guard say?"

"He said he admitted no messenger, not from Exeter, nor from Bath nor Lyonesse." Wystan spoke slowly and distinctly as if he thought Garrett had gone deaf. "No one. The people who passed through the gate yesterday were the usual comers and goers—maids to help with the heavy kitchen work and lads to work in the stables."

"No peddlers or wise women, either?" Garrett asked.

"He said no. No peddlers, no strangers," Wystan said.

"Then where else could the antidote have come from?" Garrett repeated, more to himself than Wystan.

"You think Lady Brenna made it?" Wystan asked. His face lighted with inspiration. "Or maybe they obtained it from one of the lady guests."

"'Tis possible," Garrett admitted. "I don't think the antidote came from Thomas. Wherever she and Leandra found the stuff, it isn't working. But why would she lie about this?"

The clanking of the smithy below filled the silence as Garrett wandered around the armory table, listlessly examining pieces of equipment that he and Wystan would need when they joined the king in France.

Garrett thought Wystan was right. His heart wasn't in this journey. Joining the king had been his life's goal. Now he found no merit in camping rough in Normandy, commanding rowdy men-at-arms, whipping them into fighting order, then watching them either perish in battle or turn into the victorious army, looting and ravishing the countryside.

Idly he wondered where Leandra was. He'd missed her company since they arrived at the castle. He'd last seen her in the great hall an hour ago, engaged in a game of backgammon with Reginald. The lady and the lord said little to each other, but played with silent concentration.

The sight of them together pained Garrett so much that he grabbed Wystan and dragged him to the armory on the pretense of selecting equipment for the journey.

What was Leandra feeling? Garrett wondered. Would she give him a sign when she no longer loved him? In his heart he didn't want her to. He wanted her to long for him as he longed for her. He didn't want her to be unhappy, but he wanted to think that she thought of him, that she would never forget their short time together as lovers.

A soft knock on the door interrupted the silence.

"Brenna," Wystan mouthed to Garrett across the room.

"Let her in." Garrett retreated to the armory's shadows, where she wouldn't see him when she entered.

Wystan opened the door to her. Brenna smiled up at him. "Here I am. You promised you'd show me the armory, and I came as soon as I could." She swept into the chamber. "I love seeing all of the castle. This morning I saw the brewhouse. So this is where armor and weapons are stored."

"Yes, this is where we arm ourselves." Wystan latched the door behind her.

Brenna stopped in the center of the high-ceilinged chamber, her greedy gaze seeking every detail of the room, taking in the pieces of armor, the lances neatly stacked in racks, axes hanging from wall brackets, and the spears fanned out against the tall stone walls. Then she spotted Garrett.

The wondrous delight vanished from her face. "I didn't know you were going to be here," she said with the fallen look of one who has been betrayed. She turned on Wystan. "You tricked me!"

"Garrett wants to ask you some questions," Wystan said, wisely blocking the door.

"There's no need for questions." Brenna's hands plucked at the folds of her skirt. "I told you about Leofric. I've kept your secret about the May Day festival. What more do you want of me?"

"I want to know about the antidote."

Brenna's face paled. "What about the antidote?"

"Did you make it?"

Brenna turned to escape, charging headlong into Wystan. Firmly he took her arms and turned her to face Garrett.

"Tell me the truth now," Garrett demanded softly, walking calmly toward her. If he didn't frighten her, maybe she would relent and tell the truth. "Remember, Brenna, you have wrecked all my plans and caused your cousin great pain. You owe me the truth."

"Uh, why would I make an antidote?" Brenna stammered. Her eyes grew as round as a jongleur's tambourines.

Garrett's heart leapt, but he was careful not to betray his hope. She was stalling, groping for a lie to tell. He continued to move closer to her. "Because Leandra asked you to. Because she thought that if I thought I'd taken the antidote, I'd fall out of love with her. She wants to set me free."

Brenna nodded. Then some second thought made her shake her head. "Not exactly."

"Then tell me exactly," Garrett whispered, his nose now a cat's whisker from hers.

"Well." Brenna began to wring her hands. "Leandra made me promise not to tell."

Garrett straightened, a huff of exasperation escaping him.

A TENDER MAGIC

"These belatedly acquired scruples do not become you, Brenna."

"All right, I made the antidote," Brenna snapped. "Is that what you want to hear?"

Garrett grabbed her shoulders and gave her a little shake. "Tell me why?"

"Because she hated to see you in pain," Brenna said. "I don't know it all. She doesn't tell me everything. She said something about the ring. That you couldn't put it on her finger. She hoped that you would believe in the antidote and forget your love for her. Then you'd be free to love again."

Garrett studied her face, peered into her guileless gray eyes. She looked frightened enough to be telling the truth, but how could he believe her? The only thing she'd ever told the truth about was Leofric's evil plan. There was one way.

Garrett whipped out his sword. Brenna screamed and cringed against Wystan.

"Garrett . . . ?" Wystan protested, a look of shock and reproach on his face.

Garrett held the sword forth, its cruciform clear. "Swear on the cross that you tell the truth."

Brenna whimpered.

Garrett's eyes narrowed. He shook the sword at her. "Unless you lie, swear, Brenna, here and now. Put your hands on the hilt and swear."

Trembling uncontrollably, Brenna stretched out her hands, touching the sword lightly, as if she expected it to sear her. "I swear."

"To what?" Garrett wanted no mistake about this.

"To giving you and Leandra a fake antidote." Brenna gulped, her eyes anxiously scanning Garrett's face.

He let out a deep breath. Something seemed wrong with her reply, yet the answer was what he wanted to hear. He had to turn away, unwilling to allow either Brenna or Wystan to see the mixed emotions that coursed through him. Leandra wanted to free him. She had so little faith in his love that she thought a useless concoction and a silly untruth would bring an end to it.

"Bring me the blue bottle of antidote," he demanded.

"Of course." Brenna's sigh of relief echoed through the armory, and she turned, frantically snatching for the door latch behind Wystan.

"Tell your cousin I want to talk to her. No, on second thought, don't tell her," Garrett added. "I will seek her out for myself."

"Yes," Brenna gasped, nodding her head in agreement so violently her dark curls blurred. "Do that, Sir Garrett."

Chapter 22

Somehow, my dear, I think you're not concentrating on the game." Reginald frowned and began to replace the pieces on the backgammon board. "My envoy assured me you are quite a competent player. You and he played in Lyonesse, I believe."

"Prenuptial distractions, my lord," Leandra pleaded. She'd lost the third game of backgammon to Reginald. She smiled at him meekly, dismayed by the annoyance she saw in his eyes. Despite her determination to please him, to be the smiling bride that he wanted, she seemed unable to offer him her best. She seemed to disappoint him at every turn—from losing backgammon to missing his grand kill in the hunt.

"Of course, I understand, my dear," Reginald said. His voice was kind, but the furrow in his brow convinced Leandra that he was nearing the end of his patience.

"Would you like to take the air along the battlements?" he suggested. "Something less taxing than a board game."

Fresh air sounded good. "Yes, I would—"

"Please allow me to escort you, my lady," Garrett said, suddenly looming over their game table, his hands clasped behind him. Leandra found the smile he bestowed on them disturbingly polite and circumspect.

Leandra glanced beyond him, where Brenna appeared. Frantically her cousin made hand motions and mimed words of warning that Leandra could not understand. But alarm fluttered in her heart. She looked uncertainly from Garrett to Reginald.

"Excellent idea, Bernay," Reginald said. The thought of being rid of her seemed to appeal to him. "You're well-qualified to introduce Lady Leandra to the castle's fortifications. I'd like to check on the training of my falcons. Lady Brenna, I see you waving there to your cousin. Would you like to see the mews? Or would you care to go with Sir Garrett and your cousin?"

"Oh, I'd be glad to see the mews, my lord," Brenna said with a cautious glance in Leandra's direction. Leandra nodded imperceptibly to her cousin.

Many of the guests and nobles in the hall heard Lord Reginald accept Garrett's invitation for Leandra, and no one seemed to take it amiss when they left the hall together.

Garrett led the way up the dark spiral staircase, his hand holding hers, steady, firm, almost demanding her to follow him away from the others.

When they reached the castle wall, a gusty spring breeze cooled Leandra's hot face and cleared her head. She tugged her hand away from Garrett's, but he refused to release her. He greeted a guard on the battlement and led Leandra away from him toward a tower overlooking the winding river below. The sun hung low on the horizon.

"How do you feel?" he asked, innocently enough.

"I'm fine." Leandra wondered uneasily what he really wanted to know. What was his purpose for asking for this interview?

"I mean, has the antidote worked?" He eyed her intently.

"Oh, well, yes." Leandra silently scolded herself. She should have known he wouldn't accept anything without questions.

"In what way?" he asked, stopping to lean against the stone wall. The pleasant mask slipped away. He folded his arms across his chest and regarded her as if he were about to interrogate an enemy spy. "Do I appear different to you? Have I grown shorter? Are my eyes not quite so blue as you recall? Am I not as fair to look upon as you once thought?"

"Uh," Leandra stammered, uncertain what he wanted her to say. She decided on the truth. "You seem harder. Crueler."

"Oh?" Garrett's brow rose and his voice dripped with skepticism.

"I mean, when we were lovers—when we were in the village—you were gentle and good-humored. You laughed often."

"So did you, then." He leaned closer, scrutinizing her face.

"So I appear different to you, too," Leandra said. Suddenly she understood what he wanted from her. "See, the antidote is working."

Garrett straightened. His expression remained doubtful. "Yes, that must be it. We're falling out of love. How feeble our love must have been to be killed by vinegar and spices from the kitchen." He held up the blue bottle.

Leandra stared, stunned and disbelieving.

"Brenna told me. But not willingly," Garrett continued. The anger in his voice frightened her. "Don't blame your cousin. This ruse bears your self-sacrificing mark."

"'Twas the only thing to do." A pang of disappointment pierced Leandra's heart. She had wanted so much to spare him more anguish. "After the hunt and Leofric and the ring. Truly, Garrett. I conceived the plan for your sake. If you believed in the antidote as you did in the fake love potion, you would cease to love me when you drank it." Leandra hesitated for a moment. "That's why Brenna and I decided the antidote should smell so bad."

Abruptly he leaned toward her again, the intensity in his face so frightening that Leandra edged away from him.

"Say that again," he demanded.

"What?"

"The part about falling in love *believing* in a fake love potion. What did you mean, 'fake'?"

Leandra opened her mouth and closed it again. The more she said or did, the worse things got. Soon she and Brenna would both be sent back to Lyonesse, right back where they started, fighting pirates alone. What did he know? What did she dare say?

"Uh, what did Brenna tell you?" Leandra asked. Why did

she feel as if someone were unraveling her gown, revealing her lies, baring her soul?

"Forget about Brenna." Garrett prowled toward Leandra. She backed away and stopped only when her back met a stone wall. "I want to know about the love potion from your lips. Everything."

Several ideas flashed through Leandra's head. She could deny everything. She could admit to only what she had admitted to already. She could tell the truth. Inwardly, she groaned. If he hadn't stopped loving her by now, he would by the time she finished her story.

"As you wish." Leandra drew a deep breath. "I decided to give us a fake antidote because we received a fake potion."

When Garrett did not explode in anger, didn't even blink, Leandra was encouraged. "You see, Brenna never really gave us the love potion I obtained from Vivian. It's still right here."

She drew the tiny silver phial from the cuff of her green surcoat to verify her statement—she would leave no doubt this time.

"Garrett, you were right," Leandra said, brave enough at last to hazard a look into his face, looming above hers. "Don't you see? We fell in love because we thought we were supposed to."

Garrett held her gaze. She could feel his eyes on her face, searching, uncertain, probing. She looked into his, more aware than ever how much she loved him, potion or no.

At last he shook his head and turned away. "No! No!"

"It's true," Leandra said, and she told him all the reasons Brenna had confessed for making them believe they had been given a love potion.

"When did you learn this?" he demanded without looking at her.

"The day we arrived here," Leandra admitted.

"You've known all this time and didn't tell me?"

Leandra shook her head. "All of this happened because I brought the love potion along in the first place. Brenna is so afraid of you. I decided to say nothing."

"So you still have the real potion?" Garrett looked at the silver phial in her hand. Scorn hardened his face. "Do you plan to give it to Lord Reginald? From what I've seen, you're going to need it. He seems less than enthusiastic about your charms."

Garrett's words stung. "That's exactly what I intend to do," Leandra snapped back, tucking the phial away again. "We can just forget about everything that's happened. Lord Reginald will fall in love with me and I with him, and you can sail off to France just as you wanted."

"Not if I tell him that he is being deceived." Garrett faced her defiantly. "Do you think I would stand by and let my liege lord be given a potion he knows nothing of? Never! I will not allow such dishonesty."

"You'll never know when it's given," Leandra boasted.

"Like tonight at the banquet?"

"Perhaps. Why should I tell you when?" She turned and swept back down along the battlements, thrusting her chin forward and fighting the tears that threatened. Thank heavens she still had the potion. Everything would be fine once she had given the elixir to Reginald.

All she had to do was slip the potion into Reginald's cup when Garrett was looking away. Even if he accused her, no one would believe him.

Then, when she and Reginald stood before the altar of the Tremelyn village cathedral, the Earl of Tremelyn would love her and she would love him. The joy in their faces would make them the envy of everyone present. That was the way she had wanted things from the beginning. Her plan would work yet. Thankfully, she reached her bedchamber before the tears streamed unchecked down her cheeks. If this was what she wanted, then why couldn't she stop weeping?

Reginald and Leandra stood before the doors of Tremelyn's great hall, waiting to make their formal entrance. The earl took her cold hand in his warm one and gazed straight into her eyes, his well-meaning sincerity obvious. "You look beautiful, my dear."

"Thank you, my lord." Leandra smiled demurely. He lied so nobly. What a gallant lord he was. How fortunate she was to be marrying a man who could look her in the face and speak such an untruth with so much caring. She looked ghastly.

Brenna had blurted out as much as they dressed. Sure enough, Leandra's polished metal mirror had reflected eyes swollen and red from shedding tears she didn't understand, eyes set in a face pale and mournful. She had never really regained her color since the day Garrett threw the phial into the stream, the day she had accepted their destiny to love from afar. Poor Lord Reginald. He had never seen her at her best. She hoped she'd be able to make that up to him soon. She touched the phial tucked in the cuff of her gold damask surcoat to reassure herself.

"Indeed, Lord Reginald," Brenna said. "Doesn't this surcoat bring out the whiteness of Leandra's skin?" She scurried to Leandra's side and began to tug at the hem of the gold-colored garment. "Smile, cousin," she hissed. "This banquet is in your honor."

"I am smiling," Leandra said, annoyed with the way her cousin fussed over her.

"More," Brenna demanded, and gave Leandra's gown an emphatic tug.

Obligingly, Leandra stretched her lips across her teeth in what she was certain was a parody of a smile. She held it successfully until she saw Garrett approaching them. He strode down the passage, handsome and elegant in a stylish, short blue velvet jacket and blue hose. The fake smile fell away and Leandra stared, first dispirited by his frown, then unable to take her eyes from his fine length of leg. He had held her between those strong thighs once. Sweet Mother, the man still set her insides aflutter every time she saw him. She turned away. Please don't let my thoughts show on my face, she prayed silently.

"Bernay, so here you are, to be Lady Brenna's partner for the banquet," Reginald said, stepping forward to welcome his knight with a clap on the back.

"What?" Brenna yelped. Her mouth fell slack in surprise.

"I asked Sir Garrett to be your dinner partner, my dear," Reginald said. "After all, he was my representative and your escort. I thought it only fitting."

"Of course, how thoughtful, my lord," Leandra said, filling the silence that followed Reginald's words. For once her cousin seemed at a loss for words. Brenna snapped her gaping mouth shut and stared up at Garrett, fear draining the color from her face.

"Shall we enter the hall, then?" Reginald offered his arm to Leandra.

She nodded, her cheeks already aching from the artificial smile she had forced to return to her lips. The blue-liveried pages swung open the doors, and the Earl of Tremelyn, with his betrothed, her cousin, and his favorite knight, entered the great hall of the castle, accompanied by a trumpet fanfare.

Roses and lilies littered the rush-strewn floor. Leandra greeted the guests, nobles, and vassals. From the overhead beams silk banners fluttered, shiny and rich in the glow of a galaxy of candles. Splendid new tapestries hung along the walls. The lavishness of the decorations touched her heart. Reginald offered an opulent show—for himself, of course, but for her as well.

The prenuptial banquet went smoothly, the food abundant and sumptuous, the entertainment boisterous and amusing. Leandra smiled on and gave a little sigh of relief until Brenna started to shout at the entertainers. The jugglers delighted her, as did a sword dance and play about St. George and the dragon. Her cheers echoed from the rafters when the venerable physician brought the play's champion back to life with a magic spell.

So excited was Brenna that Leandra feared her cousin would embarrass them all by climbing over the table to join the mummers and learn their secrets. But Lord Reginald took her cousin's enthusiasm without upset, laughing with her and calling the mummers to the table. He requested a repeat of the dance and an explanation of their tricks.

To Leandra's relief, the earl turned to her, smiling. "'Tis refreshing to have ladies at the head table again and youth to liven the company."

"I am glad you are pleased, my lord," Leandra said, grateful once more for his good humor and noting his patience with Brenna.

Garrett frowned into his goblet and drained the last of the spiced wine. Brusquely he motioned for the page to refill his cup and everyone's at the table. All evening he'd been spying on Leandra, waiting to see her attempt to slip the potion into Lord Reginald's cup. No doubt she would do it tonight, just before the wedding. Tomorrow she would have no time before the ceremony, and he doubted she would trust such a deed to a servant—or to Brenna.

Garrett thanked the page for the wine and looked about the hall, noting that Wystan had a maid by his side, the daughter of an older knight. Not a bad match, Garrett thought.

Indifferently, he leaned forward to look across Brenna at Leandra, who sat between her cousin and Lord Reginald. As he stared, Leandra bent over her trencher and stared back, unblinking and unembarrassed. There was no mistaking the challenge in her eyes. He sat back, faced forward and sipped his wine. When would she slip Reginald the potion? What moment of distraction would she choose? And after she acted, what would he say?

Some puppeteers jogged into the center of the hall and set their stage in place. Garrett found himself caught up in the humor of the puppets' antics, but he didn't forget to give Leandra a sidelong look from time to time. Soon the entire crowd was laughing, hands pressed against their sides and tears of merriment streaming down their faces. But Leandra's smile remained fixed, almost stoic.

When the puppet stage disappeared in pieces, a fire-eating sword swallower entered, twirling blades aflame. Garrett noted that Leandra lost interest in the amusements and began to stare down into her cup. The acrobats flipped and tumbled around the fire eater. But Leandra studied the goblet as if it held some special fascination.

Then a jester, clad in red and yellow, added to the confusion, capering around the room, ringing his bells and mocking the guests at each table.

Brenna jumped up from her seat. "Sir Jester, come bless the bride and bridegroom," she called, unladylike, across the great hall. Garrett cringed, taking pity on whatever man wed Leandra's cousin. 'Twould need to be a courageous soul who had no fear of finding himself and his lady the center of attention.

The jester waved his bell-adorned scepter and loped across the hall to the head table.

He bowed to Brenna, to all at the table, and irreverently began to chant nonsense that sounded something like a Latin liturgy in a voice mimicking a priest's. Then he shook his scepter, bells tingling, and waved it over Leandra and Reginald's heads. Guests applauded. Reginald grinned at Leandra, and with effort she returned his smile.

Next, to Garrett's horror, the jester began to do the same over Brenna and him. He protested, nearly knocking over the table to fend aside the jester's scepter. Brenna had gone still and silent. Thwarted, the jester cackled and danced away. Garrett settled into his chair again. When he looked back to Leandra and Reginald, the earl was laughing with Brenna at the jester's hasty retreat. Leandra was tucking the phial back into her sleeve.

Swearing under his breath, Garrett almost jumped from his chair again. In that moment of distraction—when he and Reginald watched the jester—she had slipped Reginald the potion. His decision must be made. Did he tell Reginald? Did he do the truthful, loyal thing and call to light Leandra's deception?

Garrett rubbed his hand across his brow. 'Twas his sworn duty to say something. But to do so endangered Leandra's happiness. What purpose did that serve?

His heart pounded against his ribs as he turned to Leandra to see whether she had drunk from her own goblet yet. He must decide. In a moment, in a quick sip, it would be too late.

Leandra gazed at him with a challenging, military glint in

her eye. She waited, almost daring him to take some action. Then, as Garrett watched, the earl turned away to speak to the vassal seated on his other side. Leandra took out the silver phial once more and poured the last drops into Brenna's goblet.

Garrett's heart stopped, terrified to even contemplate the glimmer of hope that he saw.

"What are you doing?" Brenna hissed. Swiftly she exchanged her goblet for Leandra's. Leandra switched them back. With a frown, Brenna shoved the goblet away and folded her hands on the table.

"To the fertility of the bride and bridegroom," the jester shouted, gamboling by and grabbing Brenna's cup. He held the shining goblet high before the crowd.

The guests roared approval.

"Indeed," agreed Reginald, raising his cup.

Garrett, Brenna, and Leandra stared in frozen, open-mouthed horror as the two men lifted their goblets. In that slow stretch of time like that experienced in battle—when split-second actions transpired in endless moments—the candlelight glinted off the two silver cups. The rings on Reginald's hand sparkled; the jester's bells jingled as the two men tipped their heads back. In the goblets the potion-laced wine rolled toward the brim, neared their lips. Garrett didn't even want to imagine what Vivian's elixir would do if shared by the jester and Lord Reginald.

Brenna moved first. She snatched the goblet from the jester, a few drops of wine sloshing to the white tablecloth. "That's mine you fool," she snapped.

Then Garrett saw his opportunity. He jumped to his feet, raising his own goblet high over the table so that all could see him. He wondered why he had not seen the sense in this sooner. His voice boomed throughout the hall. "Yes, a toast to the health and happiness of the Earl and the next Countess of Tremelyn."

Brenna looked down at her wine and hesitated. At a gesture from Leandra, a page hastily handed a wine goblet to the bewildered jester.

"Drink, Brenna," Garrett growled. "Drink."

"But—" Brenna protested.

"Drink, Brenna." Leandra raised her cup and leaned toward her cousin to speak low and quiet. "Or pack your things for Lyonesse." Garrett saw the mixture of loving compassion and iron will play across Leandra's face.

Wavering, Brenna glanced at her cousin, then at the smiling earl. "Oh, rot me," the dark-haired maid muttered. "Why not?" She lifted the cup to her lips. "To the next Countess of Tremelyn."

In the great hall of Tremelyn the entire company—even the sullen-faced Brenna—drained their goblets in tribute to the earl, his betrothed, and the coming nuptials.

When the dancing began, Brenna tapped her toes and drummed her fingers on the table. Reginald seemed unable to keep his eyes from straying toward her. Brenna, aware of his admiration, fluttered her eyelashes at him. Garrett had seldom seen such a blatant flirtation.

But he suffered no outrage. Promptly Reginald politely asked Leandra permission to dance with her cousin. With the first genuine smile Garrett had seen on Leandra's face in days, she assented. Brenna simpered at Reginald's invitation but accepted with a giggle and more eyelash fluttering.

As the pair moved onto the dance floor, Reginald put a hand on Garrett's shoulder. "Thank you for the toast. 'Twas a noble salute."

Garrett leaned toward the earl. His conscience still troubled him, and he knew he must say something. "My lord, I think you should know—"

"I know, Garrett," the earl said with a wink of his eye. "The ladies of Lyonesse weave quite a spell, don't they?"

Brenna drew the laughing Earl of Tremelyn out onto the dance floor.

Garrett stared after them for a moment, wondering how much Reginald knew or thought he knew. With a shrug he gave up and looked to Leandra.

"You are not angry?" she asked, her hand still on her goblet. "I betrayed your lord."

"No, I am not angry," Garrett whispered, his heart so full of relief and love for Leandra that his voice nearly failed him. He reached across Brenna's empty chair for her hand. "I only hope that the potion works as well for them as it worked for us."

Then Leandra did truly smile, a brilliant, beaming expression with happiness shining in her eyes. At last she reached for the hand Garrett offered. They linked little fingers—like true lovers.

"Sir Garrett, I wish to have a word alone with my betrothed." A frown crinkled Reginald's brow as he gazed upon Leandra and Garrett at the table.

The matins bells could be heard tolling from the cathedral. The dancing was over and the great hall had emptied except for a few revelers who remained by the fire to drink.

Leandra exchanged an apprehensive glance with Garrett.

Garrett protested. "My lord, perhaps it is I who should speak—"

"No, Garrett, this is between Leandra and I," Reginald said. "See Lady Brenna to her chamber."

Brenna pouted. "Do I have to go with him, Reginald?"

"Only for now, Brenna," Reginald assured her. Apologetically he took her hand and gave it a light, quick kiss. "We will meet again soon."

Brenna blushed and giggled, then rose to obey.

Leandra saw the question in Garrett's eyes this time. Was this the potion's doing? Leandra gave a little shrug. Did she wish his company? Leandra shook her head.

Brenna bade all good night. With interest Leandra watched Reginald's gaze follow Brenna as Garrett led her away. She turned at the door of the great hall and gave the earl a fingery wave.

"She is a lovely child, your cousin," Reginald murmured, returning the wave with a bemused smile, completely unembarrassed about the absurdity of a fifty-year-old earl wiggling his fingers in the air. "So spontaneous. So free. I'm glad you brought her along."

"I'm glad you enjoy her company." Leandra clasped her hands nervously in her lap, less certain than he about the wisdom of her actions. From the day she had obtained the potion, she had been prepared to deceive Reginald. Had he seen her pour the potion into his cup? Then she should be prepared to suffer the consequences.

The door closed behind Garrett and Brenna.

"My lord, you wished a word with me."

"Yes." Reginald cleared his throat and tapped his fingers impatiently on the table. "I'm not a young man, you know. But I'm still vital. I still have my wits about me and most of my teeth," he added.

Puzzled, Leandra agreed. "Indeed, my lord. You are fit and handsome."

He paid no heed to her flattery. "From the beginning your father and I were concerned with the alliance of Lyonesse and Tremelyn. I assumed you understood all of this. Of course, I didn't know of Brenna then."

"Yes, of course," Leandra said. "The alliance is my concern also."

"And you consented to this marriage willingly?"

"Yes, I consider our betrothal a great honor and—"

"*But* your attraction for Sir Garrett has been clear from the first day you arrived."

Leandra gulped. "Have I been so conspicuous?"

Reginald went on as if he expected no reply. "You smile only when he hovers over you. As for Garrett, he can hardly keep himself from your side when the two of you are in the same room."

His mention of Garrett unsettled Leandra. She knew she had risked herself, Lyonesse, and even Brenna, when she poured the potion, but she wished to avoid danger to Garrett if possible. "Sir Garrett is a loyal knight. He has never—"

"Oh, he's behaved honorably. Any other man I would know was guilty. This attraction hasn't been so obvious that there is talk . . . yet." Reginald regarded her intently, as though he intended to let no gesture, no blink of the eye go unnoticed.

The guilt of pouring the potion into his cup overwhelmed her, and she had to look away.

"Tell me, honestly, have you had a change of heart?"

"My lord, nothing has been more important to me than winning your affection," Leandra began, choosing her words carefully. "But . . ."

"Out with it, Leandra. Do you favor Garrett? Tell me yes, so that I may be free to pursue your cousin."

Leandra closed her mouth and stared at the earl. He stared back at her. No spell clouded his dark eyes. He knew she and Garrett loved each other. Had he known all along? His eyes were sharp, keen, and filled with complete understanding. Indeed, the man had his wits about him. A new kind of affection for the earl began to grow in Leandra's heart.

"I hope I do not offend you with that confession, Leandra. But it's been clear to me from the beginning that Garrett had already won your heart. 'Tis my regret. But I'm to blame. What folly to send a man like him to you."

A half smile came to Leandra's lips and embarrassment burned her cheeks. "'Twas no folly, my lord."

"No? I thought so. You do favor Garrett. So that leaves only one thing to settle."

"And that is?" Dare she hope that he would free her from her vows?

He twisted the oaken ring on his finger. "Will you allow me to keep the ring as a token of Lyonesse's and Tremelyn's alliance? Marriage with Brenna will seal it, of course. Do you think your father will consent?"

Suddenly Reginald leaned close and confided, "My first envoy informed me that you know your father's mind well. Your word is as good as his."

"True. Are you asking for Brenna's hand in marriage?"

"Indeed, I am, Leandra."

"Then I consent," she said. "On behalf of my father. He would do nothing to stand in the way of his niece's happiness or that of a beloved ally."

"Excellent. Good." Reginald sat back in his chair and waxed thoughtful. "Strange, is it not, how the heart defies the worldly powers? It has no respect for vows or titles, for money or age."

"Or hair color, either," Leandra added, thinking of Garrett's preference for dark hair.

A look of bewilderment crossed Reginald's face. "Probably not hair color, either."

He raised a hand to give Leandra a comradely slap on the back, then apparently thought better of it. "Sir Garrett will be speaking to you soon. Or he will when I finish with him.

"Tomorrow we will celebrate a double wedding. What do you think your cousin, Lady Brenna, will say to that?"

Epilogue

Well, of course I said yes immediately," Brenna recited for all her new ladies-in-waiting and turned to grin at Leandra. "After all, what maid would pass up the chance to be a countess? 'Twas a beautiful wedding, was it not?"

The twittering ladies agreed. The royal dressing room buzzed with women's voices. Bawdy laughter rang out and rich fabrics rustled as the two brides—Brenna and Leandra —were dressed for their bedding ceremony.

"There's something I think you should know," Brenna said, her lips next to Leandra's ear so that the noble ladies could not hear. "It *does* grow."

Leandra frowned, uncertain at first what her cousin meant. Then she understood and smiled. "I know."

"You know?" Brenna stepped back and looked Leandra over as if she hadn't seen her for years. "Did Amice tell you, too? She told me she hadn't. No? Oh, I know, 'twas May Day, no doubt. I thought so. That sly Garrett. I knew he wasn't too good."

"It wasn't like that," Leandra said, trying to be serious and dignified about this moment, but a smile teased the corners of her mouth upward once more. She was Lady Bernay now, and the knowledge pleased her so much she could hardly keep a frown on her face for long.

"Of course, it was like that," Brenna mocked. An impish grin spread across her face. "He's a handsome man, just a little too perfect to my taste. But Reginald, now he has faults. For one thing, he's a little old. But he knows how to make up for it." Brenna held out her left hand to admire her diamond-encrusted wedding ring.

"Look at this. He let me pick it from all the jewels in Tremelyn's coffers," Brenna prattled. "I can't believe you made Sir Garrett put that golden circle on your finger again."

"I am satisfied," Leandra said, knowing that Brenna would never understand no matter how many times she tried to explain that she wanted only the ring that Garrett first gave her. "'Twas meant to be mine and I wish for no other."

"Well, if it's what you wanted," Brenna said.

"Shhhh!" hissed the woman keeping watch at the chamber door. She waved warning at the women in the room. "Here comes the priest with the earl and Sir Garrett."

Fussily the ladies arranged themselves in order of social magnitude and composed their faces into appropriate noble expressions.

Brenna and Leandra turned to each other, both suddenly aware that on the morrow their lives would be forever parted. One would begin her reign as countess, and the other would return to rule Lyonesse.

Brenna sobered, almost as if the immensity of the change daunted her as nothing else ever had. "I am sorry for all the pain I brought," she whispered. Tears welled in her eyes. "I meant no harm. Truly, cousin. All has turned out favorably, has it not? Even Leofric received justice. What else can you call it?"

Just that morning a message arrived at the castle from the Earl of Casseldorne, Leofric's father. As the earl told it, Leofric had been found on the steps of a nearby Franciscan hermitage, battered and beaten—minus the little finger of his left hand. He refused to speak of the two days he had been missing, and he desperately begged the brothers to allow him to take the vows of poverty. He even promised to sign his inheritance over to the order, his father wrote in anger.

"'Twas justice, indeed," Leandra agreed. She suspected that Leofric owed his life to Lord Reginald. Murder of a wedding guest would have obliged the earl and all his knights to swoop down on the outlaws. So instead of death

the miscreants had wisely settled for torture and ransom—
the offering paid to the Church. "A life of poverty and
humility is a dear price for a man like Leofric."

"Enter, my lords," invited the senior lady-in-waiting who
stood at the door. "Lady Brenna, your husband has arrived."

Leandra embraced her cousin. "Be well and be happy."
Brenna nodded. Head held high, lashes fluttering to hold
back tears, she turned and went to take the hands of the Earl
of Tremelyn. Garrett joined Leandra and they followed the
other women.

Kneeling at the bedside, the newly wedded couple bowed
their heads as the priest intoned prayers for happiness and
children, for good health and children, for prosperity and
for children. Leandra couldn't imagine Brenna as a mother,
but she marveled to see her cousin so docile and demure at
the earl's side. Reginald smiled lovingly at his bride. This
marriage was bound to be good for Brenna.

Prayers complete, the priest sprinkled the bed with holy
water and censed the room. A little thrill of excitement
shivered through Leandra when Garrett squeezed her hand.
"We're next," he murmured.

In their chamber as Leandra and Garrett knelt by their
bed, waiting for the priest's blessing, her apprehension grew.
Since her talk with Reginald after the banquet, she had not
seen Garrett alone. The only glimpses she had of his feelings
about the sudden turn of events had come during the
ceremony—a solemn, almost grim twist to his lips and the
warm steadiness of his hands as he slipped the ring on her
finger once more.

Again the priest's prayers went on and on and Leandra's
unease increased. The sharp scent of incense stung her nose.

Finally the bed-blessing ceremony was over and everyone
departed in a flurry of knowing smiles and best wishes.
Garrett closed the door and lingered there, his back to her,
his broad shoulders straight and tense.

"Are you satisfied?" he asked without turning to face her.
"You have what you wanted from the beginning, a knight for
Lyonesse."

Leandra swallowed with difficulty. When Garrett had made the final toast at the banquet she had been reassured that he wanted this marriage as much as she did. Now she was no longer so certain of that. He had ambitions that she and Lyonesse could never satisfy, and she wondered once more what had passed between Reginald and Garrett.

"Tell me exactly what Lord Reginald said to you last night," she babbled, clasping her hands before her. "And France? Do you sail for France?"

"He said very little really." Garrett turned with a frown. Leandra knew that the interview must have been difficult for him. "He invited me to sail with the next company of knights requested by the king." Garrett glanced briefly at Leandra as though he anticipated some objection from her. "But that won't come for some time."

"Oh, that was generous of him," Leandra said, toying with the folds of her silken bed gown. She could not ask a knight to be anything less than a king's warrior—not even her husband.

"I asked him to bestow Chycliff on Wystan when he is knighted next Eastertide. He agreed."

Leandra almost started in surprise. "But why give up your ancestral home?" Garrett had refused what she knew he wanted most in the world.

"I could hardly accept reward for an undertaking at which I failed so miserably," he said with a shake of his head. "I was to bring Reginald his bride, safe and smiling. Instead I presented him with a scheming maid who wanted a knight for her realm and carried a love potion in her cuff. Not to mention a cousin bent on finding a husband."

Dismay slowed Leandra's heartbeat, but pride stiffened her back bone. "Then, if you didn't wish to marry, why did you make the toast last night? Why did you help me almost throw Brenna into Reginald's arms?"

Garrett studied her in silence. "I never said I didn't wish for this marriage, Leandra. There's been little else in my head since we were crowned May Queen and Lord."

Leandra's heart quickened as she admired him still standing at the door.

"But I failed in my mission." For the first time he shrugged, seemed to almost relax. "I find I have another duty now."

"Lyonesse?" Leandra asked, hope glimmering. "I hope you will share the responsibilities with me."

"'Tis a duty more demanding than protecting Lyonesse," he said. "I'm charged with being your husband."

Leandra smiled hesitantly.

Garrett's gaze endured, so compelling that she had to look away, immediately aware that she wore nothing beneath the loose silk bed gown. A gentle draft stirred the hem of the garment, tickling her ankles. Instinctively she pressed her legs together. Garrett remained at the door, but she could feel his scrutiny peel away the fabric. He made no move, but she could almost feel his fingertips brush along her arms.

Taking a deep breath, she resisted the urge to grab a bed curtain to hide behind. "No need to stare so, Sir Knight. There is nothing here that you have not seen already," Leandra said boldly, with false courage. Still, she could not meet his gaze.

"Perhaps." He spoke softly, his voice hoarse, a sinister smile coming to his lips. He advanced toward her purposefully. Leandra stepped back only to find her back against the bedpost. "But I have not seen enough yet to tire of it. Moreover, you must pay the price now for making me love you. I remember well that May Day night. I recall clearly that you liked the touching."

He grasped the bedpost just above her head and leaned forward, his nearness warm and enveloping, teasing every particle of her to tingling awareness. He did not touch her, but she desperately wanted him to. She knew that when they finally held each other everything would be right. Finally she looked into his face, so new to her, yet so familiar and beloved. His wicked smile softened.

Leandra summoned her courage and spread her hand over his blue jacket, against his heart. "I touch your heart first," she whispered. "Then I give you mine."

Garrett made no reply, only took her chin between his forefinger and thumb and lifted her face to his. Firm and sensitive, his lips moved over hers, masterfully banishing every fear that lingered in her. She sighed, her body dissolving, so that she possessed no more strength than a puppet held on her feet only by Garrett's grip on her chin.

He began to kiss her brow, tiny feathery kisses, descending to her eyelids, her nose, her cheeks. Eagerly she offered him her throat.

A chuckle rumbled deep and sweet inside him, vibrating through Leandra's hand, still pressed against his heart.

"I knew you wouldn't play coy games." He took her throat, his fingers working through her hair to the back of her neck. He whispered against her collarbone, "Tonight, sweeting, we resume the lesson we began on May Day."

When Leandra felt the palm of his hand, bare and hot, on her shoulder, then down her back, she knew he had untied the ribbons of her gown. Soon she would truly wear nothing but Garrett's touch.

"Remember our first night together." His kisses trailed across her breasts, light and caressing, down her belly, warm. Large hands spread over her ribs, possessive hands. He knelt before her, his golden hair gleaming in the candlelight, his hands slipping low over her hips. Lips found her navel.

Leandra gasped, pressed her head back against the bedpost.

"We only explored a few of the wonders of lovemaking," he murmured.

The silk gown pooled around her ankles. He pressed her back against the bedpost. His hands ran over her lightly; his breath brushed her hidden curls. The new sensation startled a groan from Leandra. She laced her fingers through his hair, tugging him away before her strength deserted her. Only the bedpost supported her now. When the flood of moistness came, she understood the meaning of it. She wanted to tell him she was melting, but words refused to come to her lips.

Somehow, he knew, too. He stood, swept her up in his arms and laid her on the bed.

"There will be some pain," he warned, his lips against her

ear. "But only this once. Then delight will be ours. I promise."

He left her for a moment to divest himself of his own clothes. Leandra watched, curious, ready now to see if what she already knew was true. Indeed, Brenna's words were accurate and she stared unabashedly at Garrett, also ready to make love. When he saw her gazing at him, he smiled and put her hand on the part of him that he'd kept in mystery before. He was smooth and hard, round and full, warm and alive.

"I take pleasure in your touch as you do in mine," he told her as she held him. "I guide your hands. So you must guide me."

She agreed and when the time came, he covered her, his thighs against the inside of hers this time.

The first taste of his entrance only made her want more. She wrapped her arms around his waist to entice him. He slipped his hands beneath her hips. His second thrust brought the pain, sharp and sweet, taking away her breath. He pulled back, and for a moment Leandra feared he was going to withdraw. She clung to him, her hands slipping down his back, and she whispered words of need against his cheek.

His mouth found hers, kissing her tenderly before he began the final lesson. Leandra followed Garrett's lead and accepted her own body's promptings, as he told her to. Pleasure flourished inside as she moved with him. Their breaths mingled, quick and warm, until the final sigh came, together.

Leandra lay adrift in pleasure, in Garrett's arms, caring for nothing but the moment, the here and now of their love.

Garrett watched her, wondering at the changes in her since they had faced each other in the streets of Lyonesse. She was softer somehow, and warmer, even sweeter, if that was possible. Lightly he stroked her belly, and she stretched nearly purring under his hand. "What a fierce, loving mother you will be, Leandra," he whispered against her lips. "Indulgent, yet strong, like a lioness."

She brushed a kiss along his square chin. "Hmmm. Lioness? I thought I was a scheming maid with a love potion. But this is the real magic. Not the potion, but the loving."

"I never thought of it like that until last May Day." Garrett eyed the smooth supple limbs she lazed against him. Desire stirred again. "But I knew then that you cast some kind of spell. You were so determined to have a knight for Lyonesse."

"You will share it with me, won't you?" Leandra asked. She raised herself up on one elbow, her breast plump against his arm, and peered into his face. "The burdens of Lyonesse?"

"I have pledged my life to do so," Garrett said, smiling up at her. "Did you ever doubt I would?"

"No, I have *never* doubted you, Sir Garrett Bernay," Leandra said with no hesitation. "Only you doubted yourself."

Garrett drew a deep breath of satisfaction. "I only ask one thing, lioness."

"What's that?" Leandra rested her head on his shoulder and her eyelids drooped sleepily.

"No more use of potions from Vivian."

Her lids never even fluttered. "Not even the seasickness remedy when you sail for France?"

"With that exception, only." Garrett smiled resignedly to himself. Was she always going to be one step ahead of him?

Unexpectedly Leandra sat up, pressed his hand against her heart, and regarded him squarely in the eye. "I swear I'll never seek out a potion again, except for the seasickness remedy. The only magic I'll ever practice will come from my heart."

"And from mine, also. 'Tis all we need."

When they finished another long kiss, Leandra clung to him breathlessly. Garrett held her close, admiring the curve on her lips.

"Mercy, Sir Knight," she whispered without opening her eyes. "You need no potion to put a lasting smile on my lips."

Linda Madl

Speak of Love

*"This is a delightful tale--humor offsets
mystery and weaves a page turner.
Highly recommended."*
--*Rendezvous*

A Tender Magic

"Linda Madl weaves an irresistible spell!"
--Betina Krahn, author of
My Warrior's Heart

Available from Pocket Books